The tank came to life, showing the skeletal wreck of the spaceship *Spica*, lit by the object they had followed.

Something enormous. Perhaps twenty times the length of the *Spica*.

The head had bulging armored turrets placed like eyes, glowing dully red. A bright-plated tail had arched to sting the wreck, and a jet of violet fire blazed out of it. Where it struck, the wreckage glowed red, turning yellow, finally shining white.

A thin-seeming tongue stabbed out to suck up the molten metal.

Quin stared till the last bright blobs were gone, when the red-glowing eyes were visible among the stars. They seemed to swell. They spread apart. Its nightmare jaws loomed near. Like a great snake striking, its tongue stabbed into his face.

The holotank blanked out.

LIFEBURST

a novel by

JACK WILLIAMSON

A Del Rey Book

BALLANTINE BOOKS • NEW YORK

A Del Rey Book
Published by Ballantine Books

Library of Congress Catalog Card Number: 84-3088

ISBN 0-345-32977-5

Manufactured in the United States of America

First Hardcover Edition: November 1984
First Paperback Edition: November 1985

Cover art by Don Dixon

CONTENTS

EVENTS IN THE RISE AND FALL OF THE SUN TYCOONS

1923 (Oldstyle)   In flight from the Cheka, or so he says, "Ivan Ivanoff" reaches Hong Kong on a forged Portuguese passport. A wiry little man with a strong nose and a spent pistol bullet lodged in the socket of his blind right eye, he speaks seven languages, all of them loudly but badly, Russian no better than the rest. He carries diamonds he says are Czarist sewed into the lining of his astrakhan cap. Confounding foes with a wild eloquence and a one-eyed leer, he recovers his health and takes the name of his Eurasian mistress. As Ivan Kwan, he sets out to regain the imperial station he claims the Bolsheviks have raped away.

Cycle of the Elderhood 77:54:03
Among the ice-moons of the outermost planet of a G2 core-star in Draco, a young heatseeker queen yields to her princely suitor. Consuming the male in the way of her kind, she then sets out in solitary flight to found a new hive. Her destination is the Sun.

1951   Ivan Kwan's three sons, banker, mathematician, and shipping magnate, sign a secret charter to form the House of Kwan, pledging themselves to live for his imperial plan.

1969–1974   Sergei, the banker's black sheep heir, refuses to sign the Kwan charter. Drummed out of the family, he leaves Hong Kong. Fails as poet, fails as artist, fails as impresario. Destitute and sick, he finds refuge with Penny Morang, an unemployed cocktail waitress in Little Rock, Arkansas. John Kwan is born on her father's hardscrabble Ozark farm.

1977–1986   John Kwan, entranced by TV coverage of the Voyager flybys of Jupiter, Saturn, and Uranus, discovers the wonder of space. When his father dies, leaving them on welfare, his mother takes him to Hong Kong. Possessing his great-grandfather's "Romanoff nose," he is welcomed into the House of Kwan.

Cycle of the Elderhood 77:54:05
Goldengene, a graduate student of galactic dynamics at a Newmarch university, is assigned to duty as the Newling attaché at Point Vermillion, an isolated observatory maintained on the northward fringes of the solar halo, to watch for the approaching Black Companion. Her people, the Newlings, are refugees from the seeker conquest of their natal star, and she is alert for possible pursuit.

1996   Smolensk-Atlanta Incident. City of Smolensk hit by robotic missile launched by protestors trying to vandalize it. Atlanta destroyed in retaliation. Millions are killed, more millions injured, but total nuclear holocaust is averted.

1997   Antinuclear Gottesvolk Movement spreads from East Germany, its underground leaders proclaiming the fall of Marxism and the rise of the Republic of God.

1999   Sri Lanka Accords. All nuclear weapons and nuclear materials are transferred to Supranational Nucleonics Repository. To assure compliance, all national space programs are terminated.

2000   John Kwan secures funds for a civilian space project, Kwan Planetary Laboratories, headquartered in Hong Kong and dedicated to his dreams of space conquest.

Sun Year 1   Kwan Labs engineers invent kwanlon, a monomolecular fiber with theoretical strength enough to link Earth with geosynchronous satellites.

Cycle of the Elderhood 77:54:06
The Council of the Elderhood receives reports of primitive spacecraft in flight between inner planets of the core-star. The Eldermost establishes the core-star observatory to determine the nature and intentions of these evolving spacefolk.

Sun Year 3   House of Kwan forms subsidiary, Sun Power, Inc., to hang skywires. "Ladders to the planets," these will be the means to realize old Ivan's dream.

Sun Year 7   Moon mines in production. Mars Station planted.

Sun Year 13   Solar power beamed to Earth. Kwan Labs designs genetic tests to select individuals able to live and work effectively in minimum-gravity environments.

Sun Year 17   Comet Yamamoto captured and steered into Earth orbit to supply water, oxygen, and other volatiles for the Company's space operation.

Sun Year 19   First test skywire fails when unpredicted harmonics snap ballast link. Falling cable drags satellite out of orbit. Cable burns in atmosphere, but satellite strikes Quito. Killed and injured number 2 million.

Sun Year 23 Successful skywire dropped from satellite station Kilimanjaro High to Kenya Down.

Sun Year 25 Sun Company obtains outlawed nuclear materials from Nucleonics Repository to be used as fuel for reactors located in the ballast masses that support the skyweb, 100,000 kilometers out from Earth. Secretly, House of Kwan diverts nuclear arms into highside arsenals.

Sun Years 28–31 Vogelkop Accords signed at Vogelkop Down. In return for energy, ores, and manufactures from space, the power-starved signatory nations yield terminal concessions, police privileges, and diplomatic recognition to Sun Company.

Sun Year 33 Company heiress Sonya Kwan marries financier Li Chang Chen.

Sun Year 39 The Holyfolk Front, a radicalized revival of the Gottesvolk Movement, begins underground campaign to liberate the mother planet from space dominion. Members take "Earthblood oath" to destroy the Company and the House of Kwan.

Sun Year 41 Sun Security is set up to counter Holyfolk terrorism.

Sun Year 47 Kwan Labs improve genetic tests and introduce the laser-printed Sunmark to identify individuals with "genes fit for space."

Sun Year 53 Kerry Kwan, chairman of the Company and Director-General of Sun Security, becomes first Sun Tycoon. Claims that evolving genetic differences will soon separate Sunbred and Earthbred populations.

Sun Year 55 Metal-rich asteroid Kwan Moon towed into Earth orbit.

Sun Year 58   Kwan Moon mines in production. Gravity power replaces solar power. Efficient infall energy generated by ore buckets sliding down skywires.

Sun Year 60   Kwan Labs engineers test first successful fusion-powered ion drive. Lunar skywire hung. First manned flight beyond Mars.

Sun Year 62   Dissension splits the House of Kwan. Chen faction secures control. Boris Chen ousts Kerry Kwan, becoming the second Sun Tycoon.

Sun Year 71   Unmanned Pluto probe detects laser bursts from far beyond its flight range. Kwan Labs engineers interpret burst as signals from alien spacecraft.

Sun Year 77   First Holyfolk Rebellion breaks out in Quito Nuevo, spreads to three continents. Crushed by worldwide power blackouts and threat of space bombardment. Resulting famines and disorders widely fatal.

Sun Year 79   Fernando Kwan commands first starside expedition, leaving Cotopaxi High with three spacecraft to search for solar halo. Fusion cruiser *Spica* reported lost in encounter with alien spacecraft.

Sun Year 81   With two remaining cruisers, *Capella* and *Aldebaran*, Kwan reaches the small halo iceball he names Janoort. He plants Halo Station as a starside defense outpost against unidentified space aliens.

Sun Year 82   Fernando Kwan returns Sunside to challenge Tycoon Chen. Chen accuses him of inventing space aliens as a solarpolitical ploy. Fernando ousts him, becoming the third Sun Tycoon.

Sun Year 84   Quin Dain is born aboard S.S. *Aldebaran*, relief craft en route to Halo Station.

Sun Year 88   Fanatic Holyfolk leader, "The Revelator," creates world panic with illicit holo broadcasts predicting invasion of Earth by demons from space.

Sun Year 89   Revelationists, known as *Los Santíssimos* in Spanish America, are suppressed by "warning shots"— missile strikes from Cotopaxi High against selected target cities. Estimated casualties, 18 million dead.

Sun Year 93   Mars skyline hung. Contra-Neptune Relay Station put in place, enabling laser and radio contact with Halo Station.

Cycle of the Elderhood 77:54:08:01
Newling attache Goldengene reported killed in seeker attack on Point Vermillion. Survivors warn of twin dangers to Elderhood. Black Companion is nearing passage and marauding heatseeker is at large in the halo.

Sun Year 95   Revelator preaches that space aliens are the demons of the old religions, attacking mankind under Satan's command. He claims they interbreed with human space explorers, that Sunfolk have demon blood.

Cycle of the Elderhood 77:54:08:02
Seeker queen establishes hive in Trojan asteroid.

Sun Year 107   Fall of the skyweb and death of the last Tycoon.

S HE ADORED THE PRINCE.

He was a guest in the hive, bolder and hotter in the belly than any of her swarming siblings. A magnificent creature, armored in glistening crimson, gold scales flashing, fangs and talons black as space, he pursued her almost from the moment she burst from her egg.

He vanquished all the other suitors rash enough to challenge him, and entranced her with the ballads of his hunting adventures in their halo fringe. Though the vermin surviving there were tiny things, their cunning and their rarity made them exciting game.

When her sweet sisters tried to warn her of his hot-bellied passion, she suspected them of jealousy. Ignoring them, scorning all the would-be lovers he had beaten, she left her mother's hive with him.

In love too long, intoxicated even by their shared peril, they dared too much. They dived too near the maddening fire of their star. Caressing each other with the wild ferocity of the seeker kind, kissing and touching and parting, they laughed at the madness of regeneration, insanely hoping to defeat it forever.

Passion overtook them on a cold flight-food moon where they had alighted to feast on the creamy snow. She had been teasing him, flashing the flaming colors of love. Tempting her wickedly, he kept stroking her shimmering labrum. Trembling with her own hot desire, she tried to lock herself and fly away.

Tried too late. The flame of his semen ignited a nova inside her. Crazed, yielding to delirium, she seized him with all her talons, his splendid head between her jaws, and crushed all his ripeness into her. Screaming, burning, stabbing deeper, he fought till he died.

He was dead, and joy was gone.

She woke to that fatal fact when the madness had ebbed. It chilled the fire in her bowels. Until that dreadful instant, her whole world had loved her. Secure in her royal mother's devotion and the hive's safe warmth, a happy sharer at the family feasts of rich life-metals the workers brought from the starward planets, she had known neither care nor fear.

Lying alone and forlorn, there in that deep pit where the blaze of their union had thawed the snow, feeling dead as the bright shards of his armor still clutched in her claws, she longed for all she had lost. In sad recollection, she was hatched again into the hive's happy music. She rode once more into space on a grumbling worker's back and learned to fly again, riding her blazing jets.

In wistful retrospection, she danced around their playground moons again in the splendid constellations of her gifted sisters, renewing the racial rituals of life and love and death. In joyous unison, they memorized the classic sagas of their warrior kind. She lost herself again in the sacred games of fight-and-kill in the tunnels of their hive. Wickedly she flirted again with the bright-shining rivals of her prince, teasingly testing his devotion.

All that, forever ended.

Her sisters would scorn her now, and her former suitors would shun her for killing their noble companion. The food worlds would be forbidden, and the hive would be shut against her, a dreadful trap where even the last sad relic of her once-loving mother would be lurking to assail her.

In that bitter aftermath, too sick even to suck at the last of her lover's freezing juices, she lay there amid the glittering bits of his empty armor till the furious princes swarmed down to drive her into the interstellar night, away from all she had ever loved.

Flying out into the dead emptiness of space, she clung to all those sad recollections until a new and dreadful hunger overwhelmed them with a terrible imperative, driving her on through the heatless dark to seek a place for her own new hive, a world where her firstborn neuter foragers might find life-metals and flight food for new generations as splendidly daring as their noble father had been.

As ruthless as her own fatal lust, that new ravening chose a star where she could sense no rival hive. Driven by it, helpless as a hatchling, she flew out across the halo where her prince had hunted and on into the black gulf beyond.

The flight took too long. Unfed, her prince's precious seed had to burrow too soon into her own willing flesh. The first ecstatic agonies of that gave her a proud theme for her new saga, but they soon became eternities of delirium.

Nightmare dreads swarmed like maddened males around her, haunting her back into awareness. Her mass sacs had drained too fast. Her inner fires had grown too cold. She was too young, not yet fit for all the fearful hazards she must overcome. She thought the star ahead might have no planets fit to feed her brood. Some rival queen might get there first. Some native race might possess weapons not recorded in the sagas.

The gas giants cheered her when she found them, until she came near enough to sense points of heat far out in this new halo, most of them fixed but a few in motion almost as swift as her own. Enemy princes, out of a hive she hadn't seen, swarming to kill her?

Yet, whatever the hazards, her time was too near to let her turn back. There was no other star near enough to reach before her flight sacs were altogether empty, before the fire metals cooled in her belly, before she died, consumed by her own dying brood. Agony and terror spurred her on, until she could sense sizes and make out shapes.

What she sensed killed her dread and edged her hunger. For these were no defending warriors. Nesting on the snow-clumps of the halo, or sometimes in flight between them, these were tiny creatures, strangely slow in flight and harmless as the idiot midges in the ballads of her hunter prince.

Some of them, surely, would be fat enough for food.

Janoort. *Ice haloid on inner fringe of Oort halo, 600 AU out from the Sun (600 times as far out as Earth is). A mix of water, ammonia, and methane ices surrounding a heavier core formed of interstellar dust. Diameter, 129 kilometers; mean density, .9; surface gravity, 2 cm/sec^2; day, 19.08 hours. Site of Halo Station.*

THE LIFE OF THE STATION HUNG BY A KWANLON thread. So Kerry used to say. That thread wound the master magnets in the fusion reactors that fought the interstellar cold. If it ever broke, there would be no light or heat, no food, no air.

Yet Kerry seldom seemed to worry.

"*Por Dios*, we'll hold out." He used to grin at Quin, while he sniffed his hot-smelling starmist. "Hoping somebody learns to spin a better thread."

"I will," Quin promised. "When I grow up."

He was five years old.

"Somebody will." Kerry's blue eyes looked far away. "Somebody at the Kwan Labs most likely. Back Sunside."

"I'm going Sunside," Quin said. "I'll find the thread and send it back."

"Maybe you will." He breathed his reeking starmist. "But you'll have to grow up first."

Quin might have been born on Halo Station if the old *Aldebaran* had been a faster ship, but he had come prematurely while they were still in space, six months out from Cotopaxi High and weeks before they found Janoort. His mother never told him who his father was, and he always wondered.

Nobody Earthbred. He felt certain of that, because the Earthbred weren't allowed in Sun country except to be servants. A dashing Sunblood lover? A space lord, maybe, with fabulous wealth in Company shares?

Even one of the Kwans?

People said they all had the Romanoff nose. Inherited from a mad monk named Rasputin. When he asked about that, Kerry gave him a Sun-dollar coin that had an image of the first Tycoon under its shiny plastic. He frowned at the bright gold head with its considerable nose, and hurried to the mirror to peer at his own. It looked very ordinary.

Yet he kept on wondering.

His mother never said why she'd come so far away from home. That always troubled him, because she was never well or really happy at the station. He used to think she must be homesick for Earth and the skyweb and all the Sunside planets. Longing sadly, he imagined, for all the splendor she had left behind.

Once she let him see an old holo of her, taken back Earthside. In Sun country, she said, near Vogelkop Down. Staring, he hardly knew her. She was thin and pale now, with wrinkles around her eyes and her pale hair worn in a knot at the back of her neck. In the holo, she looked so lovely he ached for her.

The camera had caught her wading off a tropical beach, white water swirling around her knees, her hair bright as gold, loose and blowing in the wind. Her beauty seemed to light everything around her. The sky was strangely blue, with giant trees called palms leaning over the breaking waves and magic towers of white-shining cloud climbing under a dazzling Sun.

Such wonders always awed him. Wind! Clouds! Water not frozen. The endless flatness of the sea and the blue of the sky and the flying thing she called a gull—he used to shiver with awe, trying to imagine that impossible world below the skyweb.

Hope was like a hunger in him, a burning urge to get back Sunside, to see the marvels his mother had known, to ride the skywires and explore the old Earth. Perhaps he could find his father and learn who he was born to be. Secretly he always believed his destined future would be there among the Sunfolk, enjoying all the splendor and the power of the Company.

Once he told his mother he wanted to go home.

"No!" Her breath drew in and her thin face twisted. "Never!"

That was all she said. He never spoke to her again about that secret dream, or even asked her about anything Sunside. He didn't want to hurt her, and he saw that she was trying to forget something very painful.

Only three weeks old when they got to the station, he grew up there, a prisoner in the narrow plastic rooms and tunnels that held air people could breathe. There was no child-sized space gear, and he never got outside.

Listening to others who would talk of the strange old Earth and all the far-off Sunside worlds, he felt more and more afraid he would never get there. Yet most of the time he wasn't unhappy. There were only a few children at the station. His mother said all of them were spoiled.

There was school, a dozen kids of every age, in just one frost-walled cave-room. The instructors were staff people, teaching how to stay alive in the halo. How not to be killed by the airless emptiness and the terrible cold outside the thin station walls. How to run the machines that had to keep running to keep anybody alive.

In school and out, his best teacher was Kerry McLenn. An old hand at the station, Kerry had come out with

Admiral Fernando Kwan on the discovery expedition.
Quin's mother married him the year he was four. To be
his new father, she said.

"He isn't," Quin protested. "He never will be. My real
father—"

His mother's hurt face stopped him. Kerry grinned and
boxed him gently and promised that they would be friends.
They always were, but Quin could never call him father.

They lived under the ice, in places lined with plastic
foam to keep the cold out and the precious air sealed
inside. The floors had velfast carpets that let them walk
in boots with velfast soles. Weighing only a few ounces,
he could fly down the tunnels when he liked, never touching anything.

In most of the station, the labs and shops and processors, kids weren't wanted. People were too busy. The pit
and refinery were too dangerous. The ship and the power
tunnels were forbidden territory. But even when he was
small Kerry would take him along to the hydroponic gardens when he was feeding and harvesting the tangle of
vines that grew most of their food. Some grew flowers;
he loved the colors and odors when they bloomed, and
he came to love being with Kerry.

Once Kerry took him far down into the frost-walled
cave above the ice-pit to watch the hoists and drills and
pumps digging down toward the far core of Janoort. The
air felt bitter, and his breath made a fog. The ammonia
reek burned his eyes and choked his nose, but he wanted
to know all about the slurry coming up through the white-
caked pipes to be processed into water and air and foods
for people and the gardens. Even into plastics, vital because heavy metals were so rare and precious.

Kerry was a big man with a good smell. He wore a
shapeless red rag of a cap. When he took it off, his head
was brown and shiny, hairless as an onion. His eyes looked
strange, with no brows or lashes, but they were nice eyes,
blue and kind and bright.

He didn't seem to mind that he had no rating and wore

no Sunmark. Mostly he seemed happy, though sometimes he woke silent and slow to move, his strange eyes hooded and gloomy. Brooding, Quin used to think, over his youth and the far Earth. Longing, anyhow, for the stuff he called starmist.

"Not for you, *muchachito*."

A sort of poison, he explained, not really good for anybody. Some plants made poisons for the bugs that ate them, and some people got addicted to the poisons. Starmist came from mutant plants. He had brought illegal seed with him to space.

"I got to using it back in the barrios," he said. "When we had no food."

The first sniff of it lit his eyes and made him merry. Breathing it, he laughed a lot and liked his work. He was nearly always busy about the machines. He used to call himself Kerry Can Do. He could fix or even build nearly anything, and he could explain all the gear that kept the station alive and even how the skywires worked, back Sunside.

When Quin was old enough, Kerry brought him along to the observatory dome. It was a clear plastic bubble thirty meters across. They came up through the floor. It was cold and still. They had to keep very quiet, not to jar the instruments. The lights were red and dim, to let them see the sky.

Black and dreadful, it terrified him. He knew the station existed to watch for strange creatures watching it from their strange homes out toward the stars. Now he felt their strange eyes on him. Cold and trembling, he clung to Kerry's hand.

"*Amigos, muchacho.*" Kerry wasn't frightened. "They've never tried to hurt us. I think they'll be friends— if we ever meet them."

Trying not to be afraid, he listened to Kerry and began to feel the wonder of the sky. The stars were near and splendid, the Milky Way a great arch of shining silver dust. He kept trying to see the halo. Billions or maybe trillions of iceballs like their own Janoort, closer than any of the stars. He never found even one.

"They're all too far," Kerry said. "It's more luck than anything that we ever found Janoort."

The daytime Sun was only another star, but bright enough to light the signal dishes and the telescopes and the lidar search gear standing in the vacuum outside. The ice around the station was a dirty gray where sunlight struck, the craters pools of night.

The Sun was never high, because the station was so near Janoort's starside pole. Through the brief days, it crawled low above the ice horizon, just long enough for signals to and from Fleet Command. Most of the time, the scopes and dishes were aimed the other way, searching for whatever was out in the halo.

The ice sloped down fast all around the dome, because Janoort was so tiny, but they could see the nose of the ship, a shining blade stabbing into the blackness above the close horizon. When he learned to read he could make out her name, *Capella*, black-lettered across the gold-winged Sun-disk.

"She's our life," Kerry told him. "It's her fusion engines that give us heat and light and all the energy that keeps us going. Without her engines, we'd be dead."

Sometimes Kerry went aboard to help with a repair job. Once Quin tried to follow him, swimming down the plastic tunnel to the hatch. The watchman scowled and said he had no business on the ship.

Nearly every day, he went with Kerry to work out in the gym. Built mostly to be an air storage tank and heat sink, it was a big balloon with kwanlon woven into the plastic, black on the outside to radiate waste heat—even on icy Janoort, the station had to be cooled.

Inside, there were ropes and swings and nets, and a squirrel cage where they could spin to weigh as much as they wanted. Kerry rode his bike on a track around it. A whiff of starmist could make him sing, and Quin loved the way his happy voice boomed against the walls.

Sometimes the songs were Spanish. Strange sad songs about Earthbred people in love, hiding from *El Cabrón* and *los demonios del Sol*, fighting and dying in the barrios. He had learned them when he was a child in the barrios outside Azteca Down.

"Can I go Sunside?" Quin asked him once. "Ever?"

"Not likely, boy." He laughed. "Not likely!"

Quin wanted to know why.

"Too far," Kerry said. "Even the Sunlight takes three days to get here."

"But you got here. Mother did. Ships take people back."

"On Company business. Or for Sun dollars we don't have. You're crazy, boy, to think about it."

"I'm not crazy," Quin insisted. "When I grow up, I'm going."

"You'll be sorry if you do." Kerry had grown very serious. "You know why I sniff starmist? It's to help me forget Azteca Down."

He brewed and fermented the hot-fuming stuff from the roots and leaves and berries of special plants he grew among the hydroponic vines. He never used it at home, because Quin's mother hated its bitter reek, but he always had it with him in a little flat squeeze-bottle.

Quin liked its peppery pungence, though once when he breathed it too deep it made him sick. Nobody minded when Kerry used it in the gardens. Sometimes when they were there together Quin could get him to talk about the Sunside.

"I'm not Sunbred," he said once, when they were gathering a bale of the ripe, rich-smelling leaves. "You can see that on my face."

All the other grownups wore what they called the Sunspot. A small round spot on the right cheek that sparkled like golden frost when light struck it. Kerry's lean brown cheek was bare.

"Dad used to say he was Irish, but I was born in the barrio. We stayed alive however we could. When Mom was young and pretty enough, she had a pass to work in

Sun Country. Cancelled when she got pregnant with me.
I grew up dreaming about space—I guess the way you
dream about the Sunside."

He shook his head at Quin, blue eyes solemn.

"People said I was crazy. No way I could get to space,
any more than you'll ever get back to Coto High. When
you hear what Azteca Down was like—what it was for
me—you'll be happy to be here."

Quin shook his head.

"*Caramba!* Listen to me, boy! Our barrio was bad.
Bad! A shacktown just outside the infall dumps. Under
a gravity power line. Big ore buckets screaming down it,
one every minute, day and night. Meteor metal for the
Earthside mills and power for everybody. Not so nice for
us, because the buckets used to get hot and come apart
on the brakeline, spilling rocks on us. Yet—"

He opened his bottle and squeezed a careful drop into
his palm and smiled when he sniffed the rich aroma.

"I never minded that." His voice had fallen to a rusty
whisper. "Even when people got hurt and Dad cursed the
Tycoon, I loved to watch the buckets howling down the
line. Because they came from space.

"Mom and Dad never understood. They hated the Sunfolk, fat and pompous inside their walls and fences. Because we had so little. That crazy little shack built of
salvaged junk. Leaky when it rained. Icy in the winter,
because we couldn't pay for heat. What we ate was mostly
garbage out of the luxury lodges in Sun Country, where
the only Earthfolk were cooks and waiters and such.

"I learned to read." He smiled, thinking of it. "Out of
a book I found in a garbage bin. A lot of it was gone, and
I never really understood what was left, but the hero had
a three-word motto I've always remembered. 'Silence,
exile, cunning.' I still think about it. We're in exile here,
if people ever were. Silence means caution. Remember
that, boy. We never ask for trouble. With cunning enough,
we can hope to survive. Three words to remember."

He paused to breathe the starmist, looking hard at Quin.

"Words to help us stay alive, here in the halo."

I won't need them, Quin told himself. Not when I get back Sunside.

"The Tycoon back then was old Boris Chen." Kerry inhaled again out of his hand. "In the barrio, people called him *El Cabrón*. Yet I never really hated him, because Mom got me into a school he'd endowed for poor kids like I was. Dad said it was only to train slaves for the Company, but we got hot lunches and I learned a lot. Till the Santissimos wrecked the place, and it closed down.

"If I hated anybody then, it was them—the Holyfolk. For the way they hated the Tycoon and the Company and everything in space. But I never said much about what I felt, because of Mom and Dad and their friends."

His eyes seemed very solemn now.

"One friend was named Saladin. A cell name, I found out later. He called himself a medic. Ran what he called the Sunmark Clinic. Promising to help people pass the tests for space and become Sunfolk. I used to wonder why he hadn't got his own Sunmark. I finally guessed that he was a Santissimo agent.

"Mom and Dad must have been Santissimos themselves, though they never told me. There was a pit under the floor where sometimes they hid things I learned not to talk about. Illegal leaflets. Heavy little boxes that must have been weapons or explosives.

"Dad built me a little green wagon out of junk parts. I used to pull it through the alleys, looking for garbage fit to eat—that's what I had to say. But sometimes I had to haul those boxes, hidden under the garbage. I guessed they came from Dr. Saladin, though I wasn't supposed to know."

He shook his hairless head, squinting off into a gloomy tunnel.

"Bad times, *muchacho*. Times I wish I could forget. One night a man and a girl came panting into the shack.

Limping and bloody. Mom got them under the floor, not half a minute ahead of the cops. They kicked our door in and found Mom peeling rotten potatoes. Held their noses and took Dad away.

"He never came back.

"Mom was strange after that. She kept going to Dr. Saladin, and finally took me. A thin little man with eyes that frightened me. Hard and bright and black. Narrow and terrible when he talked about the Kwans and the Company. I knew why he had no Sunmark when I saw how much he hated them.

"Scared as I was, I asked him if he could help me get a Sunmark. He looked at Mom with a queer little smile and promised that he would. Finally, he did help me into space. To be a spy, I found out, for the Santissimos.

"Mom never wanted me to go. Space would kill me in a year or two, she told me, unless I happened to have good Sun genes. Even if I had them, *La Seguridad* would kill me if they caught me out in the skyweb without a Sunmark or a travel pass.

"Saladin's clinic didn't even try to treat my genes— that was just a cover for what they called the movement. But I didn't care. For maybe just a year in space—"

"A whole year!"

"To me, that was worth all the risks. I kept on begging till Mom let Saladin's people tattoo a fake Sunspot on my face. His people gave me a fake travel pass and stowed me away in a new escape pod waiting shipment out to Coto High for the *Aldebaran*. The Tycoon's flagship— though he was still Admiral Fernando Kwan, not the Tycoon yet.

"Headed for the halo!"

Kerry breathed deep again from his big brown hand.

"You can't guess how thrilled I was. A raw Earthsider kid, just turned fifteen, on that great expedition." His smile went away. "Too much I didn't know. The Santissimos had filled the mass tanks with explosives to blow up the admiral and his ship.

"I had a little gadget they told me was a special signal set. I was to signal when we took off with the admiral aboard. When we finally got away, I was so excited I forgot. Anyhow, I'd had enough of Saladin.

"Later, hiding in the pod, I ran out of drinking water. Tried to get water out of the mass tank and found the explosive. Scared me witless. I expected to be tortured and killed. In no hurry for that, I dug through the aid locker and found a Metabrake needle. Shot myself with too much of it—that's what happened to my hair."

With a half-sad grin at himself, Kerry slid the red cap back and ran his hard brown hand across his slick brown head.

"It kept me alive. On Metabrake, you don't need food or even much air. We were two months out when they found me. My fake Sunspot was peeling by then, and my fake travel pass was just a quick ticket to die. Ship Security took me to Jean Charbon—captain of the ship. He was going to give me another shot of Metabrake and cycle me out through the waste lock.

"Jason saved me."

Kerry's brown face twisted, as if he had tasted something bitter.

"Jason Kwan, the admiral's son. Maybe six years old. A wicked little imp, but cute as a kitten with his new Sunspot. Cunning enough, and charming when he tried. Aboard because his mother didn't want him back Sunside. The admiral doted on him.

"Little Jason saved my life. Not because he loved me. Charbon had scolded him for stealing an officer's laser-gun. The sly little brat took me to the admiral, trying to spite Charbon.

"Old Fernando brought me into his quarters, just to please Jason. He somehow got to like me. Laughed at the peeling Sunspot and wanted to know why I'd stowed away. He said my genes couldn't have been all that bad, or the Metabrake would have already killed me.

"I told him about the explosive in the mass tank. It

turned out the radio gadget had been meant to set it off. Ship Security wanted to kill me, but old Fernando slowed them up. Talked to me a lot, asking questions as if he really cared why people joined the Santissimos. Came to believe I never wanted to be one of them. Finally made me his cabin boy, and let me study in his own library.

"So here I am." Kerry grinned, happy about it, and then leaned to look at Quin hard.

"*Muchachito*, I wanted you to know how bad things are, back Sunside. See?"

Quin nodded because he didn't like to argue, but the barrios weren't where he meant to go. His father must have worn the Sunmark. When he learned where he belonged, it would be in the skyweb, an altogether better place than Azteca Down. A thousand times better than Halo Station, with the starsiders watching out of the dark. He still felt cold inside when he thought about them.

He saw Kerry squirting another hot brown drop into his hand. That meant he still had time to talk, and Quin decided to ask what he thought the starsiders were.

"Nobody knows."

"Mother says they hit your ships on the way here."

"Something did."

Quin waited while he exhaled a fragrant cloud.

"We were cruising a million kilometers apart to give us long baselines for the lidar gear. Flashing our lasers ahead and watching for echoes. Most of a year out from Coto, with never a hint of anything ahead. Till the old *Spica* reported contact.

"Her signal officer was Reynard Charbon—Captain Charbon's son. Running the search gear, he'd got something that unnerved him. A laser burst that came back down his search beam, too strong to be an echo. It was on his search frequency, but modulated in a way he didn't understand. The Doppler shift showed its source approaching him, coming ten times faster than his ship was flying.

"Zar—Bela Zar was captain of the *Spica*—Zar wanted

orders. The admiral told them to keep contact and report everything. Another Doppler showed that unknown source slowing to intercept them. A little later, they got an actual echo from an unidentified object drifting with them, only sixty kilometers off.

"That was the last we heard. Radio and lasercom went dead. Stayed dead. We closed in on the *Spica*'s trajectory, shooting search beams at where it should have been. No echo of anything. We couldn't find the *Spica*. Karl Rohn— he was commander of the other ship—Rohn lost his nerve. Wanted our two ships to give up and run."

Kerry's grin grew wider.

"But old Fernando never ran from anything. We came on out, toward where the halo had to be, till we picked up the echos and found Janoort. No sign of any starsiders here. None that anything alive had ever been here. We landed. Built the station. Fernando left Jean Charbon in command. Went back home and got to be Sun Tycoon.

"And here we are."

"If they took the *Spica*—" Quin shivered a little, wondering what sort of things could have been born in the halo. "Aren't you afraid they might come here to hurt us?"

"Afraid?" Kerry took a tiny sip from his tiny bottle. His face relaxed and his eyes half shut, he worked it in his mouth before he swallowed and licked his lips and blinked a little sleepily at Quin.

"I used to be afraid. When I was a kid, back in the barrio. Afraid of the meteor stuff at first, when the broken ore buckets rained it out of the sky. Afraid of the Security cops. Afraid of the Santissimos, most of all."

He was wiping his hand on a big red neckerchief.

"But we've got neighbors, boy. Somewhere out there." He waved the rich-smelling cloth in the starside direction. "Probably smarter than we are, with know-how enough to live in the halo. I expect they could kill us if they had to, but I hope they never do. Old Charbon still lives in terror of them, but me—I'm keen to meet them."

Quin got to know Charbon in the classroom, there to lecture on astronomy and space navigation. A short fat man with sleek black hair, short of breath when he moved too fast, strutting in his too-tight black-and-gold uniforms until he looked ridiculous. Sometimes jolly, he was arrogant with his men and shrill when anybody angered him.

Kerry never did. Charbon loved wine and good food, and Kerry had come to be his special friend, helping with the grapes and truffles and spices he grew in the gardens from his own store of Earthside seeds and cells.

Often with them, Quin came to share some of the same fear and hate that haunted old Charbon. Talking about the starsiders, the little commander forgot to be jolly. His puffy face twitched and his black eyes glazed when he remembered what the space creatures had done to his son, and his voice rose higher.

"*Diables!*" he exploded when Kerry tried to say he hoped the aliens might become friends. "*Bien la même!* They're the same wicked things the Revelator rants about. They took the *Spica* and murdered my Reynard. That's why I stayed here. To hold the station and hunt them down and make them pay."

"He's sick," Quin's mother said.

"He's insane about the aliens." Kerry nodded. "I like him when he's working in the garden or having me for dinner, but he's no good for us here. Because he's burning inside. Crazy for revenge."

"Still—" Quin looked at Kerry and then at his mother, wondering why they weren't afraid. "If the things are out there watching—"

"They can't be looking for us." Kerry shrugged, grinning at him. "Not very hard, because we aren't hiding. We've had the search gear going ever since we landed. Shooting laser pulses out to probe for haloids. With never another reflection from anything at all. If we've got neighbors, I'd love to meet them. Could be they want to meet us. That might be why they took the *Spica*."

"If they ever do want us—"

"Forget it, boy." Kerry laughed at him. "Halo Station is a great place to be."

Quin didn't argue, but sometimes he had nightmares about the outsiders. They came out of dark space, flying on black flapping wings. When he tried to hide, they searched him out with monstrous eyes that blazed like lasers. They caught him up with great sharp claws, cruel and cold, that froze him into ice. He couldn't move or even breathe, while the whole hideous swarm came flapping and howling in to eat him while he was still half alive.

The year he was seven, they caught the starbird.

Begging for the starward mission, Quicksmith flickered nervously in spite of himself. He felt too anxious for it and nearly sure the director would turn him down. To his surprise, the old fellow kept on listening. That cheered him for a time. Then he began to wonder why.

The core-star observatory had the shape of a tiny solar system, the various facilities in orbit around a small haloid. The director's lab was a huge crystal shell that let them see the star itself, near and bright. In airless space, they spoke with photon radiation.

"An urgent undertaking." Quicksmith let his eagerness shimmer. "A great chance for me to serve the Elderhood—and to make my own name."

The director swam a little higher, regarding him with an air of easy toleration that had begun to vex him. Coming from a race that was nearly ageless, the old scholar had a patience Quicksmith couldn't afford.

"Sir—please! Really, we can't let it wait."

"Our sponsors have advised us to scrub it." The director spoke at last, glowing with a bland indifference to his anxieties. "Too chancy."

"Risky, maybe," he agreed. "But I can't hope to live forever."

"You're young." The director paused to survey him with a philosophic deliberation. "You'll live a lot longer if you learn to take your time."

"I don't have your kind of time." He tried to slow his voice. "And I doubt that the planetics do."

"They do display a reckless haste." The director dimmed. "This incursion into the halo shows amazing progress since their first nuclear experiments were detected. They do require closer observation."

"Which is why I'm begging you to reconsider—"

"We've been reconsidering." The director's troubled stare shifted to the search instruments. "But avoidable violence has to be avoided. Our sponsor advise us not to risk another chance contact."

"Waiting for the Elderhood—" He tried to shade his hot vexation. "The planetic hulk is still out there. Empty and drifting. Crying for examination. I'd expect no contact, because the other planetics have never come near it. They're probably afraid to. It can tell us more about them than we'll ever learn in any other way."

"Perhaps." A tolerant twinkle. "But we're still talking to the specimens we rescued—"

"They'll never tell us much." He flashed disdain. "I've worked with them, or tried to. A dimwitted lot. Attacking us with no provocation. Killing each other now, in their stupid efforts to escape."

"Don't judge them too soon." The director shone mild dissent. "Though they do require caution, I'm beginning to admire them. At least for their hardiness in getting out here in such crude spacecraft."

"Savages!" Quenching his tensions, Quicksmith wondered again what the old fellow wanted of him. "They've always been surprising. With their heavy-metals technology and their habits of murderous aggression. They surely need watching."

"The Elderhood has files enough on too many such primitives killing themselves with their own technology." The commander paused to inspect him again, with an air of benevolent concern. "That's why they want us to be cautious."

"I'll take care," he promised. "All I'll require is a cutter to put me on the hulk and come back to pick me up again when

I'm ready. The odds are they'll never know I've been there. If anything goes wrong, the life at risk is mine."

The great eyes blinked and blinked again, until his impatience was hard to restrain.

"Good enough!" The blaze of approval amazed him. "Invading the halo, these creatures do require closer study. I simply wanted to be certain of your dedication to a mission most of us would shrink from. I trust your competence, and I'm going to let you go.

"The cutter will be ready when you are."

Starbird. *Space alien discovered aboard drifting wreckage of Sun Fleet cruiser* Spica. *The creature was apparently intelligent and actively engaged in dismantling what was left of the ship. Trying to establish communication, Captain Caffodio brought the creature to Janoort, then back to the skyweb, finally to Zurich Down, where it died. Major problems of its biology, habitat, and purpose aboard* Spica *remain unsolved.*

THE SUPPLY SHIP FOR HALO STATION WAS DUE TO COME every two years. It was always delayed, for reasons that rarely got past the censors. Even with no trouble, the flight took many months for such early fusion craft as the old *Aldebaran*.

Captain Caffodio had been delayed in space. The linguist Aurelia Zinn was aboard, with signal equipment designed to probe the halo for intelligence. Three AU out of Halo Station, her search gear picked up an unknown object. When her signals brought no response, Captain Caffodio braked for contact.

What he found was the dismantled remains of the lost *Spica*, still drifting near its flight trajectory. Closing, he sent Dr. Zinn with her husband and two crewmen in a minishuttle to board the wreck. Though they found no apparent battle damage, the hulk had been stripped.

Escape pods gone. Hatches open, air pressure lost. Temperatures near absolute zero. Crew missing. Supplies, records, and astrogation gear removed, and even wide sections of the hull itself. All without a clue, until Zinn reached the aft compartments.

Her headlamps found the alien there. It had been disassembling the fusion engines and the ion drive. Parts removed had been neatly bundled with plastic thread, "fibers almost invisibly thin, but stronger than kwanlon." The creature recoiled from their lights and took off toward a hole in the hull, propelled by a jet that condensed into a cloud of white vapor.

Perhaps blinded by her lights, it collided with a bulkhead. The men tackled it, finding it surprisingly weak and apparently unarmed. They took it back to the *Aldebaran*. Captain Caffodio locked it in an empty mass tank and brought it on to Janoort. Quin's mother saw it there when Caffodio called her aboard to help with their examination. She came back pale and dazed, and Quin saw her swallow one of the pills meant to keep her fit for space.

When she felt like talking, she told them about the starbird— Aurelia Zinn had named it that. The mass tank had a queer ammoniac reek that took her breath. She found the creature huddled away from the lights the medic had strung in the tank. When she dropped inside, it roused and turned to face her.

"Tall! Taller than a man when it stood up." She was still trembling, and Quin thought she needed another pill. "But not so massive. It seems—flimsy. The body's nearly round, covered with what looks like fine scales, maybe metallic, patterned black and white. It has three lower limbs, more like tentacles than legs—the medic says they're hollow. Drive jets with fingers.

"Its eyes—they're strange! Mirrors, really, round and enormous. Telescopes, I imagine. The thing must have evolved far out in the dark, where distances are vast. I think it tried to speak to us. Though not with sound, because it lives without air.

"It came a little toward me. Those vast eyes shimmered at me, flushed with rainbow colors in queer patterns. Speaking, I think, with light. It must have seen I didn't understand. In a moment it was shrinking away again, folding its eyes—an odd word to use, but they're only thin membranes, and they rolled up like petals of a fading flower.

"I feel so terribly sorry—"

She shook her head, and her eyes looked wet.

"It wants to talk. We want to talk. But we haven't got a chance. Not that I can see. Its ammonia stink drove me out of the tank, but Dr. Zinn got masks for us, and we went back together. I made her dim the lights—I think they've blinded the creature.

"We spent two hours with it in the tank. Trying anything I thought wouldn't hurt it. Voice. Radio. Laserphone. Colored lights of our own. With no response at all. Not even when I touched it. I think it's sick, and I feel sick about it—"

"Hurt, perhaps?" Kerry said. "Hurt by the spacemen when they tackled it."

"Poisoned, too, I imagine." She nodded. "By our free oxygen. It couldn't be used to that."

Caffodio spent several weeks at the station, overhauling his fusion drive and refilling the other mass tanks. When Fleet Command heard about the alien, he was ordered to keep it alive and bring it back Sunside to be studied at Kwan Labs.

Aurelia's husband, Tikon Zinn, had come to be the new signal officer. She was staying, too, for their four-year duty tour, to flash her contact codes into the halo and wait for responses from anything intelligent. They began setting up their gear, and Quin's mother went back on the ship to care for the starsider.

She kept the lights low and had the air vented out of the tank. In a spacesuit, she returned to the tank to study

it yet again. It still seemed alive, though she couldn't be
sure it was conscious.

"Caffodio thinks I understand it. Not that I do. He
wants me to go back Sunside with him, to take care of
it." She was looking at him, her eyes dark-rimmed and
strangely sad. "I'm going, Quin. Going home."

Home! The word set fireworks off in his imagination.
Skywires and space cities. Earth, with the near Sun warm-
ing everything. Seas and blue skies and clouds with thunder. Air with gulls flying in it—

He saw Kerry's face.

"Aren't we all—?" His voice caught. "Am I—?"

She drew him hard against her, not saying anything.

"We don't know, Quin." Kerry frowned with trouble.
"Your mother will decide. We've a few days left before
the ship takes off."

Quin clung to her, the hard lump still in his throat.

"Your mother has to go," Kerry was saying, his own
voice unsteady. "Not just because of the alien. She
shouldn't—should never have come out. Or stayed so
long. Because her genes—her genes aren't entirely right
for space."

"That's why—" His mother sobbed, her thin body
trembling. "Why we don't know—"

Kerry moved closer, his arm around them both. A good
strong arm. The starmist sweetness of his red neckerchief
was a good smell, and Quin breathed it in.

"It's your genes, boy, that have to be tested," Kerry
told him. "Half come from your mother. Mixed with the
other half from your father. He must have had fine Sun
genes, because you've always been so well, but your
mother will have to run a lab test before we really know."

Quin stared up at him, still bewildered.

"Listen, *niñito*." He held them tighter, speaking very
carefully. "The genes are a code. A blueprint for what
you'll grow up to be. Your mother's are mostly good, or
she couldn't have lived here so long. But some—

"Some are wrong."

His tight face twitched, and Quin thought he needed more starmist.

"It has been hard for her, Quin. She does her work and doesn't say much, but she has never been well here. When the genes don't fit, space can hurt your body in all sorts of ways. You feel sick. Your bones lose calcium, and your glands act up. If the genes are wrong enough, space can kill you."

"Is—is Mother—"

Looking into her thin gray face, Quin couldn't go on.

"It's hard, boy. Harder for women than men. She could have died, having you. She's been off the Earth seven years now—" His frown bit deeper. "Much too long for her. If she doesn't go now, I'm afraid she'd never last till the next ship comes."

At the table next morning, Quin could see how sick she was. Not a bit like she looked in that old holo. Her eyes were puffy and red from crying, and she couldn't eat. Kerry was trying to help her pack, but there wasn't much she wanted to take.

In her lab after breakfast, she made Quin strip to the waist. The room seemed cold and he saw she didn't feel like talking. He watched her boot up the computer and uncover the machines that would tell what he was born to be, Earthbred or Sunbred. Her hands were trembling.

He shivered a little, afraid to learn what he was. He wanted terribly to go Sunside, to ride the skywires and find his father and somehow earn his own golden Sunmark, but he didn't want to be Earthbred. Not if it meant that he'd be sent out of Sun Country to live in the barrios where Kerry had grown up, with rocks falling out of the sky and only garbage to eat.

The lab had a queer chemical stink, and the sensors felt icy cold on his face and his chest. There was a queer computer game he had to play, with graphic shapes that kept fading out of the monitor as fast as he could build them. There were questions he had to answer, about bright dots that danced and vanished in the holo tank. And a chair where he sat with a bandage over his eyes, while she kept spinning it and asking him the direction of the Sun.

She took blood with a little needle. Staring at it, dark red in the tube, he wondered if the color could tell her whether it was Earthblood. With a sad little smile for him, she put the tube in a machine and watched bright numbers that flickered on it and then sat a long time at the computer while he waited, sweating even in the icy air.

Her eyes were wet when she looked around at him, but she was trying to smile.

"Okay, Quin." Her voice was a shivery whisper. "Your genes test as high as Kerry's, with none of those that hurt me so. You're born for space, and you must stay here."

He was almost crying, too. Because he longed so terribly to go Sunside with her.

"Quin—Quin! I'll miss you so." Her thin arm went around him. "I do wish you could come. For a few years, anyhow. But I wouldn't be able to care for you. There's too much trouble on Earth, and there'd be problems—problems . . ."

Her voice died before she said what the problems were. He gulped and caught his breath to ask her if he could ever wear the golden Sunmark.

"Your genes are okay." Her face looked sadder, and she was shaking her head. "But good genes aren't enough. Not anymore. You have to be listed by Security in their genetic register, with proof of Sunblood paternity."

He had never heard the word.

"That means—" She hugged him tighter and let him go. "You'd have to have a father." Her voice had fallen and she was suddenly busy, shutting off the machines. "Not that it matters. You'll never need the mark. Not out here."

It did matter. It mattered dreadfully, but he didn't try to tell her so.

Before the *Aldebaran* took off, she let Kerry and him come aboard to see her cabin. It seemed very bare and tiny, but she was going to be chief medic, in charge of the starbird. If she stayed well enough. Quin wanted to see the alien, but she said it mustn't be disturbed.

He kissed her, trying not to cry. She hugged Kerry a long time, and kissed him again before they had to leave the ship. The station seemed cold and terribly lonely without her, even when Kerry called him over to meet a thin little girl with long black hair and sad blue-black eyes, who stood clinging to her father's fingers.

"Quin, here's Mindi. Mindi Zinn. Just your own age. Her folks came out to stay at the station, and she'll be a new friend for you."

Her parents were saying good-bye to people leaving on the ship. With tear-smears around her eyes, she looked pale and cold and scared. Her lower lip was trembling, pinched between her teeth. Quin felt sorry for her, but she wouldn't shake his hand.

"I don't like you." Her chin jutted stubbornly. "I don't like Halo Station. I want to go home."

Her mother bent to tell her the station was going to be an exciting new home, but she stood sobbing, watching until the last crewman had gone aboard and the valves had clanged shut and the *Aldebaran* was gone. She wouldn't even look at him.

Yet they got to be friends. Both her parents were busy, her father in charge of the Sunside laser and radio links as well as the search for new haloids and her mother looking for anything intelligent in the halo. Too busy to be with her, they let her begin coming to the gym with Kerry and him.

She was shy at first, unhappy about everything she had left Sunside, but she let Quin show her how to work out in the spinning cage and tumble through the rings and do stunts on the ropes and bars. He showed her the station, and she told him about her old home in Sun Country and the skylabs where her parents used to work.

One day she smiled and said she liked him.

The Sunside laserlinks were for official business and

Fleet people only. They couldn't call Quin's mother. Two years had gone and he was nine before the *Aldebaran* got back with letters from her. She and the starbird had finished the voyage alive, she wrote, though it died without ever coming out of its coma.

"It didn't belong Sunside," she wrote. "Any more than I belong starside."

She missed him terribly, but she was well again. With a new job at the Kwan Labs Earthside facility at Zurich Down, she was working on the starbird's remains. "Very little left to study, because the creature was so fragile and decayed so fast. We'll never know much about them, unless we discover others."

Jomo Uruhu had come out to be the new fusion engineer. Quin got to know him when he began teaching classes in math and science. His English was strange, because he had spoken Swahili and Chinese in his own Earthside schools, but he was very patient and exact about everything. He called Quin his child, *mtoto wangu*, and Quin came to love him.

Like Quin's mother, he didn't want to talk about Old Earth. Maybe because his people had been Earthbred. He had passed gene tests and Security checks and used a quota to get his Sunmark. He wore it proudly, though its laser shimmer under his dark skin was hard to see.

When Quin had learned enough, Jomo began taking him to the engine room on the *Capella* to let him learn about fusion power. Though all he did at first was clean the decks, he loved being there. He wasn't so happy with what he began to learn about the fusion engines.

All three had been running when the ship landed, but Jomo said he couldn't keep them going forever. Number Three had already been cannibalized for parts to repair the other two. Just one, he said, was enough to light most of the station and keep the air fit to breathe. As long as it would run.

But if all three went down—

"One day, one engine, station plenty safe." Quin was

getting used to his way of talking. "Maybe two days, still plenty safe. Three days, four days—" He shook his head. "No more light for hydroponics. No more slurry out of pit. Eight days, maybe ten days, plenty trouble begin. Nothing come from processors. No food, no water, no oxygen."

Nearly all the time, he kept both engines going. When one of them failed, when the pumps and the processors stopped and the lights went out on the hydroponic levels, Jomo worked till it was fixed. Quin stayed with him, handing him tools and watching all he did.

Calmer than Quin was, Jomo never seemed to hurry and never stopped to rest. Sometimes he hummed the Bantu songs his mother had sung when he was a child. Sometimes, when a fitting slipped or stuck, he chanted magic spells he had learned from his Kikuyu grandfather. Sometimes he talked to Quin.

"Risky business!" he used to mutter. "One day no power. One day all lights out. One day big freeze. One bad day we die. If we let last reactor stop." Deft hands never pausing, he would turn his head to grin at Quin. "Never fret, *mtoto wangu*. Better stay dead haloside than come Earthside alive."

The relief ship should have come back the year Quin was eleven. It didn't. Fleet Command didn't say why.

"Revelator trouble," Jomo guessed. "Revelator trouble for Sun Tycoon. Always plenty trouble they never tell about. Sun Security plenty busy, back Sunside. Fleet Command forget Halo Station."

There was never much official news about any Revelator trouble, but still, for most of another year, the ship didn't come. There was a shortage of everything the processors couldn't make. Even the replacement coils of superconductor cable Jomo needed for the engines.

Secretly Quin felt glad for every new delay, because Mindi's father was due for relief and her mother had given up getting the starsiders to answer the contact signals.

They were going back Sunside and taking Mindi with them. There was no way he could go.

Mindi still liked him, maybe as much as he liked her. They had played together in the gym and studied together in school. Though her mother never wanted her in the dome, Kerry had begun letting both of them come with him when he had to fix the instruments. When he had time, he began teaching them how to run the signal gear.

Growing up, Mindi was growing beautiful, though she didn't seem to know it. She hated the freckles the Sun lamps gave her. She thought her eyes were too dark, and she didn't like the mane of rich black hair her mother wouldn't let her cut.

The year Quin was twelve, both reactors stopped. He and Mindi were in the gym balloon, racing their bikes around the track, when all the lights flickered and went out. They went flying off the track and into the net. The emergency lights didn't come on. When Quin got his breath back and got untangled from his bike, they were still in the dark.

"Quin—" He heard her frightened gasp. "You okay?"

He found her by her voice, and she was suddenly in his arms.

"Kiss me!" she whispered. "If we're going to die—"

Outpost Vermillion, in Octant Three, was an isolated snow-fluff nearly a light-year out from the Sun, on the far north fringe of Newmarch, the halo sector the Newlings had claimed. The staff lived and worked in a long hollow cylinder thrust through the heart of the tiny haloid which gave them food and fuel and reaction mass.

They were dedicated experts from all through the Elder-hood, in exile there on the halo frontier to watch for the return of the Black Companion. Until it appeared, they kept busy enough, probing the black hole growing at the galactic core and observing all they could of the whole evolving cosmos.

Their racial origins were various and ancient, but the forebears of most had managed the difficult evolutionary jump into space from birth on some planetary surface. The chief's folk, who called themselves the Eldren, had come in frozen sleep from the Andromeda galaxy.

The approaching heatseeker queen was picked up by Goldengene, a very junior observer. Her people were the Newlings. Recent arrivals in the halo, they were refugees from the seeker conquest of their native star system. Flickering with alarm, she carried her news to the chief.

"Seekers?" To her astonishment, he seemed pleased. "Coming, I trust, on a mission of friendship with the Elderhood."

"Sir!" She flashed blue with shock. "Coming more likely to wipe us out."

"Please, child!" he winked benignly at her. "Why say that?"

"It's no friendly signal, sir." Awe of him dimmed her voice. "Only a radiant point approaching from our own native star. Its spectrum is typical of a seeker's ion jet, with a Doppler shift that shows deceleration from an interstellar crossing. Still coming fast and already near. Now changing course, heading straight at us."

"My dear child!" His name was Sagacious Sage; the staff wits mistranslated it as Hard-Shelled Numskull. Born in the waters of that long-lost Andromedan planet, his people had brought their natal environment with them into space. He lived inside a silicon sphere, swimming in a replicated bit of his ancestral sea. "Why such agitation?"

Though Goldengene required no shell, her folk still wore the shape of their own marine ancestry. Sleekly tapered, golden-furred, she rode the thrust of the ionic jet in her tapered tail. Her flippers shimmered now with her soundless speech.

"I think the thing's a seeker queen. Seekers frighten me."

"Child, child! Quiet yourself." His whole globe shone with silvery serenity. "The seekers have never harmed the Elderhood. We must assume they never will." His people had undertaken their own desperate flight from Andromeda to escape predators not much different from the seekers, but that had been most of a billion years ago. "All of our races have outgrown their violent origins."

"Sir, you don't know the seekers. They'll never outgrow theirs."

"My charming little infant." His globe shone golden. "You must learn to trust the way of the Elderhood. If these seekers are still as young and blind as you say, we must help them discover their own better destiny."

"Destiny?" She tried to quench her indignant flash. "All they seek is heat. The warmth of what they eat. Their special infrared senses are acute enough to find a single Newling, even trying to hide on an ice haloid. Sir, if you had suffered what we did—"

For a moment her glow went dark.

"They took our planets and swarmed out to take our halo. Too fast for us, because they have their own scale of time. Hunting us down, apparently only for sport. We messaged all the stars around us, begging for aid. All our friends were too far off. The signals took too long. With no hope of help, we tried to fight—"

"Please, child. Please!" His azure flash reproved her. "You should have known the ways of war would win you nothing. If instead you had simply tried to understand your newborn fellow creatures—"

"Sir, we did." She tried to filter her impatience. "We observed them long enough to learn their language. They never talked to us. We found that they can be killed—monstrous as they are. They kill each other mating. The last survivors of our kind did invent a weapon."

Diffidence dimmed her light.

"I think—I've been told the weapon might have saved our halo, dreadful as the creatures are, if we had been allowed to keep trying it. But our first attacks had failed, and the Elderhood offered us refuge only on condition that we renounce violence. Most of us were gone by then. Those last few were desperate. The weapon was unproven. After a bitter debate, we agreed.

"Before we left, the inventors of the weapon sent a message to the seekers. Informing them that we had it. Advising them that it would be used to stop them if they tried to follow. I'm going out now to remind this creature of our warning."

"Child, you mustn't!" he shimmered gently. "If you try to play their infantile games, you can only harm yourself. You should have been taught that weapons are not the elder way."

"I have no weapon here. All I plan is to warn the creature off."

"At least, my dear, you must wait until we can inform the Eldermost."

"We Newlings are a free people." Her pride shone bright. "Though we do have leaders, they issue no orders. Anyhow, sir, the creature is already near. On her own scale of time, she won't wait for us to talk. If we let her hive and breed, the elder way would be suicide."

"Really, child! Really—"

Ignoring all his protests, she twinkled affectionate farewells to her friends on the staff and set out alone to face the invader. The creature slowed to meet her. They caught faint snatches of her signals to it, but none of them knew the seeker language. They detected no response. Just short of collision, she braked her own velocity and turned out of its path.

Veering suddenly, it pursued her.

"Goldengene to Outpost Vermill—" They got bits of that last message. "—sure she understood, from the way her radiation changed. But—" Her voice winked out and returned. "—empty mass sacs. Jaws big enough to crush a battle craft—"

The final scrap came even more faintly, rising high into the violet.

"—ask the Eldermost—"

Goldengene was screaming when her transmission ceased.

Kwanlon. *Synthetic fiber formed of graphite bonded to monomolecular silicon. Extraordinary modulus of tensile strength approaches quantum limits, enabling use as skyline cable. Undoped kwanlon is an electrical insulator. Properly doped, it becomes a superconductor, stable at temperatures up to 80°C. Used for power lines and for windings in fusion reactors.*

3

THEY DIDN'T DIE. THE EMERGENCY LIGHTS CAME DIMLY on, almost too soon. Leaving Mindi to get their bikes out of the net, Quin hurried back to the ship to help with the down reactor. Jomo was already there, and Kerry came in just behind Quin.

A chancy task. The superconductor coils in the old reactors had to carry enormous currents. So long as they stayed superconductive, that vast power was safely contained. Any uncontrolled failure, however, could explode the coils like energy bombs.

Older than the station, the engines had been running far too long. Too often, some tiny molecular displacement began to kill conductivity. When that happened, the safety relays had only fractional seconds to bleed deadly energy away.

31

This time they had limited the damage. There was standby power from the fuel cells. Running on liquid oxygen and hydrogen from storage tanks buried under the ice, these provided power and allowed at least a brief time for emergency repairs.

"Plenty good luck for us." Jomo's Sunmark shone faintly through a sweat-filmed grin. "Overhaul already done on Engine Number Two. Tests all *kamili*. She plenty ready to go."

The dim lights sank dimmer, while he pulled current to bring Number Two's magnetic flux up to the enormous density it took to bring the hydride fuels to the fusion point. With a fading crackle of static and a whine of tiny pumps injecting fuel, the engine started. The gloom drew back. Quin heard fans and voices and breathed fresh air.

The station was alive again.

He watched and helped when he could while Jomo located the failing loop in Number One, cut it out, and burned in another he had cannibalized from Number Three. Its flux came smoothly up, with never even a flicker.

"All plenty okay now, *mtoto wangu!*" Jomo wiped his hands, beaming at him. Though he felt much too old to be anybody's child, he didn't say so. "No fret, no sweat. Both engines plenty good, everything *safi*."

Till they go out again.

He didn't say that either, but it was a worry he could never entirely forget.

The relief ship arrived at last, still the old *Aldebaran*, Captain Tetsu Jensai now in command. Coming in to land, he called to report that his lidar had picked up the *Spica*'s hulk. The wreck, though somehow slowed in its encounter with the aliens, was still drifting near its old trajectory. That would carry it past Janoort, and Kerry wanted to salvage it.

"Metal we can use," he told Charbon. "No freight due."

"Junk," the commander objected. "Stripped twice. By the aliens when they took it. Again by Caffodio, when he caught the creature there. Nothing left we'd ever need."

"Someday, sir. Someday we might. When people come out to settle the halo."

"*Mon ami*, we are neither junkmen nor colonists." Heavy-handed with his crew, Charbon was commonly amiable with Kerry. "We are here, you recall, only to defend our planets and the Company."

"The halo's big enough for everybody." Kerry knew how to argue without vexing him. "If the aliens get to be friends, perhaps we can trade heavy metals for living space. The metals in that hulk could be precious."

He offered his starmist bottle.

"*Merci, mon ami.*" Charbon waved the flat little bottle away. "If you find comfort in that brimstone stuff, *c'est très bien*. We all require some refuge from this frozen hell, but I prefer *la boisson*."

"Drink your wine." Kerry nodded cheerily. "But we do need that hulk. It's passing in easy range of our mini-shuttle. With only one or two crewmen to help, I could tow it into orbit—"

"*Mon ami!*" Charbon's temper had begun to show. "If the aliens want the wreck, *très bon*. Sniff your starmist and forget your crazy notion of new kingdoms in the halo."

The *Aldebaran* slid down at last to her plastic landing pad. When the mail came off, Quin had letters from his mother. She was still at Zurich Down, a researcher at the Kwan Labs there.

"I'm an Earthsider now," she wrote. "And happy about it."

Smiling out of a new holo, she looked younger than he recalled her, so lovely he ached again to see her.

"Dear Quin, I do miss you," the letter continued. "I used to wish you could somehow come to live with me, but I see no hope for that. Things here are bad and getting worse. Not that I want you to worry about us. I suppose you hear a lot about the Holyfolk terrorists, but the Tycoon's beefing up Security. I think we're safe enough here in Sun Country."

There was only one letter for Kerry. His eyes got wet

when he read it, and Quin saw his face twitch and set. He turned away to take a long breath of starmist before he let Quin see the single sheet.

"Kerry—Kerry, dear—" Her hand had been unsteady. "It's dreadfully hard to tell you this. Because I love both so much. You and dear little Quin. It killed me to leave you. Yet it had to happen—you always told me that, and I've grown to see it better now. Your lives will always be starside, and mine will be here.

"Please—please help Quin understand."

She had a new husband. His name was Olaf Thorsen. She'd met him at the labs, where he was a kwanlon chemist. His speciality was superconduction. In the holo she sent, they were standing outside a Sun Country lodge, smiling at each other. He was a big blond man with a Sunmark that shone like a yellow moon on his slick pink cheek. They looked happy. Quin wanted to say he understood, but he couldn't trust his aching throat.

He didn't sleep much that night. Olaf Thorsen must be okay, if his mother loved him, but he still missed her more than he let Kerry know, and the letter had rekindled all his old yearning for the satellite cities and the skywires and all the marvels he couldn't even imagine on the strange far Earth.

The wrong of it rankled in him. Security would have a Sunmark for Mindi when she got back to Cotopaxi High, because both her parents were listed on the Sunblood register and would be there to sign for her. But he was exiled forever. Needing a father terribly, he couldn't help feeling bitter at his mother for all she hadn't told him, a little bitter even at Mindi.

When he came out late for breakfast, Kerry asked if he was sick.

"Okay," he muttered. "I'll be okay."

Kerry must have slept no better. The red neckerchief was strong with starmist, and his lashless eyes looked dark-rimmed and sad.

Sorry for him, Quin tried hard to content himself with

Janoort. Jomo was letting him stand regular shifts on the engines now, and he had learned to run the lidar gear. Kerry and Charbon were still spraying the starside dark with the lidar search beams, Charbon alert for enemies, Kerry hoping for friends.

The *Aldebaran* was there two weeks, unloading cargo and taking on reaction mass. When her crewmen came off to visit the station, one of them was Jason Kwan.

"The Tycoon's son." Kerry smiled in wry recollection. "The vicious little brat that saved my life on the discovery flight. Grown up now. Grown worse, I gather from Jensai and Charbon. The Tycoon got him on the ship as a student pilot to get him out of trouble back Sunside. Seems he's been charged with killing a Fleet officer in a quarrel over the officer's wife. Charbon hates him, and he warned me to stay clear of him."

Quin was at a telescope in the dome next morning, following what was left of the *Spica* and plotting its positions, when Charbon brought Jason to see the search gear. Quin couldn't help turning to stare.

Jason Kwan!

The Tycoon's son, trim and tall in a gold-braided uniform, a lasergun worn at his hip. Handsome in a careless way even with the jutting Romanoff nose, the bronze hair long, bronze moustache flowing wide, neat bronze beard trimmed to an arrogant point. Quin had never seen a moustache, and the bright Sunmark struck him through with envy.

They ignored him, but he overheard Jason needling Charbon. A reckless glint in his bright green eyes, he was playing on Charbon's terror of the starsiders, inquiring with elaborate irony how he meant to defend the station if they ever did attack. The little commander was pink in the face and seething inside, but trying hard not to show what he felt. Listening, expecting an explosion, Quin was relieved when Kerry came in.

"Your old stowaway!" Jason recognized him. "Off my father's ship." He turned to goad Charbon again. "Remember how eager you were to cycle him through the disposal lock?"

"*C'est*—" Charbon's voice had risen squeakily. "*C'est une bagatelle*." He gulped to swallow his rage. "We're good friends now."

Trying to rescue him, Kerry introduced Quin. Jason stared at him indifferently, the tawny-green eyes impersonal as a cat's. Quin hated him instantly, for that cold stare and the arrogant slant of the jutting nose and careless malice toward Charbon.

Yet he was a Kwan, the Tycoon's heir. He had all Quin had longed for, even to the Romanoff nose. Drawn in spite of himself, Quin offered to let him see the *Spica*. Still taunting Charbon, he turned from the telescope to ask if he thought the aliens were back aboard the wreck.

"Not likely, sir." Kerry spoke quickly. "Since the star-bird was caught, they've had three years and more to come back for anything they wanted."

Jason asked when it would pass Janoort.

"Forty-one hours from now," Quin told him. "Half a million kilometers out."

"Could we take a look—"

"*Impossible!*" Charbon stalked away. "That has been decided."

Jason shrugged, seeming pleased with himself. Quin saw Kerry reaching for his starmist, as eager as Charbon clearly was to be rid of Jason.

"Let 'em go." A shrug of casual contempt. "If they've no time for me—"

Jason smiled at Quin, and the smile transformed him. The arrogance turned to genial warmth. Impersonal no longer, the green eyes welcomed him into all the grace and splendor of Jason's world. His first dislike dissolved into awed admiration.

"Quin, would you care to show me around?"

"Sunner Kwan—" Awed at this great good luck, he had to catch his breath. "I'd love to."

Jason had a holo camera, but he didn't want to take

the gym or the gardens or the slush pit. Nothing seemed to interest him till Quin took him on the old *Capella*. He smirked at Jomo's English, but when he heard that Quin was a helper in the engine room his boredom disappeared.

"How's this, kid?" His green gaze sharpened. "You can really run fusion engines?"

"We do our best."

He wanted to know if the *Capella* had a fusion-powered minishuttle.

"It's kept out at the end of a tunnel now," Quin told him. "Operating off an insulating pad so the jet won't sublime too much ice. Used to service the orbital signal gear."

"Could it get out to the wreck?"

"My stepfather wanted to take it out, to tow the hulk into orbit, but Captain Charbon—"

"Old Charbon?" A sardonic hoot. "Let's take a look."

"Sir, the air valve would be locked—"

"I'll manage the lock." He touched his black-belted lasergun. "Come along, kid."

They swam down the tunnel. His lasergun made a blinding flash. Smoke exploded, and he pulled the valve open. Eyes stinging, Quin followed him into the shuttle.

"Odd-looking junk." He scowled at the tiny engine. "You can really run it, kid?"

"As long as it runs. On the last trip out, Kerry had a problem with the master magnet. He did get home, and I helped Jomo rewind the magnet and the spare."

He peered uneasily at Jason.

"Sir, I don't want trouble—"

"Listen, kid! I'm the Tycoon's son." Jason chuckled. "Trouble never troubles me."

"But, sir, I'm not anybody—"

"Maybe not yet." Jason squinted shrewdly at him. "But I'd bet you'd like to have a Sunmark."

"I would." Quin couldn't help confessing that, a quiver in his voice. "I'd give nearly anything—"

"All right, kid!" A hearty clap on his shoulder. "I'll get

you that, if you'll go along with me. Let's fly out to the wreck and catch ourselves a starbird."

"But, sir—"

The promise of a Sunmark had taken his voice and set his whole world to spinning. Terribly, he wanted to escape his long confinement to Janoort, to be as bold and forceful as Jason seemed to be. Maybe even to earn some high place in the House of Kwan. If he could ever find his father—

A crazy thought.

"I couldn't." He shook his head. "We'd be stealing the shuttle."

"From the Company?" Jason laughed. "The Tycoon owns enough of the Company."

"It's not very likely we'd find another starbird—"

"No matter." Jason shrugged. "We can always tell 'em how it got away. So let's go, kid! If you know how to seal the valve and uncouple the anchor and get the engine going—"

Jason smiled, and everything seemed possible.

"I—" A hoarse little whisper. "I do."

The shuttle slid off the pad and into space. Though he did get the engine going, it was cranky as the old *Capella*'s. He had to stand over it, reading the magnetic flux, listening to the whine of the pumps, rechecking voltages, fine-tuning the fuel flow, watching the thrust meter.

Yet he got brief glimpses of Janoort through the aft port. A ragged gray ball, half dimly lit by the far Sun, half only a blot across the stars, already tiny when he found it and shrinking fast. Seeing it gave him a queer-feeling emptiness mixed with a strange elation. The only world he had ever known, dwindling to a speck that would soon be lost among the stars. Losing it might hurt. Yet, with Jason for a friend, all the dazzling Sunside worlds were almost in reach.

Or seemed to be—

"Listen, kid." Hearing Jason's lazy voice on the intercom, he winced from a pang of doubt. "I'm reading

thrust at only a quarter G. Eight hours out to the wreck.
Can't you do better?"

"Maybe—" He hesitated. "But with this rewound magnet—"

"Push it, kid."

"The old coils could recrystalize. Fail again."

"I'll take that chance."

He pushed the thrust to half a G, and even a little
beyond, before the little light winked red to warn him of
some crystal flaw, threatening superconductivity. Gingerly he eased it a little back. The warning light went out,
and he began to enjoy the flight. Alert to everything,
asking the engine for all it could do, yet careful not to
ask too much, he began to feel a sort of kinship with the
brave little craft.

He felt grateful even to Jason. The Tycoon's dashing
son, his comrade now, sharing high adventure. The un-
likely chance he'd always longed for, to get out of the
tunnels and back to the fabulous Sunside worlds.

An hour out, with the robot pilot set, Jason came back
to rummage through the locker and share what he found,
hard biscuits and fruit-flavored synthetic juice.

"To our own starsider!" Jason lifted his frost-filmed
squeeze-bulb. "If we do meet him—though I rather hope
we don't."

"If you hope that—" Quin shook his head at the bronze-
bearded smile, suddenly troubled again, wondering if Jason really shared the elation he had begun to feel. If Jason
had already done so much, could anything thrill him? The
tall Sunner was still beyond his understanding, and it took
all his courage to go on. "—why are we here?"

"An impudent question."

"I'm sorry, sir—"

"It's okay, kid." The smile flashed brighter. "I guess
you've earned an answer." Jason paused, greenish eyes
narrowed until they looked catlike again. "Old Fernando
can't hang on forever. I'm planning on his place, but the
succession's never automatic. He got elected when he

brought the starbird back. I'll need the same sort of smash. Something to show the Seven I'm better than he ever was.

"Get it, kid?"

Quin nodded. He wasn't sure he liked it, but he listened wistfully while Jason talked about the House of Kwan and the Seven who controlled it. The savage rivalries among its members. Bribery and blackmail and betrayal. The Revelator and the Holyfolk, now at war to break the Company. Lies and spies and assassins.

Absorbed, envious of dramas and rewards he could hardly imagine, wondering if he could ever be as intrepid as Jason seemed, he was sorry when the radio began yelping in the cockpit. Jason went back to it. He heard Charbon's angry voice squealing out of a speaker. The words weren't clear, but he heard the cool sarcasm of Jason's answer.

"Starbirds, Captain? If you're afraid of starbirds in the wreck, we'll clear them out. If you aren't, we'll bring you one for a pet."

A shriller squeak from Charbon.

"Afraid for me? In this tin bucket? I race for sport."

The signal set clicked off, but Jason stayed in the cockpit, nosing them toward the wreck. Alone with the little engine, Quin felt his unease returning. Away from that hypnotic smile, he didn't really like Jason. Or trust him, either. Not when he'd had time to think.

The relief ship would soon be taking off, with Jason safe on board. In spite of that casual promise of Sunmark, Quin felt sadly certain now that he would be left behind, with too much to pay for. Kerry would be hurt. Even Jomo, he thought, would be disappointed in his *mtoto wangu*.

He began to feel sick.

"Here she is!" Jason roused him. "Cut the power and take a look."

They were drifting beside the wreck. It seemed smaller than he expected, much less complete. A naked metal skeleton, most of its thin shell cut away, bright where the Sun hit, the rest a black outline against the stars. He wondered if the starsiders had come back to take more of it since Caffodio caught the starbird.

"No monsters here." Jason was aiming his camera through the ports. "No room for them to hide."

"We do have space gear, sir," Quin reminded him. "One suit, anyhow. There in the lock."

"The holos will be all I need."

Quin watched him with the camera, watched the hulk's slow spin, watched the Sun searching every shadow out. He saw no aliens. Only scrap metal. The aliens might come back for whatever they wanted, but would be drifting on into the halo, lost to Kerry and his dream of a finer human future.

"Kid!" Jason's shout rang hollow in the narrow hull. "I see a signal on the console that says we're running low on oxygen. Take us back. Start your engine—and push it hard."

They had stayed too long, and he had to push the engine too hard. That small red caution light winked and winked again. He had to cut the thrust, back to half a G, back and back again.

"Push it, kid!" Jason kept urging. "Push it harder! While we've still got air to breathe."

He pushed it too much harder. In spite of all his cutting back, the master magnet kept running far too hot. At last he could see Janoort through the port, swelling from a faint gray star to a small gray snowball, but it swelled too slowly. While it still looked small enough for his hand to grasp and throw, the magnet exploded.

Hot smoke blinded him. Hauling at the manual quencher, he lurched out into the empty cabin. Gasping for his breath, he heard Jason bumping about inside the air lock.

"Too bad, kid."

His stinging eyes couldn't see anything, but he heard the little servos humming, cycling the lock. Before the valve clunked shut, Jason's casual drawl came through again.

"Hard to leave you, kid, but of course you're too small to fit the suit. A nice fit for me, and I've got to get back before Jensai takes off and leaves me stranded in your stinking little icebox.

"Sorry for you, kid..."

Runesong and Cyan Gem were Newlings, linguists, and sisters. Sisters, too, of Goldengene, who had chosen to serve out on the halo fringe at Point Vermillion, watching for the Black Companion.

Beginning their own careers, they had come to the core-star observatory to work with the rescued planetics. Young in the Elderhood, they felt a kinship to these striving primitives, and they hoped to help bridge the cultural gulf.

Runesong had grown discouraged with their slow progress. Restive, as well, under the authority of her elder sister, who now had the planetics in charge, she asked the director for a new assignment.

"The creatures do poorly in captivity," she told him. "I want to get closer to them, the way they are in nature. The captives are terrified and uncooperative, but those on the inner-fringe haloid are trying to talk. We keep picking up naive contact signals. Really, sir, shouldn't we answer?"

"You Newlings." His authority shone, serenely green. "You've still to learn the elder way. Patience, caution, peace. Our sponsors have warned us not to betray anything about who and where we are."

"Caution!" Her wings flushed with indignation. "I think you overdo it. Their own signals are announcing their presence to the whole halo. Begging, no doubt, for our friendship."

"Or trying to lure us into some trap, hoping to avenge the loss of that ship?"

"Without contact, we'll never know what they are."

"You Newlings are always too hasty."

"Our lives are brief."

"Too brief for reflection." The director's huge eyes blinked blue, reproving her. "We'll want better evidence than any I've seen that these beings are fit for the Elderhood. More likely they're sanguinary brutes who've blundered on more technology than they can handle."

"I'd take that risk."

"If you're asking for risks—" The director scanned her, winking indigo. "Perhaps you'd like to undertake a scouting mission."

Wings lifted, she waited.

"We've been hesitant to ask for volunteers," he told her, "because the task appears forbiddingly dangerous. We've lost one watcher. A young engineer who risked himself to study the planetic ship—"

"Quicksmith." A shadow of sadness. "An old friend, working with us on planetic technology."

"A tragic incident." The great eyes blinked. "We offered more than once to take him off the hulk. He always wanted more time. Finally, when we saw more planetics coming, it was too late to send the cutter. He must have been captured. I'm afraid he fared badly afterward."

The director cringed from what he imagined.

"No matter," she said. "I'll try to do better."

"You Newlings amaze me." She saw a fleeting glint of humor in his eyes. "Perhaps you'll really have a better chance. Because of what you are."

"Primitive, you mean?"

"In ways we almost admire." He shrugged, with a shimmer of admiration that astonished her. "Your readiness for risk. Your physical tolerance for radiations and gravities and atmospheres that probably killed our unfortunate colleague."

She asked for instructions.

"Get as near as you dare. If possible, near enough to inspect the facilities that enable the planetics to launch and control their clumsy spacecraft."

His eyes closed to probing points.

"I must warn you again of hazards that appall me."

"They're worth the risk," she told him. "Worth knowing better."

Metabrake.   *A drug regimen used to induce human hibernation during space emergencies. It lowers body temperature and slows all metabolic processes, reducing needs for oxygen, water, and food. Side effects varied, sometimes fatal. Survival depends on age, health, tissue mass, competent medical care, and duration of coma. In exceptional cases, revival has been successful after almost a year.*

GASPING FOR LIFE IN THE SEARING SMOKE, BLISTERED hands fumbling clumsily, Quin pulled the hot master magnet and hooked up the rewound spare. The flux came up when he ran a test, but then the overload light flickered again. Microscopic crystals had begun to obstruct the current. He had to cut back the thrust, cut it back again, until it was nearly too weak to feel.

Streaming eyes still half blind, he staggered to the cockpit and blinked into the console screen until he found the faint gray fleck that had to be Janoort. Too groggy for numbers, he knew it was too far, the thrust too feeble, the air too foul. Yet, by blundering trial and dazing error, he worked that faint far point into the target circle and engaged the pilot.

Reeling to the locker, he looked for Metabrake—and

came back to dim awareness in the station hospital with a plastic tent around him and stinging needles in his arms. His head throbbed. His eyes ached. He dozed and woke and dozed again, till he caught the hot scent of starmist and found Kerry with him.

"A damn fool!" His raw throat hurt. "I was an idiot, stealing the shuttle. I—I'm sorry, Kerry—sorry—"

"*Poco tonto*." Kerry shrugged, not visibly angry. "We're happy enough just to have you back. Your friend Jason had told us you were dead."

"How—" His lungs hurt when he tried to get his breath. "How—"

"Easy, *niño*." Kerry grinned. "You don't need to talk. Not yet. I know how you feel. I saw you when we took you off the shuttle, and I've had Metabrake myself. But Nurse Engel says you're coming out okay."

He waited, feeling a dim relief.

"Jason beat you back," Kerry told him. "In the escape gear he took off the shuttle. Arrived just in time to catch his ship. With a great tale to tell. Said he caught a space alien hiding in the wreck. Said its lasers hit the shuttle before he'd even seen it. Burned through the hull.

"He said the thing killed you."

Eyes shut, he could see Jason's bronze grin, hear the indolent highside voice, "Sorry, kid."

"Clever as ever!" Kerry opened a hard-clenched fist to inhale starmist. "We had to believe him. Said he tried to help you till the alien crawled out of the wreck, laser still blazing. Said he outran it with his rocket thruster, dodged behind the wreck of the shuttle, and finally got away."

"A lie—" he managed to whisper. "No alien—"

"The Kwans don't lie." Kerry's voice had grown sardonic. "But our scopes didn't pick up any laser battle. The shuttle shows no laser marks. Neither do you. We know that, here and now. Nobody will, back Sunside."

Painfully whispering, he asked about Mindi Zinn.

"Gone. With her folks. I went out to the pad to see

them off. Heard her asking Jason about what happened, crying when he told her how you died."

Kerry shrugged, eyeing him wryly.

"*Mal suerte*, as we used to say in the barrio. Hard luck, boy. I've been watching you and Mindi. I can guess how you feel about her, but the best you can do is forget. She's growing up adorable, but she won't be for you."

For Jason, maybe?

That was too painful even to think. Of course she was too young for Jason—or would he think so? Whatever happened on the long voyage Sunside, she would be growing up among such Sunsiders as Jason was, dazzled by them as he himself had been.

He knew he should forget. Yet, dozing and waking again after Kerry was gone, waiting for Nurse Engel and her kind-handed care, he couldn't erase the day she first told him she had to go home with her parents.

Kerry had helped him build wings for Mindi and himself, and they had been flying, alone together in the great dim cavern of the gym. It was wonderful fun, soaring free in Janoort's gentle gravity, till he saw the hurt on her face and asked what was wrong. She told him, and tried to look happy about it.

"Mom's promised me a great birthday gift, when we get—get home." Her voice quivered, and he saw her biting her lip the way she did when something hurt. "My own Sunmark!"

"I wish you could stay..."

But of course she was far too young to stay alone. Besides, she said, her folks wanted her to have a chance. The station kids, kids like Quin, had no chance. So her mother said. Not for culture or careers or anything at all.

All alone, they soared high into the whispery chill of the huge balloon and floated a long time there. Her face and her hair had a strange flower odor. She laughed when he asked about it, and said she had stolen a vial of her mother's precious wildwood scent, because she wanted to smell good for him. That was soon lost in the faint sharp stinks of plastic and ammonia and old sweat. It was always cold in the gym because it cooled air for all the station. Drifting, hands clasped, needing only now and then to flap the wings, they talked about their fine times together.

"You said you didn't like me," he teased her. "The day we met."

"Oh, Quin! If I did—"

She tried to laugh, but she was sobbing and shivering. Quin pulled her to him. They kissed. She promised to come back when she was old enough. He whispered that he would follow her Sunside when he could. Lying now in the oxygen tent, he remembered her in his arms, so warm and strong and wonderful, remembered the wildwood and ammonia and the salt taste of their tears.

Longing for her now, he thought he might never see her again. Certainly not with any aid from Jason Kwan to get his own passage Sunside. Dozing and waking, he tried not to think of his own eager folly, but Jason haunted his uneasy dreams, carrying a tantalizing Sunmark, a bright gold coin that he offered and snatched away.

Nurse Engel kept the counteractants pumping into his blood, flushing the Metabrake out. His head cleared. He sat up in bed. She helped him walk. Kerry returned to cheer him. Charbon came to question him, fearful at first that the hulk was really still infested with space aliens.

"*Le coquin!*" Convinced at last that there had been no monsters, the fat commander seethed again with hate for Jason. "Gone back now, carrying his lies to the Tycoon."

"Can't you call Sunside? With the truth?"

"*Peut-être.*" Charbon shrugged. "*Mais non.* If the Tycoon loves his son, he will not want the truth."

Out of the hospital finally, trying to forget his bitterness at Jason and shake off his own clinging shame, Quin went back to his classes and his shifts with Jomo in the engine room. Kerry let him come to the dome when he had time, to learn about the lidar gear. The search beams were still probing.

"Sending Zinn's contact code," Kerry said. "An invitation to talk. The signals begin with small prime numbers and the powers of two. They work through the values of *pi* and *e* to geometric figures and finally to pictures."

A troubled frown.

"Creatures able to capture the *Spica* and curious enough to take it apart—we know they're there. They've got to be near enough to get our signals and smart enough to read them. But they don't answer."

"Afraid of us?"

"Could be." Kerry shrugged. "If they've guessed what we did to the poor thing we caught. Or maybe—" He reached for his starmist. "*Quién sabe?* Who knows what they are or what they think of us? Could be they live on a scale of space and time that will let them take a century or a thousand years to look us over."

When the *Aldebaran* came again, Kerry had a letter. He read it, scowling through a cloud of starmist, and read it again. Finally, the scowl grown grimly quizzical, he handed it to Quin.

"From your mother."

She wrote that she and Olaf were still at the Kwan Labs. Olaf was deep in his superconductor research. With her studies of the starbird all wrapped up, she was teaching classes and beginning a new research study of the emerging genetic differences between Earthfolk and Sunfolk.

"A dreadful shock," she wrote, "when I heard from Jason Kwan that Quin is dead." Reading that, Quin felt cold inside. "I've always been so sad about leaving him to grow up so far away, always hoped in spite of everything that some change could let him come Sunside."

The letter quivered in his fingers, blurred with tears of anger.

"The news of aliens still about the wreck was a total surprise. The attack on Jason and Quin—a dreadful surprise. At least to me, because the starbird we met seemed so utterly harmless.

"I've bad news about the Zinns. They seem to have quarreled with Jason on the ship. I think because they blamed him for Quin's death, and because he was doing too much to console their teenage daughter.

"Aurelia held a press conference when she got back here to the Labs, reporting her work on Janoort and urging new funding for the contact program. She thinks the aliens could become friends, and she was unwise enough to question what Jason said about that alien attacker.

"She and Tikon weren't actually arrested, but Security detained them for interrogation. That inquiry is still in progress—I suppose you remember what Security is. The daughter has gone to stay with her uncle. Her aunt's husband. He has got rich, trading with the Earthfolk."

Quin went to Charbon, begging permission to call and tell his mother he was still alive.

"*Je vous plains*," the little commander muttered uncomfortably. "*Impossible*. You know the lasercom net is not for personal matters. You may write, if you want to risk a problem with the censors and the Kwans."

He wrote his mother. Wondering if Mindi recalled him well enough to care, he began a letter to her. He still longed somehow to find his way Sunside and see her again—but such notions were nonsense. He tore the letter up and tried to forget.

There were other women at the station, though not many. There was Lyris Engel, his gentle-handed hospital nurse, mixed up for months with Mindi in his dreams but already married to the new medic when they came to the station.

And there was Dolores Delayo.

A magnificent blonde with long straight hair as golden as her Sunmark, she ran the computers in processing and scheduled crop rotation in the gardens and sang sad songs of her own composing, tragic ballads about unlucky women who had loved the old Tycoons.

The year he was sixteen he and Dolores began working out in the gym together. He gave her the wings he had made for Mindi and listened to her songs. Out of the gym, her husky voice was not very musical, but the echo from the curving walls transformed it to a haunting wail that somehow rekindled all his old dreams of a Company father and a fabulous future waiting for him, if he could only come Sunside to claim it.

One night in the garden supply room, with big plastic drums of plant food all around them and the ammoniac reek of fertilizer strong in the steamy air, she taught him how to make love. Nearly every night for the next month they were there again, sweat-bathed and breathing hard, floating locked together in the dark, Mindi almost forgotten—until she told him they had to break it off, because she was going to marry Jomo.

He felt stunned, bitter at her and even at Jomo, till Mindi came back to life in his mind. Going to classes, helping Kerry in the dome, now standing shifts in the engine room alone, he was learning all he could and still dreaming in spite of everything of Mindi and the Sunside.

The old *Aldebaran* got back at last, only two months late. A lump in his throat, he waited for the mail. A letter from his mother. He found her in a new holo when he ripped into the envelope, standing with another woman amid the strangeness of an Earthside park. Grass like velfast carpet but impossibly green, and a miraculous tree soaring into blazing blue. The woman with her—

Mindi!

He looked again, trying to be sure. Taller and thinner than he recalled her, black hair longer, loose and blowing in the wind. Her face was graver, the freckles gone. He thought she looked sad.

"Quin—dear Quin!" his mother wrote. "It was dreadful being told you were dead. Even harder, I think, for your friend Mindi than it was for Olaf and me. She's a student now, here at Zurich, doing solid research and recovering well from a dreadful experience—"

The Security clerk called his name again and tossed another letter at him. Addressed in Mindi's slanted hand.

An ache in his throat, he tore it open. It began happily enough:

"Dearest Quin, your mother has just brought your letter to me. It's so great to know you're okay—I'm still shaking, and the paper's hard to see. I'm fine now. Here at the Labs, taking courses with your mother and working part time as her research assistant.

"But two years ago—"

The rest of the letter was written in a different ink.

"A bad thing I have to tell you, Quin. A horrible thing. Nearly more than I can bear to think about, even now. My parents—"

A blotted word he couldn't read.

"Their troubles began on the ship, before we got to Cotopaxi High. A quarrel with Jason Kwan. They were fools, of course, to tangle with him, but my mother didn't believe what he said about the starsider attacking the minishuttle. When we landed, Security detained them both.

"Part of it was solarpolitics. The old conflict between the Kwans and the Chens. My mother had to answer charges that her contact research helped the Revelator support his weird claim that we have demon blood.

"While Security had them, I went to stay with my uncle in Azteca. He's always busy but kinder to me than my aunt. When my parents were finally set free, they came Earthside on vacation. A holiday they needed. The ordeal had worn them out, and their careers were in danger.

"I went to join them at Zurich Down. They had reservations at the Sun Country lodge where they'd first met, back when they were just learning to ski. Skiing was great fun, they said, a lot like flying in the Janoort gym, and they wanted me to learn.

"Of course we'd heard a lot about Holyfolk terrorists, but the area was supposed to be secure. We had no notion of any danger, not till a snowslide stopped the bus. A gang of men climbed on with gas guns that knocked out everybody. When the rest of us woke up, my parents were gone.

"Kidnapped—it was awful, Quin!

"Security couldn't do much. They had aircraft overhead and armored hovervans sealing off the roads and agents everywhere, but the activists have too many sympathizers. Suspects were arrested. Some I guess were tortured, but none of them talked. It was weeks before we even got a ransom demand.

"The Company never pays ransom—that's what they say—but my uncle somehow learned where they'd been hidden. Finally they were found—dead, Quin. Both dead. The Security people wouldn't let me see them. Their bodies were in a mountain cave where they'd been beaten and chained and left to die of cold and hunger.

"The killers weren't caught. They never are.

"An awful thing, Quin. I spent months back with my uncle, getting over it. When I was able, he sent me back to your mother, here at the Labs. She has been wonderful, and the hard work here is good for me.

"Not that I'm over it yet. I guess I'll never be. I still dream about those masked men climbing into the bus, slapping the Sunmark on my mother's face and calling her a bride of Satan.

"A horrible thing!

"I'm sick, Quin. Sick of everything here Sunside. I'd give anything to get back to you. But of course there's no chance of it, not the way things are. The relief ships are too uncertain, too many years apart. I'm not even sure they'll keep on coming—"

The ink was different again.

"Quin—" A blot on the paper. "I've been thinking about us. Thinking a lot. I know Sunside life is changing me. I suppose you're changing just as much. It was awful to leave you, a lot worse when I thought you were dead. But the way things are—"

Another blot.

"The best we can do is try to forget. As much as we can. Enough, anyhow, to let us make our own lives—though we had wonderful times together, times I know we'll always want to remember. It hurts me to write it, because I do love you so, but good-bye—good-bye, dear Quin." A postscript, in another ink.

"Don't try to answer. For both our sakes. You'll know why."

Wondering why, he didn't sleep that night.

"*Que lástima!*" At breakfast next morning, Kerry blinked grimly from a cloud of starmist, looking as trouble-worn as he felt. "A hard thing, boy. But Mindi's right. Her life will be there. You have to pity her, and all the Sunside. Sick and dying, the Kwans and the Revelator fighting over the carrion."

Quin was shaking his head.

"Face it, boy! If the Kwans say you're dead, officially you are. The censors won't pass contradictions. Letters from you could make trouble for Mindi. Maybe even for your mother."

Chilled inside, he envied Kerry for the comforts of starmist.

"If you've got to dream," Kerry urged him, "dream about our future in the halo. Planting humanity on a hundred or a thousand new snowballs when we find them. New worlds scattered too far apart for any new breed of Sunfolk or Holyfolk to exploit and destroy them."

Raising an odorous palm, Kerry studied him.

"Think about it, boy."

He nodded unhappily. "I hope your luck—"

"*Madre de Dios!*" Kerry exploded. "You'll never get back there. Didn't Jason teach you that?"

"He made a fool of me, and I'm still ashamed. But I'm going back. Whenever, however I can."

"If you had been there—" Kerry shook his head and stopped to breathe his starmist. "A jungle in the sky, with Kwans and Chens for tigers in it. If you want that, boy—you're an idiot."

"If I am—I just can't help it."

The next arrival of the old *Aldebaran* was delayed again, this time by an engine failure in space. Quin was nearly twenty when she came in, commanded now by Admiral Megali Meng. Aching with eagerness, he waited for the mail. There was only one letter, that from his mother. Nothing from Mindi.

No surprise, yet he felt sick with disappointment.

"We're still at Kwan Labs," his mother wrote. "These days I don't see much of Olaf, because his work absorbs him so. Something big but very secret. He can't even talk about it."

He scanned anxiously for news of Mindi.

"The Zinn girl's been gone a year and more. Back to her uncle. Against my advice, because she had grown up into a very lovely young woman with great ability. She could have made a fine career in planetary science. When we talked about you, she said she had a new life to live. She didn't explain, I've heard no more, except a news report about the murder of her aunt."

The night before Meng was to take off for the Sunside, he and Kerry were on duty together. Janoort had no dawns; its sky was always black and blazing till the tiny Sun stabbed across the near horizon. Their long shift almost over, the dome was still dark except for the red-glowing instruments. Cold and very still. With the search gear on automatic, he had been updating a subroutine for the sky-sweep program. Now it was done. Looking out, he could see the lights around the *Aldebaran*, still taking on re-action mass. He was half asleep when she lifted.

The alert bell roused him. Buzzers were rasping, signal lights flashing. The printer came to chattering life. Kerry was already bent over it. He stood there a long time, intent and oddly calm, before he turned.

"We got something." He spoke very softly, but Quin could sense his wonder. "I don't know what."

"An echo?"

"No echo. Not from any beam of ours..."

Kerry's voice trailed off, and he turned to stare into the diamond-sifted dark in the direction the telescopes were pointing, as if trying to see more than they could.

"What—"

"Laser bursts. Very faint. Pulsed like search signals—
but not like ours." Kerry bent a long time, squinting at
the printout. When he looked up again, the red glow was
strong enough to show his strange expression. "Somebody—something out there is probing for us."

Still far out from her new hive star, the gravid queen came
upon a halo snow-mass large enough to fill her empty sacs.
She caught a faint warmth in it, a tempting hint of the food-
metal she was famished for. New agonies of hunger awakened
in her swelling belly. She veered to devour it.

The midge surprised her, darting out of it to meet her. A
tiny thing, yet bright with its own tantalizing warmth. Her
hunger turned to ravening fire, she swerved to meet it. Its
chirping checked her. Faint at first, and utterly perplexing,
because it spoke words she understood.

"—warning you to stay away. We are the Newlings. This
is our own halo fringe, which we call Newmarch. I speak for
my people and the Elderhood. We are the owners of this core-
star and every world around it. You are warned to turn away
and leave us as we are—"

Her blast of scorn drowned its insufferable squeak, but only
for an instant.

"We know you well, because once we owned the star where
you were born. We fought to keep it when your kind hived
there. You were too many and too savage for us, yet we were
learning as we lost. We invented a weapon. Striking with it,
we might have stopped you.

"We came here instead, because our friends in the Elderhood urged us not to kill. Choosing to follow their way, we
left our home star and all its worlds to you, but we brought
our weapon with us and we warned you not to follow—"

The midge had veered aside, and she dived to intercept it.

"Turn away!" It shrilled that fantastic challenge. "You are
not to enter our new halo—"

Outraged at its pygmy insolence, she recalled the story of

the midges, comic foils in her sacred mother's saga. Vexatious motes, they had swarmed around the early hives, trailing false food scents and squeaking their hilarious boasts and threats, until the heroes of the saga grew ill with eating them.

"—leave us in peace," the mock-heroic mite kept on shrilling, as priceless as those fatuous gnats. "Go while you can. Respecting the way of the Elderhood, we withhold our weapon and offer our aid. If your flight stuff is depleted, we can point your way to an unclaimed snow-mass where you may fill your sacs—"

She saw it freeze, paralyzed by her bellow of radiation. Her tongue stabbed at it.

"Stay away!" It tried to dodge. "We won't allow—"

Her closing jaws stopped its feeble shriek.

A disappointing morsel, no longer comic, even its warmth a fraud. Crushing it, she caught not even a flavor of metal. Its mass was nearly too tiny to matter, but she gulped it into her empty sacs.

No longer amused, she burned its insipidity off her jaws and turned again toward the snow lump. More midges were bursting from it. Not so bold as the first had been, too slow to get away. Undeceived by their false warmth, she checked herself to swallow the lump before she followed them.

Flat-tasting as the gnat had been, the little object lacked even a flavor of the nutritious power-metals her embryonic brood was burning for. Yet her long starvation drove her to lick up its last brittle bits. They were flight-mass at least, enough to carry her on toward the core-star. Even here, she could sense its tempting redolence.

Hot metal enough, now near enough. Radiant food for her soon-due hatchlings. They were big in her belly, already gnawing toward the agony and wonder of birth. No braggart gnat could ever match their warrior fury, but perhaps these lazy midges would be cunning enough to furnish sport for her hunter princes.

She paused to snap the slowest up, but only for a moment. Her time had drawn too near.

Solar Halo.   *Vast cloud of "dirty snowballs" formed when the planets were, when grains of interstellar dust and frozen gases clotted together in the outer fringes of the solar nebula. Existence theorized by twentieth-century astronomer Jan Oort, who explained comets as halo bodies vaporized and visible when they wander near the Sun. The halo is estimated to contain 100 to 1000 Earth masses condensed into many billion haloids moving in orbits up to 100,000 astronomical units from the Sun.*

5

"**P**ROBING?" QUIN ECHOED. "PROBING FOR US?"

A hot drop of starmist shone on Kerry's trembling palm, a bright-red bead in the instrument glow.

"What does it mean?"

"Hard to say." With a dazed headshake, he turned to peer into the dark beyond the dome. "They're aware of us. But I don't know—"

He stood there a long time, blankly staring, before he remembered to lift his hand and inhale.

"What will they do?" Quin had caught his troubled tension. "What can they do?"

"I suppose they're curious, like we are." He turned back slowly, red shadows shifting on his bald skull. "I hope they'll let us stay. Maybe even aid us. But I guess Charbon could be right. They may want to run us out."

Struck with sudden hope, Quin felt his own heart pounding. Enemies or friends, these strangers in space would surely give Janoort a new importance. More Fleet craft could be arriving. People who knew the halo—such people as he was—could be useful to the Company. Somehow, with luck enough, the space creatures might open his own way Sunside.

Charbon came plunging out of the tunnel when Kerry called him, fatter now than ever and wheezing for his breath. Time and wine had changed him, bleached his thinning hair, creased and mottled his oily skin, swelled dark sacs beneath his haunted eyes. He blinked wildly now at Kerry.

"*Quelle autre chose?*"

"Search beams, sir. From starside. Spying us out."

"*Les diables!* The things that killed my *pauvre* Reynard."

In terror of alien starcraft or missiles perhaps already homing on the station's own search beams, he ordered all transmissions killed until the source of the alien signal could be pinpointed.

"Impossible, sir," Kerry objected. "With no echo time—"

"We do have direction."

"But no key to distance."

"How near—"

"*Quién sabe?*" Kerry shrugged, lashless eyes squinting into Charbon's wasted face. "It's a very feeble signal. No stronger than our own search beams would be at a couple of hundred AU. If the alien station is strong enough, it could be a thousand AU."

"But the creatures could be—close!" They were still in the dome, and the little commander looked feeble and ill in its crimson dimness. "*Les voilà!* Here to tackle us, when they're done taking the *Spica* apart—"

He paused to peer at Quin.

"If Jason Kwan really found the monsters on it—"

"Quin says he didn't."

"*Le cochon*, I know he lied." Charbon turned to blink uneasily into the starside gloom. "Yet I feel the creatures skulking all around us."

"Could be, sir," Kerry agreed. "With our own beams off, we're blind."

"Keep 'em off," he rapped. "Till I can get war cruisers here from Fleet Command."

"Sir, do we really need fighting craft?" Kerry spoke softly, cautious of Charbon's emotion. "I mean, sir, the starsiders have never hurt us here. Perhaps they want peace—"

"*Nom de Dieu! Les diables!* You babble of peace when they killed my son! You'd have us sit here unarmed, at the mercy of monsters who know no mercy?"

"Not entirely unarmed, sir," Kerry objected, still mildly. "We have the search lasers. Powerful enough to damage objects several thousand kilometers—"

"Objects?" Charbon snorted. "*Quelle sottise!* We fight no objects. The things will come in battlecraft, such as killed the *Spica*."

With no more discussion, he messaged Fleet Command begging for forces to hold Janoort and challenge the aliens in space. Waiting again for signals to creep Sunside and back, he kept the station on alert, kept the search beams off, kept radar and lidar gear dishes scanning for attackers, kept asking Kerry about those alien transmissions.

"Still there, sir."

Now spelling Kerry in the dome, Quin heard that curt report a dozen times.

"Patterned pulses, though the patterns make no sense to me. Could be from a thousand AU out. Could be from one. *Quién sabe?*"

Charbon was waiting in the dome at every sudden Sunrise, but nothing came from the Company for half a dozen days, then half a dozen more. The far Sun was nearly down and he had given up and gone, on the day the printer clanged and clattered with the message.

"*Escuche, niño!*" Kerry called from the computer,

where he was setting up a scanner program. "Your friend Jason Kwan will be coming back to the halo."

Quin felt a flash of that old hate, and then a wary joy. He was older now, maybe smarter. With a second chance at Jason, perhaps he could somehow even the score. This time, at least, he could try not to be such an utter fool.

"I'm surprised," he said. "Since he knows we met no monster in the wreck."

"Perhaps his career needs a new one." Squinting into the red glow of the consoles, Kerry's face wore a quizzical grin. "He's got himself a new title. Admiral of the Halo. He's coming out on a faster craft. To take things over. To replace Charbon and deal with the aliens. Till he gets here, we're to keep alert and silent. No search beams, no contact program, nothing except essential signals back to Fleet Command."

"*Le gros cochon!*" Charbon scowled at the printout when Kerry gave it to him. "Yet if he can beat the star-beasts and avenge my son, *très bon*. Until he arrives, *à la garde!*"

"How, sir? We're blind without the lidar."

"Man the telescopes. Scan the halo."

"Blind," Kerry muttered. "We couldn't see a planet coming at us, unless it got close enough to blot out the stars."

Waiting for Jason Kwan, or for anything alien, they watched the red wink of the instruments, watched the starside sky. All that came of it was that faint and enigmatic laser pulse.

Scanning for them? Probing the Sunside planets beyond them? Starfolk speaking to one another? Calling, maybe, to mankind? Quin had time enough to wonder. When Kerry was on duty with him through those empty nights, they talked about the possible starsiders. And about Jason Kwan.

"Don't fight him, boy." He spoke gently through a fragrant haze of starmist. "I know he did you dirty, but he's older now. Admiral of the Halo. With connections to get us new engines. To build up the base. To probe on beyond."

"I can't quite forget what he did to me."

"*No le hace*, boy. All that matters is the halo—"

"Not to me," Quin confessed. "I'm going Sunside. When I can."

"If you do, you're still a fool."

"Maybe. But still I want to see."

"If you'd seen the barrios . . ." A sad little shrug. "Mankind gone wrong. People got too smart for the nature that made them. Too smart, boy, when they killed off the lions and the whales and all their wilderness. Yet not smart enough to survive out here.

"Unless they let us lead the way."

"If enough people come—" Quin shook his head, troubled. "Won't things go the same way here?"

"*Nunca*, boy. Never." Kerry exhaled an odorous cloud. "Because the halo's different. A million times the room we had on old Earth. Scattered too far to let anything ruin it all. With its own new rules that will make people different."

Quin waited to see what he meant.

"On old Earth, people had to learn its cruel old rules. They had to live and breed and fight like jungle animals. Or else they didn't survive. Under the halo rules, if they're what I think they'll have to be, people must learn to fuse hydrogen and educate themselves and respect their neighbors and their whole ecology. We can do that, boy. Some of us can. If we're smart enough and bold enough to try."

"Maybe," he muttered. "If the starsiders—" He stopped and looked into the starry dark beyond the dome. "If they let us stay."

"I think they must," Kerry said. "Evolving to fit the halo, they must have learned its rules. They haven't hurt us, remember, except when we hit them first. I think we can trust them."

"The Kwans and the Company will never do that."

"Their last misfortune, if they don't." Kerry's face grew

very sober. "If Jason is coming out to hit the spacefolk, I imagine he'll be sorry."

Kerry took a deep breath of starmist and leaned to grip his arm.

"Listen to me, boy. We've got a grand chance here, but things are going to be hard till we get a better start. That's why we need you so. There aren't many of us, and we've got too much to do. Think about it, boy."

"I—I'm sorry, Kerry." He had to gulp. "That's your dream. But I've got my own."

Jason Kwan came out from Cotopaxi High in command of the *Solar Kwan*, the first of the new Kwan-class cruisers. She had three times the acceleration of the old *Aldebaran*, her flight time only four months. Quin was standing with Kerry in the dome when she came in. A clean silver needle, not yet tarnished by the solar plasmas, drifting slowly down to the broad patch of orange-colored plastic laid to shield the ice from hot ionic jets. Quin was still on duty when Charbon brought Jason into the dome.

At first he looked so much the same that Quin felt a tingling flash of that old bitterness. Trim and fit in a gold-and-black flight suit with the black-rimmed Sun-disks of his rank on the collar. Arrogant as ever, with that imperious nose, yet handsome enough. Bronze hair flowing, narrow beard neatly trimmed, green eyes bright as his gold Sunmark.

He didn't know Quin.

"Sir, don't you remember Dain?" Charbon was smiling, as if old dislike had been forgotten. "He went with you out to the hulk."

"Dain?" Jason stared. "I thought you were dead."

"I could have been. Thanks to you."

"My apology." Blandly casual, Jason reached for his hand. "You know I'd have let you take the space gear if you'd been the right size for it."

"You said you saw me dead," Quin accused him. "Killed by a space alien."

"Politics."

Jason shrugged. His old smile was still appealing. Quin finally took his offered hand.

"My report of our adventure helped get me these." He touched the Sun-disks. "I'll grant I owe you something, Dain. A debt I want to pay. Come aboard for a drink, and we'll talk about it."

"Thanks," Quin muttered. "But if I'm dead—"

Later, though, he tried to think better of Jason. Grown up now, perhaps he had really changed. A power now in the House of Kwan, he would be flying back Sunside.

Next day Quin went aboard the *Solar Kwan* and asked to see the admiral. A junior officer let him wait in the master cabin, amid luxury he had never seen. Bending to rub the luster of an oddly patterned tabletop, he started almost guiltily at Jason's genial-seeming hail.

"Welcome, Dain!"

Jason came diving in with a lazy, athletic grace, enjoying the gentle gravity. Cordial enough, he glided across to shake hands before he settled himself with that opulent table between them.

"Inlaid hardwood." He nodded at it. "Which I guess you don't see here. You'll have a highball?"

"Please."

Smiling uneasily, Quin felt mixed emotions. Envious in spite of himself, he felt awed, even half afraid. Jason was the Tycoon's son. He had lived in the skyweb, had done everything. Caught again with that careless charm, Quin tried to forget what Jason had done to him.

"My first highball," he admitted. "One of our chemists distills what he calls drinking alcohol, but it's too raw for me."

A steward brought the drinks in slender squeeze-bulbs on a velfast mat. Quin sucked too much. Trying not to cough, he saw Jason's veiled amusement, instantly erased.

"Getting to my point—" Jason paused to look at him, green eyes shrewd. "I spent most of today with poor old

Charbon, discussing those laser transmissions. What do you think they mean?"

"We're encountering intelligence," he said. "Beings maybe like the one we caught. Watching us while we look for them. Kerry doesn't think they'll be hostile. But what they're like and what they want—" He shook his head. "I couldn't guess."

"I mean to find out." Jason sucked at his drink. His fingernails were gilded, Quin saw, shining brighter than his Sunmark. "My orders were to resupply Halo Station, relieve Charbon, and investigate anything alien. I'm going on out to identify the source of those pulses."

The green eyes narrowed, watching him.

"Care to come?"

That was a stronger jolt than the highball.

"Think about it, Dain. I had to leave Coto without a full crew. I need a fusion engineer. Your friend Uruhu doesn't want the job, but he says you're as good as he is. Even with no academic degrees." Jason bent closer. "If you still want that Sunmark—"

His heart was pounding, but he had to shake his head.

"Once," he muttered. "That was enough."

"I said I was sorry." With an indolent sweep of the gilded hand, Jason waved guilt away. "Forget it, kid. We were green punks then. That trip was a crazy stunt, and I guess we're both lucky that it ended like it did."

"You are."

"I played it right." Happy with himself, Jason shook back his shining hair. "Now I'd like to share my luck." A tight little smile. "As I recall, you wanted to get back Sunside."

"Still—I still do!" The words burst out in spite of him. "I'd give anything—nearly anything—"

"Just stay aboard." Jason's glittering fingers flicked toward the starside sky. "We're going to locate the aliens. If they want a fight, we've got projectile weapons and missile weapons and laser weapons—"

Quin sat still, remembering.

"Come along, kid." Jason bent closer, genially urgent. "If you think I've done you wrong, I want to make it up. When we get back to Coto, I'll see you get that Sunmark."

"If I could believe—"

In his mind, he was back again aboard the minishuttle, choking in the smoke of the burned-out master magnet, Jason in the escape gear, leaving him to die. He had to shake his head.

Jason's smile had faded.

"Listen, kid!" The brittle highside voice grew colder. "Say no and you'll never get your Sunmark. I'll be the next Tycoon, and I'll see to that."

"Thanks—" Hoarse and suddenly trembling, Quin pushed away from the table. "That helps me say no."

"Your own choice, kid. If you prefer this chunk of ice to your own Sunmark, welcome to it. But I'd say you're a fool."

"Maybe—maybe I am."

"Twice, kid. Twice!" Jason rang for the steward to escort him off the ship, and the mocking voice rang after him. "If I ever have to report you dead again, you'll never be able to say I lied."

Supplies came off the *Solar Kwan*, and half a dozen newcomers reporting for relief duty at the station. A new signal officer among them, and a fusion engineer. The engineer was Tony Caffodio. A lean dark youth whose father had been an admiral. Quin took him aboard the *Capella* to meet Jomo. His first glimpse of the old engines touched off an indignant outburst.

"Kwan politics!" His black eyes blazed. "My father saw these bundles of junk and ordered them scrapped— fifteen years ago!" He gave Jomo a look of rueful astonishment. "You still trust your lives—all our lives—to these?"

"We fix 'em." Jomo grinned. "So long we fix 'em, all *hali njema*."

"A holy miracle, if you can."

"*Uganga*," Jomo said solemnly. "*Kiinimacho*."

"Whatever you say." An impassive nod. "But compared to those new engines of Olaf Thorsen's—"

"Thorsen?" Quin stared.

"You've heard of him, way out here?"

"He's married to my mother."

"Huh?" He blinked at Quin. "I never knew Nadya Dain had a son. But I did work with Thorsen on the plasma polarizers for the Kwan-class spacecraft. A hundred years ahead of anything this wreckage ever was. The man's a genius. If he ever learns his solarpolitics—"

"He's in trouble?"

"We're all in trouble." His face clouded. "Back Sunside. I've been hoping to get out here ever since I used to hear my father talk about his own halo voyages."

Thin lips set, he shook his head at the engines.

"I didn't know that much about your problems here."

Jason Kwan finished loading reaction mass and took off toward the cluster. Standing with Kerry in the dome, watching the *Solar Kwan* flash and vanish in the black sky, Quin felt trapped and useless. Halo Station seemed tinier than ever, and he longed for something larger.

When news did come, it was not at night, nor from Jason. Quin was just relieving Kerry. The signal gear was tracking the Sunside relays. The receiver chimed with a message from Fleet Command. The censors had encrypted it, and they had to wait for Charbon to run it through the decoder.

Kerry's gaunt jaw gaped as he read it.

"They've bypassed us—" The printout shook in his fingers. "Another starsider has been caught. A different species, hardier than the other. Caught by the Contra-Neptune crew. It came in behind a tender and flew close around the station, spying on the docks and the radio dishes. Something silver-scaled and moving like a fish, the men said. They called it a skyfish.

"They knocked it out with a signal laser. Dragged it into the lock. Helpless then, but it did survive. They put it aboard the tender and shipped it back to Coto."

Charbon paused to stare out into the starside blackness. Unshaven, he looked paler and older and sicker than ever. "All that happened months ago. About the time, in fact, that Admiral Kwan passed Contra-Neptune on his flight here. The censors have been sitting on it, while linguists tried to interrogate the creature."

Quin wondered if one of them had been his mother.

"How had it got there?" Kerry was asking. "On some kind of spacecraft?"

"No detail. But Fleet Command's alarmed. With the alien transmissions we've been picking up, and no word from the *Solar Kwan*, they're finally convinced that we're under attack."

"They'll send us new support?"

Looking sicker, Charbon shook his head.

"They're pulling out of the halo. Shutting down Halo Station. My orders are to prepare for evacuation. Captain Vira Brun, already in flight on the *Martian Kwan*, is receiving orders to take us home."

At the core-star observatory, Cyan Gem had made disappointing progress with the surviving planetic bipeds. The creatures were oddly fragile and strangely self-destructive. Most of them were too stupid or too ill or too hostile for any intellectual contact. The exception was one tall male—whose fellows punished him savagely when he tried to talk to her.

They shut him out of the cages where they gathered for their fantastic rituals, howled at him when they found him alone, sometimes pelted him with waste food or even excrement. With one faithful female, he retreated to his cage, unlatching the gate only for their language lessons.

For Cyan Gem, those lessons were painful ordeals. The creatures spoke with sound vibration created in the noxious atmosphere they required, insufferably hot and laced with corrosive oxygen under nearly unendurable pressure.

Yet she did endure it. For a time, the lessons had gone well. Even the female began to take part. When the creature saw that some grunt or squeal had been understood, she would strike her forelimbs vigorously together, battering the super-heated gas with dazing vibrations.

That pathetic female died while the tank was darkened during one of the regular periods her companions required for their peculiar recuperative and mating behavior. Sadly for her on that occasion, the innate ferocity of her fellow beings kept them active in the dark.

When the lights came on, Cyan Gem found that the latch had been broken and the pair attacked with a sliver of iron that had somehow escaped discovery. The male's body was adrift in those noxious gases, near death from loss of vital body fluid.

Like any primitive, he had fought. The contents of the cage were fluid-splashed and disarrayed. Five other males and two females had swollen contusions and bleeding wounds that betrayed their guilt.

She found the body of the missing mate in another cage, surrounded with a group of the creatures howling in apparent excitement. It had been battered and partially dismembered. The sliver of metal was still embedded in one of the eyes.

She removed the injured male to a separate tank and gave him fluid transfusions from the bodies of his enemies. Recovering reluctantly, he tried twice to destroy himself, opening the fluid channels in his forelimbs with small blades he had used to remove hair from his face.

Patiently, in spite of blazing light and searing heat and sickening stenches, she returned again and again, coaxing him to resume their contacts. She brought him the last choice bits of food and drink from the planetic craft. She invented equipment to translate her own voice into air vibration, his into light. She showed him artifacts of the Elderhood. Ill and dull as he had become, her persistence was rewarded.

She learned his language.

He had a name. Its wave forms were difficult to translate, but he said it was also the name of a small wild creature on the surface of his native world. He had been a communicator on the captured ship. Surprising her again, he wanted no revenge for the death of his mate.

"Do no harm to my people," he begged her. "No more than you must. Living in terror and expecting nothing better, they are not responsible."

The planetics, he told her, had come in three ships. Only one had been taken. He asked eagerly for news of the others, admitting that all the captives still hoped to rejoin their own kind. The hostility of his companions had begun when they feared he might betray their plots to escape.

When he learned that those sister craft had reached an inner fringe haloid and left a small colony there, he begged to be put with them there and tried again to destroy himself when she told him that was impossible. She revived him with fluid transfusions from his few surviving fellows and the news that another planetic craft had been reported, approaching from toward the colony.

"My own people!" Quivering with joy, he seemed almost eldred. "Coming to take me home!"

"We can't let you go," she told him. "Not yet."

"Are your people afraid?" His amusement made a harsh vibration. "Hiding from us?"

Trying to explain that no general contact could even be considered until the Council of the Elderhood had received her own reports, she begged him to be patient. Unfortunately, the incredible brevity of planetic lifespans made patience impossible.

"I'm already old," he told her. "Dying while your Elderhood debates me."

She saw him growing ill again, his integument withered, the hair grown long and white even on his face since she had taken the instrument with which he had removed it. Feeling some sympathy, she had to explain that she had found no reason to welcome his kind into the Elderhood.

"Your spacecraft was not invited into the halo," she told him. "You invaded and attacked us with no provocation."

"We aren't invaders." He trembled with evident dismay. "We came only as explorers. We fired on your craft only because our officers misunderstood your laser signals. We thought you were firing on us."

He kept begging her to let him message the approaching craft. When it came near, she persuaded the director to agree. Shaking with elation, the creature called his fellow planetics. He spoke well of the Elderhood—hoping, she saw, to negotiate his own freedom.

The battle in space, he insisted, had resulted only from a tragic blunder. He and the rest of his crew, rescued from the wreck, had been receiving excellent care. The halo peoples wanted the friendship of all planetics.

The planetic commander answered at once, expressing regret for past conflict and hope for future amity. He was anxious, he said, to learn the arts and sciences of the halo civilization. In return, he could promise generous shipments of the heavy metals and other products of the inner planets.

The director allowed the planetic craft to continue its approach until its bristling guns and missile launchers armaments began to be alarming. The planetics were then asked to hold their distance until pledges of amity could be completed and confirmed by the Elderhood.

Cyan Gem heard the brief reply.

"Tough luck, Charbon, and I'm sorry for you. These queer snowballs may look like paradise to you, but we Kwans make our own human history."

Bewildered at first, she understood when the planetics opened fire.

Skyfish. *A creature of the halo, captured in space and brought back to the Kwan Labs by Nadya Dain. Described as "elegant in form, enigmatic in behavior, obviously intelligent yet inexplicably silent." Body length nearly two meters, Earth weight 39 kilograms. Body form said to resemble fish or elongated raindrop. Winglike flippers flex to serve as signal dishes for electronic communication. Body structure tapers back to propulsion jet believed to employ organic superconductors. Species thought to have originated on some planetary surface and engineered its own adaptations to the halo environment.*

6

"**H**OME?" QUIN LET ELATION LIFT HIM. "A SHIP ON the way to take us Sunside—"

Seeing Kerry's taut face and Charbon's consternation, he stabbed his boot to catch the velfast floor.

"*Quel malheur!*" Charbon's sick eyes blinked again at the printout. "*Les cochons!* Spying on us. Closing in out of space—"

"Are they, sir?" Kerry frowned. "We know too little—"

"We know they killed my son."

"A tragedy." He nodded soberly. "But that was twenty years ago. They have not attacked again. Sir—" His voice grew anxious. "We can't surrender the halo, just because of a signal we don't understand—"

"I do not surrender." Charbon swung to glare into the

starside night. "*Jamais!* Not without a settlement for my son. Yet—" He shrugged, swinging slowly back, that flash of defiance fading. "*Tout de même*, if the Tycoon commands us to withdraw . . ."

Muttering, breathing hard, he shuffled across the dome and dropped into the tunnel. Beaten, Quin thought. Perhaps even secretly relieved that his long war against the things of space seemed about to end.

"I'm sorry, Kerry." Quin turned uneasily to him. "But you know I always wanted to go home—"

"If you call the Sunside home . . ." Kerry's dry voice trailed off while he shook starmist into his palm. "I'm sorry for you, boy."

"It's what I want," Quin had to say. "All I ever wanted."

"Don't pack yet." With a sad little grin for him, Kerry inhaled another bitter breath. "Vira Brun will be three more months on the way. Admiral Kwan could contact the starsiders before she gets here. If he does—*quién sabe?*"

His hard brown hands spread wide.

"Whatever happens," he added quietly, "I don't intend to be evacuated."

Waiting for Vira Brun, they kept alert. Those enigmatic laser bursts had ceased. Listening night after night to the faint, far-off hiss of the galactic core, Quin could only wonder what they had meant.

Every midnight, he tried to be on hand with Charbon and Kerry to pick up Jason's transmissions and send them on down the relay chain toward Cotopaxi High. Always brief and curtly formal, the signals arrived precisely timed to fit Janoort's spin.

"Admiral Jason Kwan to Fleet Command." His laconic highside voice was digitized for the lasers, but it came through crisply clear; to Quin it had a ring of casual arrogance. "In flight toward alien installation." He always gave his flight coordinates, and always ended with the same ritual formula, "Concluding transmission from Jason

Kwan, Admiral of the Halo, acting to serve the Company and defend the Sun Tycoon."

Sometimes, waiting, Quin wished—almost wished—he had been with the expedition. In spite of everything, Jason's Kwan audacity and charm were still appealing. He was doing things. Feeling trapped and useless on Janoort, Quin couldn't help an ache of regret for high adventure missed.

Noël Michel was the new lasercom officer who had come out on the *Solar Kwan*. A slim young woman with a warm round face and mild brown eyes, she was lively and brightly attractive. Quin loved the crisp highside ring in her softly childish voice, and he felt fascinated with all her Sunside sophistication.

"She's lovely." Kerry was enchanted. "Lovely as your mother was. I like the way she laughs—with very little to laugh about."

He invited her to dinner. Quin cleaned their apartment, with the ventilators open wide to thin the starmist reek from Kerry's room. Kerry himself fussed over gourmet dishes Charbon had taught him how to make. Somehow, he had a bottle of Charbon's precious wine.

Noël seemed delighted with the dinner and happy with Kerry himself. She even said she liked the lingering scents of starmist. Afterward, while Kerry had gone back to the dome to pick up Jason Kwan's midnight message, she talked to Quin about the Sunside.

Thirstily he drank up all she said. She had lived in the skyweb, had known all the fabulous magnificence he had only dreamed about.

If—

His old hopes were suddenly soaring. If the evacuation took him back Sunside, if he could earn his Sunmark and find his mother, if she would say who his father had been, if he could somehow find or earn the heritage he longed for—

Too many ifs. Common sense told him that, yet the dream was too dear to be denied.

"I've known Jason most of my life," Noël was saying. "Finally too well." Her lips set hard, and he saw her flinch as if with pain. It was a moment before she went on. "My father was Kwan kin, and we met Jason at a kinship festival when I was still a girl."

Kwan kinship came by nomination, she explained, not by birth; her grandfather had won nomination for steering the Kwan Moon into Earth orbit, her father for designing the laserlink relay system.

"Jason was just back from the halo when we first met. His father was the new Tycoon, and he already meant to be the next one. I was thrilled when he smiled at me. So handsome! So daring—"

Her voice turned ironic.

"The great space hero!"

He saw her lips compress again. In a moment, however, she had shrugged off whatever she felt. Yet he had seen real pain in her eyes. He wondered how gravely Jason had hurt her.

"Of course my father said I was too young for him, and it was years before I saw him again. Except in holo tanks. He was always in the news. Always exciting. Racing rockets, exploring asteroids, sometimes brawling— he's got a savage temper, and he has killed men.

"He always had stunning women around him—I used to envy them all, and I longed for all Jason gave them. He had magic. Always climbing higher in the system, higher in his father's favor. A general in Sun Security. Admiral of the Asteroids. Elected to the Seven."

Quin had to ask about the Seven. His old illusions not entirely quenched, he wanted to know all he could learn about the remote impossible highside world of the Sunfolk and the Kwans and the Chens and the Company.

"The House of Kwan is a social machine," she said. "Rebuilt from old Ivan's original grand design. It began with only four people. The old man and his sons, signing the Charter. It grew with time. Shrewdly run, at least for the first hundred years. Misfits dumped and good new blood brought in. The House has thirty members now, all chosen from the kinship—my father lived and schemed to get into the Thirty, but he was never quite elected."

She shrugged, a little wistfully.

"He never found out why, or who had schemed against him. The Kwans keep their secrets. Dad never even learned how the Seven are chosen out of the Thirty. They are three Seconds, three Signers, and the Head. The Head has to be one of the Signers. He interprets the Charter. Rules the House. Approves or vetoes. Nowadays, he names the Sun Tycoon—names himself, of course."

Listening, Quin had been absorbed.

"The House of Kwan—" She made a wry face and shook her head at him, as if amused at his awe. "Once a machine for power. It spun the skywires and claimed the planets and discovered Janoort. But machines break down when incompetents try to run them. I'm afraid the House is breaking down."

"The Kwans?" He stared. "Incompetent?"

"Are sharks competent?" Bitterness flashed in her eyes. "The Kwans have always been superb power grabbers. Experts in the politics of perjury and succession by assassination." She leaned intently toward him. "I think you know Jason?"

"Too well."

"He should be—be in prison now." He saw her lips quiver. "Or spaced for treason. If his doting father hadn't sent him here to the halo, out of harm's way."

"Treason?"

"Jason—"

Something stopped her voice. She sat for a moment staring blankly past him, her face set hard, before she caught her breath and looked soberly back at him. Slowly she relaxed. Sipping her drink, she raised the bulb in bright-eyed approval of Charbon's wine.

"Plotting to grab the old Tycoon's place." Her voice was smoother, but old emotion still quivered in it. "Probably clever enough to get it. Letting or, more likely, helping his most dangerous rivals get rid of themselves.

"One was Uri Chen—he's the son of old Boris, the Tycoon old Fernando overturned. Uri was a few years younger than Jason. Just as ambitious, but not so bold. Nor quite so smart—or Jason might be dead."

Drinking in her words, thirsty for every revelation, he felt a chill of dim foreboding. Keenly as he longed for the Sunside, it struck him now that the House of Kwan was a deadly maze, filled with traps and hazards he was unprepared to face, more perilous than the halo.

"He and Uri played a game," she was saying. "The prize was a place among the Signers. Uri's last move was to plant a bomb in Leonid Chen's Sun Country villa, with evidence arranged to fix the blame on Holyfolk terrorists.

"Jason's move won the game."

Quin waited, watching the play of feeling on her vivid features. He saw that Jason still haunted her.

"Coto gossip." A wry little shrug. "He's far too cagey to confirm anything, even talking to me. But I gathered from his hints that he had known about the bomb. He even called Security, just too late. Uri was caught and convicted.

"With Leonid blown up and Uri blown through the execution lock, he's got two rivals out of the way with no actual evidence against him. The rumors won't matter, not to a Kwan. Risking his neck here in the halo, flying out to challenge our enemies in space, he's still scheming."

"Isn't anybody—" Quin was appalled. "Isn't anybody decent?"

"My parents were." Silent for a moment, she shook her head. "The sharks never give the innocents much of a chance. But Jason—"

Her face set tight again.

"I knew—thought I knew what he was." Her voice had changed, and he heard the pain in it. "I loved him, Quin. Thought I did. That's most of the reason I volunteered for duty here. I couldn't help wanting the months in space with him—"

A moment of silence, her wounded eyes wide and empty.

"I've told Kerry." He saw her lip quivering. "Since I've said so much, you may as well know. Jason—" Her husky whisper caught. "We were lovers through the first weeks of the voyage. Till I learned what his other lovers were."

Kerry came back from the dome and poured the rest of the wine. Noël was calmer by then, but still distressed when he told her how he longed to see the Sunside.

"Please, Quin—don't even think about it. The high-siders do have things to enjoy, but they pay high. Higher every day, with old Fernando sick and all the Earth at the brink of revolt. People poisoned with hate and fear, suspecting one another, till your best friends turn cold.

"I'm so glad to get away. Glad!"

She paused to smile at Kerry, her lips a little parted, her Sunmark flashing. Quin left them alone together.

Midnight after midnight, those curt reports kept coming in. Jason was fifty AU farther into the halo, seventy, ninety. Watching Kerry and Charbon, Quin saw their spirits lifting. The alien base seemed too far to be a threat. Kerry began to hope that Fleet Command might cancel the evacuation order.

Quin himself, uneasily eager, always managed to be waiting for the Sun's brief rise above the ice and the flight reports from Vira Brun. Hoping for his chance to get Sunside, he went back aboard the old *Capella* when he could, to learn what Tony Caffodio knew about solar-politics and Olaf Thorsen and the new technologies of fusion engineering.

Kerry and Noël were always together. A month before the *Martian Kwan* was due, they decided to marry.

"To make the most," Kerry said, "of whatever time we have." Quin heard him warning her that things could get grim if the supply ships quit coming.

"They can get grimmer, back Sunside." She shrugged and turned to smile at Quin. "We're going to be halonials—a new word, but one I like. Our children will be the people of the halo."

Kerry drew her to him, his own smile bleak.

"Even if we fail—" She caught his hand. "We'll never be sorry."

Charbon read the brief ceremony. To make space for them, Quin moved into the tiny room that had once been Jomo's. Watching them together, he felt a little envious.

With Vira Brun still two weeks away, Jason reported that he was nearing the alien base.

"Our spy drone has an object imaged." His casual highside voice had a ring of easy satisfaction. "A sphere. Diameter ten kilometers. Evidently artificial. Probing with various frequences, we failed to penetrate it. Nature unknown, though our engineers suggest that it's an insulating shell built to protect a halo snowball from energies that might evaporate it.

"We've been seen. We are detecting laser beams scanning us. Not from the sphere itself, but from a point nearly a hundred kilometers out. Maybe a satellite station."

Hardly three hours later:

"Contact!" Excitement had quickened the brittle rhythm of his speech. "Contact with the *Spica*'s missing people. With Reynard Charbon—he's old Jean's son, the lost lasercom officer. He's calling now with signal gear he says the aliens took off the *Spica*. Telling a surprising story.

"The *Spica* was disabled by an accident, he says, not by attack. He says her officers were unduly alarmed when they saw the alien starcraft. Trying to escape, they overloaded the drive. The engines failed, with damage they couldn't repair.

"The aliens were never hostile. So Reynard swears. Instead, they rescued the crew. Most of the ship's people are still alive and well. The aliens have learned enough English to describe what he calls their pan-galactic culture. Their union is called the Elderhood.

"He is hoping mankind will be invited to join. Our planets are too hostile for the aliens to visit, but they've watched our evolution. He says he has been urging them to open contact. We can trade them heavy elements that are rare out here. In return, they could offer us their own science and art and culture. A treasure hoard that Charbon says he can't yet evaluate—can't even understand.

"He's eager to see us. He has already arranged for us to dock and begin negotiations. We're to pick up a few of the crew who'll be returning Sunside with what they have learned. Charbon himself has offered to remain, as our first ambassador to the Elderhood. He believes members of my own crew may also ask to stay, when they've met our new friends—"

Jason seemed to gasp.

"Sorry!" He was suddenly breathless. "No more now. Something new coming in from Reynard. Details later. Get this report to Charbon's father—he should be happy. Relay it back to Coto. And forgive my incoherence. Because I'm still giddy. Can't express my own elation. Nothing in history quite—quite so epochal. Mankind is coming of age!"

Dazed by the message, Quin sent it on to Cotopaxi High.

"Reynard!" Charbon came back to the dome, a squeeze-bulb in his hand, already rosily tipsy. "*C'est très bien!* Alive and well! When I believed him murdered."

Kerry was afloat in a pungent haze of starmist.

"Wonderful news! Think what it means! Halo Station will surely be the transfer point between Sunside and the Elderhood. The gateway for humanity, moving from the planets out to space."

For Quin, it seemed too sudden. Those promised gifts of the Elderhood were too strange and too far for him to grasp. But—a wild elation lifted him. If Halo Station should become a gateway for commerce with the halo, he could surely find his way Sunside, to learn at last what he was born to be.

That sleepless night crawled away. With Kerry and Charbon, he waited in the dome. All silent, each lost in his own soaring anticipations. Kerry breathed his starmist till the air was heavy with it. Charbon finished his wine.

Slowly, slowly, Janoort turned. The stars blazed, slowly wheeling. Jason's position, the position of the alien base, slid slowly down. Just before it was lost below the near horizon, the lasercom crackled back to life.

"—trapped!" Jason's voice, now a breathless rasp. "They've opened laser fire. From all around us. From the base. From that ice asteroid. From out in space. We're betrayed! Fighting—fighting for our lives.

"Tricked! Very neatly, though Bela Zar tried to warn us. Tried too late. Remember Bela Zar? *Spica*'s captain. One of the captives now. He somehow got out of confinement. Reached Charbon's mike. Gasped out his story—all he had time for. Before the space devils stopped him. Killed him, I imagine.

"But not before he told us what the aliens are. Monstrous! Worse than the Revelator ever claimed. That Reynard—a devil himself. Feeding us all those fantastic lies. Zar says the aliens did attack the *Spica*. Took the crew. Tortured most of them to death.

"Most didn't break. Charbon did. Brainwashed, Zar says. Their puppet now. A dirty traitor to the Tycoon and all mankind. Squealing on his fellow humans. Cuddling up to things Zar says he can't describe. Selling us out. Spilling everything he knows about human technology and human defenses. Coaching alien spies. Helping them plan the conquest of mankind—Zar said they want to keep us in slavery, to dig heavy metals on worlds too big and hot for them.

"Reynard Charbon—a name to live in infamy! He has coaxed us into a hellish trap. The aliens have weapons. Queer devices of their own. Lasers and missiles off the *Spica*. Now—"

Seconds of thermal noise, then sounds of other voices.

"We're hit—hard hit!" Jason again, hoarse and desperate. "But not dead yet. Not quite yet. But we're going silent. For evasive action. Will report again when possible." His voice grew sharper. "Hit again—harder—"

His voice was cut off.

Old Charbon stumbled toward the tunnel, shattered, sobbing, reeling with his wine. Quin and Kerry waited in the dome until Janoort's spin broke the transmission link, but nothing else came in. That night they were listening again.

All they heard was the thin galactic hiss.

Commander Sage died in Outpost Vermillion, along with nearly half his staff. The seeker queen caught most of the rest in flight. Greenvane, the senior supervisor, urged his remaining companions to scatter themselves and drift cold, hoping some fortunate few might escape.

He reached Northpoint exhausted and alone, far behind the warning signals Sage and the others had spent their lives to send. Northpoint was the major center of the Newlings, yet hardly a city. Half a dozen small haloids had been towed into a tiny swarm, each mirror-armored to save it from sublimation.

It was hardly a capital; the Newlings were too few and scattered too widely across their empty spaces to need much formal organization. As one proud proverb ran, they required no masters because each reigned as her own mistress. Half a score of orbital shells housed the institutions of their loose union.

On arrival, Greenvane went first to the clustered globes that held the deputations of the Elderhood, along with the varied life support facilities its diverse races required. He felt grateful for emergency aid, but the staff members disheartened him with an air of untroubled duty-as-usual.

He asked to see Swift, the senior resident deputy. Swift's people were sexless Eternals, whose remote origins must have been planetic, because they still required the ambient pressure and controlled external temperature of a dirigible crystal habitat.

Speaking with a flow of luminescence along the undulant antennae blooming from a convoluted braincase, Swift assured him that Sage's last messages had been received and relayed. The Council of the Elderhood would no doubt be called into session to consider whether any action should be taken. Luckily, it added, Northpoint was safely out of the creature's apparent path.

"Sir! Safe?" Greenvane spread flashing wings to let his consternation show. "You can't imagine the invader. The thing's enormous and appalling, with no redeeming hint of evolution toward eldredship. I watched it kill a Newling who was trying— too boldly—to warn it away from the halo. Watched it swallow Point Vermillion. We're all in danger, until—unless we can put an end to it."

"Too large a problem for us." The bright antennae rippled to a shrug. "I trust the Council will consider conciliation—"

"Conciliation?" Greenvane blazed. "I saw that tried by the unfortunate Newling. Our survival can't wait for the Council to debate and do nothing. We must act—"

"With what?" Swift shrugged again, as if its capsule had been adequate armor against all harm. "I imagine all our races have evolved through stages where aggression seemed essential for survival—the same feral stage where this intruder appears to be trapped. But, here in the halo, we've left aggression far behind us."

"Sir, I'm afraid it's catching up. These creatures beat the Newlings—"

"Because the Newlings tried to fight." Swift ignored his yellow flash. "Their error, and nearly fatal. Even the Newlings are sadly immature, not far beyond the levels of primal savagery. Speaking for myself, I still question the wisdom of their admission to our society."

"On some level, sir, the halo has to be defended—"

"We've no defense establishment here." The rhythmic streams of body-color seemed almost smug. "None anywhere, able to engage such a primitive thing on its own primitive terms."

"In that case, sir—must we allow our own destruction?"

"Really, Greenvane!" Swift's eye-ring burned with stern reproof. "Asking that, you are failing to display your own eldership. Surely, until the Council sits, the halo's large enough for all of us."

"Large enough?" He let his indignation flare. "You don't know these invaders. Nearly mindless seekers of heat, all they do is eat and fight and breed. The Newlings warn us, sir, that we'll all be in danger, all across the halo, because they kill for sport—"

"Greenfoil—" A bright pink flower unfolded, gently interrupting him. "Or is it Greenglint?—you forget the elder way, which admits no violence. When we come upon such unevolved primitives, we must seek to elevate them."

"Elevate them?" His scorn burned crimson. "How—"

"If you were truly eldren, Greenteil, you would not be inquiring."

The antennae paled, withdrawing into the pale braincase to end the interview.

Fermi Paradox. *(Attributed to twentieth-century physicist Enrico Fermi.) An apparent contradiction between two lines of thought about intelligence existing elsewhere. Earthlike planets are assumed to be numerous. The cosmological principle implies that life and mind should have evolved everywhere. Even one technological culture surpassing the human level could logically expand to fill the galaxy in only a few million years. Yet the life of Earth appears to have originated and evolved though several billion years in total isolation. The paradox was once cited in support of opinion that mankind is unique and alone.*

7

OLD EARTH!

His far home, mother of mankind, world of long yearning and bright imagination. Now at last—if Halo Station had to be evacuated—he could really hope to see her from the skyweb, her dazzle against the dark and the glory of her Sunlit curve. Down in Sun Country, he would finally feel her mighty grasp, explore the limitless flatness he knew only from holos, discover all her marvels of tree and mountain, ocean and cloud, the splendor of her blue-shining sky.

If his luck broke right.

He changed to the day shift, to be on duty when Captain Brun's flight reports came in. She was a stocky, mannish woman, when the *Martian Kwan* was near enough to let him get her image in the tank. No longer young, she had short white hair around a broad, hard face.

Her transmissions were crisply brief, giving only her flight coordinates, asking only for late news of Jason Kwan, with no visible concern when he had none. She was flying a mission for the Tycoon and the Company, and she seemed untroubled by anything else.

Waiting for her, he tried to face his own uncertain future with the same sort of steadiness. That wasn't easy. To Kerry and Jomo and Noël, the Sunside was a jungle of kwanlon and orbital metal, ruled by ruthless predators. A picture so cruel that he had to reject it.

The Sunfolk, he told himself, were the selected best of mankind, evolved for space, the Sunmark their shining sign. Jomo and Noël had earned that splendid symbol. His mother had. Doubtless his father. Born to it, he would surely find more good than bad among its wearers.

He tried never to question the distant destiny he longed for. Tried not to think too much of the cruel pain giving up Janoort might bring Kerry and Noël and most of those he loved. Tried to shake off a nagging sense of disloyalty to them—after all, he told himself, the evacuation was nothing he could stop.

When his doubts grew darkest, he thought of Mindi Zinn. She would be a stranger, living a life of her own, maybe impossible even for him to find. Yet she had loved him once. Somehow, sometime, somewhere—he had to see her again!

Standing long shifts now, waiting for Vira Brun, waiting for the transmissions that never came from Jason Kwan, he was often in the dome when old Captain Charbon arrived to hope for another midnight signal from his son. Quin had to pity him. Sleepless, unshaven and haggard, nearly always the worse for his wine, yet clinging to an insane faith.

"*Bien sûr!*" His voice had grown rustily hoarse. "*Certainement*, Admiral Kwan will soon return to confess that *les cochons* deceived him. *Oui*, to tell us that my Reynard was never a traitor, but instead a loyal servant of the Company."

Waiting, waiting—till one sudden dawn when Quin came in with Kerry to find Charbon high off the floor. Launched perhaps by some careless movement, he was adrift in the gentle gravity, staring out into the dead-black sky, eyes fixed glassily on whatever he imagined there. He looked dismal, shriveled, haunted.

"Captain?" Kerry called. "Captain Charbon?"

He seemed not to hear. Unaware of anything, he rose very slowly, hung lax in the air, fell very slowly, bounced and rose and fell again, lifeless as an unstrung puppet.

"Sir!" Kerry's voice lifted. "We're here to relieve you."

Gasping in a startled way, Charbon stabbed his boot at the floor and turned himself clumsily, gaping at nothing. The instrument lights shone dimly through his loose white hair, giving him a dull-red halo. He gulped as if to speak, but no words came.

"Captain, are you sick?"

He blinked, discovering them.

"Beaten." A slow dry whisper. "*C'est fini.* No news from Admiral Kwan. *Jamais!* I was imbecile to hope. *Les cochons!* They have destroyed my Reynard. Destroyed his soul. Destroyed Admiral Kwan. As they plan to destroy us all.

"*En finir avec!*"

Muttering that, he stumbled into the tunnel. His aides called back from the *Capella* to say he was ill. They were Security men, sweating out their duty tours for hazard pay and promised promotion, none of them with Fleet training to relieve him on lasercom duty. Kerry took the next night shift. When Quin came in at dawn, he found the air heavy with starmist and Kerry on the intercom, shouting at Charbon's aides.

"*Caramba!*" He scowled at Quin. "When we've got a new object in the lidar scopes, they tell me the Captain is still indisposed. Indisposed? They mean *borracho!* Dead to everything."

"Jason's ship?" he asked. "Coming back?"

"Not likely." He shook his head, scowling out at the old *Capella*. "This thing's coming out of the north, sixty degrees from Jason's last position."

"The aliens he went to look for?"

"Not likely. The wrong direction for their base."

"So what—"

"*Quién sabe?*" Kerry shrugged uneasily, shuffling toward the tunnel. "All I see is a moving point. Faintly radiant in the infrared. Decelerating now, but still moving faster than I can believe. With Charbon unfit for anything, all we can do is report it to Captain Brun. I've got the data taped, ready for you to transmit when the window opens."

Janoort turned. The hot Sun-point rose over the snow. The *Martian Kwan* lifted into the window. He sent Kerry's tape.

"Data received." In the holo tank, Vira Brun's heavy, black-browed face reflected no emotion. "You will continue urgent efforts to identify approaching object. We are launching a fusion-driven spy drone to intercept it. Meantime, you will continue to record any data you can."

That night, and the next, Charbon was still indisposed. Kerry stood the long night shifts. He reported nothing from the alien base, nothing from Jason Kwan. Only a faint and redly radiant point, that unknown object crept slowly on across the stars.

"Veering! It's veering toward us now!" Quin had found him puffing starmist, tired eyes squinting into mystery. "But not exactly. Moving more toward where the wreck of the *Spica* ought to be."

"The skyfish?" he whispered. "Coming back for another look?"

"Watch it." Kerry moved toward the tunnel. "We're too far to get much on the lidar, but tape anything you see. Brun's drone ought to get more than we can."

Alone in the dome's crimson dimness, Quin kept the

lidar gear going, watched the monitors, watched the slow slide of the nightside stars. Midnight passed, with nothing from Jason Kwan, nothing from any alien. Slowing faster than any ship could, the object crept upon the computed position of the wreck. The two points merged. The single image brightened.

He saw no more—till a gong called him to the holocom station. The holo tank came to life. He saw the skeletal wreck of the *Spica*. Almost in line with Brun's ship, they were picking up the probe's signal beam.

Near the camera, the wreckage spun very slowly in the starry dark. Somehow, it had grown luminous. Lit, he saw, by the object they had followed out of the north. When he found it, his breath stopped.

Something enormous, though oddly hard to see at first. Its dim loom was ten times the length of the skeleton ship. Maybe twenty. He made out a faint barrel shape. A jet of violet fire blazed out of it, lighting the wreckage. Where it struck, the old ribs and plates and beams were glowing red, turning yellow, finally shining white.

That glow lit—a creature!

No starbird, no skyfish. Slowly revealed, it dazed him. The head had bulging armored turrets placed like eyes, glowing dully red. Nightmare jaws yawned wide. That massive barrel was its body, tapering into a bright-plated tail that had arched as if to sting the wreck with that incandescent jet.

It was winged, he thought, though the wing-shapes were folded into the great body's shadow and almost impossible to see. The light revealed limbs. Four of them, jointless as snakes, slenderly powerful, darting to seize the wreck with immense black talons.

It consumed the hulk.

In that jet's blue blaze, the old ribs and plates and scraps flowed into hot white blobs. Hovering closer, dark wings spread now as if to catch the gases exploding into space, the creature opened its appalling jaws. A thin-seeming tongue stabbed out to suck up the molten metal.

He stared till the last bright blobs were gone. No longer lit, the creature faded back into the dark, until only its red-glowing eyes were left among the stars. They seemed to swell. They spread apart. Its shadow blotted out the stars. Its jaws loomed near. Like a great snake striking, its tongue stabbed into his face.

The tank blacked out.

He had shrunk back from it, hands flung up. Trembling now, he stared into the empty tank. It had all happened too fast, so fast it seemed an evil dream. Yet it was too strange, too terribly real, to have been imagined.

Dazed and shaking, he tried to call Charbon. A sleepy-sounding yeoman told him the captain was unwell and unfit to be disturbed. Nobody had been left in charge. The yeoman turned surly when he kept insisting, and finally told him to take a dive into the sky.

He went back to the lidar scopes. The moving point had vanished. The red shine of those vast eyes—had they been searchlights? Looking for food? Dark now, because the creature had fed?

Still shivering inside, he kept his own search gear going. Nothing more came in. Nothing from Jason Kwan. Nothing from the position of the alien base. Nothing from where the wreck had been. At last the far Sun struck across the cratered ice. The *Martian Kwan* came into line of sight. Braking to land, now only a few hours out.

"We've lost our drone," Vira Brun told him. "Do you have additional data on that object?"

Light still took nearly a second to reach her, nearly another to return. Waiting for her responses, as she waited for his, he saw a long pale scar that ran beneath the Sun-mark on her leathery cheek, saw scattered black bristles along her upper lip.

"I saw what happened to the wreck. Though I can't—" He had to shake his head. "Can't quite believe—can't believe such a thing could be alive."

"Alive?" Her hard face reflected nothing. "What was alive?"

Feeling breathless and none too steady, he tried to describe the thing he had seen. Her eyes narrowed warily. He couldn't tell what she thought, but he felt a flash of admiration for her iron calm.

"Captain," he finished, "didn't you see it?"

"I was not on duty." She paused, peering sharply at him. "Our technician reported that the unknown object seemed to strike the wreck and our drone in an extraordinary triple collision, which stopped transmission."

"Didn't he see its shape?"

"He reports a malfunction in our equipment. He got no details."

"I think—I know I saw something alive." He tried to seem as cool as she was. "A creature of space. Shaped a little like an insect. Red-glowing eyes. A blazing jet for a sting. It's big! Bigger than any spacecraft. It eats metal— it fused the wreck and sucked up the hot metal. Moving faster than anything should, it came on to hit the drone."

Waiting again for her reaction, he saw none at all.

"Captain—" He had to catch his breath. "Don't you believe—"

"That hardly matters." She shrugged, frowning out of the tank. "I'm sure the event was extraordinary. The technician seems to have seen something that left him disturbed and incoherent. We have him under sedation now."

"Captain!" He kept trying to match her calm. "That creature's real. Real—and frightening. Now flying blind, I imagine, without the search beam it used to locate the wreck. It could attack Janoort. It could hit your ship."

More long seconds of her impassive frown.

"Mr. Dain, we're all at risk." She seemed to be reproving him. "A time may come when the human species is at home in space. If we survive. If we adapt. But that's not yet. Out here, we're meeting circumstances new to us. Circumstances we must accept if we care to stay."

"Captain," he protested, "if you'd seen that creature—"

"I hope I never do."

For a moment, almost smiling, she looked likable.

"There's a rule of the Fleet's you ought to be aware of. Rather, a rule of the Chens." Her stern calm had returned. "You'll be in trouble with the censor if you try to report what you say you saw. Better forget it," she added. "For your own sake. Maybe for mine."

"Why?" he whispered.

"Solarpolitics. An old and bitter issue. The Kwans hold that space aliens do exist. The Chens hold that they don't. They accuse the Kwans of fabricating evidence to support the Revelator, with his crazy claims of demons in space."

"The skyfish is no fabrication. My own mother took it back Sunside."

"Your mother?" Her hard face showed slight surprise. "Dr. Nadya Dain?"

Nodding, he waited again.

"I know her. I advised her once to drop the skyfish— whatever it is—before the Chens wrecked her career."

"Are they so powerful?"

"They are. In the House. In Security. Even though we now have a Kwan Tycoon. That's why I'm advising you to forget whatever you saw. The Chens won't let you talk."

Still half doubtful, he stood staring into the tank.

"If they had seen that creature—"

Two more seconds, and her face set harder.

"I suspect that one of them did. My probe technician is named Nicholas Chen." Abruptly she was moving in the tank, "Dain, you will inform Captain Charbon of our arrival time. He is to have all station personnel alerted for a quick evacuation."

Searching for the Newling weapon, Greenvane went from Deputy Swift to the contact agency, which housed a handful of specialists who had come to share the arts and sciences of the Elderhood. He found a sibling there, Fireflake, the halo historian.

Their people were a clonefolk born of planetic predators, driven from their home star when it turned nova. Cloning had fixed the adaptations that enabled their survival, but also stopped their evolution. After almost a billion years in space, their jungle origins were still revealed in the muscular power beneath their life-support harness and their gem-bright scales.

Though they were among the senior races in the Elderhood, they had always been oddballs, respected for their abilities, yet set apart by their genetic sameness and such primal survivals as their singular and seemingly fruitless sexuality. Living long and slow to clone, they had never been numerous. Never claiming domains of their own, they were a race of savants scattered through the whole halo.

Though Greenvane had never met Fireflake, as clones they had known each other forever. She slid out of her harness and into his, flowing into her female shape to greet him. Relaxing from their first passionate embrace, he began his story of the seeker queen and his own close escape from Outpost Vermillion.

"We've had the news." She held him wrapped in her hot coils, her whisper an electric tingle. "No problem of ours."

"It will be," he said. "A grave problem for all the Elderhood. But perhaps it can be solved, if we act now."

"So let us act, lizardheart." Murmuring that old term of endearment, she caught his ear with bright black fangs. "Here and now."

"Against the seekers." He writhed back from her voltaic allure. "The Newlings had a weapon. Goldengene insisted that it still exists. If it can be found—"

"Later, lizardheart."

Her prehensile tail wrapped him in tingly fire. He couldn't help responding, and they said no more of any Newling weapon until she was back in her own harness, aglow with contentment.

"I came here to study Newling history," she told him then. "Since we heard of the seeker attack, I've been searching for anything about the weapon. What I've found is mostly frustration. The Newling survivors got here in just one ship, with most of their records lost on the way."

"Goldengene said they still have the weapon."

"The hulk of their escape craft is here, preserved as a museum. I've talked to the curator and dug through everything there. I find no weapon. No convincing evidence, in fact, that there ever was a weapon."

"Goldengene seemed sure—"

"The curator isn't. She's an aging female named Whitescribe. Custodian of what the Newlings know about their tragic past. Which isn't much. Their lives are short, and their minds decay with age. Whitescribe's ramblings make very little sense. She hinted once that the weapon had been destroyed."

"You must have other sources?"

"I've looked into the archives at the mission. Reports of the initial contacts. Descriptions of the seekers and their nuclear metabolism."

"How could such uneldren things evolve?"

"The Newling refugees believed the seekers' remote ancestors must have been engineered as self-replicating weapons."

"Are they machines?"

"Half mechanical, half biological." Her reply was brief, and he felt her heat returning. "If it matters."

"To the Elderhood, it does." He tried to slow his own response. "Machines can be stopped."

"Our agents ruled that stopping the seekers would be genocide. Refuge, in fact, was offered only on condition that the Newlings opt for the elder way.

"Our own way, lizardheart." She nipped his ear again. "If we ourselves were evolved for violence, it's a sweeter sort. Come back to me."

"Not quite yet." He slid aside. "Not till you tell me what you know about the weapon."

"Frostheart!" Her next nip was painful. "There's nothing I know."

"This curator—"

"If you ask for her senile maunderings, she tells how the hunted Newlings found two seekers dead. A young queen and a drone frozen on a snow haloid, where their mating battle had been fatal to both. Newling biologists risked their own lives to obtain tissue specimens from which they made a virus that they hoped would be fatal."

"It wasn't?"

"Never fully tested." Her impatient tail flicked to tease him. "So Whitescribe says. Or maybe imagines. Fired into adult seekers, she says, it had no effect. Its creators believed it would kill seeker eggs or seeker hatchlings, but that was an experiment they never completed."

He recoiled, asking why.

"Frozenheart, the seekers themselves are the reason. The breeding queens and their young are hived in fortress asteroids, remote from their prey. The attacker would have had to penetrate the swarm and fight a way through guarded tunnels into the natal chambers.

"The last of the Newlings were preparing for that desperate assault when they were offered sanctuary here. Accepting its conditions, renouncing violence, they fled from the seekers in the craft they had built for the attack."

"So what became of the weapon?"

"If old Whitescribe ever knew, she has long since forgotten. She did give me the freedom of the old escape ship. I found no killer virus. No clear description of it. I've talked to scores of Newlings. Many of them seem inclined to agree with my own notion that the thing's a myth—a pathetic bit of compensation for their racial defeat. It's a matter of ethnic pride."

"If that's just a notion, let's go back to the Newling ship—"

He saw her sleek bright coils transforming.

"I'll be the male, lizardheart. Female, perhaps you'll recall that we ourselves are elderlings, quite unfit to fight the seekers even if weapons were thrust upon us."

Yielding to his fire, Greenvane let her body flow.

Sun Company. *A corporate arm of the House of Kwan, the Company dominated Earth through the Sun Century. It conquered the planets and reached the halo. Loyalist historians praise it for ending the wars between nations and fostering a magnificent age of progress and peace. Clerics condemn it as a satanic tyranny, ascribing its fall to divine judgment executed by "the monsters of God."*

CHARBON'S AIDES HAD DRIED HIM OUT TO MEET THE *Martian Kwan.* Clambering unsteadily out of the tunnel, he failed to catch the floor and drifted, helpless, until an aide gripped his arm to draw him back.

"*C'est fini.*" He blinked at Quin, his eyes bloodshot and glassy. "I have spoken to Brun. She is arriving to relieve me. She is evacuating everybody. Janoort will be abandoned."

"Sir!" Quin felt a pang of concern for Kerry and Noël. For Jomo and all the others who had staked their lives on the halo. "Some will want to stay—"

"*Chose impossible.*" His voice rose peevishly, as if he needed a drink. "*Voyez!*" He gestured at the aide, who was posting a sheet of a yellow-flashing plastic. "Our orders."

NOTICE TO CIVILIANS

All civilian personnel resident at Halo Station
will be prepared by 2100 hours Sun Time today for
medical inspection and evacuation aboard S.S.
Martian Kwan. Transport will be under Metabrake
regimen, with no clothing or personal items required. Each individual may, however, present one
parcel of personal items for shipment Sunside, with
advance inspection and approval required. Bulk
limit: 5 liters. Weight limit, 5 kg.

(SIGNED) Jean Charbon, Station Commander.

"Metabrake?" Quin stared at Charbon. "Will that be
necessary?"

"*Inévitable*." A helpless shrug. "Brun had expected the
Capella to carry a share of the evacuated personnel, but
Uruhu informs me that the old hulk is unfit for flight. The
Martian Kwan cannot carry so many in normal trans-
port."

"Captain, Metabrake kills a lot of people."

He shrugged again. "*Par malheur*."

"I've taken Metabrake." Quin stared for a moment at
the yellow-blinking order, recalling his own slow recov-
ery. "I'd risk it again. Just because I want so much to get
Sunside. I'd probably live. But the children, and older
people—sir, you'll have to let them stay."

"*C'est impossible*. Halo Station is to be effaced."

"Effaced? Is that necessary?"

"*Il est à regretter*." His shoulders lifted in weary apology. "I spoke to Brun about my friend McLenn and his
charming bride and their dream of life in the halo. She
deplored her orders, but Janoort must be left as we found
it. With no trace that might betray us to *les bêtes*."

"The *Capella*, sir? If she can't fly—"

"We are to overload her master magnets and leave her
to explode."

"Sir, people will surely resist—"

"*Inutile*," He was turning waspish. "Brun will tolerate

no *folie*. Your orders will now come from her." Nodding at the lasercom, he turned to go.

"Captain, please—" Quin had started to follow, still protesting. A shock of recollection checked him. He couldn't speak of what the drone had showed him. Yet that nightmare creature still haunted his imagination. Invisible now, since it had fed. Still many billion kilometers away. But it would surely grow hungry again. If it found Janoort—

Evacuation under Metabrake might be the best thing for everybody. He said no more. Pity touched him. Stumbling almost blindly into the tunnel, Charbon looked like a child crushed by punishment too cruel to endure.

Back at the instruments, he tried to call Kerry and Noël. No answer. He searched again for where the wreck had been drifting. Nothing there. He tried the *Martian Kwan*, still in line of sight, and got the howl of a scrambled signal. Charbon and Brun, he thought, discussing the evacuation.

Jomo startled him, popping out of the tunnel.

"Metabrake! Damn *uovu!*" Anger burning in his eyes, he flourished a laser welder. Another was slung over his shoulder. "Damn Charbon. Damn Tycoon. All damn plenty wicked. All *dubwana.*"

He thrust one of the welders at Quin.

"Come along, *mwenzi!* Come along quick. Kerry want everybody. Quick to gym. All civilian personnel, we all *kukita.*"

Mwenzi! Quin felt a flash of gratitude. A comrade at last, no longer a child, he took the welder and followed Jomo into the tunnel.

They found most of the civilians gathered in the gym balloon, massed on nets and tracks, hanging on to ropes and bars, floating free. Perhaps two hundred people. Far too many for normal transport in the limited passenger space on the *Martian Kwan*. A dozen children among them, too young for Metabrake.

"*Maasi!*" Jomo muttered. "Rebellion against the *kuchukiza* Company."

Quin wasn't ready for that. Clinging to a bar beside Jomo, he felt lost in a tangle of helpless regret and uncertain longing. The old lure of the Sunside burned bright in his imagination. Yet—

He couldn't abandon the people he loved.

Kerry stood perched on the high bar that supported squirrel cages and trapezes, Noël beside him. Voice booming back from the tall curve of the walls, he was telling what he knew about Vira Brun's orders and the evacuation plan.

He called Jomo to speak about the old *Capella*'s engines.

"No damn good for ion drive." Jomo grinned, waiting for the echoes to amplify his voice. "For station power, maybe *wingi*. Today, all *safi*. Maybe tomorrow, all *safi*. Damn flux loss come, we fix flux loss."

Dark arms spread, he grinned wider.

"Maybe we stay lucky. Maybe fix master magnets. Maybe fix and fix again. Fix till spare parts gone. But no spare parts to fix ion drive. All used up for plasma pumps."

He shook his fist toward the sky and swam toward Kerry, booming louder.

"Metabrake no damn good for anybody. Make me too damn *mgonjwa*. Make everybody too damn *mgonjwa*. Too damn sick. I vote we stay while engines run." He caught the bar and perched beside Noël and Kerry. "Stay till engines stop."

Silence crackled in the gloomy cavern, while people thought of that. Quin launched himself across it. Jomo reached to catch his hand. Perched beside Noël, he heard a few scattered handclaps, a few cheers, then more and more, gathering till they boomed against the walls.

"I saw Charbon," he whispered to Kerry. "He has orders from Brun. Orders to demolish everything here—

With only a bleak little nod, Kerry turned from him to wave for quiet and introduce Noël. She was shy and hard to hear at first, but soon eloquent, speaking of the Revelator and the Holyfolk and the rising tide of their rebellion against the Sun Tycoon.

"I'll never—never go back!" Her voice had begun to peal against the echoes, clear and strong. "If we live close to danger here, it's a cleaner danger than I've always lived in, back Sunside. The Sunside kills your mind and your pride and your soul in a hundred nasty ways, while you think you're still alive. Here—while the engines run— we can stay sane and free."

When the cheering stopped, Kerry spoke again.

"To those who choose to go." His voice boomed loud against that high curve. "I understand. This looks like your last chance. Metabrake may look safer than the station. We wish you well.

"To you who want to stay." His husky-throated phrases came more slowly. "We can't promise much but hardship and desperation. A hard fight just to stay alive. But at least a few of us have chosen, and I say we should proclaim our freedom.

"And save Janoort!"

A moment of silence. A few startled questions. Two or three frightened people dived for the doorway. But then scattered claps and cheers began among the drill gang, men who had come from the pit in thermal armor. Others joined, until the echoes roared. Shouting drillers wanted to name Kerry the Tycoon of Janoort.

He didn't want the title, but nobody else seemed willing to face Charbon and Vira Brun and Sun Security. He had been at the station since it began. People trusted him. When he offered at last to serve as foreman of Free Janoort, he got the job by acclamation.

Quin went with him back to the dome. Two Security aides halted them at the tunnel mouth, frowning at Quin's welder. Charbon was on the lasercom. No words came through the baffle, but Quin saw him start and scowl at Kerry. He hung up and shuffled to meet them.

"*S'il vous plaît, mon ami!*" His haggard eyes blinked

uneasily. "I'm no longer your commander. Brun is landing soon. She will load reaction mass while we process the civilians for Metabrake. The evacuation cannot be delayed."

He scowled at Quin.

"Dain, I left you on duty here—"

"Captain," Kerry said, "I am taking command of Halo Station."

"You?" Charbon's pale smile was gone. "*Mon ami*, I've heard about your mob of mutineers—"

"Sir, we've declared our independence."

"*Démence!*" He pursed his lips and shook his head with what looked like amazed regret. "An act of madness. Brun has orders to leave Janoort as we found it. Bare."

Kerry stood silent, his face set hard.

"Please, *mon ami*—please!" Charbon looked distressed. "Brun will never let you delay the operation. I beg you, before she arrives—"

"She won't be arriving," Kerry said. "Unless we let her land long enough to pick up those who wish to leave."

"*Un accès des folies,* beyond comprehension."

Charbon shrugged and turned to scowl at his aides, who stood armed and alert. Facing them, Quin had leveled the welder. His heart was hammering. Kerry had taught him how to use it years before, when they were running new water lines to the gardens, but now his sweaty finger trembled on the switch. Thinking of what its laser blade would do to human flesh, he had to gulp against a wave of nausea.

"*Non, non!*"

Charbon swung uncertainly back to wave his weapon down, wave the aides into the tunnel. His drawn face twitched, tears welled out of his bloodshot eyes.

"*Mon—mon vieux*, please!" Imploringly he opened his hands toward Kerry. "We've been friends too long. I cannot fight you. But I beg you—beg you again. Forget your treason before you die for it."

"Perhaps I will." Kerry grinned bleakly. "But not quite yet."

Charbon dropped through the door, and they were alone in the red-lit dome.

"A miserable *borracho*," Kerry muttered. "But you've got to pity him."

"Kerry—" On impulse, Quin caught his arm. "There's something I've got to tell you. Something I'm half afraid to say. But perhaps it could persuade you that we ought to go with Brun."

"Boy!" Kerry stiffened, offended. "Are you crazy?"

Quin told him what the spy drone had imaged.

"A nightmare thing—but real!" Recalling it had shaken him again. "Gone now from the scopes, but still out there. If it should find the station—"

Kerry squinted hard at him, then turned slowly to peer out into the dark and swung slowly back, his lean face grim.

"Have you reported this?"

"I called Captain Brun. Her probe technician saw something so disturbing he had to be sedated. Yet she told me to forget it. Because of solarpolitics—whatever that is. She says the Chen censors won't let anybody say space aliens exist."

Watching Kerry, he caught an anxious breath.

"I saw the thing. Really!"

"No doubt you saw something." Absently, Kerry was shaking a drop of starmist into his hand. "We'll never know all that's out there. Better, maybe, if we don't. But the halo's big enough so perhaps we don't have to care."

The starmist forgotten, Kerry looked harder at him.

"Quin boy, if you want to go back—"

"I'd be a coward, leaving you here—"

"We may die here." Kerry's hard brown grin amazed him. "But you can die in flight, from Brun's Metabrake. Or back Sunside, in a hundred ways. But if you really want to go, if you get lucky enough and fight hard enough, there is a way you might save all our lives."

Puzzled, Quin stared.

"You know the old *Capella*."

"Too well." A stab of concern. "Another reason to leave—"

"For you to go, if you're willing. Those old engines have got to be replaced." Fragrant with starmist, Kerry's brown hand seized his arm. "That's your mission, boy. Go Sunside. Get fusion power for us. Get it back to us."

"If—if I can."

"Most likely you can't." Kerry shrugged. "But better engines do exist. Designed by Olaf Thorsen—your mother's new husband. He built the drives for the Kwan-class ships. If you get back with engines like that—"

"I—I'll try."

"*Adelante!*" Kerry waved him toward the tunnel. "Let's get moving. You've had a long shift. Go get your breakfast. And pack your five kilograms for the evacuation." With an easy-seeming grin, he shuffled toward the lasercom. "We're getting set for the showdown with Brun."

Quin dropped out of the dome, feeling too jittery to look for breakfast or think what to pack. Too much was happening, too fast. But—

If luck did strike, if he could really discover his father and find the status he longed for, back among the Sunfolk, it might be easy enough simply to have fusion machines and fusion know-how sent out to keep the station alive.

Or was that just a child's wild dream?

Leaving the dome, he found the tunnels almost empty and felt an air of desperate tension. At the passage toward the old *Capella*, two welder-armed men ordered him to halt. Jomo recognized him.

"*Salamu, mwenzi!* We watch the ship. Wait for fight. Maybe win. Maybe not." A sweaty grin. "*Sasa hiva*, soon we know."

Quin went back to the dome. Kerry was there at the lasercom, Noël waiting beside him. Charbon and his staff had gone aboard the *Capella*, with the handful of civilians who wanted to leave.

Kerry, she said, was trying to call Captain Brun.

"She'll be landing in an hour—"

"If we let her." Kerry turned to squint into the gloomy sky. "So the showdown is now. We can put up a fight if she wants a fight. I hope she won't. Noël's going to state our case, if we can get her to listen."

The holophone buzzed. Kerry spoke into the baffled headset and swung back to them.

"Brun's busy. Talking to Charbon, I imagine. She'll get our message when she's free."

While they waited, Noël said she had met Brun long ago.

"My father introduced us at some Kwan reception." A wistful little headshake. "Vira—from the way he spoke her name, I knew he loved her. When he died, I found her picture and letters from her in his papers. I imagine she might have been my mother, if she hadn't been in love with Mars."

Kerry looked puzzled.

"Mars—her letters are full of it. People back in Coto used to call her Madam Mars. Because she wanted to terraform the planet. A Kwan Labs project, till she made it her baby. She spent most of her career on it. Tried to enlist my father. He told her it was hopeless. The thing was never funded, not beyond the pilot plant. Finally killed."

"If she's that obsessed—" Kerry frowned uneasily. "What sympathy can we expect?"

"Maybe none." Noël shook her head. "She's hard to know."

The holophone purred again, and Brun's image flashed into the tank. Her rough-chiseled face seemed to soften when she saw Noël, turned wary again when she looked at Kerry.

"You asked to talk?"

"We want Janoort," Kerry said. "We'll fight for that."

"With what?"

"With all we have."

"You can't win. You can only kill yourselves."

"If we die, that's our choice."

"Noël—" A wistful-seeming pause. "I knew your father, years ago. I'm surprised to find you here."

"I came out with Admiral Kwan. Janoort is now my home. All we want is Halo Station. Left as it is. A place where we can try to stay alive." She turned to smile at Kerry. "We are married—"

"You've married this outlaw?"

"Kerry McLenn." She drew him to her side. "Just elected foreman of Free Janoort."

"Free Janoort?" The grizzled head turned grim. "Your good father was no mutineer, and we've no time for nonsense. Our mission will not be delayed."

"Captain," Noël said, "most of us are staying—"

"You'd be idiots." Brun cut her sharply off. "I'll make you this concession—if you surrender at once and proceed with medical inspections for Metabrake passage, I'll delay any official inquiry into the mutiny until we reach Coto High.

"If you refuse—"

"We refuse," Kerry said. "But we can offer a swap of our own."

"We make no deals with mutineers."

"Captain Brun, we aren't helpless." His voice was mildly quiet. "Our signal gear is tracking you. At close range, it's hot enough to hurt you. You can order Charbon to cut our power off, but the standby system can keep us alive. Long enough, I think."

"Long enough?" A level scowl. "For what?"

"You need processed reaction mass for your return flight. You might thaw raw stuff off the haloid, but that could ruin your engines. We'd like to swap the mass you need for our lives."

She stared hard at him. Quin thought he saw a flash of anger, but in a moment it was erased. No emotion showing, she combed blunt fingers back through her short white hair and turned in the tank to glance at Noël.

"Agreed." She spoke abruptly, her voice not quite so bleak. "Your friend Charbon has been urging this. Now I see the force of his advice." She looked at Noël. "If you're sure you want to die here."

"We'll live here," Noël said. "While we can."

"Perhaps—perhaps you can." She swung to Kerry, her hard-bitten features almost friendly. "Let's clarify our terms. You'll allow us to land, to load reaction mass and offer a general amnesty. We'll leave you here with your energy sources intact—and I hope they keep you alive longer than I think they will."

"Thank you, Captain." Kerry grinned. "We've made our choice. We'll take our chances."

Brun looked again at Noël.

"Little Noël." Her head shook slowly, almost sadly. "Grown up lovely." Her searching eyes seemed wistful. "Once—" Emotion shook her voice. "Once I did love your father."

Gnats!

First that impudent midge out at the halo fringe. Now this odd little morsel, the wreck of a midget ship, the evident work of insect artisans. The whole star system must be infested with them.

She hated them.

The metal of their toy spacecraft lay cold in her belly. Too little of it and too dead for food. Too cold to stop the fangs of her starvelings, gnawing at her own exhausted flesh. She had fasted far too long.

She craved live metal, hot with the radiance of its own eternal fire. Without it, her brood would hatch deformed and dying. If they hatched at all. Her own fire chilled, she could perish here in view of this good star, her long flight for nothing, the prince's precious seed wasted in her, her noble kind defeated, all the undiscovered worlds ahead left unclaimed and dead.

Driving on against such stark forebodings, she began crooning the lullabies of generations. Even here in airlessness, her unborn inheritors were listening through her body, and the songs would help her form them. Proud old songs, they had to be implanted deep in preawareness, to shine forever with the history of her invincible race.

Epics of the ancient wars for which her race had been created. The sad tragedy of their betrayal into mercenary slavery. The splendid saga of their final triumph over the perfidious pygmies that tried to misuse them. Listening now, her teeming heirs would be ennobled forever.

If she could bring them forth alive.

Dreams of that took the edge off her agony. Watching the star swelling ahead, she saw new glory born from her hive. Eager workers toiling, tending new generations. Her daughter queens as lovely as she had been, growing up to fulfill themselves with her own proud ferocity. Her magnificent sons, as savagely bold as the prince who died for her, fighting and dying again to make his sacred seed eternal.

Spreading her stiffened wings to soak up a little of the star's bright fire, she tried to warm away the numbness of the frigid gulf she had crossed. Hopefully, she sharpened her senses to explore the new worlds waiting.

The first planets she found were gigantic, yet dismally heatless. Faintly she sensed good metal hidden at their hearts, but it lay too deep in their vast gravity wells, guarded by fierce magnetic fields, concealed beneath insipid seas of useless scum and stormy atmospheres so cold she shivered from their perception.

Was there nothing—

Heat!

A single bright and tiny point, it swam along in space, even nearer than the planets. Tiny, yet redolent with warmth that woke new agonies in her belly. She veered toward it eagerly, till her own sardonic laughter checked her.

The insolence of gnats!

Glinting faintly in the star's light, the midget object was yet another artifact. A polished metal ball, no larger than her eye.

Spidery rods and vanes sprouted from it, almost microscopic. A doll-sized signal dish tipped toward her, faintly squeaking.

She chortled at the audacity of its unseen crew.

Their cleverness and their daring were almost endearing. Building this fantastic teetotum out in space, steering it into this vast orbit, no doubt they esteemed themselves the mistresses of their universe. In their overweening insolence, accosting even her?

What could gnats have to say?

Her first bellow stopped their silly shrilling. Burning out their fragile signal gear. Or more likely stunning them with terror. Though only for a moment. Incredibly, they tried to fight.

Their defiance delighted her.

And their midget missiles—rich with hot metal, clearly intended to fission and harm her, but rich spice instead, sharp enough to digest that cold lump in her belly. One by one, as they came, she snapped up the tiny darts.

The energy she craved, deliciously pure.

The comic little missiles kept on coming, until she saw the faint blue spark of an infinitesimal jet and then an absurd little rocket creeping away from the comic fortress.

The gnats were in flight!

They had witnessed her invincible magnificence, recognized the splendid destiny of her race, perceived their own contemptible futility. Jubilant with the poetic irony of insufferable arrogance shaping its own atonement, she gathered them with her tongue and took them at a gulp.

"Empires Die." *A critical history of the House of Kwan, writter in prison by Julian Chen. Ignoring any extraterrestrial threat, Chen blamed humanity itself for the troubles of the Tycoons and the Company. "Every empire," he wrote, "is born infected with the virus of its own dissolution."*

Quin swam aboard the *Martian Kwan*, his shaving kit and a change of underwear in a pillowcase slung over his shoulder. Kerry's starmist scent came with him from that last crushing bear hug, and Noël's parting kiss tingled on his lips. Tears had shone in Jomo's eyes, and his own were still wet.

Anxieties nagged him.

What if that nightmare creature came to feed on the station? Even if it didn't, how long could those old engines keep Janoort alive? What actual chance had he to get something better and get it here in time?

Trying not to think of the hard odds against him, he clutched the Metabrake tag.

"Okay, Dain." His tests finished, the technician had laser-burned his diagnostic data into the hard yellow plastic and tossed it at him. "Report to the medic's mate on the missile deck." He waved Quin on. "Your printout looks better than most. Ten to one you'll be alive when we get Sunside."

Grim enough, but still better than the odds for those he left behind.

"Quin Dain?" The medic's mate peered at the tag. "Captain Brun saw your name on the list. She wants to see you before we begin your injections."

The cruiser was still on the pad, still filling her mass tanks. Following to the command deck, Quin examined what he could of her, struck with all the handrails and stairs and elevators, reminders that he was leaving Janoort's easy freedom from heavy gravity.

Vira Brun sat belted into a chair behind the twinkle of instruments on a navigation console. In person, she looked older than she had seemed in the holo tank, her wispy hair thinner, her broad face wrinkled and not very happy. Silently he handed her the Metabrake tag and waited to see what she wanted.

"Dain?" Her gritty voice might have been a man's. "The foreman's stepson?"

He nodded uneasily, wondering if she meant to have him thrown off the ship.

"You volunteered for Metabrake passage?" Her tired old eyes studied him shrewdly. "Why?"

"I've always longed to go Sunside." Her eyes narrowed as if she didn't quite believe him. "My mother's back there. My father, I think. I hope to find them."

Not used to Janoort's tiny gravity, she had tossed the yellow tag at a tray on her console. Missing, it sailed toward him. He caught it and offered it back to her. She waved it aside. Still scanning him, she combed her blunt fingers back through that untidy hair.

"I understand you're a fusion engineer?"

"I've picked up whatever I could." His heart had begun to thump. "Helping run and overhaul the engines on the *Capella*."

"So I'm told." Her frown seemed doubtful. "But they're antiques. You wouldn't know much about these Kwan-class ships."

"I can learn—" He caught his breath, trying to seem calmer than he felt. "If you need an engineer—"

"In fact, we do." A fleeting glint of amusement at his anxiety. "When they told me the *Capella* couldn't fly, I sent one of our engineers to inspect her. He didn't come back. Just called to say Uruhu told me you were competent to take his place."

"I'd love the chance—"

"Report to Mr. Matsuda." She waved him toward the door. "Perhaps he can use you."

Tamako Matsuda was a lean youth with a silent smile and long black hair. He seemed to speak no English. Blinking sleepily at the yellow tag, he twittered into the intercom and beckoned Quin to wait. The medic's mate came to fit a thin little disk into his ear.

"A computer translator. Omnivox Eight. A tricky little gadget, but you'll learn to live with it."

Matsuda beckoned him into the engine room.

"Please, Dain-san." One ear still heard Matsuda's Japanese, but now a robotic soprano was trilling phrases into the other. "If honorable Dain-san—will condescend to come—to inspect ion drive devices."

He got used to the double voice. The engines excited him. Sometimes so elegantly simple that his first glance woke startled admiration. Sometimes baffling, even when Matsuda tried to explain. Probing for more, he tried to ask about the designer.

Neither voice said anything.

"Thorsen? Wasn't he Olaf Thorsen?"

"Do not know—" Matsuda looked distressed. "Do not know—honorable Thorsen."

"He's at Kwan Tech," Quin insisted. "Doing research on fusion—"

Matsuda moved on, pointing.

"Dual mass injectors here. There centrifugal filter. To purify reaction mass."

Quin following, wondering, till Matsuda turned to question him about the engines of the old *Capella*.

"Okay, Dain-san." The heavy-lidded eyes grew wider. "If you run such junk—find our engines easy. You learn maintenance and operation. Stand watch. Keep nose immaculate. We forget Metabrake."

With no more words, he offered a red-cased guide computer. Booting it up, Quin read the title on the monitor. "Operations Guide for Mark Nine Fusion-Driven Ion Drive. Compiled and revised, Sun Year 105, by Olaf Thorsen."

He couldn't help a troubled glance at Matsuda.

"Advice, Dain-san," the translator trilled. "Study engineering procedures. Forget honorable Olaf Thorsen."

The holo monitor in the engine room let him see the station as they took off. A tiny huddle on the cratered ice, briefly lit by their jets. The old *Capella*, a tarnished silver toy. The red-glowing dome. The straggle of scopes and dishes around it. An islet of light, dwindling fast.

The only home he had known.

An ache in his throat, he watched it slide away, faster, faster, till it was lost behind the jagged ice horizon. Janoort itself dwindled to a blot of darkness against the blazing stars, dwindled and vanished.

Even with the Thorsen engines, it was four months to Cotopaxi High. The ship became a second prison, narrower than Janoort. Very little happened. Trouble-free, the engines kept up their constant thrust. He watched them run and ran the tutor programs in the guide computer and tried to plan what to do when he got Sunside.

Though the thrust of the drive was hardly half Earth's gravity, it tired and depressed him. On Janoort, he had kept in shape by pushing his bike up to two or three Gs on that track in the gym, but for only an hour or so at a time. He began to wonder how well he could endure the full drag of Earth.

Was Halo Station still alive? Had Jason Kwan escaped the alien trap? Had that nightmare space-thing appeared again? Were the Kwans and the Chens and the Holyfolk still at war, back Sunside?

No news reached him, though he knew the ship must be in laserphone contact with Sun Command. Matsuda and a quiet blond girl named Lena Ladino rotated watches with him in the engine room. Off duty, they slept together. They never talked to him about Kwan Tech, where Olaf Thorsen had been an instructor. Never about their Sunside lives, or anything outside the engine room.

The ship seemed oddly empty. All the other civilian evacuees were under Metabrake, along with most of Charbon's staff. The active crew was hardly three dozen people. Duty kept them busy, and most of them avoided him. Even at mess, few of them spoke. All wore the Sunmark. Without it, he was nobody.

Except to Jean Charbon. On the second day of the flight, Charbon hailed him on the missile deck and they ate together. Moodily he said he had no duty, no friends aboard. Brun had let him bring some of his precious wine and fruit. He asked Quin to share them, and they often sat together at meals.

Quin felt more and more pity for him. Sober, Charbon was forlornly silent. The wine revealed the torment inside him. More than once, he clutched at Quin with trembling hands, haggard eyes pleading.

"*Mon fils?* What of him?"

Quin had no answer.

"*Mon cher Reynard?*" His hoarse voice quivered higher. "Alive, may one believe? Our brave ambassador to friendly aliens in the halo?"

Quin had to look away.

"Not the traitor!" Charbon clutched his arm. "*A Dieu ne plaise!* Tell me, *mon ami!* What must one believe?"

"No way to know." Quin tried to cover his discomfort. "Until we get the truth—which won't come from Jason."

Before they reached turnaround, Charbon had exhausted hope. Brun tried to find some shipboard duty he was fit for, but he wanted no duty. His wine ran out, and he asked for Metabrake. Demanded it, when the medics found him unfit even for that. When he appealed to Brun, they gave him a minimum injection. Quin sat with him in the sickbay as he went under.

"*Bon voyage, mon ami*—" His quivering hand clung to Quin's. "If I don't wake—*n'importe*."

He didn't wake. Near midpoint, the medics reported that his vital indices were failing. Brun let them try to revive him. The effort failed. On turnaround day, she called the duty crew to the disposal lock for a double funeral.

Nicholas Chen, the spy-probe technician, was also dead of Metabrake. Quin heard no official explanation, but there was a rumor that he had killed himself with a self-injected overdose, perhaps because of trouble waiting for him back Sunside.

Brun read the formal rites consecrating Chen's body and then Captain Charbon's to the House of Kwan and the symbolic Sun. To Quin, her brief official words seemed too stiff and cold. He felt a sharper grief for Charbon than he expected, his sense of loss mixed with dread. Both dead men in vastly different ways were tragic victims of the halo's dark unknowns, and the funeral became a dark reminder of all the hazards still looming over Janoort.

After the service, Brun called him aside.

"Your friend Charbon." She gripped his hand as if to console him. He had rarely seen her with the broken man, and the feeling in her words surprised him. "You did what you could."

"Very little."

"He was past needing much." Her voice had a sudden ring of bitterness. "He had been used up."

He waited, not quite sure what she meant.

"His life used up. His son's life, too. By a Company that never cares."

She was turning away.

"Captain." He seized his chance. "Have you any news? About Janoort? Admiral Kwan? That thing I thought I saw?"

"No—" She hesitated, frowning at him. "Or perhaps I do." She paused again, and spoke abruptly. "Come along, Dain. There's something I should tell you."

He followed her into her cabin, which was plainly furnished, with little to show her rank. She closed the door behind them.

"No news from starside." Looking hard at him, she combed her mannish hand back through her thin white hair. "There won't be any. Our relay link has been cut. Perhaps—though the censors would never pass a whisper of it—perhaps by the creature you saw."

"Janoort—" His voice caught. "Has it been hit?"

"Contra-Neptune was," she said. "Knocked out. That cuts off everything beyond."

"That monster knocked it out?"

"Something did." Her frown bit deeper. "It happened fast. We did get a garbled signal. Their lidar had picked up something big. Coming fast. They challenged. No answer. They opened fire. Their missiles had no visible effect. Transmission abruptly cut off.

"That's all I know." She gestured at her table. "Join me for dinner."

A command. He obeyed. The mess steward brought a very modest meal. Dumbstruck with dread for Janoort, he found no appetite. She eyed him silently, neglecting her own food, until he began to wonder why she had invited him.

"Wine?" The steward was taking his untouched plate. "A bottle Charbon gave me. He'd want you to share it."

The steward brought her a pot of hot black tea. A special brand, she said, from Sri Lanka. Sipping it, she bent gravely toward him.

"Dain—" A stiff little half-smile. "Quin, I see you're stunned. Cut off from your halo friends, probably forever. What will you do now? When we get to Coto."

Surprised, he began to like her.

"I hope to help them. Help Halo Station." He saw her doubt. "I want to get machines and know-how to generate fusion power. Get it back while they're still alive."

Her shrewd eyes narrowed.

"You think you have a chance?"

"My mother's a Kwan Labs scientist. Her husband is Olaf Thorsen—"

"The fusion engineer?" Her expression changed. "Perhaps you will have a chance."

"The Sunside—" Suddenly trusting her, he wanted to explain himself. "A wonderworld I've always longed to see. Always hoped—"

He couldn't help staring at the sparse black hairs on her thin upper lip. They checked him for an instant, and he decided not to mention his father.

"Hoped to get my own Sunmark—I did pass the tests my mother gave me, years ago."

"That could be hard." Her old head shook slowly. "Harder than you probably expect."

"I know I'll need—need a lot of luck." He tried to smooth his voice. "I'll need friends."

Her gray eyes were probing him. Used to squeeze-bottles, he felt awkward with his glass. He set it down carefully.

"There's something I might do." Her square-jawed face was still warily intent, and he couldn't keep his eyes off that sparse moustache. "I've talked to Matsuda. He says you're learning fast. Already competent." She nodded, almost smiling. "If you like, I can cut enough red tape to keep you aboard. Which could be your best chance to earn that Sunmark."

Half choked with emotion, he had to shake his head.

"That would take years. Janoort can't wait."

"If you're hoping for anything easier—" Her shadowed

eyes stabbed into his, her gritty voice turning bitter again. "You don't know the highside. Let me tell you what the Company has done to me."

He must have looked perplexed.

"I guess I've been lucky. Compared to poor old Charbon. But I've given my life to the Kwans and the Company. And I've been cheated."

Beneath that thin moustache, her leathery lip twitched.

"I do command a ship. But I might have had a family. Noël—Noël might have been my daughter." She looked abruptly away. "I might have had a son."

Waiting, uncertain what to feel, he sipped at his wine till she turned back.

"A choice I made thirty years ago." She was almost scowling. Her voice turned harsher. "I chose the Company—because of what I dreamed it ought to be. Because of what the early Kwans had been.

"Creators!" A flash of life across her deep-seamed face. "Able to invent kwanlon, spin the skyweb, explore the planets, enrich humanity.

"Long ago, Quin. Long generations ago." She was urgent now, anxious to make him understand. "Squabbling like snarling animals over what their forefathers left them, afraid to risk any new creation, these new Tycoons have forgotten what they used to be.

"They've wasted my life. Because they didn't care. You see, Quin, I was trying to terraform the planets. If you know the word—"

"I've heard you called Madam Mars."

Calmer now, she gave him a grimly rueful smile.

"We looked at Venus first. In many ways, it's the world most like Earth. In many ways. Yet far too dry. Far too hot. We considered stealing one of Saturn's ice moons and steering it back to crash into the planet.

"That would have been water for new life the genetic engineers were already designing. New creatures to transform the atmosphere, breaking carbon dixoide down into carbon for their bodies and free oxygen higher animals could breathe.

"In a thousand years—"

She bit her lip and paused to sip her tea.

"The Kwans can't see a thousand years. We had to give up Venus. So I tried Mars. It looked easier, though it's almost too small. I spent ten years on the survey. Living in pressure cells, working in space gear. Drilling and sounding the crust, analyzing everything. Enduring the cruel hell it is.

"Ten years gone.

"Survey expeditions to Hyperion and Phoebe took most of another decade. They're satellites of Saturn, small enough and far enough out to be detached and steered down to the orbit of Mars. Still big enough to give it water and atmosphere.

"More long years back Sunside, working to sell the project. To Fleet Command. The Thirty. The Tycoon himself. All for nothing." Her face set harder. "Everybody shrugged me off. Mostly in the name of what they call solarpolitics. Harping on the billions it would cost to build the fusion drives, and the hundred years they'd have to run, and all the disasters that might overtake the Company before they could hope to get a dollar out of Mars."

Her gray face twitched.

"My own great dream. Killed by all that's pulling us back from the halo now. We've slid—the Kwans have, and the Company—too far into a cycle of decay. We've lost our racial nerve. That's why Janoort has no chance—"

"But it has!" Quin told her. "Kerry and Noël—the people we left there have nerve for anything."

"I hope for you, Quin—for you and them." A quiver of feeling in her voice. "But you'll need more than I can do. With no Sunmark—"

She shook her head, pushing knobbed old fingers back through her hair. He thought he saw tears in her pale old eyes.

"I will have my mother."

"If she is at Kwan, perhaps I can help you reach her."

"Thank you, Captain—"

"Captain!" A bitter little laugh. She gripped his hand and held it hard. For a moment he thought she meant to kiss him. Instead, she swung abruptly away. "Quin, I'll do anything I can."

Heavily, as if the thrust of the ship had become too much for her, she heaved herself out of her chair. She gave him a muscular handshake and nodded for him to go.

Past turnaround, they decelerated. Watching the monitor, he saw the Sun grow brighter, day by day, until it swelled into a visible disk. He picked up the faint point of Jupiter, fainter Saturn beside it.

The last day out from the skyweb, Brun's voice rasped out of the intercom, calling him to the pilot bubble. She met him with a tight-lipped frown.

"Bad news, Quin. I called Kwan Labs, asking for your mother. They tell me she is dead."

Joyously well, her vital fires rekindled, the queen drove ahead to find a proper site for her hive. It had to be near good metal to feed her emerging brood when they began to forage.

And it had to be secure. Large enough. Its own metal hard enough to armor the tunnels she and her newborn workers would be drilling. Far enough from any possible enemy. Small enough for her warrior hatchlings to defend.

The huge outer planets were useless to her, yet one of them checked her flight, struck her through with longing for the faraway worlds of her birth. Inside a swarm of dancing moons, its globe was fat and golden, hurricane-belted and flattened from its spin, framed in splendid rings of glittering flight-mass.

Held by its awesome beauty, she alighted on an ice satellite, enchanted by the ripple of gravity waves in the ringlets, sadly recalling all the wild delights of her lost hatchlinghood in her own home hive. It had been carved into a tiny iron asteroid caught in orbit around another ice-ringed giant, even more magnificent.

Her flight sacs refilled, she still lingered there until the gnawing pressures in her belly drove her on toward her new star and its little inner planets. They were rich with radiant metals, but their sweet redolence was half spoiled with an noxious energy pollution.

The shrilling of the gnats. Their whining dissonance revolted her. In due time, her proud young sons would hunt them out. Until then, they had to be endured. Almost ill, she veered away to search for some unspoiled asteroid.

Far around the star, she found it. A good solid nugget of hard nickel-iron, torn from the fused and fractionated core of some lost protoplanet in the system's stormy origin. It was big enough to hold her hive, far enough from the ugly buzzing of the midges, rich enough to feed her until her first foragers began to emerge.

Perching on its highest iron crag, she paused to study the planets. The third was most alluring, the surface of it savory with metals the gnats must have mined. A thread of rich spice belted its equator, just outside the atmosphere. Metal motes teemed over it, riding tiny jets off the belt and swarming into space.

Angered at her, no doubt, for snapping up their puny fortress. Insolent insects! Would they dare attempt to molest her? She sharpened her perceptions to study their craft. Minute metal shells, warm enough perhaps to tempt her hunter sons, but soft inside, the infesting gnats sickening to taste and unfit for anything.

A vile nuisance, nothing more.

She bent her tail to test the asteroid. It proved safe and solid as her old home. She chose a broad flat site for it and began cutting the entry tunnel, welding blocks of waste metal into the wall that would hide and guard the hive.

Warily, before she began to enlarge the food room, she emerged to scan the planets. That odious electronic stench was unabated, but the gnats had swarmed no nearer. Wrapped in their moronic arrogance, they were not even aware of her. She imagined their mad furor when her foragers struck—

An object, approaching!

Not from the planets, it came behind her, from the direction of her own home star. For one delighted instant, she thought it must be another noble prince of her own great race, avid to court her unborn daughters. But no; it radiated no kinship signal.

Gnats, again, encased in another pygmy ship. Perhaps those same impudent insects she had met out at the halo's fringe, now in insolent pursuit. They were still far away, but she relished the chance that they meant to attack. A comic diversion she would welcome.

Her fortress and her defenders would be ready.

Happily she backed down the tunnel to drill it deeper.

Skyweb. *"Spiderweb" woven of kwanlon, secured to Earth's equator and rotating with it, supported by the centrifugal pull of the ballast sections. These extend to the space docks, some 100,000 kilometers out. Cities, factories, laboratories, and space forts are strung like beads along the vertical skywires. Elevator cables and gravity power lines branch from the equatorial plane to Sun Company terminals in all latitudes.*

10

"**M**Y MOTHER?"

Numb from the jolt, he stared at Brun.

"An explosion," she told him. "In the lab where she was working with the skyfish."

"An accident?"

"The Holyfolk, I'd imagine." Concern for him had warmed her aged face. "They hated her, for coddling a demon."

An ache in his throat, he stood groping for his mother's loveliness as she had been in that old holo, the one his father must have taken, showing her splashing along the edge of an Earthside sea, her bright hair loose and long, blowing in the Earthside wind.

Trying, he couldn't recover that glimpse of happiness. Her image came back to him pinched and sick, the way she had looked on Janoort when she kissed him good-bye and went on the ship to nurse the dying starbird.

"—better stay aboard." He heard Brun again. "We're taking off soon as we can load drive mass. I've got new orders. To relieve Contra-Neptune Station."

"If you meet the creature I saw—"

"A risk." She shrugged. "I'm afraid getting off here at Coto would be a bigger one for you."

"One I have to take."

"I wish—" A tremor in her voice. "I wish you well."

Down at the Coto docks, she made him wait in the engine room, away from the port inspectors. They were swarthy men in trim Security black, with odd-looking turbans and long black beards.

"Sikhs," she told him. "Asians, with a religion of their own. The Tycoon trusts them here, because they fight well and despise the Holyfolk and hate the Revelator."

Waiting, watching through the monitors, he sweated in anxious uncertainty. The ship, in fact, was probably safer for him than the skyweb now. No matter what Brun might meet. His mother gone, he saw no way to find his father. He felt too ignorant of everything below to make any actual plans.

Yet he couldn't quit.

Impatient for the tanks to fill, he watched the Sikhs checking the reviving Metabrake passengers as portside medics wheeled them off the ship, watched them inspecting supplies and arriving crewmen, even checking service workers who never came aboard. His spirits lifted when Matsuda bustled silently into the engine room and Brun called him to the pilot bubble.

At last, Sunside!

"I've been trying to get news for you." Her head shook wearily. "Nothing more about your mother. Nothing official about whatever hit Contra-Neptune—though the Revelator's trying to spread panic with it, claiming in his outlaw holocasts that the Lord of Darkness is coming with his legions to carry the Satan-ridden servants of the Sun to his hell beyond the stars."

"Does anybody believe?"

"Too many." A wry grimace. "The Kwans and the Chens have betrayed themselves, the Kwans building their power to fight enemies in space and the Chens fighting the Kwans with their denials that space creatures exist.

"Now, with Admiral Kwan lost and Halo Station abandoned and Contra-Neptune knocked out—the whole highside is stunned. The House is said to be paralyzed. The Tycoon may be in hiding. Fleet Command is enforcing military law."

Her lean fingers gripped his arm.

"Quin, come with us." Something like affection softened her voice. "When we get back—if we do get back—things ought to be better. With more time then, I can try to get you legalized."

"I haven't got that kind of time."

A yellow light began blinking on the console.

"Better get off, if you're going to."

Her seamed old face was twitching, but she gripped his hand and waved him out of the bubble. The impulse to say some farewell turned him back, but she was already bent over the flight computer.

The engine room holotank had let him glimpse the docks as they came in, shining silvery-bright where the Sun hit, darker than the stars where it didn't. The access tubes made a sort of crown, spread wide from the topless towers around the skywire to reach the docking craft.

The service crews and the Sikhs had gone. He limped off the ship alone, into the windy chill of the exit tube. Behind him, with a dull finality, the lock thudded shut. The drag of the skywire made him too heavy. Even that soiled pillowslip with his few possessions was suddenly a burden.

Yet he felt a wary elation. At last, whatever came, he was Sunside!

The floor beneath him was hard and slick, needing no

velfast to hold him to it. Something droned beneath it, and he felt a faint vibration. Following green-flashing arrows, he came out beneath a vast transparent kwanlar shell. Dull barriers confined him to a narrow corridor. Muffled thuds and slams came from the cargo handlers beyond them, and the icy air was sharp with highside scents—the thin, bitter stink of some construction plastic; a hot-oil reek rising through red-glowing grilles spaced along the floor; a faint sharp bite, perhaps from chemicals in shipment; stale smells of food and liquor, from some eating place he couldn't see; stale human odors and rank hints of things he didn't know.

He stopped over a grating in the floor. There was darkness beneath, and running machinery. Conveyors for cargo, perhaps. Or pipes and pumps for reaction mass. He bent to see if he could lift the grate.

If he could hide in the dark, observe, wait for a chance to steal some dockworker's uniform and identification, maybe even a weapon—

Stupidity. Caught in hiding, with no Sunmark, he would stand self-condemned.

He walked on.

Looking up through that high shell, he found the Earth. The kwanlon filament that held the docks to the spinning planet was too thin for him to see from here, the sky cities strung along it too far away. There was only Earth itself, a dazzling sphere of cloud-swirled blue, so wonderful that he paused to stare.

"Sorry, sir." The voice behind him was crisply courteous, the accent unfamiliar. "We can't allow loitering—"

Startled, he spun to find the speaker. Another lean dark Sikh, his Sunmark glinting at the edge of a thick black beard. He recoiled when he saw Quin's face, his hand darting to draw a weapon from his hip.

"Don't move!" He raised the gun. "State your business here."

All he could do was try the truth.

"My name's Quin Dain. I've just got here from Halo Station to look for my mother—"

"Documents?"

"If I may explain—"

"Visa? Work permit? Travel pass?"

"If you'll listen—"

"Stand where you are."

"I'm no criminal." He tried to seem bolder than he felt. "I was born in space. My mother wore the Sunmark. I have a right to wear it—"

"Sir, you have no rights." The dark eyes slitted. "Not here. Not without the Sunmark. Drop your bundle."

Quin dropped the pillowslip to show his empty hands.

"Sir, I came in on the *Martian Kwan*—"

"Don't talk. Lean against that wall. Both hands on it. Feet back and wide apart."

Quin obeyed, regretting that he hadn't tried the grating in the floor.

"Stand up." Finding nothing, the Sikh stepped back. "I am Sergeant Nanak Singh. Sikh Guard Batallion K." His free hand touched a round gold badge. "Don't touch that." He kicked the pillowslip against the barrier. "Just walk ahead of me."

"Where—"

"Don't talk."

Saying no more, except to rap commands, Singh marched him down the empty corridor and off it at last into a tiny room. The door hissed shut. He staggered when it plunged upward—Janoort had no elevators. He grabbed at the wall when it stopped.

"Careful!" Singh rasped. "You endanger your life."

Inspector Santokh Das was the name on the door across another corridor. The door slid open. Inside a narrow room beyond, he was halted before a second turbaned Sikh, taller and older, with white in his flowing beard.

"Inspector—" Quin groped for assurance. "I'm from out in the halo, where I couldn't get a Sunmark—"

"Extend your hand." A dull, indifferent voice. "For a bloodprint."

He pushed his forefinger into a small black cylinder and felt a needle stab it.

"Good Sunblood," he said. "My genes have been tested."

Das waved him toward a jutting lens.

"Face the holocam. State your name. Required for a voiceprint. You may add a brief statement or request permissible aid. Whatever you say will be recorded for Security."

"Thank you, Inspector." He caught his breath and tried to smile into the lens. "I'm Quin Dain. I was born in the halo. My mother was Dr. Nadya Dain—"

"Dain?" Das recoiled, as if the name offended him. "She's dead."

"She had a husband." Quin's heart began to thud. "Dr. Olaf Thorsen. A research scientist at Kwan Tech. If I may call him—"

"Thorsen?"

Das tapped a keypad on the desk and swung to face a big holo screen that mapped the highwires strung over Earth. The map dissolved into a handsome reception room. A lovely girl sat very still and very straight at a computer console there, her Sunmark blazing on a jet-black cheek.

"Kwan Tech." Her smile grew dazzling. "How may we help you?"

"Dr. Thorsen?" the Sikh asked. "Security calling Dr. Olaf Thorsen?"

For a long second she sat motionless.

"I'm extremely sorry." Her bright smile saddened. "Dr. Thorsen is not available."

Das was reaching for the keypad.

"Please—" Quin begged the girl. "Can you tell us where he is or how to reach him? It's terribly important—"

Dark eyes sadder, she shook her head.

"I'm extremely sorry, sir." Her limpid eyes lifted to

pity him. "Dr. Olaf Thorsen is not available for any kind of contact."

A key clicked. Her image shattered. The map came back. Suddenly aware than she had been a computer simulation, Quin felt close to panic. He looked behind him and found Singh standing close, the gun ready.

"Stand where you are," Das rapped. "We can allow you one more call."

"Please! Call Captain Brun, on the *Martian Kwan*. I was an engineer on her crew."

Again the map dissolved.

"Fleet Command information." The same black image smiled again. "How may we help you?"

When he asked for Captain Brun, the same pity shone again.

"I'm extremely sorry, but Captain Vira Brun is now in flight. Unavailable for contact."

Luminous with sorrow, the image flickered out.

Das sat staring at him, lips drawn pale and hard behind the gray-flecked beard.

"Dain, have you something else to say?"

"I'm innocent—innocent of anything." He felt numb, and his voice came rustily. "You have no evidence—"

"The law requires no evidence."

Das swung to face the lens.

"Case review completed," his flat voice rapped. "We find a clear violation of exclusion acts and skywire safety acts. Subject fails to establish basis for clemency or delay. Case disposition: termination approved—"

"Wait!" Quin gasped. "There is a basis for delay. Out in the halo, I saw something that should be reported to Fleet Command—"

"Case closed." Das frowned at Singh. "Take him away."

"I saw a monstrous thing." He raised his trembling voice. "Flying out of the halo. The thing that later hit Contra-Neptune—"

"Lord of Darkness!" A whisper from Singh. "You say you saw that?"

"I watched it eat the wreckage of the old *Spica*—"

Das scowled at him unhappily and swung again to the lens.

"Case disposition revised. Subject remanded to Colonel Chen." A nod to Singh. "Take him upstairs."

Narrow steel-walled corridors led them into another vast space where he heard machines and feet, muffled voices beyond high barriers. A ray of wonder broke through his dazed confusion when he glanced up through the higher kwanlon shell and found the ferry.

"Upstairs" was Earthward, because the centrifugal pull was stronger than gravity there at the fringe of the sky-web. The ferry was a slender cylinder, strung like a bright metal bead on the kwanlon cable. He glimpsed that through the crystal shell above, a thin bright line slashed toward the suspended splendor of Earth.

Singh marched him to a gymbaled seat in a pie-shaped compartment. A warning purred. Acceleration crushed him into the seat. Silently, but fast, they climbed toward the planet.

Riding the skywire!

But he had to look again at the bright yellow Sunmark mocking him from Singh's impassive face. The climb took a long time. Overwhelmed by total strangeness, helpless even to grope for anything to do, Quin found moments of escape in the motion of the ferry—the swing of the gymbaled seats, midway, when the wire began to brake their fall. The sudden flip of his orientation, when the ceiling became the floor. Another purring signal, and that heavy drag was gone. He was suddenly light again, almost free enough to fly.

"We're upstairs. Move."

Singh marched him along another narrow steel-wall corridor painted the dull green Security seemed to favor. It was silent and empty, though at regular intervals the ceiling bulged with dark boxes that he thought must contain holocams and weapons.

Walking without velfast was difficult at first, until he learned a rolling shuffle that kept him on the floor. Singh stayed behind, calling terse commands, until they reached a guarded door.

"Show respect!" He whispered. "You've been remanded to Colonel Zhelyu Celenk Chen."

No Sikh, the colonel was a heavy man in Security black, seated at a holo terminal. His potato head was sallow-skinned and huge, hairless as Kerry's. Hunched intently forward, he yelped something in a voice too high for his size. Something meaningless to Quin, until Singh jammed a translator disk into his ear and the colonel yelped again:

"Who are you?"

"My name—" His voice broke against the colonel's hard hostility. "My name is Quin Dain—"

"The traitor's son?" The colonel blinked into the monitors and stared at him again. "What's this tale of a monster in the halo?"

"I saw it, sir." He drew himself straighter to meet the colonel's cold disbelief. "Something enormous. I watched it consume the wreckage of the *Spica*—"

"Watched? How?"

"I picked up the signal from a spy probe from the *Martian Kwan*—"

"So?" The bug-eyes slitted. "Captain Brun reported no such observation."

"Her technician—" He decided not to name Nicholas Chen. "Her probe technician killed himself."

"You claim this same creature attacked Contra-Neptune?"

"Captain Brun seemed to believe—"

"I don't." The translator cut him off. "I believe you're a Holyfolk spy, inventing lies to save your slimy life."

"But, sir—"

"If the truth is in you, we know how to squeeze it out."

Four Newling sisters.

(Four had been allowed because the Newling refugees were so few.)

Goldengene, the oldest, had been heir to the gens matronage and the right of fertility. The leader of her academic classes, she won a coveted appointment as a junior cosmologist at Point Vermillion. She died there when it was destroyed.

Runesong and Cyan Gem, the middle sisters, had earned honors in science at Newmarch University and won research assistantships at the core-star observatory, studying the newly emergent planetics.

Snowhue, the youngest, stayed behind at Northpoint. Not so brilliant as her sisters, she left school young to care for her aging mother. Their home was the half-dismantled hulk of the old interstellar craft in which the Newlings had escaped the seeker conquest of their native star.

The hulk had been preserved as a museum of racial history, but the survivors were too busy to give it much attention. Most of them were more concerned, in fact, with their future in the Elderhood than with their tragic past.

In the empty hulk, she had grown up almost alone, caring for the fragile relics that nobody ever wanted to see and listening to her mother's rambling tales about them.

The display included a small scout craft that had come all the way from their lost star, flying ahead of the interstellar ship to search out cosmic debris in its path. Moored to the hulk, it was still fit for flight, and she had learned to pilot it.

Her mother was dying when they learned of Goldengene's death. Snowhue felt that the matronage and birthright should now come to her. Her mother left it instead to Cyan Gem, her elder surviving sister.

"She's my darling. Born with true genotype. You know, dear, your own genes aren't what they should have been."

Her mother gone, she stayed aboard the historic hulk, caring for the relics and recording what she knew about its interstellar trek. Greenvane and Fireflake found her there when they came to look for the Newling weapon.

"Mother used to say it had been destroyed," she told them.

"But before she died she confessed that her own mother had hidden it, because of the Elderhood. I can show it to you. But I'm not sure it should be called a weapon. It failed to stop the seekers that took our native star."

She took them to a cold cell at the back of a cargo hold filled with useless artifacts from their lost past. The device was there, still bathed in liquid helium.

"It was intended to fire missiles loaded with an artificial virus," she was saying. "Adult seekers proved immune, but it was expected to kill eggs and hatchlings. My mother said—"

The clonefolk had forgotten her. Suddenly shedding half their life-support harness, they hurled themselves together. Changing shape, they wrapped each other in blazing coils. Killing each other, she thought at first, until Greenvane thought of her long enough to flash an apology.

Their furious union amazed and appalled her, because Newling sex took place internally, the tiny males born late from aging matrons and kept as house pets until they crept whole into the wombs of those few fortunate females selected for the birthright, living there as parasites.

She recalled her own poor father, a naked, tiny, queer-odored thing expelled like a misbirth from her mother's dying body, slick and wet and red, blindly creeping nowhere, cringing from every touch, suffering pitiably until he also died.

Shivering to that chilling recollection, Snowhue stared until the spent clones uncoiled their glowing tails and slid back into their harness, sleekly neuter once more.

"Please forgive us," Greenvane shimmered contritely. "Love sometimes overcomes us."

"Yet we are resolved." Fireflake, who had been the male, shone more boldly. "Since we have the weapon, we must test it. We'll follow the queen toward the core-star and attack when she tries to hive."

Cotopaxi High. *The first and greatest city of the skyweb, headquarters of the Company and capital of the House of Kwan. With the docks for ballast, it was strung for thousands of kilometers down the skywire. Minigravity factories and Kwan Labs occupied the geosynchronous level. Company offices and low-gravity spas and tourist resorts and residential centers were spaced below them, with Sun Security and the "sky fortress" of Fleet Command nearest Earth.*

THEY DIDN'T BEAT HIM, BECAUSE THE KIND TYCOON had outlawed torture. Instead they strapped him to an iron rack, with electrodes stuck to his naked flesh and needles in his veins.

Teams of cold-eyed men in Security black yelled and growled and whispered and cajoled him. They blazed cruel lights into his eyes, battered him with accusations and demands for information, tormented him with promises of peace. Computers chirped and trilled their queries in never-ending repetition. He got no sleep, no explanations.

They never let him rest.

They wanted more than he could recall about the monster he had seen. How had he come to intercept the signal from the probe? Why had Captain Brun never reported it? Or was his whole tale only his own desperate invention?

What they already knew astonished him, as long as he could feel astonishment. They knew he had been Jason Kwan's pilot to the *Spica*'s wreck. Could he describe the aliens that attacked the shuttle? Or had there been no alien there, no actual attack? Had Jason lied?

They knew Admiral Kwan had seen him more recently at Janoort, asking him to join this new expedition into the halo. Why had he refused? What sort of aliens had the admiral been searching for? Were they actually any more real than the aliens in the wreck?

They knew Captain Brun had offered to take him back to space as a fusion engineer. Why, when he had no formal training? Why had he refused? Was he aware of her sympathies with the mutineers?

Why had he come off her ship with no Sunmark? Wasn't he aware of the penalties? Hadn't he known his mother was dead? Who had his father been? Why didn't he know? Why hadn't his mother told him?

What did he want from Olaf Thorsen? How had he hoped to get in touch? What did he know about Thorsen's solarpolitical activities and sympathies? Where was Olaf Thorsen now?

He tried at first to answer honestly, but they never appeared to believe anything he said. Later, fogged with the drugs and deadlier fatigue, he tried to invent what he thought they wanted to hear. That never pleased them.

A time came when he thought he saw Jason Kwan among his interrogators, trying to bribe him, promising him a seat among the Seven and his own Sun Country lodge if he would join the *jihad* against all space aliens.

Living through nightmare, he fled from monstrous things diving at him out of the dark, red eyes leering from Jason's face.

The questions never stopped.

"Quin?" Her voice came out of the dark, mocking him with hope. "Aren't you Quin?"

Blind in the sudden light, he lay on a hard iron shelf. The rack and the needles and his questioners were gone. Drunk from the drugs still in him, he sat up giddily on the edge of the shelf.

"Don't you remember me?"

He found her then.

Mindi Zinn!

He tried to stand, but the drugs were still in him. Yielding to the planet's gravity, he sank back and sat blinking at her. Taller than he recalled her, she looked so dazzling that he thought she had to be another dream.

"Are you—Mindi?"

"Oh, Quin!"

She came half across the cell and paused there, smiling at him. Still only half believing, he drank her in. Her dark hair, not so long as her mother had made her wear it, not so straight as it had been. Her hated freckles gone. The Sunmark bright on her cheek, new since he had seen her. The gold skysuit molded to her shape, revealing a lean allure.

"You've had a bad time." She moved a little closer. "Are you okay?"

"I don't know."

His head throbbed when he shook it. A deep relief had eased him when he knew she was real, but he still felt vaguely ill, and he had seen the round yellow badge over her heart. A charming stranger even when he recalled their kiss in the gym balloon, her violet eyes veiled against him now.

"Mindi—" Staring, still, he licked his dry lips. "You are with Security?"

"A good thing for you." A quirky smile, which he wanted to trust. "I'm arranging a parole for you."

He gaped at her blankly.

"Two conditions. First, you must say nothing more to anybody about that space monster."

"Easy enough," he muttered. "Nobody believes me."

"Second, you must promise to remain in my custody, available to Security."

"What does Security want?"

She stood a long time frowning at him, trouble in her eyes.

"We'll talk about it." A quick finger brushed her lips. "If you want the parole."

"Why not?" He tried to grin. "I promise."

"Good enough." Her nose wrinkled at the reek of the cell. "Let's get out."

She gave him a gold-rimmed badge with his holo image on it. A Security medic frowned at a computer printout and gave him a shot to pick him up. Guards in black returned his filthy pillowslip and let them through clanging doors. Outside, a ferry dropped them far down the sky-wire, to the half-G level.

The shot hadn't really picked him up. Following Mindi, he felt lightheaded, still bewildered. She was silent, watching him with a wary frown. He saw her lip pinched between her teeth, the way it had been so long ago when she said she didn't like him and didn't like Janoort.

They came off the ferry on a ring-shaped moving walk that carried them around the wire to what she said was the diplomatic district. Off the walk, down at the end of a spacious corridor, a tall barrier stopped them. It lifted when she spoke into a voice lock, and she beckoned him into luxury. He stopped behind her in a hall that seemed larger than Janoort's gym balloon.

"All this?" He turned to stare at her. "Yours?"

"Benito Barranca's." She had seemed amused at his awe, but now her face was grave again, almost grim. "My cousin by adoption. You'll meet him soon. Right now, I think you need a bath."

She let him into a wide guest room, showed him how to work the unfamiliar plumbing, laid out clothing for him.

"Benito's," she said. "You're near enough his size."

The blue flight suit seemed to fit well enough. He came barefoot out of the dressing room and found her waiting.

She had set out a pair of boots for him to wear. They were some pliant stuff with an odd sharp scent that made him think of Kerry's starmist.

"Benito's," she said. "Iguana hide. From a lizard that's nearly extinct and illegal to kill."

He pulled the boots on. They seemed too large, but his old ones, with all his filthy clothing, had already gone down the reclaimer. Wondering if he would like Benito, he followed her to another doorway and stopped to stare again. One high wall was a vast holotank that imaged an Earthside mountainscape, cragged cliffs and glaciered gorges and jagged peaks bright with sunlit snow.

The floor was something black and slick. His heart paused when he looked down through it, because he found the Earth itself underfoot, bright-veiled and strangely near, wondrous in the empty dark. The opposite wall was lined with crystal cases that held unfamiliar animal figures.

"Benito's kills," she said when she saw his puzzled gaze. "Mounted for display."

African antelope, a great-winged bird soaring over a granite rock, a sleek-limbed cheetah, a sleeker dolphin frozen in a leap above a frozen tank. Benito had taken them, she said, in Sun Country hunting reservations. She had never hunted.

She led him to seats where they could see the dazzling Earth. Looking around him, looking at her, he couldn't help a bitter laugh.

"The Sunside," he muttered. "And you, Mindi. You! Everything I always dreamed I'd find, if I ever got here. And I'm a prisoner—"

"A guest," her quick voice protested. "For now, my guest."

"Later?" He scanned her troubled face. "What must I expect."

"That depends—" White teeth caught her lip. "On a lot of things."

"Can you tell me?"

"There are things I shouldn't say." Her blue-black eyes

squinted a little, surveying him. "I suppose you should know that none of the interrogators liked what they got out of you. The Chens don't like your space monster because they claim the space aliens are all Kwan inventions. The Kwans don't like it, because it seems too alarming—they prefer such gentler creatures as the starbird and the skyfish."

Her concern seemed real.

"Quin, you're a sort of pawn. The Chens would like to kill you. The Kwans won't allow that—not yet anyhow—because they hate the Chens. Jason's friends aren't happy that you make him a liar. His enemies suspect that you've been too close to him.

"Nobody trusts you."

"Why?" He searched her face, wondering what she believed. "I don't understand—"

"You joined the mutineers on Janoort. You made your way here with no Sunmark, which is asking to be killed. You say you were looking for your mother and Olaf Thorsen. Your mother has been on the Chens' blacklist for years, because of her work with the skyfish. As for Thorsen—"

She paused, teeth against her lip.

"Can you help me find him?"

"Not likely." An ironic half-smile. "His fusion engine has made everybody unhappy, because Earthside fusion power looked like a threat to the Company's energy monopoly. Thorsen's missing now."

"What happened to him?"

"Security doesn't know."

He sat scowling at her. His mother dead, Thorsen unavailable, Mindi herself his jailor—he felt defeated and bewildered. Yet— An ache in his throat. She was near, and lovely as she had ever been. He caught a breath of the same wildwood scent she had stolen from her mother.

"Mindi—" His voice burst out. "I—I love you!"

"I loved you." Her dark head shook, he thought unhappily. "On Janoort—too long ago. We're Sunside now. And I'm in Security."

"Security—" He stared at her, choked on the word. "How did that happen?"

"Not because I volunteered." She sat a long time staring down at the round Earth, and she flinched as if with pain before she went on. "I wrote you what became of my parents. Afterward, my mother's brother took me in. He's Claudio Barranca. Benito's adoptive father.

"They're lowsiders. With no Sunmarks. But my uncle has done well enough to make up for anything. His firm is Barranca Brokers. Middlemen between the Earthside and the Company. Peddling energy and ores out of space, they've built their own commercial empire."

"Benito?" He frowned at the magnificence about them. "He lives here?"

"When he likes. His genes are as good as any. In fact he did pass the genetic test, just to show he could. He grew up at home on both levels. Here now as head of our Coto office, with good friends in the House. Even the Tycoon sees him."

"Your cousin?"

"Adoptive."

That was all she said. Wondering what Benito was to her, he looked into her face. All he could see was the bright-glinting Sunmark. He decided not to inquire. Instead, he asked:

"About Security?"

"I got involved because of what the Holyfolk did to my parents. That's all I ought to say."

"Do you know why my mother was killed?"

"Why is anybody killed?" She shrugged unhappily. "The bombs go off. Afterward the brags and threats come in. From Holyfolk or people claiming to be Holyfolk. We investigate. Seldom with success. The killers are prepared to die before they talk."

"They killed my mother?"

"So they claim." A bleak little nod. "We haven't closed the case."

"We?"

"I'm in charge. I asked for the job because I knew her. The bomb was delivered to the lab where she and Thorsen worked. Disguised as equipment they had ordered."

"They worked together?"

"The last year or so. When his enemies got his support cut off, she arranged space for him. Up in the High Lab, where she had the skyfish. The lab's sealed now, until we finish the investigation."

"The skyfish—is it alive?"

"I think so." Her nod seemed uncertain. "The firebomb must have been meant to kill it, too. The firemen thought it was dead. When your mother's assistants came in, they said it wasn't. Just in shock from the blast. A sad little thing, lying there in the cage. No sign of life that I could see. It might as well be dead."

"Could I see it?"

She paused, deciding.

"I suppose. I'd have to call to arrange it."

She left him and came back to say it was arranged.

"For this afternoon." She frowned. "Another thing, Quin. I spoke to Benito. He's having a dinner tonight. He wants you there, though I'm afraid—"

"Afraid of what?"

"Some of the guests." A troubled headshake. "Benito's dinners are special events. Interfaces, he calls them, between Sunside and Earthside. He's having all sorts of people. Some will come just to meet you."

"Me?"

"You're getting to be notorious." A wry half-smile. "In spite of the censors, rumors of your space beast are getting around. People will be asking what you saw—questions you can't answer. A condition of your parole."

He nodded.

"Careful, Quin!" Her eyes were darkly violet, and he thought her concern was real. "You have enemies—that's why I didn't want you to attend. People in the Chen camp would like to make very sure you don't say anything at all about aliens in space."

At the core-star observatory, Runesong had been eavesdropping on the electronic talk of the planetics for most of a cycle before she volunteered for her scouting mission.

Watching the creatures in their first clumsy efforts to climb off their natal planet, she saw them repeating the evolutionary history of her own race. She came to feel a sort of kinship with them.

Though their faults appalled her, she tried hard to understand and forgive. Breeding without control, killing one another, ruining their environments, they were merely following the behavior patterns of fitness for survival in their primal world.

Delighted with the chance to watch them at close range, she had been cautious at first, hiding in the long cloud of debris trailing from the disposal lock of their orbital station.

What she saw was fascinating, though they often baffled her. Their habits of waste were shocking, even after she became totally engrossed by all they revealed in what they threw away.

Worn machines that could have been repaired. Sheets of vegetable fiber, covered with their enigmatic records. Odd broken objects, each another fascinating piece in the puzzle she had come to solve. All rich with precious heavy elements that any halo culture would have preserved and recycled.

For a long time she saw no sign that she had been detected. The supply craft came and went as usual. Reading the signals they relayed from their pioneers out in halo, she found nothing to alarm her.

Cunningly, they never let her suspect that the most alluring of those discards had been tossed out to bait their trap. Even when she saw the signal laser swing upon her, she expected nothing worse than a challenge.

They fired without warning.

That first cruel slash nearly killed her. Too badly injured to call the observatory, she felt doubly wounded, the searing laser blade no worse than her sense of kinship betrayed. The planetics dragged her aboard the supply craft, carried her back to their orbital web and finally down to a crude laboratory on the surface of their planet.

Her captors were males, amazing creatures, larger than the females, hairier, ferociously aggressive, so merciless at first in their clumsy probing that she expected vivisection. No compassion delayed her death, but only their determination to make her talk.

Her rescuer was female, a creature called Doctornadyadain, who treated her more gently, lifting her out of the planet's cruel gravity, offering food and trying to heal the laser burn, even displaying affection.

Beginning to recover, she found strength to call the director.

"The creatures have hurt me," she admitted. "But their faults are forgivable. Primitive as they are, they've reached a critical point in their evolutionary progress. They need contact with the Elderhood.

"May I open contact?"

The observatory was out in the halo fringe, and his reply took many of the planet's fleeting days to reach her.

"Request denied."

The signal came very faintly through heavy interference from the crude electronics of the planetics and the radiation of the star itself.

"We are dismayed by the murderous misbehavior of the specimen planetics here in your sister's care. They have become so violent in their quarrels with one another that we must regard their presence in the halo as an actual threat to the Elderhood.

"We regret your own predicament, but you will recall that you were warned. In view of your own mistreatment, your present concern for the creatures astonishes me. We have no means, unfortunately, to offer any aid. Your orders remain in effect.

"You will not communicate."

She obeyed.

She didn't talk, yet Doctornadyadain seemed to sense the

truth. There were no more demands. Instead, the kind-seeming female continued to reveal the planetic culture, filling her cell with electric receivers she didn't need, and the books and periodicals she was learning to decode.

Touched by such consideration, she called the director again, begging him to reconsider. At least a few of the planetics had evolved far enough, she told him, to be selected for welcome into the halo and encouragement in their progress toward eventual admission to the Elderhood.

There was no reply. Frightened by the unexpected silence, she set out to rebuild some of the planetic equipment into a transceiver that could use the whole orbital web for an antenna that would reach farther into the halo.

Doctornadyadain did not stop her work, or even pry too far into the design of her equipment. Before it was finished, however, an odd-feeling package was delivered to the laboratory. She watched Doctornadyadain opening it.

Too late, she sensed what it was.

Sunblood. *A term for the complex of genes required by the space environment. These genes were not, for the most part, new mutations, but rather selections from the existing human gene pool. The "highsiders" were therefore totally human, though their fitness for space made them a new elite, bitterly resented by those less fit. To the Holyfolk, they were "spawn of Satan," wearing "the mark of the Beast."*

12

THE FERRY LIFTED THEM UP THE SKYWIRE, PAST THE geosynchronous level and on toward the docks. People on the moving ringwalks frowned at his naked face, glanced at the gold-rimmed Security badge, peered at Mindi, kept uneasily away.

She ignored that hostile wariness.

"The High Lab was planned for hazardous projects," she told him. "Located out here where the solar wind would carry wastes away. Your mother brought the sky-fish here, away from high gravity and the Holyfolk."

Outside the lab, two Security guards saluted Mindi and put a laser reader on Quin's badge before they unlocked the double valves. Inside, they stumbled into blackness. The stagnant air was icy cold, edged with a bitter stink of old fire. When Mindi found the lights, the place became a shadowy cavern whose high walls echoed every sound. The floor was bare metal.

He followed Mindi around it.

"Olaf's shop." An array of lathes and drills and presses, of dies and reels and ovens, of sinks and vats and kwanlar annealers. "Your mother was always close to me, and I got fond of Olaf. A big shaggy man with a genius for fusion engineering and a blind spot for solarpolitics.

"Or maybe I should say a genius for trouble. The propulsion system he designed for the Kwan-class cruisers made his name, but then he blundered. Stupidly, your mother told him. His little team had come up with a better superconductor for an even better fusion reactor.

"The machine he planned was too small and simple and safe to please the Kwans. Your mother warned him to drop it. Kwan Labs cut off his research funds. Security agents came to grill him. Real trouble, if Benito hadn't bailed him out."

"Benito?"

A wry half-frown at his astonishment. "Benito gave him a contract job. Just to build him a private space-plane."

She nodded at a sleek silver hull, hardly larger than the shuttle he had flown with Jason Kwan. It lay on rails outside a fat cylinder jutting out of the wall.

"Designed for flights down to Earth and back. That's her dock. She was never launched. The Company was afraid he meant to use her to test his new reactors. Or maybe to make contact with your mother's alien friends in the halo. One day Olaf and half a dozen of his best people were gone. Suspected of defecting to the Holyfolk.

"A cruel thing for your mother. She was arrested and interrogated. She claimed not to know where he'd gone or what he planned. She was finally released to carry on her work with the skyfish, but only under guard."

They went on to his mother's lab. A smaller space, still littered with wreckage from the bomb. Tall metal partitions ran half around it, black from fire and crusted with yellow blobs of dried foam from the chemical extinguishers.

"Her desk was there." Mindi pointed into an empty spot. "A powerful bomb—the Holyfolk are experts. She must have died instantly. Three helpers also killed, by smoke inhalation."

A wide black stain on the metal floor. His mother's blood? Feeling numbed, nearly ill, he turned from it to wander through the debris. Overturned workbenches. Burned and twisted metal scraps that had been scientific instruments. Broken glass crunching under his boots. Mindi followed, and he felt her sympathetic hand squeeze his.

"A long time." Gratefully he drew her closer. "I was only seven. But it hurts."

Aimlessly he kicked into the litter. Charred paper, matted and clotted with the yellow foam. Computer cubes, shattered into glinting shards. Bits of holo film, fused around the edges. Acrid dust came up. Bending to sneeze, he saw a face.

Kerry's hairless head, grinning at him through a thin smear of ash and foam. Stooping for it, he stirred through the clutter. A young child, peering wistfully out of a half-burned holo, spacebags on a berth in the narrow room behind him.

"That's you!" Mindi whispered.

"Taken—taken on Janoort." A hard lump ached in his throat. "In her cabin on the ship. The day she left. The last time I saw her."

He stooped to stir again and found another holo, hardly damaged, the colors still bright. His mother, lovely and still young, wading in foaming surf, gold hair free.

"She showed me that." His voice turned husky. "Once when I wanted to know what the Earth was like. She said my father made it. I always hoped she would tell me who—"

Tears dimmed her image. Raising the picture to blow at bits of clinging ash, he saw something on the back. A string of digits, written in faded ink. He blinked and bent to read them.

"A holophone number," Mindi told him.

"My father's?" He peered at her. "Do you think?"

She nodded, with a searching look at him. "Maybe."

The skyfish was caged in a shadowy alcove at the end of the lab. Peering through steel bars, he saw nothing in the gloom until Mindi pointed at a still gray huddle in the corner. He caught a new odor beneath that stale fire-stink, something strange, sweetish, faintly etherlike.

He dropped to his knees to see the captive. A slender, graceful shape, tapering to a narrow tail. Two gray flaps, winglike or maybe finlike, sagging to the floor. He couldn't see its face, if it had a face. He reached impulsively through the bars to touch its sleek skin and drew his hand back from a long, thin scar.

The laser burn.

Awed pity washed over him. Here was a creature of space, at home in that airless dark infinity where no human being could survive without complex equipment. It had come Sunward to do no harm, perhaps even hoping to find human friends, and all its wonder had been cruelly wasted.

"I used to come here with your mother," Mindi was saying. "She rescued it out of the lowside labs, where Security experts had failed to make it talk. They'd come to doubt its intelligence, but she found it as smart as we are.

"Maybe smarter. It has electronic senses. She was convinced it can pick up radio signals without equipment. I've seen it reading books and magazines. Riffling through the pages as if it could get them at a glance.

"But it never talked, even to your mother. The Security people had tried compulsion. Lights too bright for it and sounds that seemed to hurt it. Even a cattle prod. Your mother tried kindness. It never responded, not even to her."

"I wonder—" He stooped to stare again.

"She had a notion its people had been frightened by our invasion of the halo. She thought it must have been sent to spy on us. Determined not to give away anything that might betray its world."

Nodding, he reached again to touch it. Again, his trembling hand was stopped by the awesome mystery of it, and a throb of pity.

"Now?" he asked. "What will happen to it now?"

"Hard to say." She shrugged uneasily. "I had the lab sealed to protect it, but nobody knows what it needs. It doesn't eat. Doesn't breathe. It peeled off an antiseptic dressing your mother put on the wound. Its metabolism isn't understood. The Security scientists tried to take biopsies and serum samples. It did something to ruin their needles and blades. They tried X-rays. It emitted radiation of its own that fogged their images.

"Your mother stopped all that, but she did let Olaf set up magnetometers around it. He found powerful internal magnetic fields. Structured, he thought, like the fields in his new reactors. He wondered if its energy is nuclear. A notion pooh-poohed by everybody else, but how else could it stay alive out in space? With no food or air or source of warmth?"

Trembling with wonder of his own, he bent to stare again.

"Do you think it understands what we're saying now?"

"I hope not." She caught his arm to draw him away from the cage. He felt her hand quiver. "I can't help feeling afraid of it. Most of us are. A lot of people were appalled when they found out what your mother was letting it read. They're afraid it might escape with what it knows about us.

"That could have been the reason for the bomb."

The creature lay there, a flat gray huddle. Trying to imagine what its life in space had been, what it knew and felt about the human world, he shivered at something more than the chill in the bitter air.

"Do you think—" Dread hushed his voice, and he drew her farther away. "Will it be killed?"

"No verdict yet." A husky whisper. "The Tycoon himself has named a commission to review all the reports. They're reporting to the Thirty. Perhaps there will be a debate. Some of the Kwans want a new effort to make it talk. Till some decision is made—"

Her whisper sank lower. "I hope it isn't listening."

He shook his head and leaned to look again at the laser scar before they left it.

Benito Barranca's great dwelling was swarming with servants when they got back to it. Dark-skinned men in white jackets, preparing for the banquet. With no Sunmarks, they wore yellow badges. Security had taken Quin's translator, and he understood nothing of their speech. Mindi took him to meet a slender man who had been instructing them.

"Quin, here's Benito."

Barranca was dark as the servants. A handsome man, Quin thought, sleek hair worn long and fine teeth flashing under a neat black moustache.

"Hello, Dain." Barranca's nod seemed very casual, but the piercing eyes probed him intently. "Welcome to El Nido."

"Thank—"

Ignoring his half-extended hand, Barranca turned to take Mindi in his arms. Watching their kiss, till they swayed so close and stayed so long together that he had to look aside, Quin envied his wealth and his Sunside culture, his high place in two worlds, bitterly envied him Mindi.

Released at last, she came back to him.

"It's hours till dinner." Her voice was quiet, but her eyes held his so long he thought she must have sensed his own bitter emotion. "Perhaps you'd like to rest?"

Silently, trying to swallow a sudden savage jealousy, he followed her back to that spacious guest room. Trembling and half sick again, as if the drugs were still in him, he didn't trust himself to speak.

Too brightly, she began talking about Benito. His mother had been an Aztecan holo star. The father she claimed for him was a highsider newsman who had come to do a story on her and stayed in Azteca as her manager and lover.

"Such mixed affairs offend the Holyfolk. They called her a devil-lover. A bomb was set in her dressing room. It caught them together. Killed them both. Benito was five years old.

"Enter my uncle. Claudio Barranca. He had been funding the mother's productions. He must have been another lover—I've thought, in fact, that he has to be the actual father. Which might explain what Benito is."

They had reached the guest-room door. She paused there to look at him. Unhappily, he thought.

"Mindi—" A whisper of pain. "Are you and Benito—married?"

"Of course not, Quin!" A brittle laugh. "That's illegal. Though the Company isn't quite so murderous as the Holyfolk. The penalty is surgical removal of the Sunmark and exile from the highside."

"But you—love him?"

"Oh, Quin—" He thought he saw tears in her eyes. "It hurt me terribly to leave you on Janoort, but that's too long ago, too far away. Too much has happened."

She leaned to kiss him, lightly, briefly.

"Please! We've got to forget."

He longed to take her in his arms, but she was already opening the door. It slid shut behind him. He heard the lock click.

Alone in the room, her wildwood scent still in his nostrils, he felt miserably helpless. Barranca's vast residence was better than the Security interrogation cell, but his visible future looked no brighter.

He couldn't help hating Benito Barranca, or wondering if Mindi was really happy with him, but he saw nothing he could do about it. Pity stabbed him again, for the sky-fish lying in its cell, trapped as hopelessly as he was, waiting for a verdict that would probably be death.

Yet, if he could find his father—

He looked again at the charred holos he had brought from the High Lab. Kerry's bald grin. The big-eyed child. His mother's long-lost loveliness—and that fading holophone number on the back of the picture.

A way to reach his father? Not likely, he thought, so many years later. Yet he tapped it into the phone beside the big bed. The tank stayed dark. All he got was a computer chirping, "Speech circuits disconnected. Speech circuits—"

He slapped blindly at the keys. The chirping stopped. The tank lit with a dusky woman wailing a sad-seeming song in some language he didn't know. He left it on. A bitter aftertaste of the Security drugs again in his mouth, he sat down on the edge of the big bed, staring blankly at the tank.

The singer's head winked out of it. A news segment came on, reporting crimes incited by the Revelator. A power station sabotaged. A food factory blown up. Rioters burning cities in PanAfrica. Strike violence in Azteca.

"Here are bits of his illicit signals."

A stark hawkface flashed into the tank. Black eyes blazing, and a white-shining beard. The Revelator himself, chanting, trumpeting, singing, praying. The voice had a resonant power that became almost hypnotic. The tongue was strange at first, but then the image winked again, and it was English.

"—I am Alpha, opening a sacred way for the blessed children of God. I am Omega, rising to destroy the whelps of Satan, monsters born without souls and doomed to perish in the fall of their false heaven. I am come to cry woe, woe, woe, to all the idolators, the evil seed of the Beast.

"I proclaim their Armageddon, and the fall of their blasphemous Babylon, because I behold the approach of the great red dragon forseen by Saint John, come for them with the keys of hell. They have worn purple and scarlet and drunk the blood of martyrs and lived deliciously with sin.

"Yea, I have seen the Beast, and their fleets and all their devil-fathered minions and their hellborn Tycoon will not prevail to save them. For the Sunmark is the sign of their damnation, and they cannot be saved. They cannot repent, because they have no souls. They have heard the Revelation, but they cannot believe.

"Yet a witness lives among them, one poor damned soul who swears that he has seen the Beast. Another son of Satan, conceived in blackest hell, this man has been allowed to mock them with his warning, and still they don't believe. Until all their Babylons fall out of the sky, with all their demon princes and their scarlet whores, they never will believe.

"They plan, instead, to put this miserable wretch to death, the man who saw the Beast, because the demons that rule them forbid them to believe."

Shaken, he slapped the keys again.

It was he who had seen the Beast.

The queen had fasted too long in flight from her regal mother's star. No fresh metal in her belly, her poor starvelings had been consuming her. Her new hive was scarcely dug before the agonies of birth overwhelmed her.

Aware again, she found she had no belly. Her emerging darlings had consumed it, metabolizing even its armor to shape their shells. Disabled, even her jet sacs gone, she would never fly again.

Even her motherhood had ended. The precious sac of her prince's sperm still lay hot beneath her heart, sacred sparks that might have burned in many thousand warrior sons born to make atonement for his dreadful sacrifice, but she could never bear them now.

Crippled, she turned and tended the incubating eggs. Limping when she could to the mouth of the hive, she kept watch against predators and listened to the nauseous whine of the gnats.

And she clung to the invincible spirit of her warrior race. Her prince had not died in vain, nor would she. They both would live again, happier and more gloriously, in their hatchling daughters and sons.

Eagerly she sensed the new life stirring in her first small egg. When its incandescent shell began to crack, she helped her firstborn son break his way to freedom. Licking the clinging bits of armor from his wee body, she dropped them into his tiny jaws.

He was no prince. Only a feeble little forager. Yet her mother's heart burned with tender pride.

Synfare. *Trade name for synthetic nutrients produced from industrial and human wastes, these rumored to include the bodies of the dead. The industry was dominated by Sun Company affiliates, using power from space. It increased in importance through the Sun Century as uncontrolled populations grew and arable lands were wasted by erosion or occupied by urban expansion. At the time of the skyweb's fall, nearly 80 percent of the world's population depended on it for survival.*

DULL WITH THE DRUGS STILL IN HIM AND HEAVY WITH the drag of the wire, he found no sane plan for anything. He lay wearily back on the bed. The door was still locked when he woke, and lenses in the ceiling followed when he went to the bathroom. Hoping for news of Captain Brun and her flight, he tried the holophone again and found a documentary running.

The narrator was a computer simulation that called itself Sunner Slim, "the genie of the highwires." A lean, athletic figure with bright gold skin, it wore a Sunmark that burned like a yellow diamond. In holo minidramas, it was mining the moon, capturing asteroids and comets, pouring ores down the gravity lines.

"We risk our lives for all mankind." It smiled out of the tank, golden arms extended. One hand offered a bright yellow ingot; lightning flickered from the other. "We are the servants of Earth, givers of metal, givers of energy, givers of life—"

It vanished from the tank.

"A bulletin from Fleet Command." A human newsman, time-scarred and gravel-voiced. "Saturn Station has picked up a message from Admiral Jason Kwan, whose fusion cruiser, the *Solar Kwan*, has been out of contact for many months and feared lost in the halo.

"He reports an encounter with hostile space aliens, which he says have established a powerful base on the inner fringe of the halo. He says it was a battle force from this base that engaged our first halo expedition, back in Sun Year 79, disabling the *Spica* and capturing Captain Bela Zar and his crew.

"Admiral Kwan reports his attempt to rescue a few survivors among those space heroes. Using brainwashed captives as translators, the aliens promised friendship and vast benefits from their strange civilization. False promises. Nearly too late, the admiral found they were trying to lure him into a trap set at their base.

"Fortunately, Captain Zar was still uncorrupted, loyal to mankind. He was able to escape long enough to transmit a warning message. Admiral Kwan fought his way out of the trap. He has been flying silent since then, evading pursuit. He reports a second space battle, in which he knocked out an alien warship that had overtaken him. He is now crossing the orbit of Saturn, in flight back to Coto. Details will follow.

"We return you now to *Gifts of the Sun*."

Sunner Slim flashed back into the tank, riding an ore bucket down the wire, golden arms filled with gifts to be tossed to eager people waiting at a Company terminal. Quin heard the lock click. The door slid open. Mindi met him in the doorway.

"Ready for dinner?"

Her violet eyes seemed to warm when she saw him. Now in something softly blue and less confining than the gold skysuit, she was vibrantly desirable. But still his jailor, Barranca's lover, forever untouchable.

"You should dress."

She had brought him a dinner suit of Barranca's. Sleek black stuff that felt too stiff and too tight, frilled with bows and ribbons he didn't understand. Gold ribbons for the Sunside, Mindi told him when he came out of the dressing room, green for the Earthside.

She tied them for him. A glint of amusement in her eyes, she stood so close her blue blouse brushed him. So lovely and so near, she was sheer agony. Her wildwood scent overwhelmed him. In spite of himself, he slid his arm around her.

"No!" A sharp outcry, as if it hurt. "Don't touch me."

"Mindi—" His whisper broke. "I so wish—"

She had recoiled from him.

"This isn't Janoort." Her own voice quivered, and he thought he saw tears in her eyes. "We aren't what we were."

"I'm sorry." That was all he could say. "So terribly sorry."

Hands down, he let her finish with the ribbons.

"Let's go," she said. "The guests will be arriving."

Yet she paused at the door.

"Careful, Quin!" She caught his arm. Her hand was trembling. "This could be an ordeal for you. People digging for what you mustn't say. The Kwans trying to use you against the Chens. The Chens fighting back.

"I wish Benito didn't want you there." Teeth sunk deep into her lip, she reached to adjust a green ribbon. "I don't know why he does."

She led him into a magnificent hall that seemed even vaster than it was, because the walls were all holo screens alive with recorded views of an Earthscape that arrested him. Immense green vistas massed with strange trees, sloping up to a mountain mass that soared through layers of cloud.

"Kilimanjaro." She had seen him staring. "Recorded in a Sun Country game preserve near Kenya Down."

Opposite, he found a water hole, animals coming down trails around it, wading in to drink. Some he knew from a picture box his mother had given him on Janoort. Warthogs and waterbuck, a herd of sleek zebras, a giraffe towering out at the jungle edge, a black-maned lion half asleep on a rock, great head lifted to watch the unalarmed game.

Mindi pulled him away to meet arriving guests.

Oddly mixed, some wore Sunmarks, others badges like his own. Some in uniform, crusted with medals. Others wearing bright cords and ribbons that meant nothing to him. Many races, many nations. He caught scraps of language strange to him.

"Sunner Dain," Mindi introduced him. "Here from the halo."

People turned to look. Merely curious. Intently inquiring. Affable, anxious to talk. A bright-medaled man in Sun Fleet black had gripped his hand hard and hailed a waiter to bring him a drink before he heard the name. Admiral Chen.

Quickly Mindi took him on to another cluster. More names than he could recall. Diplomats from a dozen Earthside nations. Sleek young men from Barranca Brokers. Scholars and journalists and artists. All slightly startled at his name, all peering at him too sharply.

Mindi seemed surprisingly at ease. She greeted them by name, graciously accepting compliments, allowing her hand to be kissed. Admiring her, still yearning for her, he felt his old eagerness for the Sunside world turning bitter in his heart.

Benito came to meet them, flamboyant in black and green and gold, white teeth flashing beneath the black moustache. Quin had to look aside from the way he kissed Mindi's hand. Greeting him, Benito's voice seemed casually ironic.

"Enjoy yourself, Dain. Enjoy yourself!"

He took Mindi away with him to greet one of the Seven, just arriving. Left standing alone, Quin couldn't help wondering if the word he really meant hadn't been destroy.

Admiral Chen brought Quin a second drink he didn't really want and stayed to talk, asking about life on Janoort and what he thought about the conditions for human survival in the halo. Could all the essentials of life ever be manufactured there? Or would a colony always be dependent on supply craft from Earth?

With never a question about aliens in the halo, or even about the plight of the mutineers, the admiral seemed keenly alert for more than he meant to say. In uneasy defense, he began asking about the Company and how it ruled the Earth.

"We don't." The admiral smiled, as if amused by his effort at evasion. It struck Quin that he had the Romanoff nose. "We've never tried to rule. Rule invites rebellion. We don't even tax. Taxation invites resentment.

"The so-called Holyfolk may accuse us of despotism, but the fact is we've left Earth free. A hundred independent nations, free to speak their own tongues, praise their own gods, enforce their own laws. All we ask is trade."

Sweepingly, he gestured toward Benito.

"Barranca Brokers serve us better than missiles in the sky. They merchandise energy. Our chief export, essential to the Earthfolk." His tone turned hard. "Without it, most of them would die. With their so-called Revelator!"

A scornful snort.

"Preaching his so-called *jihad*. Which he will have to fight with sticks, because we've stopped the sort of wars nations used to fight. Simply by cutting off the energy and ores they'd need to make heavy weapons. Of course the Sun Fleet has everything we'll ever need, but we depend very largely on more subtle instruments.

"Trade, first of all. Metal and power they'd die without.

"Diplomacy." He swept his arm at Barranca's guests. "We maintain Company missions everywhere, and welcome national ambassadors to the High House.

"Education. Our enemies call it propaganda. We fund the best schools, hire the best brains, drench the whole planet in holocasts from the skyweb.

"Altogether, a very efficient solarpolitical machine. As for your halo, Sunner Dain—" The admiral spoke the Sunner with harsh emphasis, staring hard at the spot on his cheek where there was no Sunmark. "We need nothing from it. We fear nothing from it—"

Escaping that loud challenge, Quin was captured by a big-busted brunette. Naked to the waist, like several of the women, she wore her nipples gilded.

"Sunner Dain, I heard you speaking of solarpolitics." Her voice was raspy as the admiral's. "I'm solarpolitical editor for PanPlanet Holo, and I've been dying for a word with you. Not for attribution, if that's what you prefer."

He wasn't used to nudity. Though he tried not to stare, her jutting breasts kept drawing his eyes. She thrust them at him as if amused by his discomfort.

Was it true, she wanted to know, that he had seen a space monster big enough to eat a ship? When he asked who said that, she demanded more than he knew about the circumstances of his mother's death. Had the bomb really been meant to kill the skyfish? Had he seen the creature isolated in the lab? Did he think the commission should order it destroyed?

In flight from her, he blundered into a debate between two dark, intense young men without Sunmarks. Speaking some tongue he didn't know, they shifted into English when they saw his puzzlement. One introduced himself as an Aztecan journalist. The other was the highside agent for a Eurasian Synfare distributor. They got him another drink and inquired if he minded not having a Sunmark.

"Insufferable elitism!" The journalist was vehement. "Millions of us have better genes than the Tycoons. Fully qualified. But they issue no Sunmarks now. Except to the lucky ones with certified Sunfolk parents.

"Racism—"

"Nonsense!" A bull-voiced professor of biotechnics

charged into the debate, his own Sunmark blazing through a shaggy beard. "Look at history, and you'll find that the first Sunfolk came from every race. Look at facts. The real problem is ecological. Born of life's old urge to fill every ecological niche.

"Look at Synfare. Excrement reprocessed with power out of space. It created a new ecological niche that didn't exist when people had to feed themselves with farms and fisheries. The Earthfolk have multiplied to fill the niche— sixty billion of them. Rioting now for more reprocessed excrement."

He glared at the journalist.

"Look around you, sir, at the skyweb. A rich enough niche if you happen to inherit a Sunmark, but not immune to the processes of ecology. It has also filled itself. The sky cities and the Sun Countries have all the inhabitants they want."

His fat forefinger stabbed at the journalist, at the Eurasian, at Quin himself.

"Biology, gentlemen! That's why none of you will ever get a Sunmark."

Retreating again, Quin stopped to watch a herd of gazelles in leaping flight from a cheetah beyond the water hole in the holotank. He turned to see the yellow-nippled woman bearing down on him again, but Mindi called dinner before she reached him.

The endless table was waiting in a great space walled with holo recordings from a probe down on Io. A lurid landscape of sulfur lava flows, red and orange and yellow and black. A volcano sprayed bright fire high into the black sky where Jupiter blazed, near and enormous, streaked and spotted with its hurricanes.

Too many drinks had been pressed upon him. The dinner went on forever. There were too many waiters, too many dishes, too many forks, too many toasts to the Sun Tycoon.

He was seated between an inquisitive Aztecan girl who said she was a holocast dramatist and a waspish little man who called himself a presolar historian. The girl begged for all he could tell her about his life at Halo Station. Research material, she said, for a script she was calling "Isle of Eternal Night."

When she began pressing for hints about what her unlucky exiles might fear from unknown monsters of the dark, he turned to the historian. His field, he said, was the decline and fall of presolar America. A great nation once, he said, destroyed by suicidal cults of liberalism and democracy.

"Rights!" He muttered the word like an obscenity. "A national madness for what they called rights, with duty forgotten. Selfish groups of self-blinded fools, claiming idiotic rights, growing like cancers, rotting the nation. It crumbled like Athens in the Peloponnesian war, like Rome when its soul was lost—"

The words dissolved in his mental haze. Refusing more wine, guarding all he said, he watched the Aztecan girl to see which fork to use. Most of the talk he overheard was in tongues he didn't know. He stared at the sulfur flows pouring down the volcano slopes of Io, changing color as they cooled, seeing in them his old dreams of the Sunside, turned now to lurid nightmare.

A hush in the talk aroused him. He saw Admiral Chen abruptly standing, looking shaken, a hand cupped over one ear. Calling a brief excuse to Barranca, he strode out of the hall.

A startled whisper came around the table. There was news from the *Martian Kwan*. Captain Brun had reported an unidentified spacecraft flying to meet her from toward the Trojan asteroids.

Mindi and Barranca had risen to receive the excuses of other guests, also hastily departing. Quin joined them, begging permission to go.

"Stay, Dain! Stay!" Barranca seemed secretly sardonic. "Enjoy yourself."

Mindi, however, took him silently back to his room. Again she locked him in. He slept badly at first, through evil dreams in which he had been marooned on Io. He thought his unknown father was somewhere there, with a ship in which they might escape. Searching for his father, he was in flight from volcanoes erupting behind him and floods of molten sulfur racing after him.

Groggily half awake in the middle of the night, he remembered that holophone number written on the back of his mother's picture. Hoping it might help him find his father, he slept again, more soundly. When Mindi unlocked his door, he asked her to let him call.

"If you like." Her eyes looked shadowed. He wondered if she had slept any better than he. "Though I'm afraid it won't help you."

The holophone was voice-keyed. She read the number into it. He waited, watching the tank. For a time that seemed endless, there was only silent emptiness. When a voice spoke, it startled him.

"Who is this?"

The tank had lit, but only with a golden glow that formed no image. The voice was a man's, seeming puzzled and impatient.

"My name is Quin Dain—"

"Dain?" The voice quickened. "How did you know this number?"

"I found it on the back of a holo of my mother. Taken Earthside, on a beach, long ago. Taken, she told me, by my father."

"Who was your mother?"

"Nadya Dain. Dr. Nadya Dain."

Long seconds of silence.

"Twenty years—" A rusty whisper. "Twenty and more— Where have you been?"

"At Halo Station, on Janoort."

"Now? Where are you now?"

"In Cotopaxi High. At Benito Barranca's place."

"Barranca?" The voice sharpened. "What's he to you?"

"No friend. I'm here on parole from Security."

"Why are you calling?"

"Because I hoped—" He was trembling, and his voice turned hoarse. "Hoped to find my father." He gulped and asked, "Who are you?"

Silence stretched longer. He watched the pale yellow light in the tank, faintly flickering.

"That can wait." The voice came back with a ring of command. "Stay where you are."

The tank went dark.

Flying starward out of Newmarch to attack the seeker hive, Snowhue and her sleek-scaled clone companions had planned to stop at the core-star observatory to replenish their reaction mass.

A relic of her ancestral sun, the tiny explorer probe had no equipment for long-range contact with the Elderhood. Its narrow hull became their world, isolated from the universe. The two clones spent nearly all their time coiled together in serpentine union.

Snowhue, reminded forever of her own lost birthright, could only contain her envy, endure the odors of their passion, and pilot the probe.

When at last they came in range of the observatory beacon, she braked to dock and tried to call. She got no answer. Fireflake and Greenvane glided reluctantly apart into their separate harnesses to help locate it. Approaching at last, they found only a little swarm of fused and shattered fragments.

"The queen has been here." Still male from their coupling, Fireflake spoke from the telescope, the shimmer of his coils dulled with dread. "Nothing left alive."

"The queen's alive, lizardheart." Still female, Greenvane tickled him with a teasing tail. "We're lucky we got here late."

Wheeling close around the wreckage, they found no life, nothing useful, nothing even to identify the destroyer. The mass tanks had been exploded, the contents vaporized.

The clones wanted to turn back.

"We're in trouble," Snowhue admitted. "But we've mass enough left to take off toward the star—"

"With very little left for any strike against the hive," Fireflake objected. "None to get us back if things go wrong."

"If we succeed, help will come," she said. "If we don't, we'll need no help."

Yielding, her scales flushed with dread, Fireflake turned female. Male again, Greenvane slid out of his harness to console her. Snowhue stripped the tiny craft, to make the most of their remaining fuel, and jettisoned everything she could.

Again they accelerated starward, toward the asteroid where they had traced the seeker.

High House.   *Highside dwelling of the Kwans and official residence of the Sun Tycoons. Located above geosynchronous point on Cotopaxi skywire, at quarter-G level. Private dock and skywire station. Said to have had secret access.*

14

WAITING, HE ASKED MINDI FOR NEWS. FLEET COMmand was on standby alert, she said, but no more unidentifed spacecraft had been reported. Nothing more had been heard from Brun's *Martian Kwan*, nothing from the Contra-Neptune station.

Benito Barranca had gone early to the office, and they had breakfast alone.

"All natural." She spoke a little too lightly, as if to avoid anything that touched her feelings. "I learned to like our synthetics out in the halo, but Benito hates them."

Orange juice. Smoked ham. Poached eggs. Muffins with marmalade. The first tastes told him why the pioneers had tried so hard to adapt pigs and chickens to zero-G. As they ate, she asked how he had left Kerry and Jomo and her other old friends on Janoort.

"I'm afraid for them—"

The holophone sang.

"Mindi Zinn!" A golden-toned computer voice. "Mindi Zinn! The High House calling."

She baffled the audio, speaking silently. He saw her teeth sink into her lip. She turned back to him with awe in her eyes. "You're to come upstairs."

The High House! He was suddenly trembling, all his old hopes and dreams awake again.

"Who was it?"

"Somebody on the staff. They'll call back. Things have been arranged."

He waited again, afraid to hope, even to wonder. The holophone trilled again, and it was time go.

"Careful, Quin!" Impulsively Mindi paused at the door to grasp his hand. "Whoever it is, watch yourself. It may look like a break for you, but—remember! People here play dangerous games."

"At least," he muttered, "I haven't much to lose."

The High House had its own ferry station, far up the wire. A white-turbaned Sikh met them on the station platform with a quick salute for Mindi. She told the guard they were expected.

"If you are—"

A hard stare for him. The Sikh thrust a laser reader at both their badges, pricked their earlobes with a blood scanner, and made them sign a register. Calling something Quin didn't understand, he dropped a transparent barrier to let them meet another bearded Sikh.

"Sunner Dain?" Black eyes scanned him, and he heard no irony. "You may come with me." He turned to Mindi. "We assume responsibility."

"Thank you, Lieutenant." She turned to Quin. "Careful!" she whispered. "Please!"

"Sunner Dain, come with me."

The Sikh lieutenant left him to wait in a long empty room, not quite so magnificent as Barranca's halls. Alone, he had an uneasy sense of hidden lenses watching. One high wall was a computer simulation of a window into space, opening on the Earth from above the skyweb. The planet itself looked realistic, half moonlit shadow, half Sunlit, splendid against the empty dark.

The skyweb was exaggerated, a bright golden net that stretched far out from Earth's equator, beaded with brighter yellow diamonds for its cities, anchored everywhere with the Sun-disks that marked the surface terminals.

The opposite wall was recessed with huge holo portraits, gigantic heads of historic Kwans and Chens. In most of them he thought he saw a certain hawkish family likeness, Romanoff noses jutting, hooded eyes slightly slanted. They seemed to turn, watching with a shrewd intentness as he walked down the room.

Chairs were set around a tiny-seeming table, but he felt too restless to sit. Almost overwhelmed by those imperious giants, he stopped at the end of the room and turned uneasily to admire the shining simulation of their empire.

"Quin?" The raspy voice startled him. "Quin Dain?"

A lean old man in a plain tan shipsuit had come from a door beyond the table, leaning on a cane. A long yellow jacket was drawn close around him, as if he were cold. His Sunmark had dimmed, a pale yellow moon at the edge of a thin, grizzled beard. Breathtaken, Quin saw the arrogant tilt of the nose, the hooded eyes inspecting him. It could have been an aged Jason, moustache and beard and flowing hair gone white.

Fernando Kwan! He knew the face from coins and history tapes. The Sun Tycoon!

"You are Nadya—" The old voice wavered. "Nadya's son?"

"Sir—" He had to catch his breath, and his own voice came hoarsely. "Nadya Dain was my mother. I was born on the *Aldebaran*, three weeks before she got to Halo Station."

"Then you are mine." Swaying a little, the Tycoon put more weight on the cane and leaned to peer again. "A fine young man." An imperative whisper. "Come here to me."

Himself unsteady, Quin walked into his arms. A brief embrace. He caught a sharp medicinal pungence, felt thin old bones through age-wasted flesh.

"Come along." Rustily cracked, the voice had kept a ring of command. "I need to sit."

He followed around the table and through the door. The office they entered was small, at least by comparison, walled with maps and a holo screen and model spacecraft and antique paintings and shelves of old paper books. It seemed to Quin strangely out of date. He saw no computer console, only a battered wooden desk.

"Old, old!" The Tycoon sank into an equally ancient chair and paused to breathe. "All too old. The House and the Company. Even this." He breathed again, pale eyes on Quin, his unsteady hand on the time-scarred oak. "Ivan Kwan had this in Hong Kong."

Yet another wheezy breath.

"Sit, please." He waved the cane at the other chair. "I've arranged for us to be alone."

Quin sat, his heart throbbing hard.

"I never knew." He thought he saw the shine of a tear. "Even though I saw her again. Once when I wanted to see the remains of what they called the starbird. Again down in Sun Country, when I could still stand the gravity. I wish she had told me."

Quin said, "She never told me."

"Then how—" The hawk-eyes narrowed.

"I found this in the lab where she was killed." He leaned to offer the foam-stained holo. "Called the number written on the back."

Quivering fingers took the holo, turned it, turned it again. Pale eyes blinked and came back to him.

"You are my son." The shriveled face twitched. "I wish I had known while—while she was alive."

For a long time he said no more. Waiting, Quin felt a

sting of pity for him, washed away in a surge of sympathy and sorrow for his mother.

"Though it may have been—may have been better." The old head shook, lips sternly set. "I couldn't have claimed you. I can't claim you now."

The old Tycoon seemed to sigh.

"Perhaps I should tell you, if your mother never did, what we were to each other."

"Sir, if you would!"

"You needn't call me sir." A wan half-smile, while the old man decided what to say. "My wife was Mei-ling Chen. We married young. Years before I met your mother. Mei-ling had looks and charm enough then, but our marriage wasn't for love. Our parents imagined it would help them bring the House back together. A sad blunder, because the Chens never let her forget that she was one of them.

"Our first real quarrel was over Jason."

He nodded at a little niche in the wall above that odd wooden desk. It held Jason's handsome bronze-haired head, a computer-sculpture smiling with the casual arrogance Quin remembered. His own half-brother—that thought was an unpleasant jolt.

"She hated me because I let him come to space with me on the halo expedition. She wanted to keep him with her here and turn him into a Chen. I brought him back an all-out Kwan. She never forgave me." He shrugged. "Not that I cared by then."

He paused to breathe before he went on.

"When I was young enough, I loved to travel Earth-side. Mountains, the sea, the woods, and the weather. All the wonders we'll never have in space. I even loved the Earthfolk, and diplomatic dealings with them. I was good at it. Visiting lowside friends, speaking to lowside crowds, fighting the Revelator.

"That's how I met Nadya. I'd picked up an Earthside virus. The lowsiders breed a lot of bugs, along with more babies than they can feed. The medics called Nadya in—

she had turned to study mutant viruses when she found her genes weren't entirely right for space.

"We fell in love. I stretched out my convalescence." Wistfully, the old eyes smiled. "I planned to keep her near me as my official medic. Planned—" A rueful shake of the faded head. "I'd just got into office. I had a lot to learn about the limits of power."

Thin lips twitched and tightened.

"Too many Chens talked too much. Mei-ling made an ugly public scene. In spite of the bitch—because of the bitch—I needed Nadya. Begged her to help me bluff it out. She was too proud. Too proud."

A long-drawn sigh.

"She disappeared. Gone to the halo on that relief ship before I knew where she was. With never a word. About—about anything." A tremor in his voice. "Not even later, when she'd got back sick from space with the starbird to nurse. Even when we managed another night together in Zurich Down. She never let me guess—till you called the private number I'd always kept for her."

"Thank you—father!" The word came out in a quivery whisper. "I always longed to know. Always dreamed—But I never dared imagine it could be you."

"My son!" Tears again in the keen old eyes. "I see your mother in you. More Dain than Kwan." A small sad smile. "I wish—wish I could claim you."

He reached out as if to touch Quin, but his wavering hand fell back to his knees.

"Too old, Quin. Too old to fight the Chens. Or anything—" A slow headshake, while he breathed. "Mei-ling died two years ago, hating me till her last gasp. And Jason—"

Something pinched the parchment features.

"Just back from the halo. Eager to take my place."

"Father—" The word came stronger now. "There is something I think you can do—" Eagerness took his breath. "We need help, out in the halo. Power for Halo Station—"

"Mutineers!" Abruptly harsh, the Tycoon cut him off. "We've pulled out of the halo. The Fleet was ordered to evacuate all civilians. When those fools stayed, they asked to die."

"They want to live," Quin protested. "A hundred people. All my friends. Our foothold in the halo. Kerry's there—Kerry McLenn, my stepfather."

"Nadya married him?" Hostility faded into wistful recollection, the bleak voice softening. "I remember Kerry. The young Santissimo who stowed away to blow us up and then thought better of it. I never knew Nadya married him."

"He loved her," Quin said. "It hurt him terribly when she had to come home. He was always good to me. I love him, sir. And they're all in danger. Kept alive by power from balky old engines that fail and fail again. I hoped to find them a new power source."

"You're too late." The Tycoon frowned. "A long time too late."

"Sir—father—" He groped for words to save Janoort. "I've heard the Revelator screeching. I've heard about Contra-Neptune going silent. And unidentified spacecraft. If there's real danger in the halo, don't we need the station for an outpost?"

"We've pulled out to stay." A time-seamed scowl. "With the relay link broken, with Jason's hostile aliens, and now your own wild tale of something eating the old *Spica*—"

The pale eyes probed him.

"You really saw something?"

"Yes, sir. A monstrous thing." He searched for words to make it real. "Shaped a little like a scorpion with wings— why wings in space, I don't know. I watched it fuse the wreckage and suck up the hot metal.

"If you believe me—"

"I'm no Chen." The Tycoon peered at him, the old eyes bleak. "I've been to the halo. And now I've seen the secret Fleet report we got last night from Brun, on her way to Contra-Neptune. Callisto High relayed it."

"The thing I saw?"

"Take a look." He nodded at the wall screen. "Their search system picked up an object coming from toward the trailing Trojan asteroids. It didn't respond to their challenge. They veered to intercept it. Here's what their cameras got."

The screen came on. Black at first, pierced with an unsteady red point. In image after image, the point shone brighter and began to show form. A round barrel body, barely visible. Eye-shapes like jutting turrets, dimly crimson, faintly lighting the gaping jaws.

Sudden hot white spots danced across the image.

"Laser hits," the Tycoon whispered. "Hot enough at that range to burn through the armor of a Kwan-class cruiser. The thing somehow absorbed them. It kept on coming."

The image swelled. The laser flashes revealed more of it. Wings, motionless, only half extended. Four serpentine limbs, armed with triple talons. A snakelike tail, tipped with a hot blue jet.

"It kept on coming," the Tycoon whispered.

Brighter, brighter, the lasers stitched again and still again across the dark-armored barrel, the crystal wings, the bright-glinting sting. And did no harm.

The screen went black.

"The end of their transmission."

Quin hardly heard the words. Staring into the vacant dark, he thought Matsuda and Lena Ladino wouldn't be sleeping together again. Vira Brun would be as dead as her defeated dream of planets terraformed into new utopias.

"What I saw—" He shivered. "It must have been real."

"I wish it had been imagined."

"What now?" He peered into the stern old eyes. "Do you think Earth's in danger?"

The Tycoon shrugged.

"Can the Fleet—"

"The Fleet?" A sardonic rasp. "Though what it does

may not matter." The old man sagged heavily back in his chair. "If the Revelator learns about this, he'll do worse than any monster could."

"I've heard him."

"Which means this report must be kept secret." He nodded at the screen. "Even from Security. As long as we can. When it gets out—the Chens will dig it out—the Revelator could ruin us with it."

He shook his head, peering at Quin with a sad half-smile.

"You're one bright spot, my son—my new son! In the darkest time I've ever known."

"Father—" Quin breathed, "Thank you!"

"While we wait, I'll do what I can for you—" He pulled himself unsteadily forward in the creaky chair. "Though I can't keep you here at the High House. Some Chen would do you in, trying to do me in. I can order Security to expedite arrangements for your Sunmark."

The pale eyes narrowed.

"If you want the Sunmark?"

"Of course I do."

"Think about it, son." The frown bit deeper. "If things break down, those mad fools will slaughter us."

"Are you actually—" Quin stared. "Actually afraid?"

"They outnumber us, ten thousand to one. In the past, we've kept them divided by nation and race and faith. We've bribed the best of them to join us. We've hit them from the Fleet and the forts when we had to. But we and they are symbiotes. Dependent on each other. If the system ever does break down, we die together."

"Still," Quin said, "I want the Sunmark. If that can be arranged."

The Tycoon roused himself.

"I hoped you would." His faded eyes lit again. "Your mother's missing husband—what's his name?—can be listed as your legal father. My staff will get a Suncard for you, with a credit limit big enough to cover anything you want."

"Except what I really want," Quin had to say. "Help for Halo Station—"

"Better forget your mutineers." A fleshless arm brushed them aside. "Another thing, Quin." The old voice fell. "Stay away from this Barranca."

Unsteadily the Tycoon reached to touch Quin's arm.

"Keep safe, son." A husky whisper. "Keep my number. Keep in touch—"

Quin stopped listening.

Beyond that ancient desk, behind the Tycoon, a door was sliding open. Benito Barranca darted through it, clutching a lifted blade that flashed like glass.

"Sir!"

Quin gasped and pointed. The Tycoon spun his chair, scrabbled through the clutter on the desk, whirled back with a heavy black weapon.

It crashed.

But Barranca was already over him, stabbing savagely. That crystal blade turned crimson. Bright scarlet sprayed through the tan shipsuit. The frail old body jerked and sagged. The gun fell out of a lifeless hand.

"*Adiós, viejo!*" Barranca grinned at the toppling body. "God reward your sons. Jason for his idiot High House agents—they set up my game. This *bastardo* for the pawn he played."

Empty-handed, Quin staggered forward.

"Take it—" Barranca coughed red foam and tossed the dagger. "For your *linda* Mindi!"

He darted back the way he had come.

Ears ringing, Quin heard shouts and then a siren screaming. Looking down, he found the dagger in his hand.

Her heart ached for the forager, a puny little thing, not a third the size of her dead prince. Licking off the last poor shreds of its little shell, her hot tongue revealed all its pathetic imperfections.

Sexless, it could never love or breed. Nearly mindless, it would never know the splendid history of their conqueror kind. Mute, it could never learn to chant the proud old sagas. In the end, it would be only a meager morsel for some later sibling offended by its fragile impotence.

Yet it was her first, and vital to the hive.

Burning with pity and pride, she watched it wobbling to its feeble feet, flexing its tiny tail. Crooning gently to it, she woke the simple drives it must obey. When it was strong enough, she nuzzled it outside.

"You're a searcher," she told it. "A searcher for good food-metal. The heat you feel will guide you to richer stuff closer to the star. When you taste it, you will know its goodness. On your way, you must find hot metal to fill your own little belly and cold flight-mass to drive you. You will gather what is good and bring it home to me. Radiant metal to make your princely brothers and your queenly sisters beautiful and strong."

It had no voice to answer. Not even any actual understanding of its great duty to her and the hive. Yet she saw its tiny eyes shine redder, reflecting her love. She watched it spread and test its tiny wings, felt its crushed bewilderment when they found no air.

"You'll need them, baby, when you come to raid the planets, but they won't help you here."

She filled its wee flight sacs and stroked its tail to kindle its fledgling jet. Learning, it blundered into the barrier wall and tumbled back into a cloud of lifted stardust. Her heart burned hot when at last she saw it climbing off the asteroid.

It was back too soon, frail jaws empty, aquiver with terror. Voiceless, it couldn't say what had alarmed it. She left it hiding deep in the hive, while she crept out to look for the danger.

Only a gnat.

Or, in fact, a midget shipload of gnats, flying out toward the point where she had eaten their orbital fort. Creatures altogether harmless, probably not even aware of her hive in the asteroid. She coaxed her frightened forager back outside.

"You should catch them," she urged it. "Just for practice.

They aren't really fit to eat, though the sly little midges will make fine sport when your big brothers go out to hunt."

Whimpering, it wrapped its poor little tail around her leg and clung fast. She felt it trembling.

"Baby, baby!" She stroked the feeble fire in its little belly. "They can't hurt you. They can't hurt anything. Hit them, baby. Hit them hard!"

The red sparks lit its eyes again. Its wee jet puffed warm against her face, and again it lifted. She watched it hover, uncertainly searching, until at last it flew to meet the gnat-ship.

The gnats veered to meet it.

Their arrogance delighted her. Miserable pygmies, pretending to guard their star with the fortress she had eaten, daring now to challenge her brave little forager. Her heart burning hotter, she watched the encounter.

Her forager wavered when their toy lasers blazed, but only for a moment. They came straight to meet it. She watched its tiny tail bending, watched its feeding jet flash, watched the gnat-ship veiled in exploding plasma.

A tiny victory, but enough to whet its uncertain courage. Seeming stronger, bolder, it flew on toward the gnat-infested planets closer to the star.

Her own daring champion!

Pride burning fiercely, she crept back into the natal chambers to turn and warm the larger eggs that would soon be hatching queens and princes. They would people her hive with beauty and splendor, brighten it with all the ferocious passion she once had felt, but that first forager would live forever in a comic epic of its own, a hilarious saga she would be singing to delight its future siblings, even after the certain tragicomic climax, when one of them would surely snap it up.

Solarpolitics. *A Machiavellian philosophy of power developed by the leaders of the House of Kwan to advance and justify their long domination of the solar system. Denying all the dogmas of democracy, it relied on economic advantage, political corruption, and missiles in space to defend the privileged position of the Sunmarked elite above the masses of mankind.*

15

QUIN STOOD NUMB WITH SHOCK AND HORROR, WATCHing the dead Tycoon sagging slowly out of the chair into the crawling pool of blood. Reaching out to stop the toppling body, he found the sticky-hilted dagger clutched in his own quivering hand.

He flung it away. It clanged against the wall, clattered back into the red gouts around his feet. He caught a sobbing breath and choked on the acrid smoke from the ancient gun. Ears ringing, he heard the siren screech again and boots drumming down the great hall where the Tycoon had met him.

Beyond the desk, that farther door was gliding shut. He plunged at it, scraped through, and found himself in the Tycoon's bedroom. A severe little chamber, antiquated as the office. A narrow bed, an old wooden chair, shelves of books along two walls. A trail of blood led his eyes across the floor to a tall wall screen.

The screen was moving, swinging toward the wall like a closing door. He lurched after it, slipped in the blood, dragged it open again. It had hidden a long passage, dimly lit. Blood spattered the metal floor.

Benito Barranca's!

Sticky-handed, he tugged at the screen to close it after him and plunged down the passage. It turned, and he saw the killer far ahead. Reeling, stumbling, Barranca fell into the wall and slid slowly down until he sat propped against it, staring back with a sardonic red-freckled grimace.

"*Viva*—" A bubbling gasp. "*Los Santíssim*—"

Coughing red froth, he crumpled back.

Quin paused for an instant. The sirens were howling again, louder. Men shouting closer. With no time for anything, he blundered around another turn. The dark metal walls seemed featureless until he found a panel jutting, like a door ajar, propped with some object on the floor.

He hauled it open, kicked the object through, stumbled after it. The door swung shut. He was in a small square cell. He saw the six gymbaled seats and knew it was a skywire car.

Out of breath, trembling, he leaned against the wall to read the luminous legends beside a row of buttons. Dockside. High Lab. High House. Coto High. Security. Lowside. He stabbed a blood-stiffened finger at the High Lab button.

"Warning!" A cool computer voice. "Passengers must secure for acceleration."

He picked up the object that had kept the door ajar and flung himself into the nearest seat. Its moving arms secured him. The car surged upward. He studied the object. A flat little box-shape of something flexible and brown, stamped with gold-colored letters, BB. It had an odor he liked. Leather, perhaps. He couldn't be sure; leather had been rare on Janoort. It was empty, except for a narrow sheath that must have held Barranca's dagger.

Heavy from the lift of the car, he felt crushed with a greater weight of sadness for the father he had imagined all his life and known for half an hour. A hard and crafty man, ruthless with his foes. Yet pathetic, even before the killer came. Overwhelmed by age and circumstance, his space empire already crumbling. He had revealed a tender compassion for Quin's mother, concern for Quin himself.

And he was dead.

Gripped in the acceleration seat, Quin felt helpless and bewildered in the grasp of events he couldn't understand. What had driven Benito Barranca to kill? How had he been able to use this private car and the secret passages of the High House to reach the Tycoon at the precise moment when the guards had been ordered away.

A Holyfolk terrorist, striking for the Revelator? An ally of the Chens, at war with the House of Kwan? The instrument of some new junta, removing Fernando Kwan to open Jason's way?

Mindi?

It hurt too much even to wonder if she had known the Tycoon was to die. He refused to think of that.

Now, what?

He felt battered too hard. Too much had hit him, too fast. His old dream come incredibly true. His father found. The Sunmark promised. Even a hope of power for the halo. Now the Tycoon's blood drying on his hands and Barranca's splashed to lead pursuit.

The car itself a puzzle. The Tycoon's secret getaway? Maybe used long ago for meetings with his mother? Or perhaps a secret of Sun Security kept even from the Tycoon?

It climbed on. They reached turnaround. The pull of the wire slacked and reversed. The seat swung his head toward what had been the floor. The braking drag began, and still he grappled with bleak uncertainties.

How far could he ride? Dockside? That was only danger. Back down to Coto High? He couldn't help longing for Mindi. But—Barranca's lover? Security agent? He shivered.

Anywhere in that sky city he would be a baffled stranger, branded even by the nakedness of his face. Anywhere he tried to go, he would always be betrayed by everything he didn't know, hunted forever.

The High Lab?

At least a chance. Sealed until the dead Tycoon's commission settled the disposition of the skyfish, it might hide him for a time, might even let him search Thorsen's deserted workshop for fusion know-how.

The car stopped. The grille slid aside, a flat door beyond it. Listening, he heard nothing. The door gave when he pushed. Darkness, and that thin bitter stink of the dead fire and the chemical foam that put it out. He punched the down button and stepped out into silence. The grille slid back. He pushed the door shut. A click, and the car was gone.

Alone in the dark. Blind at first, he found a faint glow overhead. His eyes adjusted. He found tall partitions around him. Cluttered tables and benches stood against them, dimly lit from overhead. Thorsen's workshop. When he turned to look for the elevator door, it was already hidden behind a hinged holo tank.

Shuffling uncertainly into the gloom, he found a sink. He scrubbed his hands. The Tycoon's blood still spattered his clothing—Barranca's blue shipsuit—yet he felt a little relieved.

Outside the shop, beyond the pale loom of the unfinished spaceplane, he came into stronger light that struck the far-off ceiling above the skyfish in its cage.

He stopped in the shadow of the craft to listen and look again. No sound. No motion. He threaded his way across that vast floor toward the cage, through the scattered wreckage from the blast that had killed his mother.

The skyfish lay there, a flat gray dead-looking huddle—yet it had moved since he was here with Mindi. Its face, hidden before, had turned toward the door. He couldn't help recoiling. Yet of course, he reminded himself, no such creature could look human.

Never breathing, it needed no nostrils. Never eating—so far as his mother had learned—it needed no mouth. Adapted to airlessness, it needed no vocal organs, no ears. Communicating though a whole spectrum of radiation that ranged from the infrared through visible light and far beyond, as his mother had believed, it used its own complex electronic transmitters and receptors.

Yet it had a face that held him fascinated. Two eyes, larger than the human, gray lids vertically closed. A slender gray rope-shape, tapering from what would have been the human chin, ending with three delicate boneless-seeming fingers.

Awed, he wondered what its mind must be. Wondered at the purpose and the nerve that had brought it out of the halo to meet the human invaders of space, wondered at its stubborn defiance of torture and even of his mother's gentler persuasion to make it reveal anything. The shock of its strangeness dissolved into upwelling sympathy. Himself a friendless fugitive, he had too much in common with it.

The cage was locked. He traced wires to a wall switch a dozen meters out of the creature's reach. The floor beneath the switch was stacked with paper books, a databanker, a little holo receiver. Things his mother must have given it, taken out of its reach after her death.

The lock clicked when he tried the switch. A little uneasy, he opened the door and entered the cage. The creature didn't move. Half afraid, he knelt beside it. Again he caught its odor, clean-seeming, slightly etherlike, oddly pleasant.

Doubtfully, trembling, he reached to touch it. The gray skin was velvet-soft, neither warm nor cold. He slid his fingers beneath a drooping wing and found it pliantly flexible. He felt no pulse, no quiver, no response at all.

"Hello—" His voice came huskily. "My name is Quin Dain. Dr. Nadya Dain was my mother—if you know what mother is. I think she tried to help you. I will try to help you if I can. If you can tell me what you need—"

He detected no response.

"Can you hear me? Can you make a signal?"

Nothing.

"People have been cruel to you." He bent closer to its strange face. "People in Fleet Command. People in Sun Security. But I'm not Security. Security is hunting me now, because they think I killed the Sun Tycoon. If we could be friends, maybe—maybe we could help each other."

The thin gray wing felt dead against his hand.

"I've come back out of the halo." Could it hear sounds? He raised his voice. "I saw a terrible being there. A dreadful thing. Bigger—far bigger than a Fleet battlecraft. I watched it eat the hulk of the *Spica*—that was our explorer craft that some space people captured and stripped. It melted the wreckage, drank it up.

"Do you hear me?"

No sign of life.

"Now the thing is flying on this way. It has attacked the orbital relay station that linked us to the halo. It has knocked out a Fleet cruiser that went to meet it. Do you know—" His voice caught. "Do you know what it is? What it means to do?"

No hint of anything.

"I need help!" He was shouting now. "You need help. If we could help each other—"

He knelt a long time waiting, but the eyes stayed shut, with never a quiver of the vertical lids. The slender trunk lay lax on the floor, the delicate fingers grasping nothing. The lifeless wing sagged back to the floor when he withdrew his hand.

"You don't trust me," he muttered. "No reason you should."

He went back to the databanker and the stack of books. Squinting in the dimness, he made out titles. Science texts, one of them his mother's monograph on the starbird.

Geology, geography, biology. Histories, among them a history of the Company. A battered paper copy of *Hell Above Us: The New Revelation*.

He brought them all back into the cage and arranged them in reach of those still fingers. The fingers didn't move. He set the holo receiver beside them—

A sudden clang.

He froze, listening to the reverberations that rang against the high walls, rolled through the gloom, slowly dying. No doors opened, no lasers flashed, no Sikhs burst in. Silence came back. Breathing again, he tried to relax.

"I thought it was Security." He spoke toward the cage. "But I guess they haven't found me. Must have been just the wall. Expanding and contracting when the Sun moves across it."

No reply.

"I'll be here," he told the skyfish. "Till something happens."

How long, he wondered, could he hide here with the Sikhs on his trail? His father's blood on the sleeves of the blue shipsuit that had been Barranca's—

A faint hope woke. Could Barranca's body have been mistaken for his own? A chance of that, perhaps, if the doorway into the elevator hadn't been discovered.

He shrugged. He must try to make the best of whatever time they gave him. Leaving the cage door open, he went back to the workshop. The spaceplane filled the end of it, resting on the rails that were to guide it through the dock and out into space. Its own lock was a stubby cylinder, jutting under folded wings.

The lock was open. He climbed inside and got the lights on. Dazzled at first, he peered around the cabin. Nearly ten meters long. Galley and bar along one side, curtained berths along the other. Lustrous fabrics, shining metal, gleaming hardwoods—luxury commanded by Benito Barranca.

He climbed into the cockpit. Seats for two pilots, covered by a kwanlar dome. The instruments were lit, ruby numerals dancing in the computer clock. The whole Earth was imaged in the monitor, skywire terminals mapped across the nations, a green-glowing target pattern centered on Azteca.

Was the craft fit for flight?

Hope jolted him, abrupt as a blow. Could he launch it? Operate it? Could it—could it possibly carry him out of the High Lab, away from the Sikhs and Sun Security? Maybe even all the way back to Janoort?

Drunk with such notions, he scrambled back down the ladder well, down through the cabin deck into narrow odd-shaped holds between the huge-seeming mass tanks. He found the fusion drive.

In working order?

Heart thudding, he inspected it. Plumbing for plasma injection. Pumps and filters, their installation almost complete. Magnetohydrodynamic generator. The master magnet?

Gone.

Thorsen must have taken it, wherever he went, leaving the little craft disabled without it. That wild hope dead, he stared a long time at the empty bedplate before he went on to check the auxiliary drive.

Powered with fuel cells only. Intended only for minor course corrections, docking, landing. Useless even for a take-off from Earth.

He clambered out of the holds and back through the lock into the workshop. Shivering now in the frigid dimness, he found a switch for the overhead lights. They revealed a clutter that must have been hurriedly abandoned.

Empty shipping cartons must have held parts for the engine. Most of them were from Barranca Brokers, Ciudad Barranca, Mexamerica. A dog-eared paper notebook lay open on a stand-up desk beside another databanker. A drafting table was piled with technical handbooks and computer-drawn plans.

Clues to Thorsen's fusion know-how?

Hope still alive, he began searching for all he could learn. He found no entry code for the databanker. There were notes and plans he could decipher, but none for the essential master magnet. Thorsen and his helpers must have taken their key secrets when they fled.

He found a little stack of blankets in the corner of the shop, an opened carton of Fleet rations on a shelf above the sink. He emptied an ice-cold ration pack and climbed back aboard to search and work again.

Time passed. Once he slept until the walls alarmed him, creaking and booming again as the lab turned beneath the Sun. He started up, breathless, but no Sikhs attacked him. The skyfish lay still when he went back to look into its cage, but he thought its sleek gray head had moved again.

He carried the plans back aboard, learning all he could. He checked filters and meters. He finished coupling the tiny pumps to the mass tanks. Poring over wiring diagrams, he connected everything to the pilot computer. He ran computer checks, repaired his errors, made adjustments, until a final flight test showed all systems up. All except the most essential.

WARNING! The red legend flashed across the monitor. MAIN DRIVE DEAD.

He scowled blankly at it. The computer had been programmed for a flight to Azteca. The indicated mass in the tanks might be enough get them there. With luck enough, the auxiliary drive would let him launch the little craft, but the alerted Fleet would surely detect and overtake him before he could try for a landing anywhere.

Just possibly, he thought, the craft had range enough to reach Janoort. If he had the missing master magnet installed. If he had full mass tanks. If he had starcharts and navigation skills. Without any of them—

He stumbled out of the cockpit, feeling dull with long fatigue and penetrating cold, his fingers numb and clumsy. Aimlessly he clambered off the craft, back into the gloomy lab. There was nothing more he knew to do.

Spent, he rolled into the blankets and shivered himself into a restless sleep. He dreamed that he had the craft in space, hoping to reach Halo station. Jason Kwan was close behind him, firing lasers at him. Ahead of them, a monstrous creature was swallowing Janoort. It came fast to meet them, red eyes blazing, black talons clutching, roaring—

The roar became the boom of a gong.

"Security alert!" Groggily awake, he saw a red pattern flashing in the wall screen, heard a hard voice barking. "Emergency Zero Red!"

The gong rang again.

"Priority Alpha!" The screen burned yellow, green, crimson again. "Security alert! Emergency Zero—"

The voice was broken off. The screen turned black, and a different image filled it.

The skyfish!

It was floating in the dark, riding on a thin white cloud jetting from the tip of its tapered tail. Its wings were spread, alive with shimmering color. Its great eyes were open, luminous, unearthly with their vertical lids, fixed intently upon him.

"We greet you, Quin Dain, son of most unlucky Dr. Nadya Dain."

Its voice unnerved him. His mother's, remembered from his childhood. He wondered for an instant if this was more of his dream.

"We speak to you, Quin Dain, because you were born in the halo." Pulsing, swirling, the light of the wings waxed and waned to the rhythm of the voice. "We speak because you seem eldren, as your mother was.

"We have never spoken, not even to her, but we must speak now because of the disaster your people name Emergency Zero Red. We speak because your people and our own share the same danger, a greater danger than anything the Elderhood should fear from you."

The precious little forager, born from her very first egg!

Its siblings would soon begin emerging. Farther-ranging foragers, skillful workers and nurses, shining fighters, all immensely larger and more richly gifted with the awesome splendors of her race, all burning to serve her infant princes and her coming queens. Each one she would cherish in its turn, but this small hero had been the first, and her belly quaked for it.

"Watch yourself, little one!" she flashed after it. "Watch your flight sacs. Watch out for gravity wells too deep for you. Find food for all of us, and come back safe."

Its small wings dipped as if to answer. It flew on starward, wavering uncertainly as it searched the space ahead. It flew too fast.

"Caution, baby! Caution!" she called again. "Don't waste mass. Don't take risks, till you learn your limits."

The little wings waggled again, too jauntily. It flew on, still too fast. She had to let it go. Flightless, her belly gone, there was nothing more she could do to aid or guard it.

She could only watch. Even after she had crawled back into the natal chamber to tend her larger, later eggs, her fond imagination followed it toward the starward asteroids. Surely, even with its own untrained perceptions, it could evade any hazard from the gnats and find ores rich enough to feed its siblings when they hatched.

A time came when she thought it should be back, but her yearning senses caught no hint of it. At last, overwhelmed with unease, she left the red-glowing eggs and crept back to the lip of the hive. She couldn't see it.

Panic-stricken, she scanned the orbits of the asteriod swarm. It wasn't there. Turning farther starward, she winced at the idiot din from the planet of the gnats.

She found her intrepid forager.

Too intrepid, it was diving into the silly web the things had woven around the middle of their world. Terror for it chilled her heart. Though the gnats themselves could hardly harm it, it was blundering into trouble through its own sweet simplicity.

It should never have dropped so deep into such a hazardous gravity well. Not until it had learned to conserve the mass in its tiny sacs a little more cunningly. Or learned at least to refill them from the wide icecaps she could see at the poles.

Or perhaps—

Perhaps it had already learned, because its skill and daring dazzled her. The gnats had strung their moronic web beneath a circle of tiny moonlets moving fast enough to hold it suspended. Many of the moonlets were radiant, made of rich enough stuff to feed the hive, yet small enough for her infant to take.

It was claiming them!

Diving too deep, too near all the dangers its tiny mind could never understand, it was burning the filaments between the moonlets and the web. Working with a cunning she had never expected, it was severing each strand at the chosen moment that would toss its moonlet out toward the hive.

What a saga this would make! A feat to be celebrated by all her unhatched future generations. Never in all history had any epic hero been such a puny little nestling, so brilliantly bold, serving a hive so well.

Aglow with anxious pride, forgetting her own loss and pain, she began to shape the new saga in her mind. Beginning with the noble death of its dedicated father, the exposition would recount her own lonely flight from star to star, the future hero only a magic spark in her belly.

She recast the pathos of its little life, the brief drama climbing toward this high climax. Laughing at the imagined antics of the gnats in the comic interludes, she tried the ring of the old heroic meters and began searching out metaphors and fit similes to celebrate the courage and the triumph of her first-hatched forager.

Mercifully, the pestiferous whining of the gnats had been stilled. Most of it had come from the idiotic skyweb, falling now as her small hero detached its anchor moons. Her own tragedy had not been in vain—

Dread quenched her blaze of glory. The daring little infant had flown too low, stayed too long. Its feeble jet had begun to flicker. The gravity well had trapped it.

Yet she tried to hope that even now it might somehow save

itself, folding its baby wings against the first savage wrench of entry, then extending them to glide safely to the polar snows, fresh mass that could rekindle its dying jet.

It seemed happily unaware of danger. Rigid with horror, she watched it coming on around the planet, busily clipping those unseen threads. One by one, the little moons flew free, tossed out toward her.

She screamed a frantic warning, but of course the baby was too far to hear. She saw it falling. Tangled, perhaps, in some invisible scrap of the web. She saw its feeble wings crushed and twisted, burned away.

Tumbling and torn, its brave little body blazed down through the deadly atmosphere and skittered at last into something dark and flat at the tip of an odd white line that had followed it all around the planet.

Vapor, she knew in an instant, vapor rising where the web was coming down. Sadly she saw the dramatic irony of that narrow cloud. Dying for want of flight-mass, her pathetic little hero had fallen into a liquid ocean of it, dead before it could drink.

Her darling dead—

But not forever. Her pain dissolved into happy laughter at the gnats. Sublimely arrogant, trapping her little innocent in that idiotic web, they had given it eternal fire as the tragicomic hero of the founding of her hive. Her heart burned again with a mother's undying joy.

Survival Paradox. *Survival during the pretechnological stages of evolution commonly depends on unrestrained reproduction and aggression. As technology advances, however, that becomes the way to extinction. Only through some sane resolution of the paradox can life survive into the post-technological stage.*

16

GROGGY WITH SHOCK, HE TURNED TO LOOK FOR THE actual skyfish.

"Quin, dear!" The screen called to him with his mother's own voice, urgently imperative. "Stand where you are. You must listen to the electronic instrument, because we cannot utter sound."

The cage was far across the floor, beyond the empty spot where his mother's desk had been. When he found the skyfish, its eerie eyes were open wide, watching him. One finlike wing was lifting. It cupped toward him, aglow with color, winking to the rhythm of the voice behind him.

"Stand, Quin," it begged him. "Watch. Hear."

Awe gripped him.

"I'm listening." Unsteadily, trembling a little with that

old eagerness to learn and the secret terror of what he might find, he swung back to the wall screen. "If you can tell me what's happening."

"You should fear the space marauder."

"We do," he muttered. "And we fear you."

"Dear Quin!" His mother's voice, a little impatient with all he didn't know, the way she was when she tried to explain the Sunside. He saw her in his mind for a moment, more real than the skyfish, hunched and almost shivering in the old yellow sweater she wore over her dropsuit because she was always cold.

"If you fear us, we have more to fear from you." Her voice showed hurt. "The marauder, however, is a greater danger to the whole halo."

"Is it—" Dread took his breath. "Is it the monster I saw? Out beyond Halo Station?"

"If you saw a being greater than your battlecraft. She did pass near your halo colony."

"She?"

"The marauder is female. She comes to plant a new dwelling for her kind. She has made a place—a nest, perhaps you would say—among the asteroids your astronomers call the trailing Trojans. There she will replicate."

"It eats—" Wonder took his voice. "Eats metal?"

"She seeks radiation sources." His mother's voice, very patient. "Heavy metals, because her metabolism is based on nuclear reactions. She is drawn to anything warm. On her way here, she attacked our observatory on the halo fringe. Coming on toward the star, she attacked your orbital relay station. And now—"

His mother's voice fell sadly, the way it sometimes fell when she spoke of Sun Country on the far-off Earth.

"Now one of her children has come to raid your planet."

"How—" He shook his head, trying not to believe. "How do you know?"

"We perceive a wide spectrum of electromagnetic radiation. Your atmosphere was blinding to us, but here we have been able to use the skyweb as an antenna." The bright wings dimmed. "Now it is being destroyed."

"Destroyed?" His eyes shut for an instant, against the strange-eyed image in the screen and the shock of what it said. "The thing has got here to Earth?"

"If you wish to see—"

The skyfish vanished from the tank. In its place he saw the whole planet, diminished as it had looked from the Coto docks. Something hung beside it, a bright point swimming in black space. The bright point was swelling.

"An image of the attacker." His mother's voice, strangely calm. "Transmitted from your Fleet station at the Cotopaxi docks. The creature is flying around the planet, severing the wires to detach the ballast masses."

"Why?" Stunned, he turned to peer toward the skyfish. "Why?"

Its wings still winking, it now lay on the floor just outside the cage. The borrowed voice still came from the screen behind him.

"It seeks metal to feed its mother. The supporting masses contain radiant residues from nuclear reactors which once operated in them. The creature is detaching each section at the instant when momentum will carry it outward toward the nest."

That bright point blurred and flickered in the screen. Back in focus, at a higher power, it took a shape that dazed him. A shape like the one the holo probe had showed him. Shimmering wings half extended, cruel jaws agape, enormous eyes redly glowing.

"The visual image." His mother's voice, as softly patient as when she was teaching him to read. "If you wish the audio, here is what we receive."

Incoherent commands blasted out of the speaker. Hoarse shouts in many tongues. A military band blaring "The Sun Forever." A snatch of the Revelator's voice, ranting that the Beast of Satan had come to gather Sunmarked souls into its high hell. People screaming somewhere. A burst of harsh laughter.

"Sir, we have been firing." A clipped highside voice, brittle with tension. "No good, sir. No damned good. Because it snaps up the missiles like tossed sweetmeats!"

Silence, and then his mother's voice, explaining.

"The attack began over the Pacific. The marauder has followed the rotation of the planet, cutting the ballast lines above each city. Cotopaxi High will be the last."

"Can't it be stopped?" He stood dazed, eyes fixed on that nightmare swelling in the screen. "Your own people—can't they do something?"

"We have tried. We had a weapon..." A tired little sigh, like his mother's when something bad couldn't be helped. "You yourselves defeated us."

"How can that be?"

Silence, while that hideous image grew in the screen. Broken shards of sound. Air hissing and metal thudding, perhaps from a cycling lock. A muffled explosion. Male voices chanting what he thought must be a Muslim call to prayer.

"We are the Newlings." His mother's voice again, wistfully fond, as it had been when she remembered happy times in Sun Country. "We are new among the eldren. The Elderhood gave us space on the halo fringe—"

The voice paused. The attacking seeker had grown large and dreadful in the screen. He stumbled away from it, toward the cage and the small gray huddle on the floor.

"If it's hitting Coto—"

"Patience, Quin. Patience." A narrow wing tipped to flicker at him, and his mother's quiet voice came from the screen behind him. "The creature cannot be stopped."

A wave of pity swept him, and an ache of admiration. Far from its strange home, captured, wounded, tortured, the little being had kept its silence with a stubborn fortitude that filled his eyes with sympathetic tears.

"Maybe—" he whispered. "I think I can open the lock and set you free. If you can fly—"

"We cannot. We were wounded by the Fleet planetics

when they took us. Security planetics injured us again. Our organs of flight have never healed."

"You've suffered—" He gulped at the throb in his throat. "We have the spaceplane here. I think I can launch it. If we can find supplies and fuel, perhaps I can take you home."

"Quin, Quin!" The voice his mother used to reprove some bit of nonsense. "There's nowhere you could hope to take me. Your Admiral Jason Kwan has destroyed our core-star base, and you don't know how far Newmarch is."

"We must try! Before the creature strikes—"

"The time for that has gone." Grave regret. "It has come too near. It kills such small things as we are, for a joy it finds in killing. Outside the lab, we would be eaten."

"Can't we do—anything?" He stood staring at the little gray shape by the cage. "If your people brought a weapon, can't we use it?"

"We tried." A sad little sigh. "Our sister Snowhue was flying with it to attack the seeker's hive. Her ship was attacked and she was injured. Helpless in the wreckage when we reached her last. The weapon is lost."

"This Elderhood? Can't it defend itself?"

"You don't know the eldren way." The voice was his mother's when she told him she had to leave Janoort because her genes weren't right for space. "Nor do the seekers. To the eldren races, killing is the most dreadful crime, but the seekers were created to kill. That is all they live for."

Fists knotted and quivering, because there was nothing he could do, he turned again to watch that nightmare shape growing in the screen.

"Our sister came in spite of the Elderhood, with her two eccentric companions. She was able to depart from the eldren way only because she was born imperfect." His mother's voice, solemnly wistful, the way it had been when she showed him that old holo his father had taken.

"She was near the seeker hive when your Admiral Jason Kwan came upon her—"

Startled, he couldn't say that Jason was his brother.

The flicker of the little wing had ceased for a moment, though he heard no bitterness in his mother's gentle voice.

"I'm sorry," he muttered. "I hope we aren't all alike."

He waited until the voice went on.

"You are not alike. Your mother had eldren traits that made her kin to us, and we felt affection for her. We often desired to speak with her, as I speak with you, but we had been forbidden."

"Have you other sisters?"

"We were four. Goldengene was killed by the seeker, out at the halo fringe. The next was Cyan Gem. We left her out at our core-star observatory learning to speak with one of your fellow planetics. Her hope was to find your race fit for admission to the Elderhood."

"Is there a chance?"

"If there ever was, it has been killed by your Admiral Kwan. With no provocation, he attacked and destroyed our observatory. Our contact with Cyan Gem has been broken."

Hardly hearing now, he watched the seeker's image growing until its crimson-glowing eyes and bright glinting jaws filled the holo tank. The image blurred, the focus changing. It sharpened again, diminished but swiftly swelling again.

Overwhelmed with waiting, he listened again to his mother's gentle voice.

"Snowhue was our youngest sister. With her defective genes, she was always backward. She was still at North-point when the seeker came. She had stayed to care for our aging mother—"

When he looked again at the screen, the seeker's image had vanished.

"It's gone!"

"It is here," the cool voice said. "Too near for the holocam."

Waiting, waiting, he drew an unsteady breath.

"About—about yourself? What is your name?"

"We who speak—" The voice hesitated. Not from any panic, but the way his mother used to hesitate when she wasn't sure he would understand. "Our language has no form for the one who speaks, because we share one another more totally than you planetics, but for you we shall designate the speaker now as Runesong."

"Runesong." He nodded, pleased with the sound of it, grasping to share her seeming calm. "If we can launch the ship—" he whispered. "If we could recover Snowhue's weapon—"

A sudden blaze of color.

"Watch out, Quin!" His mother's anxious voice, when she had seen him leaping too recklessly against Janoort's gentle gravity. "It's hitting—"

Her voice was cut off. The lights went out. The floor tipped and tossed him high.

"Runesong!" he called into the dark. "Runesong, can you hear me?"

But of course she couldn't speak to him, even if she did, because the screen was dead. All he could hear was the creak and rumble of the vast structures around him, yielding to shifting stresses. He knew the skywire had been severed. Afloat in the dark, he found nothing he could touch.

Pale emergency lights came on. He found the dim gleam of the spaceplane, somehow above him now. The lab had spun. Searching for the skyfish, he found a rainbow shimmer adrift in the gloom below the toppling cage. Calling to him, he thought, with a voice he couldn't hear.

The edge of a hanging partition was creeping slowly toward him. He waited, twisted in the air, reached to seize it. With a skill learned in childhood, he set his boots against it, launched himself toward the cage. He caught the door, pulled himself inside to search for the portable holo receiver he had left there. He found the books and the databanker lodged against the bars.

The receiver was gone.

"Quin, dear." His mother's voice, tenderly soothing, the way it had been when she gathered him up after some reckless collision. "Here I am."

Looking down—it seemed down—he found the little Newling. Her face was lifted toward him, the strange eyes wide and shimmering, the slender trunk wrapped around the holo set. The voice spoke from it, and the small screen held a Sun-glinting cluster of connected globes and cylinders toppling through dark space.

"The High Lab?"

"As we image it."

"The seeker?"

"It has severed the ballast wire. Coto High is falling."

"And we—"

"The highwire was cut below us. We are still attached to the docks. Their mass is dragging us out toward the Trojan asteroids and the seeker's hive."

The surprise attack demolished Cyan Gem's laboratory, but she herself escaped. She was able to rescue the planetic male, Reynard Charbon. The only survivors, they managed to board a lifetube that had been preserved from the wrecked planetic craft.

He had been hurt. Recovering, he longed for his native planet.

"I've been away half my life," he told her. "I want to see Earth again before I die."

That was impossible. The inner planets were too far for the crude little craft to reach within his probable lifetime. When she told him of the cruel misuse her sister Runesong had suffered from his people, he understood.

They set out for Cluster One.

"The dwelling of the Eldermost," she told him. "Not a seat of government, because the peoples of the halo require no government, but it is the center of our sharing."

Though it was almost as far as his native Earth, she perceived no danger of any new attack from either his fellow planetics or the seeker, and she hoped some eldren craft would come near enough to pick them up.

Alone together, they came to feel a mutual affection. She learned more of his sonic speech. They began to share their lives.

"I was a Fleet brat," he told her. "My father was an officer. We lived wherever his duty took us. Coto Base. Farside Station, out on the back of our big satellite. Fort Chen, which is anchored in orbit above the Company colony on the fourth planet.

"Between tours, we always came home to Earth. My folks had a Sun Country lodge near Kilimanjaro Down. Mom and I lived there when my father was off on long cruises, and he spent leave time with us. I thought we were a happy family, but my mother hated space.

"I used to do computer art. She wanted that for my career. She quit Dad when I decided to follow him into the Fleet. She kept the lodge and stayed lowside, collecting native arts and crafts for museums.

"On a visit to her, I met a girl. She was Aztecan. A talented artist. Beautiful. We fell desperately in love. She had no Sunmark. We couldn't marry or even live together on station, but we had a daughter. My child—"

She saw water shining in his eyes.

"I saw her only once, on my last leave before we took off for the halo. Half a lifetime ago. She'd be in her twenties now. Maybe with children of her own. I don't like to think what will happen to them if this monster gets to Earth.

"I guess I'll never know."

Sympathetically Cyan Gem extended her slender three-fingered trunk to stroke his bearded face. She told him the bitter history of the Newlings and related the misfortunes of her sisters. The seekers were invincible, she said. All the inner planets would soon be lost to them.

"If Earth is done for," he said, "a few may escape to the halo. Do you think we can be taken into the Elderhood?"

He saw sadness in her fading colors.

"Your ways of violence have destroyed our hopes for you,"

she told him. "Your own ship had to be disabled, because you were attacking our survey craft. Your people killed the investigator you discovered near it. You have captured Runesong, our own dear sister, and tortured her unspeakably. This last attack has destroyed the station we had built to foster friendly contact."

"If we had known you—" The wetness glistened in his eyes. "We were afraid, because you were too strange for us. If we had only understood..."

His voice died, and she felt his sorrow.

"Some of us," he muttered, "never tried to understand."

"We have tried not to blame you." Her eyes had lit again. "Because some of you seem so rich with eldren promise. Some of you have intelligence, altruism, creativity. Your advancing technology opened your way to us—a way you have lost."

Her wings and her eyes went dark with regret.

"You were children." Her voice came back, dimly violet. "The core-star station was to have been your school, to prepare you for the halo."

"But now—" The wetness shone on his face again. "We have lost everything?"

Her wings went dark. Very gently, her delicate fingers brushed his withered cheek.

"We see no future for you."

Mexamerica. *Chief political jurisdiction of North America since Sun Year 69. Nominally independent but dominated by the House of Kwan through Sun Company agencies. Uncontrolled population estimated at 9.7 billion in Sun Year 100, subsisting largely on synthetics produced by gravity power. Surface resources depleted, soils eroded, famines endemic.*

17

"LET'S GET OUT," HE SAID. "IF WE CAN."

"We are injured." His mother's voice, soft and oddly calm. "We cannot move ourselves."

"I'll move us both."

He had begun to feel almost at home in that huge and gloomy space since the pull of the wire was gone. As if it had been the gym balloon, he set his feet against the bars of the cage, measured distances, launched himself toward Runesong.

Adrift in the dark, she was slenderly graceful. Her whole form glowed, a liquid silver droplet that tapered to her maimed and useless tail. She felt sleek and warm when his arm slid around her, boneless and vibrant. Her odd, clean scent seemed stronger now. One wing flexed and clung to him, gently firm. The other cupped to search their way with a soft golden beam.

When that caught what had been the ceiling, he twisted in the air to get his feet ahead, to cushion their impact and push them off again. Caroming off a dark partition, they glided so near the spaceplane that he could catch the rim of the open lock.

She clung there and shone her light to help him find the launch controls. With power off, he had to toil at a stiff hand crank and haul at stubborn levers to close and clamp the inner valve. Climbing into the spacesuit, he stopped to ask Runesong if the loss of air would trouble her.

"A welcome thing." His mother's voice, murmuring from the little holo set cradled in her trunk. "We don't enjoy oxygen."

Sealed in the suit, he found the manual valve that let the air scream from around them, labored at another crank to open their way to space. Inside the tiny craft's own lock, he found its fuel cells still alive. He cycled them through and swam with Runesong into the cockpit.

At first he felt bewildered. He had flown the shuttle around Janoort, but there in this nearly powerless craft at the brink of Earth's gravity well, everything was different.

Uncertainly he bent over the flight computer. Ruby numerals still danced in the clock. A tutor program taught him how to start the auxiliary drive and launch them out of the lock, into darkness and the blaze of stars.

Friendly-seeming stars, they might have been Janoort's. He felt happily at home among them, until he found the Earth. A disk of darker darkness, bright-ringed from the Sun beyond it.

A broken line of fainter light, strangely straight, was drawn around the black equator. The Sun's blinding limb was exploding into view before he understood what it was.

Fire.

Fire blazing all across the continents, where the sky-web had fallen.

He raised a filter against that savage Sun. When his eyes had adjusted, he found the lab. The lock they had left was a black shadow-pit yawning in its great ungainly cluster of space-stained cylinders and globes. Falling fast away, it vanished in the dark. When it was gone, all he could see was the crescent Earth and the great full Moon.

"The seeker?" he whispered. "Where is the seeker?"

Runesong gave him no answer. Lying beside him in the copilot's seat, she had laid aside the holo set and stretched her slender arm to grasp the metal rim of a window. Her eyes were closed, and her radiance had faded.

He turned from her to study the tutor programs and plan their descent to Earth. The auxiliary drive made too little thrust for any quick effect. He kept it burning, braking the velocity that had held the web in space, but their first orbits swept them even farther out.

Scanning the planet as they swung around, he found no seeker. That line of fire along the equator was fading, turning to a streak of white cloud across the Sunlit face. Condensing vapor, he supposed, rising from where friction-heated ruin had come down from space.

The computer pilot engaged, he tried the ship's signal gear. Radio and holo channels were dead. All he got was crackling static. He sat a long time motionless, trying to guess what they would find if they got down alive.

Impossible. He had never known the Earthside, not even in imagination, not even as it had been before the sky world crashed. He thought of Janoort during those grim times when the reactors failed, but the plight of Earth would be altogether different. He had no way to picture it.

A dreadful loneliness crept into him. Janoort seemed farther than a dream, perhaps already dead as his old, romantic dream of a great place among the Sunfolk. Earth had nothing for him now, except whatever chance there was that he could find fusion power and reaction mass for the long flight back to Janoort.

Mindi Zinn haunted his thoughts. The only woman he had ever really wanted, now the lover of his father's killer. Perhaps even the killer's coconspirator?

He thought he would never know. Though Sun Security must have gathered evidence, it was doubtless gone, burned in the falling ruin or swept away into space. Maybe even Mindi herself. He tried to shut her image from his mind.

Runesong was his companion now. She lay beside him in the cockpit, motionless, strange eyes closed, wings lax and dull, thin fingers still grasping the window rim. Her sleek skin was cool when he reached to touch her, and he felt no response.

The catastrophe had dazed him.

Time's greatest empire, fallen in a single day. A catastrophe too vast and grim for him to comprehend. Dull with shock, he groped again to imagine the fate of the Earthfolk. It struck him that their swarming billions must be like the cells of a dismembered body, most of them doomed to perish now.

Without the skyweb—

He didn't want to picture that.

The monitor was a half-meter hemisphere, swelling from the pilot console. He had found programs to project the celestial sphere upon it, or the continents of Earth. He ran the tutor units again, trying to prepare himself to attempt the landing.

Their first orbit took two hours, the second almost as long. The third had begun before Runesong stirred beside him, her silvery body brightening. Her prehensile arm left the window rim and flexed to recover the holo set. Her radiant eyes came back to him.

"We were searching." His mother's voice, as he recalled it from lullabies she had crooned when he was very small. "The seeker is gone. We caught its last frightened outcry. It tangled itself in the cables it was cutting and went down into your Pacific Ocean."

"Will others—others be coming?"

"Not at once. We have searched all the way to the hive. We found no others."

"Perhaps your sister killed them all?"

Her silver glow grew dim, and her wings shone violet. For a long time, the holo set stayed silent.

"She failed." His mother's voice at last, sad as when she had to leave him and Kerry on Janoort. "We reached her mind again. Her ship is disabled. She is dying."

"The weapon?" he asked. "Destroyed?"

"Damaged, perhaps. Snowhue was hurt too badly to inspect it."

"Runesong—" Trembling, he reached to touch her. "Perhaps we can get the missing engine and fly out to recover the weapon—"

Her velvet skin flickered with color and faded again.

"How can you think of defeating the seeker, after so many have failed?"

"You'll be with me. We must try."

"If—" He felt her sleek flank quiver, saw her wings glow again. "If you dare!"

"First—" He frowned down at her, groping for ideas. "First we must have the reactor. Thorsen took it with him when he left the High Lab. Security never found him. We may do no better, but I think we should begin at Ciudad Barranca. It is near Azteca."

A meager hint—the fact that Benito Barranca had employed Thorsen to build the spaceplane after the Kwans cut off research funds—but he had found no better clue.

Azteca lay far north of the equatorial plane in which the skyweb had spun. Trying not to dwell on the hard odds against them, he reset the computer to bring their orbit over it.

A bright point on the maps in the monitor, the actual city was still invisible when at last he could pick out its location on the turning Earth. Hidden under clouds, it was sliding toward the sunset line.

The clouds were gone when he found it again on the planet's night face, a murky yellow glow. He knew it must be burning. They were flying lower when it came back across the sunrise line, but dark smoke had veiled it.

Their descent took too long. Waiting for feeble jets to do their work, he searched the whole signal spectrum, searched it again. Except for the hiss and rattle of static, he heard only silence. The world seemed dead.

Now and then he left the computer flying the craft while he went back to look for food and water or to relieve himself. Twice he slept in his cockpit seat, hoping Rune-song might arouse herself to wake him in emergency.

She lay still beside him, lost most of the time in her search for signals out of space. Once, when she had stirred to tell him that she still heard nothing from her people in the Elderhood, nothing from anywhere, he spoke to her about their landing.

"I think we'll be in trouble," he told her. "With no news from Earth, it's hard to guess what we can expect. Except chaos. I'm afraid for you. If anybody sees you. The Revelator has taught the Earthfolk to hate any being from space."

"If there is danger, there is danger." Color shimmered in her wings. "No Newling lives forever."

"I'd like to land where we can stay in hiding," he said. "Though I don't see much hope of that."

"Land where you can. Do what you must."

With every pass a little lower, he learned to work the electronic telescope that projected images into the monitor. Searching for mountains, for forests, he found no hidden spot. The city itself was still concealed by a gray plume that stretched far across the computer chart, but all the land around it was an open plain, patterned with lines he thought were roads and tiny rectangles that must be farms.

Roads and farms that would now be overrun, he

thought, with refugees from the burning city. People stricken with terror from the seeker attack, insane with hatred for anything from space.

Shrinking from what might happen to Runesong among them, he kept on searching till a wind shift moved the plume to uncover a broad brown patch southeast of the city. No farms patched it, no roads crossed it.

"It looks empty. I don't know why—"

Runesong lay still and dark again, her fingers on the metal window rim. Listening perhaps for signals out of space, but not to him.

He reset the computer to bring them down on that empty-seeming patch. The stubby wings extended. On the last orbit, they dipped and skipped and dipped and skipped half around the planet before he found them diving to glide low over range on range of strangely straight brown hills. The nose came up. They fell. Clustered braking rockets fired. Roaring smoke hid everything. The spaceplane lurched and creaked and stopped.

They were down.

He looked at Runesong. Not fit for Earth, she lay flat on the seat, seeming lifeless. Her great eyes were closed, her fingers still on the window rim, her head crushed back. Her colorless skin felt cold when he touched her.

Pity wrenched him, when he tried to imagine how she must feel. Alone here, maimed and helpless on a world where she was hated, her chance of escape such a fragile thread. Suddenly, her survival seemed to matter terribly.

Thorsen's reactor had to be recovered, so that he could take her home.

He turned again to look outside. Smoke from their own landing rockets still veiled everything around them. Waiting for it to clear, he felt a sudden unexpected eagerness.

Mother Earth!

In spite of everything, his old dream had come alive again. Blue sky and warm winds and unfrozen seas. Green things growing and songbirds flying. Here was the ancient cradle of all mankind.

His spirits soared, till the smoke blew away and he saw shattered stone. They were down in a narrow valley between two straight and endless ridges of broken stone. No green things grew anywhere. No birds flew. The sky was a dirty yellow when he looked up. Smoke, he guessed, from the burning city.

The rubble ridges perplexed him, until the odd scraps of rusting metal scattered over the slopes recalled what Kerry had told him, long ago on far Janoort, about ore buckets breaking on the skywire overhead and rocks raining into the barrio.

Suddenly then, he thought he understood. This area must have been a power terminal, where buckets of space waste came down the gravity lines, generating power out of space. A danger zone, closed to everybody.

Runesong was rousing. Her wings were still crushed against the seat, but a pale shimmer of life had returned. Her arm had fallen from the window rim, struggling toward the holo set. He slid it into reach.

"We're down," he told her. "To stay, till we get the reactor. Unless I find that—"

His throat constricted.

"We wait." His mother's patient voice. "We hope."

"If I don't get back—"

Her silver-shining wing lifted to brush his hand, and he felt a glow of warmth.

"We feel elderbond with you." His mother's whisper, saying she would always love him. "It lights our wings until we die."

The wing fell away from his hand.

"Quin, dear—" His mother's voice when she had to warn him not to play so near the air locks. "We have information for you. We have detected signals."

"Here on Earth?"

"The first was a call from space. From out toward the asteroids you call Trojan, where the seeker has hived. Others have answered, here on the planet."

"What do they say?"

"Content unknown." His mother's sigh, when she felt too ill to face some household task. "They are what is called scrambled, in the language of your Fleet. We are unable to decode them."

"The sources here? Can you locate them?"

"Most are far away. Perhaps on other continents. One, however, is near. The strongest signal emanates from a point west of us. We estimate the distance at seventy kilometers."

He tapped computer keys to project a map of Azteca on the pilot screen. A bright green point marked their own location. Thin green rings showed distance out. West, the seventy-kilometer line crossed a wide yellow disk. A dark-lettered legend flickered across it. *Azteca Down Terminal Concession.*

"That would be Azteca Sun Country," he told her. "Fleet units must be still active in space. Now getting back in touch with whatever Security forces they can reach here on the surface."

He scowled into the yellow sky.

"If the House of Kwan still exists, I imagine they'll be looking for Thorsen. They'll want his engine to replace the gravity power they've lost."

He frowned again at the chart. The Sun Country circle lay beyond the river and the heart of the city, a gold-tinted island in the green suburban districts. He found the Coto terminal, the Security barracks, the Kwan Trade Center, the aerospace port, found hotels and parks and residence areas.

Southward, a smaller, pale-blue patch nestled on a hill above a river bend. Ciudad Barranca. Enlarged, the chart showed Corredores Barranca, Torres Barranca, Barranca Mundial. Farther from the river, Aeropuerto Barranca—which must have been the spaceplane's intended home. Yet farther, on another hill, Casa Barranca.

He whistled, considering.

"Ciudad Barranca." He spoke aloud. "The only hope I see—"

Silence from Runesong. Her eyes were closed when he looked, and the color was gone from her wings. Her boneless arm lay lax, touching nothing. She might have been dead.

Noël tried not to hate the station, but Jason Kwan had been hard to forget. In moments when she could forget what he was, their months together on the Solar Kwan had come to seem an interlude in paradise, so precious the memory seemed sacred.

He had been handsome, bright, totally charming when he wished. He made love well. She had been totally enraptured with him and his exciting future in the House of Kwan.

She never spoke of him. Kerry adored her. She tried to feel the splendor he saw in the cold-blazing stars, his awed joy in the mystery of the near-seeming cosmos, tried hard to share his pride in coping with the cruel hazards of Janoort and his stubborn resolve to keep humankind alive in the halo.

She liked the new people around her. Jomo admired her. He called her the Princess, *binti wa mfalme*, and promised to keep the old engines going for *mwana*. Her children.

She never told him, but she wanted no children. Janoort was too small and cold and lonely, too terribly desolate. No child should be doomed to pine and die there.

She had grown up in the freedom of the skyweb and the Sun Countries. She had loved receptions, parties, balls. Loved shopping for new fashions, meeting new people, travel everywhere. Loved the great restaurants, the theater and music and art.

She never talked of all she missed. Wanting to be happy, to fit herself in, she tried to keep a neat home for Kerry, but he had lived too long without a wife and their frigid tunnels under the ice were too narrow to need much keeping.

She offered to share his duty shifts in the dome, but all he ever did there was listen for signals he never heard and watch the soul-crushing midnight for visitors that never came. She tried to help with the hydroponic gardens, but even they required skills she had never learned.

She longed for excitement, for news, for anything different, but every day had come to seem the same. Jomo's problems with the engines were too grim to be thrilling. With Contra-Neptune gone, there was no Sunside news. There would never be. If anything different ever came, it would surely be worse.

Sometimes, after her first terrible hurt began to heal, she couldn't help thinking that perhaps she should have forgiven Jason. The Tycoon's son, after all, he had never had to learn to live by the rules of lesser men. It might have been wiser to keep whatever she could have kept of his love and his intoxicating promise than to scorn it all.

But she had chosen. Desperately she tried to hide her gnawing discontent. Really, she did love Kerry. The exiles around her were generous with the little they could give. Surely she would get used to the cold, the dreadful monotony, the narrow tunnels and the never-ending danger, the strange-flavored hydroponic stuff and the Synfare from the labs.

Even if she didn't, a time would come when Jomo couldn't keep the engines going any longer and all their troubles would be over.

Azteca. *Capital and largest city of Mexamerica. Site of the continent's largest gravity power installation. Located on El Rio de Dios, formerly called the Canadian River, in Provincia Oklahoma.*

18

J UMPING FROM THE LOCK, QUIN STUMBLED UNDER THE unrelenting gravity of Earth. He had made a little backpack, Fleet rations enough to last a few days and a plastic bottle of water rolled in a blanket, and it felt too heavy for him. The distance down was hardly a meter, but broken rock slid beneath his boots. He sprawled on hands and knees.

He pulled himself up, rubbing rock particles out of his smarting palms, and looked around him. The season was late autumn here in the north hemisphere. The low Sun was far south, a dim red disk in the smoke-yellowed sky. Wind struck his face, the first wind he had ever felt. It was bitter-edged with smoke, and he shrank from its raw chill.

He looked again, wistfully, for the green he had expected on Earth. The ridges climbing all around him were useless waste from the mines and ore processors in space, crumbled lunar refuse and carbon-stained asteroid slack and black masses of brittle slag, piled where the power lines had spilled it, even its energy of gravity drained away.

The steep slopes above him were naked of life, but a few straggling weeds had grown on the valley floor. They were already dead and brown from frost. Brittle stalks shattered when his boot touched them, and dust set him to sneezing.

Depressed by the feel of winter and his cold forebodings of human doom, he tossed half the rations back into the lock and retied the backpack. Still clumsy under it, he stumbled up the ridge. Loose space waste slid under his boots. Once he tripped on a broken metal flange and fell again. He was gasping for breath when he reached the crest and turned to look back at the spaceplane.

Runesong's coffin, unless he got back. Stubby-winged, tiny-seeming, it stood far below him now at the bottom of the deep ravine, tipped a little like a toy some careless child had dropped. Hidden perhaps from observers on the ground, it would show its metal glint too well to Fleet craft in space.

She lay helpless in it.

Unless he got back—

He shrugged and looked for the city. Its yellow-brown smoke was all he could see, meeting the gray-brown ridges at the murky horizon. Shivering again from the icy gusts across the crest, he plodded north along it.

The red sun was lower and the fitful wind colder before the ridges fell away into thicker smoke. Stumbling over broken stone and broken metal, he came at last to a barrier of woven wire with sharp-spiked strands strung on insulators along the top, too tall and cruel for him to climb.

He tramped west inside it for several kilometers, until he came to a break where a recent rockfall from space had flattened and buried it. Very recent. The rubble felt hot to his hands when he fell again, and it had a hot-sulfur stink. The sun had gone, and a frosty dusk had thickened the smoke, before he heard a grinding rumble ahead.

People!

He broke through a brittle jungle of dead weeds to the edge of a low cliff and dropped flat to look. People and machines jammed a roadway that ran a few meters below him. Trucks and buses and passenger cars, bicycles and wheelbarrows and machines he had no name for. More were stopped beside the road, many wrecked or burned. The air carried an acrid stink of burned synthetics.

The machines were clots in an endless stream of people. Running, plodding, limping, falling and staggering up to stumble on again. Men and women and trotting children. Hoarsely shouting, weeping, screaming. One little group chanting in unison, chanting prayers in the Revelator's name. Staggering men, laden with cartons and cans and packs. Women with crying babies packed on their backs. Whimpering children clutching toys.

All in flight from dying Azteca.

That river of panic was yet another enemy. To reach the Sun Country or Ciudad Barranca he would have to make his way against it, into the city and out again across El Rio de Dios.

He lay there till the chill sank into his bones. Human pain and human terror numbed him, colder than the wind. He thought of many things. Thought of Kerry and Noël and Jomo. Of Dolores, who had taught him to make love. All of them—if they were still alive—waiting on far Janoort, hoping for the new reactor.

He thought of Mindi Zinn, as she had lived in his imagination before he knew about Benito. Thought of Runesong lying disabled on the yacht. Dying there, unless he got back with Thorsen's engine.

He had to move, yet he lay there, unnerved by the world's fate, until the cold spurred him back to his feet. He blundered through the weeds, down to the road. Packed, it had no room for him to move against the mob.

He had to blunder along in the muddy, weed-grown ditch beside it, through dead vehicles and people dying in them, peoply lying under makeshift tents of cardboard and blankets, people hunched and shivering over smoky little fires, people sprawled exhausted in the mud. People hideously burned, moaning where they lay. Sometimes he had to hold his breath and hasten past the swollen dead.

Power from the skyweb had once lit the road. The lamps on the tall posts were dark, yet he found light enough to let him stumble on. Headlights flickered on creeping vehicles, and the sky glowed murkily.

For a long time he spoke to nobody. The voices he heard were mostly Spanish. He had learned a little of that from Kerry long ago, but not enough to offer innocent-seeming explanations of who he was and why he had to push into the stricken city.

Fighting Earth's gravity, he grew groggy with fatigue. Limping from too many falls, tripping and reeling in the uncertain light, he envied the lucky ones moving on wheels.

A deep stream stopped him, dark water rushing under a bridge. Flowing water was itself something new, and he stood on the bank, staring into it, searching for nerve to climb back to the road and try to push across against that mad traffic.

"*Señor!*" A woman's urgent voice. "*Párate!*"

She had rushed to catch his arm. He understood that she thought he was about to jump. He saw a campfire blazing under the bridge. A lanky, black-stubbled man came stalking from it toward him.

"Thanks!" He shook his head and grinned. "*No hablo*— I don't speak Spanish."

"No Spanish?" The man came closer, squinting at him. "Sunblood?"

"No, sir." Suddenly grateful that he had no Sunmark, he turned to show his face in the fitful firelight. "But I'm a stranger."

"Stranger?" The man peered at his backpack. "You have food?"

"A few Fleet rations."

"Would you—" The man gestured at the fire. "Would you share?"

"If you'll let me rest," he muttered. "I'm too dead to go on."

He followed them back to the fire. The woman looked young when he could see her. Haggard now, her face grimed with drying blood from a deep scratch across her cheek, but she had been attractive. The man wore a torn uniform, a badge he couldn't read. Another woman lay under a blanket on a stretcher by the fire.

"Jonas Eaker." The man offered a muddy hand. "I was a fireman." He nodded at the woman on the stretcher. "Lucia, my wife. Our daughter, Carmencita." His voice hushed, he reached to touch her arm. "Her husband was a cop. Died fighting looters."

"I'm Quin Dain." He was wondering what to say about himself, but they didn't seem to care.

"We're starved." All their eyes were on his pack. "We've been through hell. Since the Behemoth wrecked the sky-web. Junk off the wires rained out of the sky. Knocked out the whole *ayuntamiento*. Everything!"

A hopeless shrug.

"Started fires. Fires we couldn't fight. No water pressure. No power for the pumps. No lights at night. The police—" He shook his head at Carmencita. "Nobody left in charge, but a few like her husband tried to control the looters and break the traffic jams.

"Not a chance. Not a holy chance."

Quin squatted by the fire, grateful for its heat. He opened his pack. Moaning, the woman on the stretcher raised herself to watch.

"Lucia—she's arthritic." Eaker shrugged, somehow apologetic for his tenderness. "Has to be carried. The whole block was burning when we got back to her. We barely got her out. Carmencita snatched up what she could. All gone now."

"*Agua, señor?*" With a broken cup, Carmencita dipped

water for him out of a blackened can beside the fire.
"*Buena*."

Blood had dried on her quivering hand.

"Drink it if you want it," Eaker urged him. "She boiled
it. You won't find much that's safe."

The water was tepid, but he gulped it gratefully and
offered three ration packs.

"*Gracias, señor!*"

Careful not to seem too greedy, Carmencita opened
one for her disabled mother.

"Rapists." Eaker dropped his voice. "We finally beat
them off."

He stopped to attack his own ration. When it was gone,
he hunkered down to talk again. His own people had been
mostly Cherokee, he said, farmers here before the Company took the land for the gravity terminal. Lucia had
come from Zacatecas when she was young to work in a
Sun Country night club.

"Beautiful then. A talented dancer. They tossed her
out because she wouldn't whore. I picked her up, hungry
on the street." He sighed, red eyes blinking at her. "We've
had a lot of happiness."

He said they were headed for a farm where his brother
lived.

"Down on the Washita, close to Chickasha. If—if we
get that far with Lucy." An uncertain whisper. "If he's
still there—"

His whisper had trailed away, but then he muttered
suddenly:

"I'm worried for Howard. A fine farmer. Raised prize
livestock. Fattened his cattle to sell in Sun Country." A
tired sigh. "No power now. Not to grow anything. And
the mobs—bound to strip him bare. Even to breeding
stock and seed corn."

Staring into the fire, he shook his head and stirred
again.

"A bad time, *señor*. A very bad time."

"Bad for me," Quin agreed, adding that he was trying

to get through the city to find a girl who had worked in Ciudad Barranca. Eaker drew a map in the dust to show the streets he should take. The river was up—this stream under the bridge was only a tributary creek. He would have to cross on Los Santos bridge. If he got there ahead of the fire. Debris off the falling wire had knocked out the Will Rogers bridge, and the fire had cut off the others.

Trusting them because he had to, Quin rolled up in his blanket and went to sleep. He woke shivering and numb to the bone. The fire was dead, ashes blown in his face. Eaker and the women were gone. They had left his water bottle, filled again, and one ration pack.

He ate that, wryly grateful to them, and climbed stiffly to the pavement, his whole body aching to the ruthless gravity. The traffic had thinned a little. He got across the bridge. Beyond it, a lone policeman challenged him.

"*Alto!*"

A haggard little man with one arm in a blood-sodden sling and an air of savage elation, he was directing traffic into a narrow lane around a pile of wrecked vehicles that had been pushed or rolled off the pavement. In broken English, he warned Quin out of the city.

"*Está prohibido.*"

Grimly he added that *ladrones* would be shot. He was still loyal to his duty, even though "*los autoidores son muertos. Y los demonios del sol, también.*" With an air of bleak satisfaction, he swung the gun in his good hand toward the rolling smoke ahead. *El monstruo* had been sent to prove *La Revelácion.* Wounded as he was, he remained a loyal *soldado del Dios.*

A fire truck interrupted him, roaring toward the bridge, sirens howling.

"*Los cabrones!*" He spat. "Running from their duty."

He limped into the road, waving his gun. The fire truck came shrieking on. Quin stumbled aside. Behind him, tires squealed and the truck crashed into the wreckage. When he looked back the wounded soldier of God was wrapped in yellow fire, howling curses in the Revelator's name.

He tramped on into broad avenues scattered with dead vehicles and roofed with rolling smoke. Shops had been looted, windows smashed. Shattered glass crunched under his boots. A frail little man with a smoke-stained white moustache stood guard in one doorway behind three dead bodies on the sidewalk.

"Watch it, mister!" He waved an antique pistol. "*Cuidado!*"

When Quin answered in English, he smiled with weary relief. He had little Spanish, and he wanted to talk. His name was Sarkis Kogian. He was Armenian. His stock was Oriental rugs. "Kashgars, Ispahans. Ghiordas prayer rugs. Genuine hand-knotted silk." His thin old voice quivered with emotion. The rugs were precious things, the secrets of their making lost before the Kwans spun the skyweb.

"If the fire comes—" Eloquently he shrugged. "I burn with them."

Limping on, Quin came into smoky canyons between rows of towering, empty-seeming hotels. Most of the inhabitants had already fled, but he came upon a small girl. Blue with cold and shivering, she stood over a body on the sidewalk, the body of a bearded man, a red-stained handkerchief spread over half the face.

"Sir?" she piped eagerly. "Are you the doctor?"

He had to say he was not a doctor.

"Father's sleeping," she told him. "Mother went for the doctor. It's a long time now. I hoped you were the doctor."

Blood had flowed around her feet.

"We are here from Auckland Down," she said. "Father had business with the Barrancas. We stayed in the hotel when the bad time came, 'cause there was nowhere to go. Today we had to leave, 'cause they said the hotel would burn. So we walked."

Trying not to sob, she looked away from the body.

"Bad men stopped us. Mad at Father 'cause he didn't understand. They pulled at his beard to see his Sunmark.

He didn't have one, 'cause he never liked the Kwans. But they shot him anyhow. They hurt him real bad.

"If the doctor—"

She couldn't stop the sobs. He wrapped his blanket around her.

"Perhaps—" It was hard to say. "I think your mother will come back."

He tramped on west till a wall of rubble blocked the streets. The smoky sky looked open beyond, the taller buildings shattered or leveled. He turned south along the barriers of debris to a broader avenue, where cranes and bulldozers had been used to clear a passage. They stood abandoned now.

Looking north through the gap, he saw a wide open space, walled with ruin. Kilometers long, it reached into towering flame and rolling smoke. Something off the broken skyweb had come down here. Firemen must have tried to reach the blaze, but they had given up and fled.

His spaceboots weren't meant for Earth. The velfast soles worn thin, every stick and bit of debris hurt his feet. Limping grimly on, looking for a way to the river bridge, he circled south again and west when he could, until two hard-eyed men stepped into his path. They wore red armbands and carried long wooden staves.

"*Alto! Ponte de cara!*"

He turned his face to let them see he had no Sunmark.

"*No hablo.*" He shrugged and spread his hands. "*No español.*"

"*Porque no?*" They scowled and peered again, and the second asked, "Why not?"

"I came from New Zealand," he said. "On business with the brokers."

"*Barranca? Bien.*" They looked at each other and gestured with their staves. "Okay, *amigo*. We are centurions of the Kingdom. A herald of the triple symbol has come to proclaim it. Come, brother. Kneel with us and seal your soul to the Revelator."

They marched him into an open space where he could

see the lurid sky. Rows of silent people knelt on a tiny patch of brown grass around the gold-colored statue of a man—stabbed with pain, he recognized his murdered father.

The statue stood on a gilded globe. A gang of men with sledges smashed at it till it caved in. The statue toppled. They shattered it to rubble on the ground.

"The park of *El Tycoon*." His escort spat on the ground. "Kneel, *amigo*. Kneel to the herald of Paradise!"

He knelt.

A black-bearded man with a red armband and a red-painted staff was climbing on the empty pedestal.

"*Óyeme!*" His voice pealed about the tower walls around the tiny park. "*Hermanos de la Revelácion—*"

Quin caught the gist of his shrill harangue. The prophecies of the Revelator had been fulfilled. The God of the triple sign, the black cross and the yellow crescent and the red disk of holy Earth—God in his wrath had sent the Behemoth of Space to free mankind from Satan and the Company. In the Revelator's sacred name, he proclaimed the fall of the Sun Tycoons and the triumph of *Los Santíssimos*.

Los demonios had been overthrown in space, but their evil seed remained on Earth. Every land must be bathed in blood and purified with fire. The holy *jihad* of God as Allah must continue until the whole planet had been cleansed in the blood of the Sunfolk.

"Kneel!" He broke into howling English. "Yield your blood to seal your sacred souls to the Triplex God. Extend your arms to the sacred blade, and bow your heads to baptism in your own sacrificial blood. Pledge your lives to slay the last of Satan's space-born spawn, and receive your own rewards in Paradise.

"*Muerte!*" he shrieked. "*Muerte! Muerte—*"

His tirade stopped. He turned to stare into the gloomy canyon behind him. A sudden rumbling filled it. Blinding light stabbed through the smoke from a high window. A few breaths later, the window vomited fire. Thunder crashed and echoed against the looming towers.

"*La Seguridad!*" the man beside him hissed. "*Los demonios*, offering us their evil blood—"

Quin ran.

Glancing back when he stopped to get his breath, he saw an ugly black battle machine roaring into the square. The banner of the Fleet fluttered on it, a bright gold Sun on a black field. A laser stabbed at it from another high window. Its long gun swung. Thunder boomed again.

The brothers of the Revelation had scattered. Nobody pursued him, but the fire was roaring closer down the smoke-filled canyons. Explosions boomed, and new towers of flame rose against the lurid sky. He limped faster.

He came into poorer streets, their pavements littered and broken, buildings already half ruined before anything fell out of space. Women stared from broken windows. Naked children huddled in doorways. Scarecrow men clustered on a corner, staring at him.

"*Adonde?*" A sick-faced youth stumbled to intercept him. "*Adonde va?*"

"Toward the bridge."

"Too late, *señor*." His arms spread and fell. "*El fuego*— the fire comes too fast."

"All these people? Why didn't they go? While they could?"

"*Señor*, we could not." A hopeless shrug. "*Somos pobres*. Many were ill. We had no wheels. No food, because the Synfare stopped. We had *nada—ninguna*—nowhere to go."

Coughing to a gust of bitter smoke, Quin slogged on through pools of filthy mud and the reek of human excrement. Blistering heat radiated across every intersection. A woman's shriek above him, cut off when her body crunched and flattened redly on the sidewalk. Frantic refugees streamed into the street, cursing or praying or dully silent, milling in aimless confusion.

Pushing on through human chaos and suffocating

smoke, he came to the bridge. Fugitives jammed it, swarming over stalled vehicles, over bloodied bodies. He plunged in among them. Guns thudded behind him. Shouts and screams and the conflagration bellowing. The human river swept him across.

On the bank beyond, he climbed aside to glance back. The dark war machine came lumbering out of roiling smoke. It roared onto the bridge. People ahead of it climbed on the railings, fell into the river, slid under its tracks.

He saw sudden yellow flame bloom beneath it. New smoke exploded. A heavy concussion jarred him. Beyond the river, a blazing tower toppled. A long section of the bridge exploded under the tank. It toppled and teetered, climbed out of the wreckage, came grinding on.

When the seeker struck Point Vermillion, Venerable Sire had been on his way to relieve his fellow Andromedan, Sagacious Sage, as research chief. Near enough to observe the attack, he escaped the queen by letting his supply craft drift cold. When she had flown on starward, he turned back home to alert the Elderhood.

Cluster One had the shape of a midget galaxy. Its core was the dwelling of the Eldermost, a heavy little asteroid born near some early star and rich in elements rare in the halo. Its spirals were mirror-shielded iceballs, gathered into orbit by the member peoples of the Elderhood to hold their missions and legations.

Arriving at the Andromedan residency, Venerable Sire found the news there ahead of him. The queen had flown far faster than he. Elderhood craft had seen her feeding on objects nearer the core-star.

He asked his minister what action had been taken.

"None," the minister replied. "Though I understand one of the Newlings wants the Council to schedule the matter for discussion."

"Discussion? I urge that we must act."

"What action is possible?"

"I don't know." His voice flickered and dimmed. "But I've seen the seeker. I watched her destroy a rash young Newling who ventured too near. I saw her swallow our observatory. I urge that something must be done."

"It's a matter for the Eldermost."

He asked the minister to request an audience.

"Not much chance of that." An indigo scowl. "The Eldermost seldom talks to anybody except a few old cronies and the Seniors of the Council."

When he insisted, the minister radiated his request. He was allowed to call. Nervous at first, because he had never spoken to the Eldermost, he began describing the invader. He/She/It interrupted to ask what had happened to the instruments and records at Point Vermillion.

"Your Ripeness, they were totally destroyed."

"They must be replaced."

"Your Ripeness, the seeker—"

"Forget the invader." The Eldermost hushed him. "Your own duties are more urgent. You will act at once to replace the equipment we lost at Point Vermillion and proceed without delay to establish a new observatory out on the halo fringe to watch for the returning Black Companion."

Revelator. *Self-styled Prophet of the Triplex God. A white-bearded mystic, living in hiding and appearing only in illicit holo broadcasts, he revised ancient texts to produce* The People's Revelation. *He led a holy* jihad *against "the demon-bred" Tycoons of the House of Kwan, promising eternal joy in the People's Eden for all who died for the holy cause. His appearances began in Sun Year 88, ceased with the skyweb's fall.*

19

QUIN TOOK COVER IN THE CHARRED RUBBLE BEHIND the broken foundation walls of a building demolished by some stray scrap of the falling skyweb. Crouching in the frosty dusk, he watched the war machine lurching toward him off the bridge. A few of the fugitives ran from it, but most stood defiantly staring.

It rumbled past him to stop a few hundred meters away. A square shape rose behind the gun turret and suddenly shone. A holo tank. The flag of the Kwans rippled in it, fading into a speaking head. Far-off as it was, he knew the golden beard, the flowing moustache, the Romanoff nose.

"Fellow Earthfolk—"

The amplified voice took a moment to reach him, roaring through the ruins, rolling back from the burning walls beyond the river. In spite of distortion, it rang with the old hypnotic power.

"Fellow citizens of Earth, I speak to you, wherever you are, from Azteca Sun Country. I am Jason Kwan, Admiral of the Halo. We are just back home from the war in space. We have witnessed frightful terrors and unspeakable disasters, but we are not defeated.

"I myself have suffered grievous loss. You may not have heard the dreadful news, because the censor tried to suppress it, but my own dear father, Tycoon Fernando, has been murdered.

"That dire crime will be avenged. Sun Security has now at last identifed his killers. Two men were involved. A Holyfolk terrorist, Benito Barranca, was found dead at the scene—killed by my father in his own defense. The accomplice is still at large.

"This second assassin is a native of the halo named Quin Dain. His motives are obscure and his whereabouts unknown. Security suspects that he got downside in time to survive. His description will be broadcast, and rewards will be offered.

"The killer of my father!" A quaver of seeming emotion. "I beg each of you to help us apprehend him. And I implore every one of you to help us cope with the most desperate emergency of all human history.

"Dear, dear brother Earthmen, I know what you have suffered from the single alien attacker that crept past our Fleet in space while we fought the monster swarms. My heart brims with feeling for all your own pain and loss, but I rejoice to be back among you.

"I beg to share my hopes and my high resolution with you. The space aliens have wounded us severely, but they are not invincible. We have beaten them in space, but we discover now that we have greater enemies here on Earth.

"Among them are the Chens!

"Would-be tyrants, traitors in the House of Kwan, they have betrayed mankind. They tried to deny that we had enemies in space. They infiltrated the Fleet and Security to destroy all the evidence of the planned space attack. With their mad ambition—with their treason!—they weakened our means to defend you.

"Yet, in spite of their black-minded arrogance, we have won the war in space. Our laser fire knocked that cowardly attacker into the Pacific Ocean. We doubt that others will dare come so near.

"Now, my dear brother Earthmen, we must join together to repair what the aliens and the Chens have done. My heart aches for each of you. But, my brother men, I have come to bring you a new age of human greatness. The skywires are lost. Our world's heart has ceased to beat. Communication has been interrupted. Transportation is stalled. Synfare factories are still. Even our limited existing stocks of natural foods are in danger of spoilage. We face famine. Suffering. Social chaos.

"Appalling news, my friends. I suffer with you. Yet this disaster is not the end. Let us make it instead a proof of our shining destiny.

"Join me, friends! With your faith and toil and courage, we can rebuild our shattered world. We can end the looting. We can find energy to make you safe again, to let our cities live again, to make food and move it. The skywires have fallen, but not the House of Kwan. My great father is dead, but I shall take the reins of life and peace. Begging your loyalty, I promise victory.

"Yet, even here on our wounded Earth, we face another foe. An enemy more evil than the Chens and more dreadful than anything in space. The sinister monster who calls himself the Revelator!

"I know most of you have heard him. Some of you may have been deluded by the sanctimony of a white-bearded face and a lying voice that speaks from nowhere.

"Listen, fellow Earthman! I have no quarrel with those who call themselves the Holyfolk. I do have a revelation of my own—one that may shock you.

"There is no Revelator!

"His holocasts have been a monstrous hoax. On the

trail of my father's killer, Sun Security has penetrated the terrorist underground. What they discovered has stunned us all. The self-proclaimed Revelator—that screeching rogue who claims to speak for his Triplex God—the Revelator is a computer simulation!

"The assassins—"

Hoots and jeers drowned Jason's booming.

"*Mentiroso!*" haggard men were howling. "Liar! Liar!"

The long gun tipped and swung to menace them. Most of them ignored it, closing in around the war machine, hurling rocks. The holo screen darkened and crumpled. The machine roared out of the mob and stopped again.

"—Fleet units still safe in orbit," Jason's voice rang out again. "Our Security forces all over the planet are restoring contact. As my father's rightful heir, I have assumed command.

"And I have means to feed you. The fall of the skyweb is a cruel loss, but I can promise power to keep our world alive—energy from a new and better source.

"Fusion—"

Dim forms had followed the machine, hurling missiles through the smoky gloom to crash and clatter on its armor. The long gun spat sudden flame, its projectile screaming toward the burning city. The jeering shadows darted closer. Rocks hailed on the machine. It roared suddenly away.

Quin lay shivering for a time in the rubble, pondering what he had heard. If Jason had recaptured Thorsen and recovered the reactor, he could hope for nothing.

But if Thorsen was still free—

Nerved again by that narrow chance, he climbed back over the shattered foundation wall. Keeping out of the mob, keeping the murky glare of the city behind him, he found a road that should lead toward Ciudad Barranca.

The smoky dusk was closing in. He limped on as long as he could see the wreckage and debris on the pavement. Blundering at last into an empty vehicle, he crawled inside and tried to start it. A feeble light came on to show the hole where a bullet must have come through the windshield and dark blood dried on the seat, but the power cells were too dead to move it.

Huddled there, too cold and tired and hungry to sleep, he tried to imagine what might happen in Jason's war with the Revelator. He could see no winner.

Though Jason had boasted of Fleet units in space, all their bases and supply facilities must have come down with the skyweb. The surviving Security forces on Earth were surely too few to crush the Holyfolk now, when the Tycoons had failed in almost a hundred years of trying.

Yet he could see no victory for the centurions and soldiers of the Triplex God. Perhaps they were elated, with all the Revelator's predictions of doom so miraculously fulfilled, but food and warmth for the Earthbound billions could hardly come so magically.

His own odds looked no better. Desperate men would be hunting him now, hungry for Jason's reward.

He slept at last, fitfully, through nightmares in which he and Mindi were in panic flight across the dying Earth, hiding from strange-winged monsters diving from the sky.

A hoarse yell woke him. Something banged on the broken windshield. Lying still, he heard boots tramping away. He dozed again, until a dismal dawn. The smoky sky had lowered, and a biting north wind swirled a few sooty snowflakes.

He drank the rest of his water and climbed out of the cab. A delivery van, he now discovered, lettered *Panadería Eldorado*. The looters had left him not even a crust of bread.

Lightheaded with hunger, he plodded stiffly on. The roadside was cluttered with things thrown away. A naked doll, toy spacecraft, clocks and pictures and holo receivers, books and tapes and wind-scattered letters. Never anything he could eat.

He came to a wide avenue with a blank wall beyond it. An endless barrier of gray concrete, three meters high, topped with sharp-spiked wire strung on insulators. It was hung with yellow-lettered signs.

SUN COMPANY CONCESSION
AZTECA TERMINAL POWER AUTHORITY
ADMISSION RESTRICTED
BY THE TYCOON'S COMMAND

He limped south outside the wall. A few kilometers
down the road he came to a gate, a huddle of people
outside. An ugly black war machine blocked the gate, Sun
banner flying, long gun leveled. A loudspeaker crashed
above the mutter of the mob.

"Warning! Stand away! Admission is restricted to Sun
citizens and Company employees, registered and identi-
fied . . . Warning! Stand away—"

The crowd was growing. Men with red armbands har-
anged it. Most carried wooden staves; a few had laser
guns.

"Fat cat *cabrones!*"

A yellow-haired man bellowing at the mob.

"*Muerte! Muerte a todos los demonios!* They've got
food—hoards of food inside the fence. Hoards of everything. All for us when we take it. *Amigos*, join the holy
jihad! If we die, the Triplex God rewards us."

Skirting the crowd, he limped on south. The streets
grew emptier. He crossed a wide park whose trees were
bare. The buildings beyond it looked newer and taller,
not yet touched by the fire. The roiling smoke was far
behind him now, and no space debris had fallen here.

A silent car raced around the corner to stop in front
of him. A green globe on top of it flashed *Guardias Barrancas*. The driver was a green-capped black.

"*Señor! Qué tiene en Ciudad Barranca?*"

"I want—" Reeling with exhaustion, he fumbled for
sanity. "I want to see Claudio Barranca."

"Sorry, mister. You ain't the only one. We're full up
with refugees."

"Let me—let me talk to him."

"*El Cacique?*" A sardonic hoot. "You think he'd talk
to a filthy rat?"

"Tell him—" He groped for words that might win him food and warmth and some shred of hope. "Tell him I'm Quin Dain. From the halo. The stepson of Dr. Olaf Thorsen."

The driver looked at his companion.

"Could be, mister." The other man shrugged and stared back at him. "What's it to *el Cacique?*"

"Tell him I know his niece. Mindi Zinn."

"*Quién?*"

"Tell him—" Quin shivered in the icy wind. "I knew his son. Benito Barranca."

"*El Señor Benito?*" The driver scowled, perhaps impressed. "*Verdad?*"

He had to take a chance. "Tell him I saw Benito Barranca dying."

"Dying?" The driver leaned to squint into his face. "*Adonde?*"

"In Coto—Coto High." His teeth chattered. "When the Tycoon was killed."

"Wait, mister." The men nodded at each other. "We'll call."

The car window slid shut. The driver reached for a microphone. Huddled against the wind, he waited a long time.

"Okay, *señor*." The driver eyed him with a wary respect. "They want you at *la quinta*."

They locked him into a metal cage in the rear of the car, let him out again on a drive before a row of tall white columns. Two more green-clad blacks escorted him into the building and up to a bedroom.

"*El Cacique* receives you as a guest." They stayed on guard at the door, as if he were a dangerous prisoner. "He'll see you when he can."

They let him shower. The steaming spray was sheer delight. They brought him a clean blue shipsuit that fitted so well he thought it must have been Benito's. A tray of hot food left him wearily content. He was sprawled on the bed, half asleep in spite of himself, when they called him.

"Come, *señor. El Cacique* wants you now."

Trying groggily to rouse himself, he followed them into an elevator and out into a long corner room rich with relics of the dying past. Deep carpets, carved marble, antique books, heavy-framed paintings dark with age. No holo tanks anywhere.

Massive chairs were drawn around a massive table, but he saw nobody. Heavier snow was swirling beyond the huge windows now, hiding everything outside. For a moment, the place became an island of refuge from the sea of terror and death he had crossed.

"*Señor?*" A gesture from his escort. "You may go in."

In a smaller room beyond an archway, Claudio Barranca pushed a hooded holophone aside and rose behind a barrier of computer consoles. A lean, compact man with a hard, dark face, his eyes the dead-black color of carbonaceous meteors.

"You say you're the Tycoon killer?"

Those cold black eyes and the coldly brittle voice shattered his brief illusion of escape. The chill still in him, he felt exhausted and inadequate, felt half sick with fear of some stupid blunder that might betray this last narrow hope.

"I'm Quin Dain." He felt too numb and dull to invent any clever deception. "Accused in the Tycoon's killing."

An expressionless nod. "I heard the admiral's holocast."

"I was there." Wondering how much to say, he tried not to shrink from those merciless eyes. "I saw the actual killer—dying." His voice caught. "It was Benito."

"My son." That dark mask had hardly changed, but savagery flared in the narrowed eyes. "A hero of *la causa.*"

Quin couldn't help recoiling.

"Sir—" He tried to steady his voice. "I've come looking for Dr. Olaf Thorsen. My dead mother's—"

"Tell me how you got here." Barranca cut him off. "How you got out of Coto."

"I was lucky." He wondered what could warm Barranca's deadly stare. "Slipping in, Benito had left an elevator blocked open. I rode that to Thorsen's lab. When Coto came down, I escaped in the spaceplane he was building for Benito."

"Benito's plane?" A tremor of surprise. "Where is it now?"

"Where I left it." He nerved himself to face that probing stare. "Sir, I'm here from Janoort. I came hoping for Thorsen's help. Out in the halo, we need his engines to keep us alive—"

"So?" A derisive rasp. "Why ask me?"

"Because—because we're fighting the aliens in space." He caught his breath.

"Sir, I'm not alone. Runesong—the being my mother called a skyfish—is with me on the spaceplane. She'll die here unless I get her back where she belongs. But her people have a weapon against the things that hit the skyweb."

"A weapon? Where?"

"Aboard the wreck of a drifting spacecraft that Jason Kwan disabled. With luck enough—"

A snort of disbelief.

"Runesong—" Desperately he plowed on. "Runesong says they can be killed. She calls them seekers. Cyborgs. They're breeding now, out in a Trojan asteroid. She says they'll be back."

Barranca stiffened, dead eyes blazing.

"They were sent." His raspy voice had risen. "They have done their work. The skyweb has fallen, and the Tycoons are dead. They will not trouble us again."

Quin looked away, into the driving snow beyond the window.

"Sir?" He nerved himself to try again. "May I see Dr. Thorsen?"

"You're two days late." That fanatic fire had faded into casual-seeming malice. "He's gone. His engine with him."

"Gone where, sir?"

"You might ask my niece." A harsh, ironic little laugh. "Mindi Zinn. Your own first love, I understand?"

"I loved her," Quin muttered. "Once."

"People did." Dark fire lit Barranca's eyes again. "She charmed me. Charmed Benito. When she came here to live after her parents died. Almost a daughter to me. We trusted her—too far."

Quin waited, uncertain what to say.

"*Puta!* Infatuating poor Benito." A burst of brittle passion. "Her devil's face! Her yellow mark! Her foul Sun kin! We should have suspected. We never did."

He quenched that flash of feeling.

"A slick little bitch." A sardonic rasp. "Our double agent in Security—long enough to sell us out. Slick enough to get away with Thorsen and his engine. Escaped while the rocks were raining out of space."

"Where did they go?"

"Would I tell you?" A scornful snarl. "The Tycoon's by-blow? I know what you are, and you're a fool to think of any reward. If you gave Benito his opening, it wasn't for love of the cause."

Barranca sat silent for a time as if to control emotion. The dead eyes turned critical.

"Kerry McLenn? Your stepfather?"

Quin nodded, cheered by a hint of feeling in that gritty voice.

"I knew him. In the barrio long ago, when he was still a child. A better man than you are, Dain, when he was eight years old. Hauling goods for the cause in his toy wagon."

Quin stared.

"You were the Santissimo agent? Your cell name was Saladin?"

"Long ago." Barranca shrugged. "McLenn served us then, but we owe you nothing now." That hint of warmth was gone. "All I want from you is Benito's spaceplane. Stolen property—"

The computer hummed, and he turned toward it.

"You Santissimos!" Desperate, Quin raised his voice. "You're finished. Admiral Kwan says your Revelator is only a hoax."

"The Kwans are damned!" Barranca swung back, glaring at him. "I know the holy Revelator. I'll follow him to Paradise."

Barranca's voice had a sudden ring of iron, and his black eyes loomed mad as the eyes of the white-bearded image Quin had seen in that computer simulation.

"We are building the Eden of the Triplex God to be an eternal haven for the chosen. We build it on the bones of the unholy, out of famine and terror and death. Those who die at His work will be born again in Paradise."

The computer kept on buzzing.

"My inquisitors will find out where you left Benito's spaceplane." Malice edged the loud mad voice. "If you die telling, you'll find no room in Eden for a hell-born bastard."

He swung to the insistent machine, and the green-clad blacks took Quin back to the room where he had been. The winter dusk had fallen. Lights came on before they reached it, flickering unsteadily.

The guards stood watch at the open door. The room was cold. He asked for food, asked for blankets. The guards merely stared. Pacing the floor to keep warm, he wondered if Barranca himself had created the computer simulation of the Revelator. The gravity of Earth grew too heavy, and he lay down across the bed.

An hour past midnight, Jason Kwan attacked.

Estrella Navarro was a raven-haired beauty, with brains enough and a mind of her own. She was born in Incamarica. Her lowsider mother had been chief design engineer for the surface power net that fed a third of the continent from the gravity terminal at Pampas Down.

Her biological sire was Maximilian Chen, a Company expert who lived with her mother while the project was under construction. When it was done, he accepted a promotion for it and returned to Coto High.

With enough of such Sunfolk, her embittered mother went on to design a new power net around Sahel Down and marry a Saudi banker who wanted no whimpering whelps of Abaddon in his house.

They sent Estrella to be raised by the Daughters of Fatima, holy zealots who tried and failed to instill their ritual contempt for the Kwans and the Company. Despising them, she used to spend her midnight prayer hours standing at the window of her convent cell, eyes lifted to the skyweb.

A splendid arch of woven fire, it spanned the whole north sky, many-colored marker lights and navigation beacons glittering like diamond frost all along the wires. The web became an enchanted kingdom in her imagination, ruled by gold-maned gods.

Jason Kwan became her idol. She kept a contraband holo of him hidden under her mattress and nursed improbable dreams that he would somehow come to carry her into that shining skyworld. Toiling toward that vision, she won a scholarship to the Kwan College of Space Medicine at Azteca Down.

Graduating with honors enough, she applied for Sun citizenship and duty in space. Her application was denied. All lowsider quotas, they told her, had been filled years ago. Lacking registered Sun paternity, she wasn't eligible even to be tested.

Grown beautiful, she rejected a handsome Synfare billionaire because he wore no Sunmark. Working as a temporary medic at the Azteca terminal hospital, she kept on waiting for her break.

She was still there when the seeker knocked her dreamworld out of the sky. Making her way through wrecked streets to the hospital, she worked without relief for thirty hours patching up the injured.

One of them was Jason Kwan.

Still on duty when his shuttle crashed, she led the rescue team that pulled him out of the wreckage. Though hurt, he was still fit enough to enjoy her eager consolations.

His cocky charm rekindled her old infatuation, and elation made her lovelier. In Jason's bed at Company House, she found her broken dreams restored. What if the aliens had crushed the Company? The Kwans had never been vanquished. Fusion power would energize his new empire.

And she would be his empress.

Armageddon.   *The final war between the hosts of the Triplex God and the space-bred hordes of Satan, foreshadowed in ancient texts, prophesied by the Revelator, fulfilled in dreadful cataclysm, and recorded in the annals of the damned. It came in an evil age when no man could buy or sell, save that he wore the mark of the Beast. The harvest of mankind was ripe, and blood came out of the winepress. The Revelator called upon the Triplex God to pour out his wrath, and there fell upon men a great hail out of heaven. The Sun Tycoons were fallen, and all their Babylons on Earth. Their plagues came in one day, death and mourning, and famine; and they were utterly burned with fire.*

20

SOMETHING WOKE HIM FROM A DREAM OF JANOORT. He had come with the engine and found Halo Station stricken. Jason's missiles had cratered the snow and brought his spaceplane down. Kerry and Noël lay dying in a shattered tunnel, blue-faced and gasping for air. Pinned under the wreckage, he couldn't move to help them.

Mindi stood near, saved from harm by her bright Sun-mark. He begged her to start the engine to let them breathe. She laughed at him instead and turned to look for Benito Barranca, who came stalking through the ruins, red knife slashing, cutting down people trying to escape.

Benito dropped the blade when he saw Mindi, and she ran into his arms. Her eager kiss changed him into Jason Kwan, who grinned at Quin indolently.

"Tough luck, brother," Jason drawled. "But you've got no Sunmark—"

Something crashed, and the dream was gone. The weight of the wreckage was the gravity of Earth. He sat up, shivering with his own sweat and blinking at the light. His prison room was cold and still and empty. The guards were gone.

Silence all around him, till something crashed again. Falling glass jangled. The lights flickered and went out. He rolled off the bed and groped in the dark for his boots. Another crash, closer. Light blazed through the window. He stumbled to look out.

A hot white point floated high in the black sky. Ciudad Barranca and the park he had crossed lay naked to its savage glare. The snow had stopped falling, but it lay white on roofs and streets and the empty park. He heard no sound, saw no motion anywhere.

The light drifted lower, slowly fading. He saw clots of shadow darting among the leafless trees, spitting fire. Night came back. He heard the war machines roaring closer. Their guns thudded, and the building shuddered. Hard-heeled boots came pounding down the corridors. Sudden light dazzled him.

"Dain?" A hoarse shout. "You're Quin Dain?"

"Who wants to know?"

"Sun Security."

"My name—" He groped for survival. "My name's McLenn."

"*Falso!*" A sharp voice out of the glare. "*Es el asesino.*"

"We've got you, Dain. Stand where you are." Boots thumped around him. "I am Captain Abu Rasul, acting for Admiral Kwan. You are under detainment, charged with killing the Sun Tycoon."

He squinted into the light, trying to see Rasul.

"I am Quin Dain," he admitted. "I didn't kill the Tycoon, but I know who did. I can tell you—"

"Save all that." Cold steel clicked around his wrists. "Just come along."

"I want to see Admiral Kwan. He knows me."

"He knows you killed his father—"

"*Fuego!*" A shout in the corridors. "*Fuego!*"

The building was on fire. They marched him down smoke-choked stairs. In the bitter air outside, he heard guns crashing. Another sudden star blazed in the sky. It showed war machines stopped in the street and a huddle of Barranca's guards, disarmed and shuffling uneasily in the snow.

"*Mueva! Pronto!*"

They shoved him into the back of a captured guard car. It lurched away, skidding on the snow, following one of the armored machines. Locked in the jolting cage, he was numb and shaking with the cold, yet he tried to see what he could.

That high star was gone, but new flames towered from burning buildings all around them. The tank led them out of Ciudad Barranca and back across the empty park. Off in the east, low clouds above Azteca were lined with lurid red. They came to the terminal concession. The mobs around it blocked the road. Blazing bonfires lit a black-clad figure on a rooftop, screeching into the night.

"*Muerte!*" A savage chorus from the mob. "*Muerte a todos!*"

Death to them all.

Men with red armbands surged toward the car, waving staves and throwing rocks. Glass sprayed him from a shattered window. A machine gun rattled. He saw men crumpling into the snow.

"*El Revelador...*" Mad voices screaming. "*... venganza de Dios...*"

The car slewed and roared into the mob, jolting over bodies. A new light bloomed overhead. They lurched between two machines now defending the gate. Inside the wall, the car stopped in a court behind a blinking sign.

Sun Security, Azteca Detention Center.

A stark prison, guarded by white-turbaned Sikhs. They tapped his name into a computer and locked him into an unheated cell. He spent the rest of the night there, shivering on a bare iron ledge.

The corridors were busy with black-bearded Sikhs and manacled prisoners. They brought him no food, no information. Noon was near before two of them unlocked the cell to march him into a grimy little office. He had to stand until Jason Kwan strolled in.

"Well, Dain!" A tone of casual mockery. "Never thought I'd meet you here."

Jason Kwan in a torn yellow dutysuit, right eye patched, one arm in a dirty sling. His visible eye was lit with a reckless elation, as if the space attack and the skyweb's fall and the Revelator's threats were a relished challenge.

"Security says you killed my father?" A tone of amused inquiry. He sat on the corner of cluttered desk, swinging a scuffed Fleet boot. "I must say you keep surprising me."

"I didn't—" He had to gulp for his voice. "I didn't kill the Tycoon."

"Security says you did." Jason seemed not to care. "They reported at first that you died on the spot." The green eye narrowed. "You admit you were there?"

"I was."

"How'd you get in?"

"The Tycoon—" His heart throbbed hard, and he had to get his breath. "The Tycoon sent for me. He had loved my mother. He said I was his son."

"Huh?" A lowering scowl. "You claim you're my half-brother?"

"That's what he believed."

"No matter to me." An untroubled shrug. "How'd you get away?"

"I hid in Thorsen's lab till the skyweb was hit. Got out in a spaceplane—"

"Thorsen's?" Jason slid off the desk. "Where is it now?"

"Where I landed. Useless, with the fusion engine gone—"

"I've got Thorsen and his engine." The nonchalance gone, hard purpose rang in Jason's voice. "I can use the spaceplane. To reach Fleet units trapped in orbit now, with their bases gone."

"I want the engine." Quin straightened himself to meet that hard green eye. "For Janoort—"

"Wake up, Dain!" A sardonic laugh. "Look where we are! Under siege here. Ten million maniacs yelling for our blood. And you're raving to rescue a handful of outlaws marooned on a snowball."

"Sir, it's not just them. With Earth in trouble, the halo can be a better place—"

"Listen, Dain." Jason strode closer. "I'm trapped here. My shuttle crashed, coming in. I've got nothing else able to climb off the Earth. The spaceplane can, if and when Barranca's maniacs break through the wall."

"So let's have it!" Brittle impatience. "Tell me where you left the craft."

"Sir, here's an offer." He tried not to tremble. "Get me back to it, with an engine to run it, and I think I can tell you who the Revelator is."

"Barranca?" Jason shrugged. "Do you really want a bargain?"

"I want a way back to Janoort."

"Okay." Behind the flowing beard and the golden Sunmark and the strong Kwan nose, Jason was suddenly radiant with that old genial charm. "Brother or not, I've always rather liked you. And I can use you now. I need that craft and a pilot for it. Play my game, and take the plane when I'm through with it."

"Thanks! But I've played your games before—"

"Think again, brother." Jason's silky voice grew softer, genial no longer. "Don't forget you've been condemned to die." Bright-nailed fingers flicked his whole existence away. "Sentenced in absentia. We've set your execution for midnight.

"Your choice, brother. Talk or die."

"Sir, Janoort can't wait—"

"You've got your option." Jason tossed the bright hair back. "Your guards will have instructions. If you decide you want to live, just let them know."

A wave at the Sikhs to take him away.

Back in his cell, they gave him a lump of hard bread and a plastic bag of water. He ate the bread slowly, chewing till it turned sweet in his mouth, and watched the two Sikhs silently watching him.

In the windowless cell, he had few clues to the time. His guards were changed. Hungry again, he knew that a good many hours had passed. He paced the cell and lay on the cold iron bench and paced again, and still he found no hope.

Two new guards arrived. The corporal unlocked his door. Midnight? Dry throat constricting, he scanned the beard-veiled faces and saw no hint of anything. Expecting to be taken away, he hardly saw the slim figure slipping past them into the cell.

"Quin—?"

An uncertain whisper. He spun to find Mindi with him in the dimness, peering at him warily. Lithely slight in a black-and-gold Security dutysuit, she recoiled from the steel clang of the closing door.

"Mindi—"

A gasp of pain. The lover of his father's killer, was she now to be his own executioner? He sat back on the cold metal bed.

"You hate me." Her gold Sunmark shone in the gloom, and her voice was very small. "I knew you would."

He could only nod.

She stood looking at him, slowly shaking her head. The dark Sikhs stood silent beyond the bars, watching them both. Faintly, through the stale prison stinks, he caught her haunting scent.

"I loved you, Quin. When I could love. I had to see you, when Jason told me you were here." She glanced at the guards. "He wants to know where you left the space-plane."

"I don't want to tell him."

"Perhaps you shouldn't." She sat far from him, on the other end of the shelf. He caught the wildwood again, a fragrance recalled from Janoort so long ago when their love was everything. "I guess you despise me."

"It's hard," he whispered. "Hard to hate you."

With a wry glance at the listening Sikhs, she dropped her voice.

"Forget the spaceplane." A tiny shrug. "With the mobs already ramming through the walls, Jason's too busy to think about it now." Her face looked pinched with pain. "While we're both alive, I want you to know why I've done what I've done.

"If—if you'll listen?"

He nodded, trying not to feel too much.

"Please, Quin! I hope you'll try to understand." She leaned to see his face. "You know what happened to my parents. A dreadful time for me. My uncle helped me through it. Brought me here and gave me everything.

"Claudio—Claudio Barranca." New tension trembled in her voice. "A strange man! Intense, gifted, always terribly busy. I never quite understood him, but he was always kind and generous to me. I loved him more than my aunt.

"My mother's sister. She had given up her Sunmark to marry him. She must have been sorry by the time I knew her. Spent most of her time in what I thought was charity work and never seemed to care much about me.

"My Uncle Claud—" A wry twist of her lips. "I used to pity him, because he seemed so terribly alone. Even before my aunt was killed. Murdered the way my parents had been, with the Holyfolk suspected. I thought they must have hated her for her Sunblood, even without the mark.

"He seemed to need me, and I—I loved him, Quin!"

A quiver in her voice.

"He was generous, with a lot to give me. He had—he seemed to have the best of both worlds. Wealth. Influence. Exciting friends downside and skyside. And Benito for a son—"

Quin flinched.

"Please!" A wistful whisper. "Hear me out."

He nodded, bleakly waiting.

"Try to see him, Quin. As I saw him then. Ben and I finished growing up together. He was good to me, fond of me. Always teasing, like an older brother. Till—till we fell in love. Not that I'd forgotten you.

"I longed—" A tremor in her voice. "Longed for you, Quin. Treasured all I could remember. But you were lost forever—I thought you were. And I let Ben take your place. He had looks and dash and style. A reckless charm that caught me—when I was with him, nothing else seemed to matter. I was happy here, with him and my uncle, till I went into Security."

She saw him stiffen.

"I had to join, Quin. Thought I had to, anyhow. A duty to my parents. The agents kept insisting because my life with my uncle and Benito gave me so many downside contacts. And I had no notion—"

Her quick little shrug was half a shudder.

"No warning of what I was about to find. Facts I couldn't believe till I read Security files. My aunt was *in* Security—she must have gone to them when she began to suspect my uncle. I saw reports from her.

"It was dreadful, Quin. Dreadful! She'd got evidence that my parents had been tortured because the Holyfolk thought they knew something about 'evil space aliens.' Security concluded that my uncle had my aunt killed because he suspected her.

"Even Benito—"

She flinched as if with actual pain, teeth sunk deep into a quivering lip.

"I couldn't believe what he was—not till I came to see the hatred in him—hatred for the Kwans and the Company—hidden under all his dash and charm. Despising even me—" Her hushed voice shook. "Because I wore the Sunmark. Because he couldn't."

Her hands quivered and clenched on the edge of the cold iron shelf.

"A terrible time, after I knew." A sharp little laugh. "Ben had begun begging me to join Security—not knowing I was already in. To penetrate it for the Santissimos. Working for the cause, he told me, would erase my yellow curse.

"At first I made excuses. I got back to Coto High for a visit with your mother and tried to get out of Security. Of course they wouldn't let me quit. Because this was the break they'd always wanted.

"Their best chance to identify the Revelator.

"I had to come back." She shivered again. Huddled on the hard bench, she sat a long time staring blankly at the blankly staring Sikhs. "You can't imagine the hell it was. Trying to pretend all the hate I didn't have and hide the fear I did. Letting Benito—letting him . . ."

Her voice died. Unhappy eyes on him, she shook her head.

"That's why," she whispered again. "Why I came here now. To tell you I had to do what I did, because I knew they'd kill me if they ever discovered what I was. But, Quin—" Her whisper quickened. "If you think I knew Ben meant to kill your father—"

Her hand reached toward his. An impulsive little gesture that she quickly checked.

"I didn't! Security had heard about a plot, but there'd been a hundred plots. I knew the Santissimos had somebody in the Tycoon's quarters. But I never guessed—guessed Ben was rash enough to strike the blow himself."

Trembling, she reached out again.

"Believe me, Quin! Please believe."

"I—" He gulped and leaned to catch her hand. "I do."

"I hoped—hoped you would." Tears shone in her eyes, and her cold fingers clung a long time before she gathered herself to go on. "I had a bad time afterward. Suspected of complicity. I was under what we call severe interrogation."

He felt her shiver.

"I thought you were really dead, till they took me to see Ben's body. His face laserburned. I said at first I thought it was you. Hoping, Quin—hoping to give you time—"

"Mindi—"

The ache in his throat stopped his voice, and his eyes stung with sudden tears. Gripping her quivering fingers, he moved to draw her closer—and checked himself when he saw the frowning Sikhs.

"Finally—" Her own voice broke. "Finally they let me go. Sent me back here to look for Benito." A bitter little smile. "I kept on digging into my uncle's links with the Santissimos. Learned more—"

A sudden muffled thunder stopped her. The building shook. Up and down the corridor, steel doors clattered. Prisoners cursed. In some near cell, one began chanting prayers to *El Dios Triplicar, en el nombre del Revelador*. He heard hoarse commands and pounding boots. Gunfire, and then a thin scream of pain. Through it all, the impassive Sikhs stood fast.

Mindi listened silently.

"One man I found was Olaf Thorsen." With a wry little shrug, she turned back to him. "With his fusion engine. Benito had bribed and tricked him into defecting. My uncle had jailed him here in the Ciudad. Hidden in a secret shop, tricked into building more engines."

"Where is he now?"

Lips tight, she shook her head at the unmoving Sikhs. Somewhere outside, the chanted prayer went on. Closer gunshots echoed in the corridor. Another dull reverberation shook the walls.

"My uncle's attacking. His Santissimo hordes—" Fine teeth against her lip. "Jason can't hold out forever."

"Barranca?" He blinked at her. "He really is the Revelator?"

"Something else I learned." She raised her voice, with a bleak little grin at the listening Sikhs. "Claudio Barranca has always been the Revelator, speaking through a computer simulation."

He saw no change in their hard stare.

"I'd guessed long ago," she said. "But we didn't get the truth till the fall of the skyweb stopped the outlaw holocasts. Barranca needed Olaf's fusion engines to power them again. Pressuring Olaf to rush more of them out, he gave himself away.

"A hard thing, Quin. I'd loved him so long I hoped I was wrong. The truth was so—cruel. He didn't seem surprised when I confronted him. He admitted that the Revelator was only a secret program in his business system. Wanted me to help him get it back on the air. And he warned me—"

Her hand had strayed to the Sunmark on her cheek.

"I said I'd talk to Olaf. We got away that night in a Security car. I told Jason what I'd found out. That's when he sent the Sikhs into Ciudad Barranca. They didn't catch Barranca—"

Boots came marching down the corridor. Two new guards arriving. Quin relaxed a little when he saw they hadn't come for him. The turbaned sergeant spoke to Mindi. Listening, she nodded slowly, teeth against her lip.

"It's over," she told him. "The Santissimos have overrun the walls. My uncle's leading them, calling himself the Revelator's son. The sergeant says Jason's forces are deserting or surrendering. All except the Sikhs."

She nodded at them, in rueful gratitude.

"Santissimos everywhere, he says. Murdering, raping. All Jason still holds is the Company center. Offices and barracks, the arsenal and the detention building. And the sergeant says—"

She caught both his hands.

"He says they're going to blow us up. They captured a nuclear device in the wreck of Jason's shuttle. My uncle

sent a warning that they've got it into the sewers, somewhere under us.

"Set to go off at midnight."

The Newlings were novices in the Elderhood, recent arrivals
in Cluster One. Their small official moonlets occupied the
orbits of a single tiny snowball. Whitewing was their Council
member, not yet at ease in office.

Aged for a Newling, she could recall eldermothers born on
the interstellar flight from their native star. Yet, too often, the
elderfolk seemed to take her for an untried child. She felt more
than annoyed when Cyan Gem arrived with her pet planetic,
begging the Council to grant probationary contact to its species.

She reviewed the filed reports that the core-star observatory
had been able to transmit before the planetic attackers destroyed
it. Grudgingly she went at last to inspect the pathetic creature
itself, in the bubble of hot and noxious gases its life required.
She listened while Cyan Gem translated its curious vibratory
speech.

She was not impressed.

Though half a cycle younger than even Cyan Gem, the
creature was feeble with age and visibly ill. Its behavior betrayed
grotesque adaptations to its primal jungles. She doubted that
such things could ever adapt to the halo, and she saw nothing
about it to justify any sort of contact.

"Why bother?" she inquired. "What have they to give us?"

"They're young," Cyan Gem admitted. "Still driven too
often by primitive reflexes. But all our races once were young.
All we ask is some initial formal contact, hoping it will lead
to recognition for them, a bit of space in the halo, and freedom
to share our culture. Their potential is surely worth tending."

Whitewing had found no potential.

"They're in trouble," Cyan Gem persisted. "Their technological ingenuity has run too far ahead of their altruism.
They are in danger now from their own creativity. They are
in more immediate danger from the heat-seeking invader that

destroyed Point Vermillion. Too soon, they'll be in even graver danger from the Black Companion."

"A necessary test." A grave blue glow. "If they survive, we'll petition the Council for trial contact. Until they do, we've job enough to establish our own evolutionary fitness."

Black Companion. *A remote binary companion of the Sun, composed of twin black holes. The Sun's orbit around it is an immense ellipse, the estimated period 30 million years. Periastron passages are never close enough to disrupt planetary orbits or even the solar halo, but they have been epochs of cataclysm. Collisions with cosmic debris around the black holes and radiation flashes from their accretion disks have caused such periodic events of mass extinction as the disappearance of the dinosaurs.*

SHRIEKING BEDLAM IN THE CORRIDORS. YELLED COM-mands and curses. Gunfire crashing. The chanted prayer became a Spanish hymn, praising *El Revelador*. Ragged voices joined. Yet the Sikh guards stood firm at their post, glaring stonily through the bars.

"I spoke to them," Mindi whispered. "Begging them to let you go. But they honor the Sikh tradition and follow the orders of the Kwan."

"If they do—" He swung to face them. "They've got instructions. To bring me to Jason, whenever I agree to guide him to the spaceplane. Tell them I'm ready!"

He saw her touch the Sunmark on her cheek. He thought she shivered, but in a moment she was back at the bars, urgently appealing in a tongue he didn't know. The sergeant scowled at him.

"Sir?" Soft English words he understood. "You now wish to obey Admiral Kwan?"

"I do."

"*Bien!*" A grim-faced nod. "Though perhaps you wait too long."

The Sikhs unlocked the door and led them down the corridor, past singing men and cursing men, frantic men snatching at them through the bars, kneeling men praying to the Triplex God. Outside, in the icy night, they crossed a vacant snow-banked yard and turned up a brightly lit street—he wondered if Jason had fusion engines running.

Sirens squalled ahead. A string of yellow-striped police cars came lurching and skidding to meet them and wailing on behind them. The sergeant paused to stare, muttering uneasily to Mindi.

"Sir—" he muttered at Quin, "I think the admiral will be leaving. I think you come too late."

"No, no!" Mindi gasped. "Admiral Kwan would never run. He'll be in Company House."

"*Bien*, Inspector Zinn." Grudging respect. "We try Company House."

Snow crunching underfoot, they tramped on.

Company House stood behind a high stone wall with sharp-spiked metal along the top. An armored machine lay wrecked and burning on the street outside, yellow flame roaring into the night, explosions crashing inside it. The sergeant marched them past it, so close Quin felt the blistering heat.

The gate before the house had been blasted open, heavy steel barriers twisted and tossed aside. In his imagination, he could hear the timer ticking on the nuclear device somewhere underfoot.

The sergeant halted them to meet a little squad of Sikhs marching out, boots crunching frozen snow. Listening to terse words from the officer, the sergeant bowed his turbaned head. Grimmer than ever, he turned back to Mindi.

"Evil news, Inspector. The Kwan has been killed."

He swung upon Quin, dark features savage.

"Son of a jackal! Tycoon killer!" He spat into the snow. "We should execute you now."

"No!" Mindi gasped. "Listen, Sergeant Badahur." Her voice lifted. "The Kwan trusted me. I know the case. The Sahib Dain is the Tycoon's—the Tycoon's kin. Pure Sunblood, though he wears no mark. He is innocent of any killing. I swear it—"

Bleakly impassive, the sergeant had reached for his sidearm. Mindi darted forward, crying out in his own tongue.

"Son of a demon!" He spat again. "Yet perhaps we need not soil our souls with his foul blood. I leave you both to the will of Sat-Kartar—and the Revelator's bomb."

He rasped an order. His men fell in behind the squad. They marched on, double time. Mindi beside him, Quin ran through the shattered gate.

A wide courtyard. Company house, a massive pile of gold and black, now white-domed with snow. A bulky armored machine stopped at the entrance. Nearer, two bodies lay sprawled on red-spattered snow. A woman bent over them.

She stood up when she heard them. Her face was lean and striking, wild with passion. Gouts of blood had splashed her cheek where a Sunmark might have been, splashed her white shipsuit and her loose black hair. In both clenched hands, she gripped a thin, red-dripping blade.

"*El Cabrón!*" A shrill half-scream. "*Y su puto!*"

"Jason—" Mindi pointed at the nearer body. He saw the golden beard, the yellow dutysuit. The snow beneath it was black with clotting blood.

The woman turned, and he looked at the other body. A slight young man, the long hair waved and bleached and matted now with blood. A gold-plated pistol lay near him. He had worn some strong cologne, and its heavy redolence hung strange in the frosty air.

"*Sí! El puerco maldito!*" The red knife slashed the air. "Escaping in the armadillo. Leaving me for *los fanaticos* to butcher." She spat at the yellow-haired body. "Leaving me—for that!"

A clang of steel from the armored machine. A tall man came plodding across the court. Unarmed, Quin saw, stolidly unhurried, scarcely glancing at the bodies.

"Olaf!" Mindi ran to meet him. "Olaf Thorsen!"

Quin followed. His mother's husband! He knew the raw-boned head from the holo she had sent him on Janoort, though the blond hair had thinned and the yellow beard was new. The Sunmark on his fair cheek shone like new gold. Grinning, he swept Mindi into bearlike arms.

"Quin—" He had squeezed her breath out, and she gasped the name. "Quin Dain."

"Nadya's boy?" Thorsen let her go and turned to goggle at him. "Here from the halo?"

"From Janoort—" Shaken with his own emotion, he had to pause for words. "I came to get—came hoping to get your fusion know-how to keep us alive."

"So you were the pilot?" Thorsen swung back to frown at Mindi. "Here in Barranca's spaceplane?" She nodded, and he peered at Quin. "The Kwan was heading for it. You think you have it safe?"

"I hope. I left it pretty well hidden. Nobody near it then. In the waste off the power wires—"

"*Ja.*" He nodded, turning to Mindi. "Down in the gravity dump. Kwan's Fleet observers thought they'd seen it. We were setting out to search—"

Gravely deliberate, he checked himself to introduce the red-spattered woman.

"Dr. Estrella Navarro. Kwan's personal physician till—"

"Till I killed him." Her voice rose jaggedly. "And his evil—creature. *Puercos sucios!* I'd kill them both a thousand times!"

"Sir—" Quin caught Thorsen's arm. "Do you have the fusion engine? Off the spaceplane?"

"*Ja*." He waved at the armored machine. "On the armadillo. Supplies, too, for the spaceplane. The Kwan hoped to get away aboard it."

"Have we time?" Mindi seized his other arm. "Before the bomb—"

He shrugged. "Perhaps there is no bomb."

"The guards said—"

"*Ja, ja*." He nodded, unalarmed. "Barranca sent an insolent message. Claiming to be now the Revelator's voice. Claiming he had a nuclear device set in the sewers."

"To detonate at midnight." She glanced at her time ring. "The Sikhs seemed convinced—"

"The Kwan wasn't. He ordered the messenger shot. He did send men to look for the bomb. They found nothing, but the rumors made panic enough. His forces surrendered or ran. All except the Sikhs. Which left him very little choice, except to try a dash for the spaceplane."

"Can we make it?"

"Perhaps." An unhurried shrug. "If you can guide us. Though I think there is no bomb."

Thorsen led them toward the armadillo. Glancing back, Quin saw Navarro kneeling in the snow at Jason's head. A numbing grief sank into him. Grief not for his dead half-brother, though even now Jason was hard for him to hate. A sense of fatal loss instead, for his father's death and the fall of the Kwan Tycoons and the end of mankind's greatest empire. This seemed a sad and shabby finish.

They climbed after Thorsen into the big machine. Gears snarled, and it lumbered back across the court. Beside the two bodies, Thorsen stopped the machine and got out. Quin didn't hear what he said to Navarro, but she climbed back with him, silently scrubbing her red fingers with a handful of snow.

"A lovely woman, when she was herself," he murmured to Quin. "A fine physician. She saved my life, in fact, when I was first here from the High Lab. Barranca had hidden me in a cellar. Let me pick up downside viruses that nearly did me in.

"*Ja,* if he hadn't called Navarro—"

He shook his head and settled himself at the wheel. Quin sat with him to help find the way. Mindi climbed into the gun turret behind them. When he looked back for Navarro, she was huddled down in a seat, both hands twisted into her flowing hair, her body jerking with sobs.

They drove through empty streets and a wide gap blasted in the high Sun County wall. Beyond the city lights, a full moon shone on still snowscapes. Dead men lay where they had fallen, and burned-out machines where they had failed, but the living had fled.

The armadillo ran quietly, with only the whine of shifting gears and the occasional muffled crunch of debris under the tracks. Thorsen had replaced the fuel cells with one of his reactors.

"We'll need no fuel," he said, "except perhaps a spoonful of snow."

He had brought Jason's map of Azteca Major, a red line drawn through the city and on to the blank space marked GRAVITY TERMINAL. It crossed the Santos bridge, which Quin had seen blown up. He traced another route to take them over the Shawnee bridge and south around the city.

They found a road and wound their way along it through dead machines. A few kilometers out, they began to come upon refugees huddled around scattered campfires. Most merely stared. Now and then bullets clanged against their armor, but Quin had begun to feel almost secure before he heard a curse from Thorsen.

The pavement erupted ahead. Bright fire gushed up. A stunning concussion dazed him. They lurched and slewed through hailing debris to stop on the brink of a sudden smoking crater.

"—land mine." Ears ringing, Quin barely heard. "Set off a second too soon."

They turned off the road. Peasants had lived here, eking survival out of tiny plots. Most of them were gone now, and the roofs had burned from the blackened mud walls of their clustered huts. But ditches and hedges and mud walls slowed the pitching machine.

A few minutes short of midnight, Mindi called a warning. Thorsen veered into a raw ravine where erosion had taken the soil.

"Heads down! Hide your eyes! In case there really is a fireball."

Eyes covered, Quin waited. Mindi's voice, small and breathless, counted seconds down to midnight. His muscles tightened when she stopped, but nothing happened.

"Only a hoax," Thorsen muttered. "Let's go on."

"Not yet!"

She counted another minute down, another, and a third. Still nothing. Gears singing, they were crawling back up the slope when he heard Mindi cry out.

"Down—"

Before he could hide his eyes, the black sky had turned blinding. Yet, still in the ravine, they had been shielded. His stinging eyes could soon see again. Trembling, he twisted in the cab to watch the fireball swell and climb behind them.

They were lurching out of the ravine before the shock reached them. The earth pitched. Dull thunder rocked them. The sky was black again before the hot wind overtook them, thick with choking dust.

"No hoax," Thorsen muttered. "Nothing stops Barranca. Millions of his people will be dying in the fallout, but I guess he has finished off the Company."

"Are we—"

"In the fallout?" A fatalistic shrug. "Perhaps we are. Perhaps we aren't. Perhaps the upper winds will drift it the other way."

The Shawnee bridge still stood. Beyond it, they crashed through a gate into a Company hunting preserve, the high fence hung with warnings that the area was reserved for exclusive use by members and guests of the House of Kwan. Poachers would be punished with death. The moonlit snowscapes lay empty inside the fence, and they found the going easier.

Thorsen talked about fusion engines.

"Can we build them on Janoort?" Quin asked. "With what we have there?"

"*Ja*." He nodded. "If you do reach the halo with what I give you. In fact, you have an advantage over us here. The monomolecular fibers for the master magnet must be annealed in a microgravity environment, to form stable superconducting cores inside stable insulating sheaths.

"Simplicity has made my difficulties," he added moodily. "It frightened the Company. My engines seemed to threaten their gravity monopoly."

He talked, too, about Quin's mother and her years of work with the skyfish.

"Nadya—Nadya loved you." He reached to clap Quin's shoulder. "She always grieved because she had to leave you. I think she hoped to learn things from the skyfish that might open wider ways to space and somehow bring you Sunside."

He steered them across a snowbanked gully.

"Too late." He sighed. "You came too late."

In a frosty dawn, they broke through the fence again, into the drop site. The Sun rose clear as they pushed up a straight white valley between two endless ridges, but a thick black cloud was climbing across the north horizon.

Smoke from the still-burning city. Mixed now with fallout from the bomb. Lingering death to the fugitive millions exposed in the open. It rose higher as they pushed north, but the cold Sun still shone when they came at last to the spaceplane.

The snow around it showed no tracks. Aboard, Quin found the skyfish where he had left her in the cockpit, crushed down into the copilot's seat by the gravity of Earth, her boneless body limp and cold and colorless.

"But she's alive—I'm sure she is," he told Mindi. "I think—I hope she'll revive again when we get back into space."

The small size of the fusion engine astonished him. Thorsen brought it aboard in a computer case—the same case in which he had smuggled it down from the High Lab. He let Quin install it and gave him tech guides for it.

Running, it brought the spaceplane to life. Lights came on. Ventilators whirred. Ruby symbols shimmered again in the flight computer monitor.

Thorsen ran a cargo loader out of the lock, down to the armadillo, and they began tranferring the cargo Jason Kwan had meant for himself. Cases of Fleet rations, cases of gourmet foods and liquors, crates and bags of staples, boxes of weapons, leather luggage gleaming with the Kwan monogram.

The enticing holos of exotic dishes on the cartons reminded Quin that he was giddy with hunger and fatigue, but with space so near again he dared not stop to eat or rest.

To fill the fuel bunkers, they hoisted snow aboard. Navarro joined Thorsen at that, climbing the steep slopes with him to set snowballs rolling. At last, the cold Sun sinking again, the bunkers were full.

They were ready for space!

Lightheaded with his mix of exhaustion and joy, Quin wanted to take off at once, but Thorsen lingered outside the lock, frowning at the cloud now climbing higher all across the north.

"The wind is shifting." He frowned at the Sun. "Yet I think we've time enough. *Ja*, time to say good-bye."

In the cabin aboard, they spread a hasty meal. Thorsen opened a bottle of Jason's wine and offered a toast.

"To mankind—wherever!" Sitting beside Navarro, he turned solemnly to Quin. "Estrella and I have decided to stay."

"Olaf, you can't!" Mindi whispered. "Not in all this terror and death." She stared at his bright Sunmark. "The Holyfolk would hunt you down."

"Perhaps." He shrugged and looked again at Quin. "Yet

space might be no kinder. Your rescue expedition is still a chancy thing."

"We have the spaceplane ready to fly—"

"Not yet tested. The supplies and the life-support gear should get the two of you to Janoort, but perhaps not four." He smiled gravely at Navarro. "We wouldn't want to die under Metabrake. Or in the jaws of those space monsters."

"There's a weapon," Quin said. "Aboard the Newling ship Jason disabled. With luck enough, we'll stop them with that."

"*Skoal!*" Thorsen lifted his glass, smiling at Navarro. "But I have spoken to Estrella—"

"*Loco, loco!*" She nodded at Mindi and Quin, tears on her dark streaked face. "I was mad. Because I had worshipped Jason since I was a child. Because he'd been my lover. Because he seemed—seemed *que maravilloso!*"

She reached blindly for Thorsen.

"Olaf—*él tiene lástima.*"

He drew her to him.

"Our place is here." He touched his Sunmark. "Estrella can take this off. Perhaps—perhaps we have a chance." With a nod to Navarro, he rose from the table. "The wind will be shifting. Better go while you can."

"I'm afraid for you." Quin shook his head. "With the whole world stricken—"

"We live in doubt." Thorsen shrugged. "And do as we must. In spite of Barranca, we'll find men still sane. They'll need Estrella's skills. *Ja*, and fusion power."

"*Vaya bien!*" Navarro followed him into the lock and turned to wave a grave farewell. "*Por los todos!*"

The mites amazed and delighted the queen.

They had lost their arrogant outpost on the halo fringe. Lost their insolent little orbital fortress. Lost that odd little web around their planet. Yet now she perceived another of their lazy little spacecraft in flight toward her hive.

It woke the warrior in her.

A lift she needed, in this time of lonely waiting. Flightless, half her body sacrificed to feed her coming queens and princes, she could feel alive only in the old sagas she recalled and the new one she was spinning to celebrate the future glory of her hive.

The joy of combat burned again, like hot metal in her. If these preposterous gnats were really daring to attack the hive, here was stuff to fill another comic canto.

Elated, she burst into her prince's grand old battle song.

Lifeburst. *The evolutionary leap into space from a planetary birthplace. The crucial event in the evolution of any race, comparable only to the earlier leap from water to dry land, it becomes possible only when primitive survival modes are superceded by intelligence, technological sophistication, and a holistic regard for the total space environment and its entire community of life and mind.*

22

IN THE COCKPIT, QUIN WAITED FOR THORSEN AND NA-varro to climb aboard the armadillo. His throat tightened when he saw them looking back to wave again before they closed the hatch to move away.

"The human future," Mindi whispered.

"Here on Earth." He shivered a little, touched with pity and dread. "If the Holyfolk don't slaughter them. If Barranca lets Olaf build his engines. If we can stop the space beasts. If civilization stays alive.

"If not—I guess we'll never know."

The machine spun on its tracks and crept up the long snowslope. Silently they followed its slow climb until it pitched out of sight, into the lee of the ridge. Gingerly, then, he tested the Thorsen reactor.

The first hot breath vaporized the snow beneath them.

Condensing steam made a white ringwall rushing out around them, rising to hide that ugly cloudwall across the north.

The spaceplane quivered and lifted.

Climbing above the steam and dust, they found the armadillo. Creeping east across the white-ridged waste from space, it left a clear trail in the snow. When Mindi gripped his arm and pointed, he saw a column of dark machines crawling out of the west, following its track.

"Holyfolk," she whispered. "In captured tanks. Too late to catch us, but they'll soon run Olaf down."

"And then—?"

She shook her head. "We'll probably never know."

At full thrust now, they climbed fast. Those dark dots vanished. West of the gray, winding streak of the river, they found the new crater, a shallow-seeming pit with dark debris splashed far out around it, a ragged blot on the snow. The smoke of Azteca was a dirty brown plume, dwindling as they climbed.

Mindi answered a call on the Fleet signal system. She spoke a long time in the baffled headset and turned at last to Quin with a rueful frown.

"The *Solar Kwan*," she said. "Jason's flagship. Trapped in orbit now, almost without supplies. They were hoping we were Jason, coming out to relieve them. They didn't know about his death."

She paused a moment, staring solemnly out across the far bright limb of the diminishing Earth, into dark infinity.

"The signal officer." Even when she turned again to him, she was still far away. "A kid I knew in Kwan Tech. We used to go dancing together. He taught me to pilot his sports rocket and gave me my first orchid."

She must have seen his twinge of jealousy.

"That was then." A wry, tiny smile. "He soon met another woman. A Brazilian beauty with a bright new Sunmark, crazy for spacemen. He took her with him to his duty station, but she was back at Rio Down when the web fell. Their two kids with her. He's desperate now for news about them."

Pain pinched her face.

"Nothing good I could say. On the ship, they'll have Metabrake when their food and air are gone. But a Sun-marked woman, there in Rio Down—"

Shivering, she stared away again.

"Humankind will have to do better," he muttered, "out in the halo."

"Something else he said." She stared away again. "He tried to call Janoort as they came home from the halo. From within a few AU." She shook her head, teeth against her lip. "No answer."

"We may be late." He had to nod. "But we'll do what we can. As long as we can."

The round Earth fell away toward the Sun until most of it was dark. He thought once that he could see other cities burning, but they were already too far for him to be sure.

Mindi ran the tutor programs, learning to spell him at the controls. In open space, the flight computer was designed to keep them on course without attention, and they set it for the trailing Trojans.

"As close as we can come," he told her. "Unless Runesong wakes. The seeker's hive is somewhere there, with whatever is left of the Newling ship, but we'd never find them on our own."

They cut the thrust back to half G and moved the skyfish to blankets spread on the chart table, the little holo set ready if she roused to use it. Watching her cold gray flesh for the shimmer of returning Newling life, they saw no color.

"Eight days to the Trojans," he told her. "Perhaps by then—"

Happy himself to be escaping Earth's unrelenting drag, he felt that they were escaping into freedom and peace. All the tensions and emotions of those last desperate days were falling away behind, almost as if he had been inhaling Kerry's starmist.

A feeling not entirely rational, he tried to tell himself. Left to the Holyfolk—and after them, perhaps, the seekers—the people of Earth were still doomed to agonies of famine and terror. Unless—

Shrinking from too many ominous uncertainties, he turned to look at Mindi, leaning over the small flat shape on the chart table. The convulsions of a dying world had mauled them both too cruelly, but that was now a chapter ended. He felt drained of all emotion except gladness.

"Mindi—"

He had only breathed her name, but she came to him, her dark eyes inquiring. For a moment, when he caught her wildwood scent, time turned back. They were on Janoort again, flying free in the gym balloon.

Trembling with that old emotion, he caught her slight body to him.

"Don't!" She twisted away. "Don't touch me—not like that!"

"Mindi!" Hurt, he drew back. "I didn't mean—"

"I'm—I'm sorry, Quin." Her breathless whisper quivered. "But I just can't—can't let you touch me—"

"I love you, Mindi. That's all I meant."

"I loved you." A sad headshake. "But now—after Benito Barranca..."

Her voice trailed away, her head slowly shaking.

"It doesn't—it shouldn't matter." Aching with pity, yet still desiring her, he muttered it huskily. "Not when you think of what we hope to do."

The engine ran steadily, and they met no raiding seekers. Turn by turn, they kept watch in the cockpit. Off duty, he explored the ship and checked the fusion engine and studied the tech guides Thorsen had left and slept when he could in the cabin Benito Barranca had designed for himself.

Mindi learned the language of the flight computer and

inventoried their supplies and watched over Runesong. She said no more about Benito Barranca, but her eyes looked haunted. Though he urged her to rest, he knew she seldom slept.

His duty shifts were bleak ordeals until at last Runesong began to show signs of revival. Her lax body warmed. Color tinged her limp gray wings. That was all, until Mindi found that her slender proboscis had slid over the table edge to let its three slim fingers touch a metal support.

On his next shift, he heard his mother's faint and weary whisper:

"Quin—"

Startled, he spun to find Runesong's trunk drawn back to touch the holo set that let her speak. Her eerie eyes had opened. Her wings were lifting, and they flickered to the rhythm of her words.

"Quin Dain, we greet you here in space."

"Are you—" He found his own voice hushed, as if afraid sounds might harm her. "Are you well?"

"We were hurt." The wings were fading, her whisper with them. "Now we heal. Slowly we heal."

"How can we help?"

"You have done all we hoped."

"If the acceleration is still too much, we can cut it again—"

"Not yet!" Her whisper quickened. "If we hope to stop the seekers, we must reach our sister Snowhue while she has life . . ."

Her voice died away, and all color with it. The gray wings collapsed, but the delicate trunk was still alive. Releasing the holo set, it glided again around the table edge to contact bare metal.

On Mindi's watch, Runesong spoke again. She had reached her sister aboard the drifting wreck. Snowhue had a lifespark left, not quite extinguished by her wounds. She would try to guide them, but her signals came feebly and far apart.

On his own next watch, Quin turned to find Runesong's

open eyes upon him, great and bright and strange. His mother's voice grown stronger, she told him more about Jason's attack on Snowhue's ship.

A brief encounter, because their closing speeds were high. They evaded his missiles, but his lasers killed the two clonefolk and injured Snowhue. Able to repair one jet, she had kept them on a flight path toward the seeker's hive till all the fuel was gone.

"Our sister seeks now to share her life with us, because she cannot live alone."

Picking up Snowhue's faint signals through the fabric of the craft, Runesong roused herself again and yet again to give them corrections for the flight computer until Quin was able to image what was left of the alien craft.

A jumble of silver-bright globes and strange-colored cylinders and laser-fused ruin, most of it something else than metal, it had never been the sort of ship he knew. Most of it had been burned or blown away.

Nosing near, he cut the braking thrust. In free fall, Runesong was alive and luminous. Dancing in the air, rebounding from the bulkheads, she begged for flight-mass. When he offered a big bubble of water, she sucked several liters of it through her trunk.

He got into Barranca's space gear. Leaving Mindi in the cockpit, he cycled Runesong with him through the lock. At ease in space, she darted ahead to find her sister. He overtook her in what must have been the main cabin.

Jason's laser had sliced half of it away. Exploding fragments had battered what was left. The sleek-scaled clones looked snakelike to him, wrapped together in an intricate love-knot, tapered coils sadly mangled, blackened and frozen rigid now.

Runesong was gathering her sister out of a shattered tangle that must have been the pilot device. A lax gray shape, almost her twin, eyes sunken and shut, one wing burned away. Runesong's wings folded around her, rosily glowing.

For a long half minute, they drifted together in the

wreckage. Runesong rippled with color, each slow pulsation brighter than the last. As he watched the strange, lifeless face, Quin saw faint light flush it, saw the huge eyes open, saw a flicker of green before they closed again.

The waves of color ceased. Glowing dully blue, Runesong's wings unfolded; Snowhue was dead. Runesong laid her gently beside the clones and launched herself away, signaling for him to follow.

They found the weapon in an unharmed compartment. A massive thing, two meters long, it had the look of a seven-barreled cannon. The thick walls of the tubes were golden; they held dark projectiles.

They hauled it into the lock.

"Snowhue's life is in us now," his mother's voice murmured solemnly when Runesong could reach the holo set again. "She is happy now, because she did not die alone."

The Trojans were still too far for the telescope, but Runesong could cup her shining wings like radar dishes to pick up infrared radiation from the seeker's asteroid. In the monitor, at last, it became a craggy dark object some thirty kilometers long, more brick-shaped than round. Its slow spin showed deep scars from old collisions.

"The seeker's nest." Runesong picked it out long before it came into the far Sun's light. "We perceive the creature, already aware of us."

When the asteroid's flattest face tipped again into Sunlight, he made out a wide ring at the its center, cratershaped.

"Nickel-iron," Runesong said. "Excavated from the nest."

The image grew. A ring of great dark metal blocks, carved from the asteroid's core and welded again to form a fortress wall. At the center of it, a round black dot swelled and swelled until it became a yawning circular pit.

They found the seeker near it.

"The queen." His mother's voice, as soft as when she used to tell him bedtime stories about Earth before the

Sun Tycoons. "Her eggs will be deep inside the hollowed satellite. She will be guarding them now, waiting for them to hatch. The eggs and hatchlings should be vulnerable to the virus in our missiles."

"We—we must get inside to reach them?"

"Our only way." A weary-sounding sigh. His mother's sigh, at times when life on Janoort had become too much for her. "When the creatures emerge from the hive, they will be fully grown, armored and immune to everything."

"Then—" His voice caught again. "I guess we must."

Mindi's fingers quivered on his arm.

"I never imagined—"

Her husky whisper died as the image of the queen grew larger, more detailed. The same nightmare thing Brun's probe had showed him. Scuttling now across its walled domain on the same jointless legs, staring with the same enormous red-glowing eyes, following to keep them in view as its world turned.

He bent closer to the monitor. Beneath the folded wings, half of it was gone—the long swollen abdomen and the tapered tail that he had seen fusing the wreckage with that incandescent jet.

"Has it been injured?"

"Only by her own offspring." His mother's patient murmur. "She must have been too long in flight before she found a place to hive, but their way of birth is always cruel. Consuming the mother, they eat even the armor. It forms the shells. After they hatch they eat the broken shards again to make their own armor."

Silent, chilled with awe at the creature's strangeness, he watched her scuttling up the inner slope of her dark fortress wall. She perched there. Her wings spread a little, as if seeking air where there was no air, following them with red-blazing eyes.

"How—" Mindi whispered. "How can we possibly—"

"We'd never get past her." He nodded. "Not with the plane. The alternative—"

He looked at Runesong, and her strange eyes shone green, peering back at him.

"That choice is not for us." His mother's voice, brushing off some needless appeal. "Yours is the younger race, nearer the needs of conflict. Our action is yours to plan."

"Okay." He nodded, with a bleak grin for Mindi. "I'll get off while we're out of her sight behind the asteroid. Approach on the surface. On her scale, I'll be small. Maybe so tiny she won't see me."

The bright wings shimmered, and his mother's voice murmured, "If you wish. We must warn you, however, that your body is imperfectly adapted for survival inside the hive."

"If I can live long enough to fire—"

He looked into Mindi's eyes. They were violet and open wide. Suddenly darker, when the pupils dilated. She swayed against him, shuddering, but in a moment she had drawn away again, turning back to Runesong.

"We'll keep the creature busy," she whispered. "If— if we have to ram!"

Runesong went with him back into the lock to show him how to work the weapon. The seven projectiles were rocket-driven darts. To take effect, they must penetrate the softer parts of the hatchlings, where the armor had not hardened.

"Suppose seven aren't enough?"

"Even one could wipe them out, Quin. They are ferocious. Even the young have been observed to attack one another. They should spread the virus among themselves."

With Mindi in the cockpit, Quin climbed into his space gear. Waiting in the open lock, he watched the rock's slow rotation. The fortress wall slid out of view, those crimson-glowing eyes still watching. Ragged peaks and dark crater-fields emerged slowly into Sunlight.

Before the hive was back in sight, he pushed the weapon out of the lock. Half a ton of mass, it was clumsy to move even in free fall. He steered it down toward black metallic cliffs. The spaceplane sank and vanished behind the saw-toothed horizon.

Afraid the queen might sense his rockets, he shut them off to move as he had learned to move long ago. Though the asteroid was smaller than Janoort, its stuff was heavier, the gentle gravity not much different. Pushing and towing the weapon, he jumped from point to point, careful not to soar too high.

A dozen kilometers to go. Eon-scarred nickel-iron, drifted deep with carbon-darkened dust. Jagged-rimmed pits, where hard metal had impacted harder metal. Wide craters and tiny ones.

The space gear was stiff and clumsy. Though Benito Barranca had been near his size, it didn't quite fit. Every time he crouched to leap, something chaffed his crotch. Before he had gone halfway, darkness overtook him.

By starlight, he leaped and caught and leaped again until the demand valve failed, perhaps from changing temperature. The valve that metered his regenerated air.

A microchip sensed the failure, and a sweet synthetic bird-voice chirped in the helmet, telling him how to find and install the spare, but he was gasping and groggy before the thing was done.

The weapon was lost, drifting away in the dark. Panic chilled him, till his searching headlamp found it. Forced to risk the jets, he flew to overtake it and tug it back to a crag where he could brace himself for another leap.

He found the spaceplane again before the sudden Sun came up. A tiny silver toy, bright against the dark, his guide to find the hive. Flashing his own headlamp to signal where he was, steering the stubborn mass of the weapon, he jumped and thrust and jumped and thrust, until at last he stopped against a knife-edged point and raised his head to look.

He found the fortress wall, not three kilometers ahead. The queen was not in view. He launched himself for his longest leap, flying low across the last long field of dark boulders and darker dust. Low and too slow.

It took him a nerve-straining time to reach the wall, but at last he stopped himself in the ragged joint between two crudely welded ship-sized blocks. Climbing sharp iron seams, nudging the weapon ahead, he came to the top.

Peering warily, he found the queen.

Crouched below him at the rim of the pit, she was a full two kilometers away, but still overwhelming. He shivered when he saw the pit. Black, circular, enormous. It was the way he had to take.

He clung there, his heart drumming hard. He felt hot in his armor, felt the trickle of sweat under his arms. The demand valve, had it stuck again? No, the microchip chirped no warning.

Terror?

He tried to think he wasn't afraid. Not, at least, for himself. For all the others, he had to be afraid. For Thorsen and his engine, perhaps all the Earth. For Kerry and Noël and the human future in the halo. Even for Runesong and the Elderhood.

For an instant, he wished he had been Jason Kwan. With Jason's ready relish for challenge and hazard, he might have felt better. But Jason Kwan was dead.

He watched the queen. One thin black wing dipped a little. One silvery leg lifted to preen it with a long black-hooked talon. The other wing dipped, and another leg preened it. Both wings lifted, as if ready—

His breath caught. The spaceplane was dropping out of the dark. Runesong and Mindi attempting their diversion. They came plunging toward the pit as if to dive inside, swerved narrowly aside to skim the fortress floor, touched down on the farther wall.

The queen scuttled at them. A little clumsily, perhaps, wings half-spread as if needed for balance since her abdomen was gone, yet still a fearful thing, huge enough to crush the tiny craft like a morsel in her black jaws, fast enough to frighten him.

He scrambled over the wall, towing the weapon. He braced himself against jagged iron, steadied the awkward mass, measured his way to the pit. Afraid she might sense the jets, he pushed off without them.

His glide took too long.

Faster than he, the queen came to the wall, swarmed up its inner slope. White steam washed her, from the spaceplane's jets. It lifted a little, dived at her head. She leaped to meet it, black talons grasping, fell back in another gust of steam.

She had seen him!

The exploding cloud glowed red from the glare of her eyes. Bursting out of it, she came scrambling back to cut him off.

Clumsy in Benito Barranca's space gear, he aimed himself at the center of that black pit, set himself to push the weapon, opened his own jets.

It seemed too far.

She came too fast.

In orbit around the Black Companion, the Sun had climbed away half a hundred times to drift for geological ages along the limits of its immense gravitic web, but never quite escaped. It slid back now, with its planets and its wide-spun halo, toward one more periastron passage.

It had been lucky. The black holes were themselves far apart. Though burning radiations and battering collisions had left a record of extinctions in the rocks of Earth, most of its orbital family had always survived to climb away again.

Another star ahead of it was not so fortunate. It had come out of Draco along a hyperbolic orbit that would bring it close and toss it out again, never to return. It passed too near the black binary. The star itself went on unscathed, but one unlucky planet struck a moon-sized mass that deflected it into a great accretion disk.

A monstrous eddy of infalling matter, the disk consumed whatever it caught, stars or worlds or satellites, tearing them apart with tidal forces, grinding them to incandescent dust, fusing that to vapor, stripping atoms into ions, finally sucking everything into the black hole at its heart.

Light itself could not escape from that, but a wink of radiation from the disk did announce the planet's death.

The Eldermost. *Founder and guiding mind of the Elderhood.*
Described by Runesong as the oldest and most powerful
intelligence ever evolved. Embodied in a massive five-meter
sphere, the Eldermost arrived in the galaxy soon after stars began
to form. Through ten billion terran years since then, He/She/It
has moved from star to star on an unending pilgrimage,
searching out newborn intelligence and fostering its peaceful
evolution. Known by the terran planetics, the Eldermost might
have been their God.

23

A STRANGE RACE.

Diving off the fortress wall toward that black pit, Quin
gripped the Newling weapon with both hands to push and
steer it. Touching helmet sensors with his head, he opened
the suit jets all the way. Too small for such a massive
load, they moved him too slowly.

The queen came faster.

Her own jet lost, she herself was handicapped. Wildly
beating, her black wings found no air. Scratching madly
for traction, her black talons kept tossing her too high
against the rock's tiny gravity, clawing at nothing.

Yet she was gaining, till the spaceplane came plunging
back to meet her. For one sick instant, he thought Mindi
really meant to ram. The black-fanged jaws gaped wider.
The tongue darted out, striking like a monstrous scarlet

snake. The spaceplane spun, jets flaring. The blast of expanding steam checked her charge.

Long enough.

Ahead of her, he steered the weapon down into darkness. The pit was an awesome maw, two hundred meters wide, its iron walls slick and darkly glistening where the far Sun struck. Too feeble for its vastness, his headlamp found nothing at all below.

He kept the suit jets pressing. Behind him, the Sunlit rim diminished. His tiny light found the black wall too near, and he veered away. The crescent rim had vanished when he looked back again. The passage had curved.

Total blackness. He had never liked the dark, not since that long-ago night when Kerry brought him into the red-lit dome to show him the search gear and tell him about the space aliens watching the station from out toward the stars. Shivering in spite of himself, he wished again for Jason's daring.

Though he knew the asteroid was hardly a dozen kilometers thick, that winding black chasm seemed bottomless. Afraid of losing himself, he kept twisting to look back, twisting and looking again. Only blackness.

If Runesong and Mindi could somehow give him time enough—

The darkness, suddenly, was no longer total. He could see the shape of the weapon he grasped, its gold turned a ghostly red. He found the wall's vast curve, lit faintly red.

They had lost that strange game to delay the seeker queen. She was following. The gleam of the weapon grew brighter. He knew she was gaining. Veering toward the wall, he found a break in its dim sweep. Denser darkness. He steered into it.

A shadowy floor, piled with shadowy masses. He spun the weapon behind him, opened his jets to brake its motion, dropped to hide among those dark shapes.

Rough ten-meter lumps of bright new metal, when he came near enough to make them out. Did the queen excrete metal? Or was this choice stuff, refined from all the ores she had excavated, stored to feed her ravenous brood?

The red light brightened, shifted, dimmed. The queen had passed him. Somewhere ahead, she would be searching or lying in wait.

"Warning!" The microchip's bird-voice, trilling in his helmet. "Heat sinks overloaded. Urgent advice: Limit activity. Avoid heat sources."

How? He felt baffled, trapped. The heat source had to be the asteroid itself, heated by the nuclear energies of the queen and her brood. All around him, doubtless more intense ahead, unavoidable.

He was no Jason, yet he had to go on. He was heaving at the weapon to set it back into motion, when the dark walls glowed again. Shrinking down, he watched the queen's return.

All he could see at first were her eyes, huge and sullenly red, soaring through the dark. A soot-colored wall loomed ahead of them. They stopped and swung. Twin crimson beams raked the stacked ingots around him.

He braced himself against a great, crimson-glinting globe to hold the weapon motionless. The probing beams paused on the ingots. They brightened, and he couldn't breathe.

But then they went on. Daring to move, he raised himself to watch them dim and wink as the creature launched herself again, flying back toward the entrance.

Frantic, he imagined. Uncertain, perhaps, that anything so tiny as he could really harm her brood. Afraid of some greater danger from the spaceplane itself. Perhaps expecting it to dive down the shaft in a suicidal assault.

When she was gone around the curve, he pushed the weapon once more into motion, following the path she had showed him.

Ahead, a new light shone.

Fainter and redder than the glare of her eyes. Braking warily, he drifted on, searching for its unseen source.

"Warning!" The chirping microchip. "Thermal safeguards overloaded. Emergency coolants in use. Indicated protection time only one hour. Urgent advice: Avoid heat sources."

Tiny jets open wide, he pushed on. The light brightened, glowing from somewhere below. It lit ink-black walls, an ink-black arch above him. Below and ahead, it revealed the rim of a wide black shelf.

Beyond that rim, he found the nest.

Red fire and red shadow at the bottom of a vast dim chasm, an abyss too vast and too dim to let him guess its dimensions. A tall mound of rounded, red-glowing things at its center. Unhatched eggs, he thought. All around them, out to the wall, new hatchlings swarmed.

A menagerie of incandescent monsters. Wasplike shapes with enormous crimson-shining bellies. Baby queens, he thought. Antlike forms with gigantic mandibles. Warriors, he imagined. Mothlike creatures with green-glowing wings. Raiders, perhaps, adapted to planetary atmospheres. Reptilians. Shining dragons. Unshaped crawlers half out of shattered shells, newborn beast-things whose function in the hive he couldn't imagine.

Afraid of delay, he tipped the weapon toward them. It had no aiming device; its Newling designers must have depended on their own electronic senses. Sighting along one golden tube, he pointed it toward the largest infant queen.

Trembling, he pressed the firing key.

A soundless explosion. The weapon recoiled. Gas erupted around him, a pink-tinted cloud that veiled everything. When it dissolved enough to let him see, he hauled at the weapon to correct the recoil, aimed at a wide-jawed fighter, fired again.

Again, when he could see again, at a fire-winged raider. At a flame-scaled dragon. At a half-hatched thing like a two-headed snake. Again and yet again into the high-piled eggs. The weapon emptied, the rosy smoke clearing, he watched the Newling virus take effect.

The baby queen burst into convulsive fury, jetting hot blue flame at a baby dragon. Clawing, stinging, the warrior flung itself on the double-bodied snake. The raider leaped and dived to assault the mounded eggs. A hatchling reptile vomited red flame into them. Pandemonium spread, until a fiery cloud concealed it.

"Warning—"

Staring, chilled with awe, he scarcely heard the microchip. But he had passed the danger level. He should seek safety with no delay.

He kicked off from the empty weapon, flying back into the dark. The thermal system had failed. No longer chilled, he was suddenly drenched and sticky with sweat. The air grown bad, he was gasping for breath.

A crimson glare ahead, the queen returning to her brood. Veering aside, he found that storage chamber, or it may have been another, piled with those great enigmatic metal masses. He hid among them, waiting for her to pass.

"Warning." A bright bird-song. "Imperative warning! Coolant entirely depleted. Imperative advice: Seek safety now. Delay may be fatal."

The great red eyes came blazing by. He flew on again, the way they had come—he thought it was the way. But he was giddy now. The suit was suffocating, yet without it he wouldn't live an instant.

Darkness forever. He had to get back to the plane, back to where there was air, back to Mindi. But the blackness never ended. He blundered into a hard iron wall. Feebly he leaped away. He pushed on. He struck another wall.

Gathering himself in the chafing armor, he wasn't sure which way to leap. In flight again, he was afraid he had taken the wrong direction. When he saw the two huge eyes swelling to meet him, he knew he was lost.

The red beams fixed him. Dimly he saw the great jaws yawning. The tongue thrust out of it, darkly scarlet in the light of the eyes, thrust and struck. A vast orifice yawned at its tip, fringed with fingers like smaller serpents.

One of them whipped around him.

He was almost glad. The seekers were beaten. With

luck enough, Runesong and Mindi might yet reach Janoort in time to save Halo Station. Whatever happened, his part was over. This agony of effort could end.

The gnats had beaten her.

Standing on the lip of her natal chamber, she saw her darlings gone mad with agony, slaughtering one another.

The braggart gnats—

Chilled where her belly had been, she recalled her dead prince's hilarious tales of the insolent little idiots screeching their fantastic threats even while he was hunting them to extinction.

Hilarious then.

Sick with the fumes of death rising around her, she shrank back from the pit's foul glow. Those arrogant brags had been no lie. Some impudent midge must have escaped to bring their coward's weapon here.

The pestiferous gnat that had darted behind her while she faced the pygmy ship, had it been the killer? One lone gnat? Could a single gnat have murdered her whole brood? Erased her life? Wasted all her prince's precious seed?

Searching for evidence, she found a tiny golden toy, falling slowly now into the charnel pit that should have been the cradle of her colony.

The weapon?

Hot with fury, she stung at it—or tried to sting. But she had no belly, no quick ionic whip to burn it into instant vapor. The best of her body gone, she was dead as her pitiful children.

Numbed with the agony of that, she wandered away from the reeking birthpit. Blindly blundering toward the door of her dead hive, with no jet to drive her, no air for her useless wings, she found the killer gnat in flight ahead.

She struck at it savagely—

And checked her striking tongue. Because the feeble creature seemed already dead. And because she recalled the codes of combat her dead prince had taught her. The defeated were carrion, food for slaves, but victors had earned the rituals of regard, the right to feast their peers, ceremonials due even when the contest had been fatal.

This hateful gnat had been the victor.

Grasping it gently, she carried it out into the light.

The midget ship was down inside her wall, as if waiting for the raider. It lifted fearfully when she started toward it. She laid the lifeless mite where it had been and crept back to her doorway.

The ship dropped again. A bright-winged midge came out of it to take the body back aboard. She watched it lift and climb and vanish, flying toward the halo. She stood there, aimless eyes on empty space where it had been.

Her belly gone, her own life-fires were cooling fast. Her limbs were already beginning to stiffen. Her body—this poor relic of it—would soon be frozen hard, and with none of her own kind here to consume it decently in the sacred rites of death.

Yet she pitied the gnats more than herself. Victors, they were due the ritual gesture she had made, but they had earned no admiration. Winning by cowardly stealth, they had broken all the classic codes. Too small to know courage or honor or pride or beauty or truth, they were worth no more of her emotion.

Her life-fires dying, she began crooning broken fragments of the old sagas, her lost pride restored in those rolling odes. A happy hatchling once more, she grew up again in her own home hive, basking in the love of her lovely sisters, thrilling to their heroic mother's epic.

She learned to fly again, carried into space by that grumbling forager. She met her own prince again, dashingly intrepid in his gold and crimson armor, besting ferocious rivals to claim her love. She tempted him again, evaded his burning lust again, until the moment of overwhelming ecstasy on that cold snow moon when she found his splendid head crushed between her jaws, the glory of his life thrust from his dying body into hers, all their joy destroyed.

Driven from her home again by the fury of his fellow hunters and the contempt of her sisters, she dared the dark infinity again to make her own hive here. She endured the sweet agonies of birth again, sacrificing herself to nourish her own precious hatchlings. She met the laggard gnats again, and watched her heroic forager giving his tiny life to serve the hive.

Now, when probing cold returned her to reality, the concluding cantos of her own saga had to be completed, revised from the dancing comic meters in which she had first composed them into the solemnities of classic tragedy. Her mind was slowing as her body froze, but she thought she should have time to finish it.

There was nothing else for her to do.

He could breathe.

Gasping for the good cool air, that was all he cared about. Runesong hung over him, wings shimmering gold and green, slim trunk wrapped around his upper arm. In a vague, far-off way, he knew she must have brought him back inside the airlock. And Mindi—

He caught her wildwood scent and felt her quick fingers shucking off his space gear.

"Quin! Can you hear me?"

Nodding feebly, he felt her lips against his face and knew that she could touch him now.

And the seekers were beaten.

"Strange creatures!" she whispered. "The queen came with you out of the hive. Crippled and barely moving. But she brought you to the ship and left you there for us to pick you up.

"I think she was dying, but she saved your life."

He relaxed again, happy with that, and drifted into dreams that he and Mindi were children again on far Janoort, learning to fly in the cold ammonia stink of the gym balloon, learning to love.

Awake again, alone in the room, he wasn't quite so happy. Awe still haunted him, a solemn dread before the strange wonder of the beings he had killed, and a solemn pity for the dying mother-being that had somehow chosen to save his life. He felt half sad that such great creatures had to be defeated.

And Janoort—could they ever reach it?

Even with the Thorsen engines, still they could fail. Not designed for such long voyages, the spaceplane had no external tanks or bunkers. They had burned too much precious mass on the flight out from Earth.

Should they try for more fuel?

Folly, he decided. Some of the Trojans were doubtless rich with ices fit for the engines, but they had no equipment to discover and refine and load new reaction mass. He wondered if they would be scrabbling through the emergency lockers for Metabrake before the voyage ended.

On his feet again, he found Mindi in the cockpit, Runesong beside her. She came into his arms, happy to let him touch her now. Yet, when she told him she had been calling back to Earth, he felt her shiver.

"I know we can't—can't ever go back." Her voice caught huskily. "But still it's hard—hard to give everything up. My whole world. The friends I had—I'm afraid most of them are dead, but still I'd like to know." Her quivery fingers clutched his arm. "I feel so lost. So dreadfully lost."

"Someday, maybe, we can go back." He ached to ease her desolation. "But now we've got to get the engine out to the halo. Hoping we're in time."

"If we're too late—" She shook her head, whispering faintly, "We'd be so terribly alone—"

Economizing reaction mass, they had to make most of the flight in free fall. It took a long time, yet to Quin it seemed too brief. They were in love, with the whole halo ahead and most of Mindi's pain left behind. Lying together in Benito Barranca's berth, they could forget the ravaged Earth and their dread of what they might find at Halo Station.

At least sometimes.

Runesong was eager to tell her people that the seekers were dead. The spaceplane in free fall, she had them cycle her back outside. For many days she drifted with them, wide wings shimmering, seeking contact.

Back aboard at last, she shone with elation.

"We have spoken to our sister, Cyan Gem. She sends most welcome news from Cluster One, where she had taken your fellow planetic, the one named Reynard Charbon, to beg recognition for your species."

His mother's voice as he recalled it from times she had felt well and happy with Kerry.

"Whitewing is the Newling Councilor. At first she saw no hope for you, but Cyan Gem kept insisting. With the news of our victory at the seeker hive, Whitewing was persuaded to take your case to the Council. Most of the members were still opposed to any contact with you. Killing the seekers, they argued, was proof itself that you had never evolved above their primal level.

"When the Council decided against you, Cyan Gem appealed to the Eldermost. He/She/It has reversed the decision. Astonishing the Council, the Eldermost has forgiven our act of genocide, justifying that leniency by the fact that it forestalls a more odious reign of genocide.

"The overwhelming reason for His/Her/Its decision is data just received from the distinguished Andromedan, Venerable Sire. On duty at the new outpost that has replaced Point Vermillion, he reports a radiation flash that pinpoints the approaching Black Companion.

"The flash came from one of the planets of a passing star, swallowed by the black binary. Anticipating the probable extinction of most forms of life on the surface of your planets, the Eldermost feels compassion for your species. He/She/It has decreed that your kind should have a chance."

The softness in his mother's voice recalled his fifth birthday in their ice-tunnel home at the station, when she had been well enough to make sweets he liked and wrap a toy snow-crawler Kerry had made for him.

"The Council, yielding to the Eldermost, is therefore offering your species probationary contact. Since we have recommended the two of you, Quin Dain and Mindi Zinn, as the best available speakers for your kind, we are instructed to inquire if you accept peaceful contact."

Looking at Mindi, he saw her awed nod.

"We do—we do accept." He gulped at a sudden tightness in his throat. "We thank you and the Council and the Eldermost. And we hope—Tell them we hope to prove worthy."

They both sat a long time staring at Runesong when she was outside the lock again, flashing wings tipped toward the halo.

"It's all—all so strange." Mindi turned at last, whispering to him. "I can't imagine all it means."

"Nor can I." A slow headshake. "But it will be—it has to be a splendid thing for us."

Burning the last of their reaction mass to brake for landing at Halo Station, they called ahead, listened in cold anxiety, called and called again. Three days out, they picked up the first reply.

"*Mtoto wangu?*" Jomo's startled voice. "You okay?"

"Okay—" Quin had to get his breath. "Are you—is the station okay?"

"All *furaha* now, since Captain Brun come."

Kerry was soon on the holophone, then Noël and finally Vira Brun, reporting events at the station and listening to their own news of the skyweb's fall and the end of the seekers and now mankind's promise of contact with the Elderhood.

"We're doing fine," Kerry told him. "*Muy bien!* Thanks to Captain Brun."

Brun's cruiser had been disabled in her encounter with the seeker. Adrift in space off the Trojans, she had picked up news of the skyweb's fall. The worst of the damage repaired, she had headed for the halo.

"Just in time," Kerry said. "In spite of all Jomo could do, our last engine had quit. Another day, and we'd have been taking Metabrake."

Nearing the station, they promised to carry Runesong

on to meet her own Newling kindred as soon as the space-plane could be supplied and refitted. She stayed outside in space when they landed, to keep in touch with the Elderhood.

Kerry and Noël met them when they came off the ship into the plastic tunnels, Noël smiling tenderly at Kerry's son in her arms.

Young Quin McLenn.

They were a month at the station. With the tech guides Quin had brought, Jomo rebuilt a lab to synthesize and draw and cure Thorsen's improve kwanlon superconductor.

"All okay, *mtoto wangu.*" He grinned, the golden glint of his Sunmark an odd anomaly there in the halo. "We build our own Thorsen engines now. *Rahisi, rahisi!*"

With sheet metal and plastic from the old *Capella* they fitted the spaceplane with external bunkers to carry added reaction mass for the long halo flight. Before that was finished, Runesong was hovering at the air lock with another call for Quin and Mindi.

"A new message from our dearest sister, Cyan Gem. She says Reynard Charbon feels exiled too long from his fellow planetics. He wishes to leave the halo. We are now asking you to take his place at the Council of the Elderhood, meeting in Cluster One, to be speakers for your species."

"I never expected—"

Quin turned to stare at Mindi.

"Why not?" She kissed him, with a breathless little laugh. "If we're to join the Elderhood—"

The little ship equipped and ready, Runesong aboard once more, they took off to meet the peoples of the halo.

Dying in the doorway of her dying hive, the queen had fixed her dimming eyes on her far home star. Its faint point had kept one warm spark alive in her chilled heart, even after her own sad saga had begun to fade from her freezing brain.

In the happy epics of her mother hive, her warrior soul still survived. These rascal gnats had beaten her, but her sisters would soon be arriving to make them repent their overweening—

Her star winked bright.

A wink that killed her soul. She knew the flash had been a planet sucked into the dark vortices her people called the Huntress Queens. Her own hatching place. Her mother was gone, her sisters, all the splendid princes who had once been proud to offer her their lives.

That flash of death had left her utterly alone.

ABOUT THE AUTHOR

Jack Williamson began writing science fiction in 1928, before it got that name. With time out for service as an Army Air Force weather forecaster during World War II and a more recent career as a college English professor, he has devoted his life to science fiction, and he says he has no regrets.

A Southwesterner, he was born in Arizona of pioneering parents who took him to a Mexican mountain ranch before he was two months old, moved from there to Pecos, Texas, and then, the year he was seven, brought him by covered wagon to the Staked Plains of eastern New Mexico, where he and his wife, Blanche, still live.

The best known of his thirty-odd novels is probably *The Humanoids*. He has been honored by the Science Fiction Writers of America with their Grand Master Nebula Award, and he has served for two terms as president of the organization. He taught one of the first college courses in science fiction and has edited a guidebook for science-fiction teachers.

Now retired from teaching, he writes on a word processor.